A GODS OF HUNGER NOVEL

DRAG ME UP

♠ ♥ ♣ ♦

R.M. VIRTUES

STRANGE HUNGERS PUBLISHING

We formally welcome you to Khaos Falls…

Author's Note

This book contains the following:

explicit sex, rough sex, on page violence, physical violence, attempted murder, on page death, gun violence, explosion, guns, stalking, harassment

Gods of Hunger is an alternate-world fantasy romance

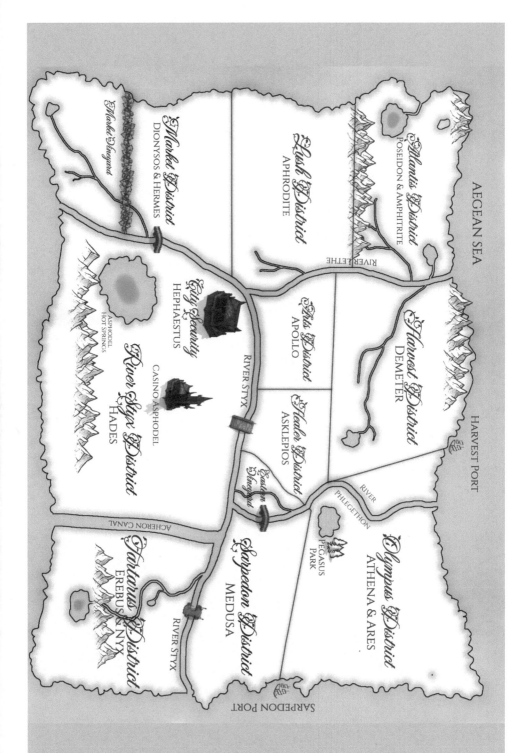

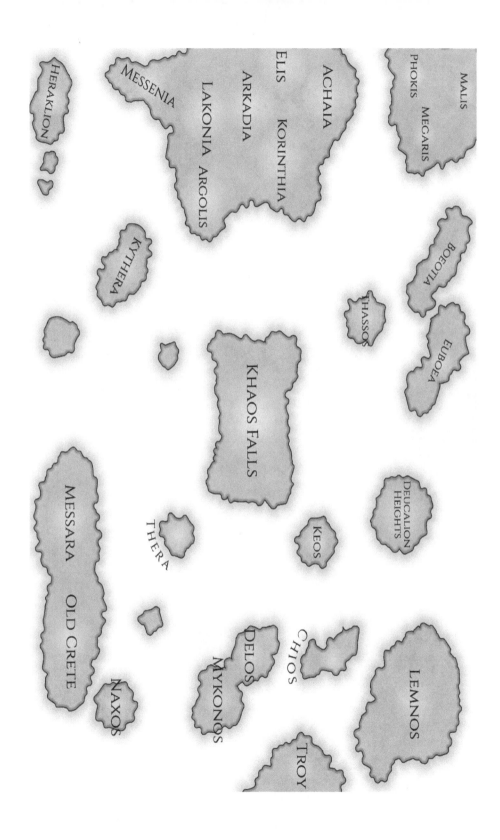

One

HADES

Hades' grip on the railing before him tightened the moment the doors to Casino Asphodel opened, his dark brown eyes narrowing on the man that walked through them. There was nothing particularly interesting about him. Young, slender, and adorned in a worn grey suit that hung off of his shoulders awkwardly, his dark hair slicked back and his shoe is untied. No, he didn't stand out at all, which made him stand out to Hades.

He brought his radio to his lips in one fluid, practiced motion. "East entrance."

"You just gonna have security question every stranger that walks through the door?"

That voice did not come from the radio. Sly and sultry, it washed over his back like warm water. In his peripheral, Hades caught the familiar reflection glancing off of the tinted glass that encased his office just before Hecate appeared beside him in the flesh.

"I'm gonna try," he returned.

His gaze remained fixed on the man in question, who was now being spoken to by two members of Hades' security team. Though they soon sent him on his way, a voice crackling through the radio once he was clear of the floor.

"All good, Boss."

Again.

Hecate turned to him, her gaze keen to inspect his current state. She knew not to ask. She knew he would try to lie despite the fact he was incapable of lying to her, and she hated to waste her own time. He could feel her attention snag on the pronounced circles around his own eyes and the intermittent twitch of his jaw. She tsked. Then she began to pick him apart, decrypt right there on the floor of his office.

He was written in a dead language. She was one of very few who could read it fluently.

"Who do you think is gonna walk in here and start trouble, sweetheart?" she asked, her voice softer now.

She may have been half a foot shorter than him, but her presence could fill the room twice over. While it tended to overwhelm and intimidate others, it surrounded Hades with the comfort of a well-worn coat. It always had, ever since they were children, and while the presence of most people exhausted him quickly, hers did the exact opposite. It renewed him.

Long fingers emerged from the shadows that hugged her dark brown skin and moved over his jaw, soft and soothing. Her gaze trailed up to meet his, and she held it there, expectant. Patient.

At last, he sighed and rubbed his eyes, signaling that his walls were down, at least low enough for her to climb. Still, she waited.

He cleared his throat. "Zeus cut Coeus out of the deal with Medusa. During the deal."

2

Hecate stalled. The softness of her touch only made the shift in her expression feel worse. "Are you fucking kidding me? Hades, lead with that."

"I didn't think it would be beneficial to have us both worrying," he huffed.

"That's how this works. You worry for the sake of worrying, and I worry with a purpose." She looked over the railing and down at the floor. "Have you seen Coeus since?"

Hades pursed his lips. "No, I haven't. None of Erebus's children actually."

"Not even Tethys?"

"Especially not Tethys."

Their jaws clenched in unison. Tethys tended to clean up on the poker tables of Asphodel at least twice a week. It had been so for the past two years, since she was old enough to enter without use of her special privileges as daughter of Nyx and Erebus, the leaders of the Tartarus District. If they weren't seeing her, it was a clear sign that something was extremely wrong. Hades almost wished he did not know what that was.

"Coeus was making the deal on her behalf," Hades continued.

"For the port," Hecate clarified.

"Yes, and I told Zeus to give it to them as a show of good faith. They're the only ones who use it, and he's taxing the hell out of them."

"But it's partly in Medusa's territory, isn't it?"

"Yes, but Medusa had no problem with it. She'd agreed to it with me directly, and I got it in writing before I allowed the deal to move forward. All Zeus needed to do was follow through, but apparently, that was too difficult a task for him."

"Did he talk to you about it?"

3

He gave her a dark look. She pinched the bridge of her nose.

Of course Zeus had not talked to him about it. Zeus hadn't said anything about it at all. It was Hephaestus who had warned Hades of this most recent act of sheer idiocy when he had been turned away from the Tartarus District's boundaries. Zeus himself had told Hades nothing, simply leaving town as he had been scheduled to do and letting the chips fall where they may, even if it meant they fell atop his brother's shoulders. There was only one viable reason too. Zeus had been afraid.

If Khaos Falls belonged to anyone, it belonged to Zeus in the Olympus District, but if Khaos Falls had a heart, it could be found in Casino Asphodel. The River Styx District was a place you didn't go unless you absolutely had to, and if you absolutely had to, it usually wasn't good. That was why they called it the Underworld. However, the exception had always been Asphodel.

Every notable figure in the city and beyond had an unofficial seat at one of the endless card tables. High rollers came in and tried their luck at card games they'd only ever seen on TV. Then, with their last several dollars, they would descend into Club Elysium for a drink and one last chance to get lucky. And regardless of whether they succeeded in either of these endeavors, the outcome was the same. The house always won. That was what kept them coming back of course — a thirst for vengeance.

Independent of Asphodel's reputation was that of Hades. Most people respected him or feared him, but few had ever actually laid eyes upon him much less had a conversation with him. He was a shadow among them, a myth, an echo of his father's death. Any distrust or dislike of him simply stemmed from a lack of interaction because without interaction, the only opinion they had to go on was that of Zeus.

4

Since he had taken over Khaos Falls, Zeus had been spinning tales that made his stepbrother out to be one of his own nightmares made flesh, and Hades did nothing to challenge that. In fact, it was his scarcity that offered these tales credibility. Paired with the fact that Hades seemed to be some all-knowing entity who could sell your secrets back to you at a higher rate, fear wasn't hard to come by. What was more terrifying than someone who could be everywhere and nowhere all at once?

They called it a tactic. Hades called it a comfort.

He found solace in this glass box suspended high above the casino floor. He could still recognize the cards on the tables with no one else the wiser, and the sound of the slots still reached his ears in a soothing symphony. He kept to himself and his small circle, which was necessary when constantly running back and forth between tending to his own district and tending to his stepbrother. Zeus may run the city, but Hades was what kept him from running it into the ground. He never received any of the credit —at least not for the good he did— but he always got things done, and if it weren't for Hades and his impeccable resilience, Zeus wouldn't be breathing much less leading Khaos Falls.

Though some might not see that as a failure, especially after this business with Tartarus.

It had been Tartarus that ruled before Zeus had, and it had been Hades who had taken the crown from their head and placed it upon his stepbrother's. Needless to say, the relationship between them was delicate at best, and so this particular betrayal was one of immeasurable proportions, as good as a bomb being lobbed onto a very rickety bridge. And by the city leader no less. Not only could it get someone killed. It was an outright act of war. And Hades had no idea what it would cost them to mend it. If it was possible at all.

Considering he was usually cleaning up multiple messes a week, Zeus's silence over the past few had indeed worried Hades but not to the point where he could have foreseen this level of foolishness.

Placing a hand against his chest, Hecate pushed Hades back and slipped between his body and the railing. Looking up at him with those vibrant eyes, she clicked her tongue.

"We'll handle this," she assured him.

"Do we have a choice?"

"Well..."

"Forget I asked."

Both of her hands now ran up along his front until they reached his tie. She took hold of it attentively, her eyes fixed on the knot, and her fingers moved in that familiar way which always kept him guessing whether she was going to straighten it or remove it. She had certainly done both in equal measure.

She straightened it this time.

"We'll keep an eye out, see what Charon can gather from the informants, but I need you to remember this." She grasped his chin before he could look away, holding his gaze. "What you're feeling right now? That worry? It isn't yours. You keep letting Zeus drop it in your pocket so he can go on playing Fate, and it isn't fair to you. It isn't fair to any of us. This city isn't a board game, Hades. You can't change the rules every time he fucks up. I know you hate hearing it, but I will say it to you every chance I get because you deserve better. We all do. And if this keeps up, a lot of people are going to get hurt."

Hades inhaled as if to retaliate, but the look in her eyes stopped him cold. What rebuttal could stand against that? She was right.

Instead, he nodded, pressing his lips to her forehead before glancing out over the casino before them. Of course, her reprimand wasn't new because the pattern wasn't new. He had spent most of his life watching over Zeus, wiping his nose and keeping his hands clean. Hecate, as well as Charon and Thanatos, had warned him against the lack of limitations that came with his fealty to Zeus, but what could he do? He'd promised his mother that he would protect his brothers, take care of them, and while Zeus needed far more support than Poseidon ever had, the point stood. Hades was only trying to keep that promise.

Hecate seemed to read his mind. "Rhea said to look out for your brothers. She never said to kill yourself doing it."

She patted his chest now before she reached into the inner pocket of her suit jacket and extracted a small envelope.

"But tonight is not for worrying," she concluded, handing it to him.

He raised a brow. "What is this?"

"Tickets."

"—Tickets?"

She gave him a disappointed look. "Ferocity debuts downstairs tonight." He only blinked. "Ferocity? The show that Dionysos has been reminding you about for the past four months? Come on, Hades."

"Shit, that's tonight?" He opened the envelope, inspecting the two cardstock strips. "And - I need tickets to get into my own theatre?"

"Dio wanted to commemorate the event. And I promised him I would get you there. He's very excited. He even had his tickets laminated."

Hades hissed. "I don't know if I can-"

"No, you can. I've already told Thana to hold down the fort, and

7

I advised the security team to contact him in case of an emergency because you are not going to stand up here all night screening people. You are coming with me."

"Hecate, I—"

"He really wants you there, Hades. He will be crushed if you break your promise to him. He doesn't ask you for much, but he asked you for this, didn't he?"

And Hecate knew that even if he could deny her every now and again, he had never been able to deny Dionysos. He'd been raising Dio and Hermes both since they were kids, rejected by Zeus in one way or another and left on their own. There was very little Hades wouldn't do for those boys if anything at all. That included attending events in his own casino that he would much rather avoid.

"Alright, but let's go upstairs first," he huffed, moving around her and snapping his fingers. Cerberus, the large black hound lying beside his desk, immediately came to his side. "I wanna change."

"Of course you do," she smirked. "From your good black suit to your other good black suit."

He matched the expression. "To my *best* black suit."

DIONYSOS STOOD at the doors of the vast theatre when Hades and Hecate finally make it downstairs. The younger, but much larger, man quickly rushed towards them before flinging himself at his uncle, wrapping his arms around Hades' middle. It drew enough attention from others that a chill ran down Hades' spine, but he reminded himself that he was feared, not fearful. This was his casino. They were merely guests.

"Very professional, my big boy," he chuckled, embracing Dionysos nonetheless.

Dio pulled back, reaching up to pat his uncle's cheeks. "We did it, Uncle. This is the biggest show in the Aegean, and we brought it here. No one else in the city has a showing! Not even Aphrodite!"

"I am very proud of you." Hades cupped Dio's face around his boyish grin. "Are your brothers here?"

Dio nodded fervently. "All of them, and Uncle Poseidon and Aunt Amphi. We brought Heph through the back, so he wouldn't have to walk up and down the stairs. Ares is with him now, and Hermes is helping backstage."

Hades released him. "Of course he is. And it looks like you've certainly filled the house."

"Oh, we sold out the first three showings already. Just make sure you sit in your seats, okay? It's the best seat in the house, even for the acrobatics, so no hiding in the skybox."

Hades gave him a pointed look. "Even for the acrobatics?"

Dio shrugged, offering his most innocent smile. "—Yes?"

"Don't worry. I'll handcuff him to the seat if I have to," Hecate assured him with a wink.

Hades rolled his eyes. "You have my word that I will sit where you assigned me to."

"Perfect! Oh!" Dio clapped his hands. "And do you mind hanging around for a bit after, Uncle? I want to introduce you to our star."

"Your star? And who would that be?"

Dio grinned. "You'll see. She's gonna be huge, I'm telling you. And she's going to make you a fortune, but that's just a bonus really. You have to meet her."

"Alright, son, I'll hang back." Hades truly would not dare

endanger Dio's happiness in any way, and he ignored the sight of Hecate's smug look in the corner of his eye. "Now get in there. We're right behind you."

Dio hugged him once more before leading them all into the theatre, and Hades followed with much more interest than he'd possessed upstairs. He glanced around as they entered, and he could not remember the last time he'd been in this particular room. Despite living right upstairs, he didn't come down here much at all, certainly not for grandiose engagements such as this. He felt - exposed, especially when he seemed to tower above everyone around him. He made the trek down towards the front rows, his eyes on the back of Hecate's head, but he felt every single glance and gawk that came his way. Some of them were simply out of curiosity. Others stemmed from assumption. Either way, he knew they would all be wondering if it was in fact the leader of the Underworld that they had spotted tonight long after the show ended.

He only allowed himself to breathe again once they reached their seats.

There was still a decent amount of space between them and the stage, and their seats were elevated well enough that he could see the entire expanse of the platform. He greeted Athena and his nephews, happy to see them all together, before shaking his youngest brother's hand and kissing his sister-in-law's cheek. Of course, the only one missing was Zeus, but Hades knew that even if he weren't out of town on business, he still wouldn't be here. And honestly, that was likely for the best.

"It's good to see you, brother," Poseidon hissed as Hades settled in between him and Hecate. "Figured you'd be up in the luxury box."

"Dio wanted us all down here," he surrendered with a wry

smile, patting Poseidon's shoulder. "I'm surprised you're here. You hate coming down to my district."

"Hate is a strong word." Still, he winced. "Atlantis keeps me busy."

It went unspoken. It always did. The truth was that Poseidon kept his distance from both of his brothers, not because he didn't love them but because he feared for them. He could never handle Zeus's chaotic recklessness, and he hated to watch Hades break himself over their middle brother's mistakes again and again. Ever since Rhea passed, he'd been even more withdrawn, which was to be expected, but that didn't make it any easier for Hades. The good thing was he rarely had to worry about Poseidon. He may not be as ruthless as Zeus or as calculating as Hades, but he had something far more valuable working for him. He was a good man.

"And you?" Hades addressed Amphitrite now. "How has the seaside been treating you, sister?"

"Like a queen," Amphitrite returned with the sweetest smile.

A good woman for a good man, Hades thought. "As it should. He better be as well."

"Always," Poseidon scoffed.

"Yeah? Is answering for her part of that working strategy?" Amphitrite grinned at them both before slipping her hand into Poseidon's.

Hades smiled too and turned back to the stage just as the lights around the theatre began to dim. Only then did he realize how excited he was to see the show. He'd never seen a production like the one Dionysos had described to him, one of acrobatics and music, performance and playacting. Written by the up-and-coming songwriter Orpheus and directed by the famous Calliope herself, it sounded like quite the spectacle, and Dio had truly sold it. Not that Hades was at all surprised. It was what his nephew did.

Between running the Market District with Hermes, running clubs like Elysium with Hecate and Aphrodite, and running his vineyards and breweries, Dio is a jack of all trades. Hades may have raised him, but his skills were something his uncle could never take credit for. He was simply made to entertain, to make people happy. The difference was that he never sacrificed parts of himself to do so. Hecate always pointed it out, saying that Hades might learn a thing or two. Hades wished he knew how.

The show opened with a desolate piano and two bodies swaying in the center of the stage. Within minutes, the anticipation was palpable, and the tension was like a thick smoke filling the room. Hades could feel the air buzzing around him as the music built, and he was helpless to tear his eyes away for anything. It seemed everyone was. Even Ares had a look of awe on his face as more performers flitted across the stage. Although soon enough, those performers were soaring through the air far above them, moving as well as they had on the ground, and all that they did was surreal. It was almost superhuman.

The room was soon a chorus of gasps and shrieks above the music of the show as they climbed towards a climactic crescendo. In the midst of it all, Hades found that his eyes were continually drawn to one particular figure at the head of each scene. He didn't know if this was the star Dio spoke about, but she was very much a star, and every move she made was fluid as if she had been born to move like that, like water, even —and especially— through the air.

It was mesmerizing to watch, this allure she exuded, bending the air around her to her will. He could tell: it wasn't simply a show or performance to her. This was where she lived and thrived, and to be invited inside was a privilege she had granted them explicitly. He was grateful.

When she descended upon the open space between the seats and the stage, interacting with the crowd without ever breaking stride, Hades was ensnared. In the wash of the lights, he could make out thick curls sitting atop her head like a crown and a wicked curve to her red-painted lips. When her eyes met his, alive and passionate, he felt barer than he ever had, as if she was looking right through him and into the abyss beneath. Clearing his throat, he dropped his gaze and tried to gather his wits, but that look left something in its wake that gnawed at him insistently. Like a mark. Or a wound.

When he looked up again, she had moved away down the floor, but his gaze chased her with reckless abandon. Yes, she must certainly be the star. At the very least, she is the one he wanted to meet.

Two

PERSEPHONE

Persephone peered around the thick purple curtains and out into the theatre as she took a few deep breaths. Intermission had just begun, but few people were racing for the doors. Instead, there was an excited buzz filling the space, the energy electric as it danced across her skin. She searched for Aphrodite in the crowd, but while she remembered the seat number on the ticket she'd given her, she had no clue where anything in this theatre was located. She looked diligently nonetheless, only giving up when Calliope called her name.

"Did you see him?" Calliope questioned, excitement in her eyes.

"Who?" Persephone returned as she began touching up her makeup, catching the other woman's gaze in the mirror before her.

"Hades. Front row."

"Front row?"

Dionysos had mentioned to Persephone that his uncle, owner of the casino and leader of the district, would be coming to the show, but she had tried not to think about it since. It had been weird enough to hear him refer to Hades, the stuff of legends and scary stories through each and every one of Khaos Falls' districts, as something as mundane as his uncle. To think further about it would have certainly smothered what confidence she had left. Trying to protect that confidence already felt like cupping her hands around a flame in the middle of a blizzard.

"Does he - look like he's enjoying it?" she asked tentatively.

"I would say so." Calliope's voice hit a higher pitch. "He looks very engaged."

"Well - good. Right? That's what we want?"

"Absolutely. If we can extend this residency, we have a better chance of him signing the next show here too. This is the best venue in Khaos Falls and one of the best in the Aegean."

Granted, it was probably the only venue in the city that could handle one of Calliope's shows, but Persephone didn't point that out. Khaos Falls was one of the most lucrative cities in the world, and along with Casino Asphodel itself, the Pantheon Theatre was famous. It had seen many of the greatest names in entertainment, and now they were joining that company. Persephone was still processing it.

"Keep it up," Calliope encouraged her, squeezing her shoulders. "You're killing it."

"I got you," Persephone managed.

As Calliope moved off, Persephone straightened and looked at herself in the mirror. It was hard to reconcile with the fact that she made it here after clawing her way through the mud just for a chance. Part of her still waited all too patiently for the other shoe to drop, waking up each morning with the anticipation that it had all been a dream. She inhaled.

I deserve to be here.

Turning away with a smile, she returned to the gap in the curtains.

Her mother wasn't there of course although Persephone suspected that Adonis might be, and not just to report back to the elder. He still called every now and again, trying to mend a bridge that he'd charred to ash long ago. If he had it his way, she would be at home cooking his dinner right now instead of in front of a sold-out audience. And as for her mother, well... Demeter had nearly torn down the walls of their dining hall when Persephone had expressed her desire to pursue performing arts despite the fact she had already done what Demeter had wanted, wasting six years on a business degree she'd never use. Demeter had frozen Persephone's accounts the moment the mere idea of attending Terpsichore's School of the Arts had formed in her daughter's mind, which was how Zeus had gotten through the door with his little proposal.

Zeus.

He wasn't here tonight either, but she wasn't entirely convinced that he wouldn't be keeping an eye on her if he weren't away on business for the next two weeks. She also didn't doubt the job had fallen to someone else in his stead as it had for Demeter. They'd been playing that game of "pin the tail on her whereabouts" since she got back from Deucalion Heights, where Calliope's production company was currently based. She was learning to tolerate it.

Despite that, she couldn't help but smirk in between acts. After all, she'd done it. She'd scored the lead in one of Calliope's renowned shows, and she'd been able to bring it to her hometown, even if it didn't come free. Even if it came with chains.

Tonight wasn't about that though.

"Five minutes!" somebody called into the room, sending everybody bustling.

16

"Five minutes," Persephone repeated to herself. "You got this. Come on."

Tonight was about making a good impression. While Calliope might run the most coveted production company in the Aegean with dozens of independent shows under its umbrella, the Pantheon was one of the most coveted venues, and not simply because of its elegant beauty and famed design. It was also owned and run by a man Persephone had been led to believe was a figment of Khaos Falls's imagination.

If she went only by the stories she'd heard, she would conclude that Hades didn't exist at all. Aphrodite had met him several times for matters of business and described him in explicit detail, but a secondhand account hardly instilled an unshakable belief, even if it had come from her best friend. All her life prior to that, he'd been an urban legend, the story you told kids to keep them away from The Underworld and all of its temptations. Demeter had only ever told her once. She was not to ever, for any reason at all, step foot over the River Styx.

Now she was scheduled to be here four nights a week for six weeks straight, more if things went well.

Judging by Calliope's energy currently, things were going very well. And now Persephone had just been alerted to the fact that not only was Hades himself there in the building. He was sitting in the front row.

She almost managed to forget once the third act started. This was not only the closing act but the cultivation of her most challenging work. It was an entire dance routine orchestrated among the silks strung from the high ceiling of the Pantheon. Calliope and Orpheus had taken great risks in writing and directing it, the aerials far more advanced than any other show they had ever done, and they were trusting her with it. Persephone fell into it headfirst.

She loved being in the air. Flying was her first love — or perhaps more accurately, defying gravity was. The higher she went, the lighter she felt. She climbed through the sky, her svelte figure entwined in the soft fabric as she hung and dipped, contorting into a complex tale that read differently for all who are watching.

That was what she adored about Ferocity and all of Calliope's shows. They combined so many mediums to tell a story, and it did so with acrobatics and allure and arduous temptation. The music lifted her as much as the silks did, and her movements were as crucial as the dialogue of a play. In fact, they were the dialogue, and she delivered them with passion poured over each and every line.

The crowd grew smaller below her, as did the others on the stage, but the intensity of their eyes followed her to the apex. It was the only thing that could touch her here. It was the only thing that could reach.

Yet once she was on the ground again, her feet carrying her across the stage and down the stairs, she was reminded, rather harshly, of their guest of honor. And once she spotted him, the title hardly fit his vast presence.

It wasn't hard to single him out, taller than all of them in his tailored black suit. The stubble that lined his sharp face blended beneath the lights, his dark hair cut in a smooth tapered fade. It seemed he had enough bulk on him to hold his own in a fight, but he looked wily as a fox just the same. And all of it dressed in dark brown skin that looked as soft as the satin of his tie. Even in the flesh, he appeared every bit like a myth, cloaked in shadow and smoke yet as luminescent as a god. It simply wasn't fair.

No wonder they said he didn't exist. How could he?

18

She didn't know how long she looked, but when she met his gaze, the air around them seemed to shift. The whole room did. Those eyes were the worst thing about him. Or the best thing. She wasn't sure, but either way, there was something so dynamic about these two dark orbs that sent chills down her spine and beads of sweat down her back. She felt stained by them, marked across her skin by the allure they exuded. It was almost as though there were embers underneath the onyx, a faint glow hungry for kindling. They bore into her with insurmountable intensity, and she felt it long after he looked away.

—Why did he look away?

Someone had to nudge her calf before she reeled it in, returning mind and body to the performance. For the first time that night, she was out of breath. After that, she couldn't even remember finishing the show.

She had just wrapped up washing her face when Dionysos walked into the outer dressing room, rushing towards her with that charming grin on his baby face. She liked him a lot and enjoyed his company, but more so, she enjoyed his energy. He picked her up off of her feet the moment she turned to face him, and she laughed furiously as she was swung around. Once she was back on the ground, she kissed his cheek and extended her deepest gratitude.

"You made all this what it is," he breathed, glancing over his shoulders as if to make sure no one else heard him. "You stole the show. Everyone out there is talking about you, Seph. You were amazing."

"Thank you, Dio, for all of this," she replied, patting his shoulders. "I - don't even know what to say. I can't believe we did it. I was so nervous."

"Not a soul alive would've guessed. You were fucking

awesome. And listen, after party in your honor downstairs in Elysium. Drinks are on the house. We're gonna celebrate tonight and all the nights to come!"

Persephone hesitated. "Oh, I don't know. I'm really tired, and-"

"Hey, come on. This is all about you. Listen, just a few drinks with everyone, some pictures, and I'll get you home myself. I promise. But first, Uncle wants to meet you. He loved the show. And trust me. He's a tough critic, so this is good news."

She froze, eyes widening as she stared at him. "—what?"

"Yeah, he loved you!" She figured he must be embellishing. "He's already asked about the next run. Go ahead and get dressed, and you can meet us right outside, alright?"

All Persephone could do was nod as he kissed each of her cheeks and raced off, patting other performers on the shoulder as he passed and leaving a trail of excitement in his wake. She watched him disappear from view before she started to panic, racing back into her private dressing room to retrieve her evening gown. Aphrodite wouldn't let her leave home without one, no doubt foreseeing this aspect of newfound notoriety. She was grateful for that now.

Why Hades would want to meet her was beyond Persephone though. She may have been the lead, but this whole thing was Calliope's masterful work. She would certainly be a much better conversationalist than Persephone. It was why Persephone had been drawn to this type of performance to begin with. She would much rather memorize lines than make up her own, but not having to say lines at all was ideal. Dancing came naturally to her. Talking never had.

Demeter had always said she wasn't a people person, her tongue too sharp and her intentions too blunt. That truth had never bothered her until this very moment. What if she said something foolish, and it cost the production? What if she ruined what they had accomplished tonight in one fell swoop?

Perhaps she was overreacting, but she could not possibly make that determination herself. She was dialing Aphrodite's number the moment she closed the door, but before she could complete the call, it opened again, and the woman herself strode in with a big grin. Her thick, brown hair fell in waves around her flawless face, her brown skin glowing and her bright brown eyes gleaming with a characteristic mischief. Aphrodite was the embodiment of divinity. It was no wonder she was more celebrated in this city than anyone, Zeus included. This was the kind of person Hades should be standing outside to see.

"Girl, are you aware that the leader of the Underworld is waiting for you outside?" Aphrodite immediately hissed before they embraced each other in a giddy hug. "He is dying to meet you!"

"How you know?" Persephone questioned sarcastically, already wound up with emotion.

"He keeps asking for you. Dio is out there talking you up, and for good reason." Pulling back, Aphrodite met her gaze. "You killed it tonight. I mean I knew you didn't snatch the lead off a fluke, but I was completely awestruck, Seph. You did the damn thing. I've never seen you do anything like that."

Persephone dropped her gaze as it all sunk in. This was a triumph in every sense of the word, but she'd never truly considered what might come with it. Again, avoiding people was half the reason she ended up in the air, but this? This was something else entirely. This was networking. This was politics. This was her mother's territory, and Persephone had been fleeing from that her whole life.

21

Aphrodite seemed to notice she was shaking. "What are you so nervous about?"

Persephone gave her a dumbstruck look. "Are you serious? It's Hades!"

"Okay. Narrow it down." She was so good at this, guiding Persephone through her worst anxieties. It was like a superpower.

"Well, first of all, he's in charge of our residency here. If I mess this up—"

"You won't."

"But if I do, I could ruin it for everyone."

Aphrodite didn't appear at all worried, but of course she didn't. She never did. Persephone was the one who worried. She was the thinker. Aphrodite was the doer.

"Next?" Aphrodite urged, eyes fully prepared to roll.

Persephone scowled at her. "Next, do you know how much trouble this can be if someone sees us together and reports that shit back?"

"What trouble? He runs the casino, and you work here. It's business as far as anyone else is concerned. Everyone knows all that man does is work."

"And what about my mother, huh?"

Aphrodite shrugged. "What about her? What can she do to you that she ain't already done?"

Persephone chewed her lip. "And Zeus?"

"Who cares about Zeus!" Aphrodite scoffed, exasperated.

"Um, I'm willing to bet that Hades cares."

Yet another piece of the puzzle that was the legend of Hades. He was Zeus's secret weapon. And the most dangerous man in Khaos Falls which Persephone pointed out to Aphrodite.

"Doesn't mean he's dangerous to you. He's got a code, unlike

22

his brother." Aphrodite softened nonetheless. "Seph, chill, alright? I wouldn't even be debating this if I thought it would hurt you in any way. The man just wants to meet you, that's all. And if nothing else, it will be good for what you're trying to do here. Have a drink, talk some shit, and then we can go home. It doesn't have to be anything worth worrying about."

"But - what if he doesn't just want to meet me? What if he's only doing this to gather information for Zeus?"

"I seriously doubt that. Spying on a girl for his brother? That is beneath him on so many levels, and I don't think Zeus wants him or anyone else knowing how much of a dog he's been. Besides, trashing his marriage is the only thing Zeus seems perfectly capable of doing on his own, so."

"Okay, but what if?"

Aphrodite's eyes did roll now. "It's not like he's gonna kick you to the curb. If anything, it's more reason to keep you employed here, so it works out either way, girl. Plus, if anyone can sniff that out, it would be you, and then at least you'd know, right? You won't be walking in here every night clueless."

"I'll just walk in here every night thinking about it." Persephone huffed. "Even if he isn't a - spy, I still gotta deal with Zeus. How long do you think Hades will like me around if I start bringing trouble to his doorstep?"

"It's Zeus. If anyone knows that bastard is trouble, it's Hades. That ain't on you. And if Hades likes you as much as I know he will, you don't gotta worry about that anyway."

"'Dite, that's not the point here. I-"

"Okay, listen." Aphrodite gripped Persephone's shoulders, forcing her to stop as their eyes met. "Forget everything else right now. Do you wanna meet him or not?" Persephone looked away

23

before she shrugged her shoulders. "If you do this, you do it because you want to. And if you dont want to, I'll go out there right now and tell him you're not coming, but it is completely up to you. You don't owe anybody anything. Not him, not your mother, and certainly not Zeus."

Persephone nodded, swallowing hard. She had pushed this worry to its absolute limits, and now she was all out of arguments. That didn't negate the fact. Meeting new people had always been difficult, but trusting new people was nearly impossible. Trusting Zeus had only enforced the latter, and this felt all too close to doing so again. She just didn't want to find herself in another helpless situation due to her own naivety. She definitely didn't want to risk everything she'd worked for, not to fulfill some childish curiosity about the leader of the Underworld.

But she didn't want to live in fear either.

A slow grin began to spread across her face.

"I am really curious though."

Aphrodite squealed and hugged her again, and Persephone couldn't help but join in with a laugh. If there is one thing she did trust, it was her best friend's judgment. Most of the time.

"Then let's go, girl!" Aphrodite snapped, pushing her playfully towards the clothes rack. "He's waitin'!"

Demeter always said that Persephone's curiosity would get her into trouble. Although to date, Persephone would have to disagree. At the very least, she would say it was well worth whatever trouble it brought. She had always loved mysteries. It was part of the vast fantasy world she'd fallen in love with as a child. Before she could ever be comfortable in her own skin, she had grown comfortable in her books which had fueled her daydreams and given her new worlds to escape to, worlds where she could be free from standards she would never meet set by people she could never satisfy. From poetry to plays and everything in between, she could be whoever she wanted there, including herself.

That escape was crucial in the years when her father still lived in the house of Demeter, angry at his wife's power and angrier with the mere existence of his daughter, the daughter he'd never wanted. Even once he left them, Persephone clung to her fantasies. Now, she got to recreate them for others. She'd fallen in love with the fathomless possibility of something more. And the flying too.

"Ugh, I don't even know what to say," she groaned.

"Be mysterious. Don't say shit."

Persephone snorted, shoving her best friend away playfully as the other woman giggled.

"If I were you, I'd probably just stare at him. That man is beautiful," Aphrodite went on.

"He's also thee scary story we were told growing up."

She smirked. "That's the best reason to meet him."

Rolling her eyes, Persephone pulled the dress on, allowing Aphrodite to straighten her out and fix her hair. There really was no use debating it further. She'd never know Hades' intentions if she didn't make it out to see him, and she couldn't just blow it off. She needed the clout here in the casino. If nothing else, she was doing this for the sake of her livelihood.

By the time Aphrodite shoved Persephone out of her dressing room, much of the cast had gone, and she wondered if maybe she'd kept him waiting too long. However, as she and Aphrodite exit out the side door into one of the entrance halls, she found Hades standing there, alone, with no Dionysos in sight. The two women stopped before him, and while Persephone only looked up at him in silent appraisal, Aphrodite spoke.

"A gentleman," she said softly. "Where did the rest of the entourage go?"

Hades smiled, and Persephone had to force herself to blink. Up close, those eyes were far more dangerous than she'd initially realized. And far easier to get lost in. And that smile... it was something else. She wondered if he knew how many weapons he had just on his face alone. She wondered if he'd sharpened them himself. Or if he'd sharpened them just for her.

Oh, by the Fates.

"Dionysos took them downstairs," Hades replied, his voice smooth as silk and thick as honey. It was everything Persephone expected and nothing she was prepared for. "You know how restless he gets. It's a pleasure to see you, Aphrodite. It isn't a common occurrence."

"Unfortunately not," Aphrodite concedes with a curt nod. "We like to keep to ourselves, don't we? —But, we did have a common cause tonight it seems. Hades, let me formally introduce you to Persephone, that star of the show you've been waiting on."

Persephone finally looked away, and she heard him clear his throat before holding his hand out to her. She had to fight the urge to snatch it out of the air the moment it entered her line of sight, taking her time slipping her much smaller hand into his. It grounded her enough to look at him. Only - then it wasn't grounding anymore at all. He was smiling another kind of smile, something soft and disarming. It was a stark contrast to the first, which had been sharp and all too charming, like a serpent before it struck. She liked this one better.

"It's a pleasure to meet you, Persephone," he said in a voice to match, licking his lips. "You were absolutely stunning tonight. I have never seen anything like what you did out there."

"Thank you-" Persephone started but stopped herself.

"Hades is fine."

"Hades." She tested it on her tongue, and it felt like one of those summoning games they played as children. "I'm glad that you enjoyed it. Dionysos says you're a tough critic."

"Does he? I'll have to talk to him about that."

The three of them laughed before Aphrodite did what Persephone feared she would do.

"Listen, I've gotta make a call, but I'll meet you both downstairs, I'm sure?"

She said it like it was the most natural thing in the world to her, winking at Persephone. Hades nodded, still smiling that impeccable smile.

"I'll get her there in one piece, I promise," he said, and Persephone only just realized she hadn't retracted her hand yet. She did so slowly.

"On your best behavior," Aphrodite warned him although her lips quirked up at the edges.

"I would offer nothing less."

Aphrodite kissed Persephone's cheek before sauntering away, and while Persephone knew damn well that she was going directly down to the club without making any kind of call, she simply waved her off. After all, she hadn't lied. She was very interested in what a conversation with Hades could hold, even if it was just unraveling a small part of the mystery he was encased in. Not to mention Aphrodite was right.

He was beautiful, impossibly so, especially when he was looking at her like that. She couldn't quite pinpoint what it was, but it looked a lot like wonder. And so maybe rather than worry herself sick, she could take a night off from worrying altogether about

27

everything going on beyond Asphodel, especially Zeus and her current predicament. After all, it wasn't like this was serious. It was only a few drinks with the leader of the Underworld. If he turned out to be a threat, it was better she found out now rather than later because there was one thing Hades would soon learn. She didn't go down without a fight.

Three

HADES

Dionysos hadn't at all exaggerated about this star of the show he'd mentioned. What he'd failed to disclose was exactly who this star was. When Aphrodite introduced them, Hades nearly choked. Here he was, standing in front of Persephone, the daughter of Demeter.

"Bad blood" didn't even begin to encompass the relationship between their districts. Or more accurately, between Demeter and the sons of Rhea. While it had begun long before Hades and Zeus took control —and he imagines it would linger long after— Demeter had always looked down at both men as if they were dirt on her shoe. Due to this dynamic, business between the three districts was always handled by Hecate and Hestia, Demeter's sister and right hand.

Although slight and quiet, it was no secret just how clever and cunning the Hestia could be, certainly not to Hades. He knew everything about everyone, or at least as much as he could know without intimate conversation, but that still added up to a whole lot. Information was the most valuable currency in Khaos Falls, and in that, Hades was surely the wealthiest.

He'd never known nearly enough about Persephone however.

Demeter had always managed to keep her daughter sheltered from the world, him included, and Hades had never come across her in all of his time running the Styx District. He reckoned she was a smart girl who stayed on the right side of the river. Now, it seemed that she had come across to conquer what was found here.

She was succeeding thus far, in more ways than one.

He had to wonder just how angry Demeter would be if she found out that he was currently alone with her daughter, walking through the service halls of his casino in The Underworld and towards Elysium of all places. Each aspect of that reality, every word in that sentence, must have been a strike against his character. He found it mildly exciting.

As if Demeter could think any lower of him.

"So this was your first show with Calliope?" he asked, breaking the silence as they walked through the empty halls. "You looked like you'd been doing those moves for years."

She chuckled, and his heart thudded against his ribcage. "I mean, we did some primers before we came back to Khaos Falls, but this was the first show with all three acts and the more sophisticated acrobatics. It was a whole lot of training."

"It certainly paid off."

He smiled over at her. She'd seemed so much larger on that stage, her mere presence commanding the room in a way he'd never seen. She hadn't lost much of it now, but it was nice to see her up close and at her most human. It was almost as if she was completely unaware of it, her power, which was such a rare quality in Khaos Falls. One would think modesty was banned there.

"Dio was talking about another production Calliope's working on," he went on.

"Yeah, she has some ideas," she confirmed with a nod. "She wanted to see how this one went first before she set anything in stone."

"From what I understand, we've never packed the theatre like that. Even when we've sold out tickets, we've never filled every seat. I'm assuming it went well, and it will continue to for the duration of your time here. Of course, we would extend it then."

He felt her look at him suddenly. "Really? You're thinking about it?"

He shrugged. "What's there to think about? You did in one night what most shows here haven't done in their entire residency. It's good business... And I really enjoyed it."

"Ah, so it's a personal indulgence too, is it?"

He didn't skip a beat, meeting her eyes. "Very much so."

He knows they're approaching Elysium simply by the increasing volume of the music up ahead. He hadn't planned to come to Dio's little after-party, but he supposed plans had changed. For once.

That looked to be the theme of tonight. Hecate would surely never let him live this down, but he didn't dwell on it right now. This was the first time his shoulders hadn't been wound up by his ears in a long while. It was also the first time he wasn't thinking about Zeus.

As he started down the last flight of stairs leading into Elysium, she grabbed his arm. When he turned, fighting to ignore the thrill that ran through him at her touch, he found that something in her face has shifted drastically although it seemed like she was trying to hide it.

31

"On second thought..." she mused, biting her lip. "I'm a bit too worn out for too much interaction, you know?"

"It's your party," he said, amusement in his eyes. "Do you want them to think you're a diva?"

"I promise I'll make it up to them after the next show."

He surveyed her quietly for a moment. He imagined she was thinking what he was thinking, that if Demeter found out she was sharing drinks with him, she would lose her mind and rain chaos down upon them both. Now that he was being forced to confront that reality, he berated himself for having overlooked it in the first place. That was alarming in and of itself. He never overlooked anything.

Nonetheless, that childish excitement remained despite the acknowledgment that it could have very mature consequences. He reminded himself to be wary of that.

"Would you like to have a drink with me upstairs then? In my box."

She raised her brows. "In your box?"

"That's right," he nodded. "In my box. You can still observe your whole party without the whole party observing you. Is that acceptable?"

She shrugged, but he saw her lips twitch. "Yeah, I think that's acceptable."

"Alright, come on. You're explaining it to my nephew though." He led her back into the hall and to the elevator at the end. "And tell Aphrodite. I don't want her thinking I stole you away."

"A very good point."

Apollo had modeled Hades' Elysium skybox in the same way he had modeled Hades' main office, close enough to the ground floor to see everything and yet far enough to feel untouchable. By the time the elevator opened up directly into the box, there was already a bartender prepared to take their drink orders behind the small bar. Once they called out their orders, Hades led her to the window.

He could easily gauge that they were at capacity —if not over it — which wasn't too common on a weeknight. It didn't surprise him however, considering the high traffic upstairs earlier in the night and the sold-out seats in the theatre.

He immediately began trying to identify faces before remembering his promise to Hecate, but it was difficult when he was being thrust back into it. He forced himself to take a seat beside Persephone in the booth bordering the window as the bartender brought over their drinks. When he looked over at her again, his curiosity — or perhaps his nerves— got the best of him.

"What do you think your mother would say if she hears you had a drink with me?" he inquired.

"A good question," she hummed. "Probably the same thing she said about me performing for a living."

"She didn't approve." It was more statement than question.

"Not at all."

"Yet you did it anyway."

"Yet I did it anyway." She seemed to be warring with something, but he waited. "I don't think I could've lived with myself if I hadn't."

That, he could understand. "And how did you wind up with Calliope?"

She smiled this proud little smile, and he wished more than anything that he could preserve it, place it in a jar and marvel at it each day and all hours of the—

Her voice brought him out of his thoughts.

"I did three years at Terpsichore's school before Calliope came

33

to see me, asked what I thought about an alternative path to my degree. She wanted me to audition for Ferocity, and if I got it, it would be counted as my final-year performance project. I'd still get my degree at the end of the year."

He smiled too, brushing his thumb along the side of his glass. "I'm assuming you got it."

She nodded giddily. "I did. Just before we got here. I haven't seen my mother since I got back to town, but... Sorry. I don't wanna bore you with the details."

"No, no. Trust me, you aren't."

A smirk flitted across her face. "Oh, right, you like collecting information, don't you?"

He laughed, sipping from his glass. "I promise all of this is off the record."

"Hey, I don't mind. If anyone would be worried about our dirty laundry getting aired out, it's my mother."

"And you don't seem too worried at all."

"I've been out of my mama's house for a while now. I'm not saying she won't call me the moment she finds out I've been here, my meeting you aside, because of course she will, but what can she do? Unless..." Her look suddenly turns mischievous, and she could hardly hide her smile. "Is the wraith of Khaos Falls afraid of my mother?"

He chuckled softly, more intrigued by the title than anything else. "I don't underestimate her."

"Then you're as smart as everyone says you are."

"Oh? And what else does everyone say about me?"

She tilted her head. "I'm sure you know all of the legends they tell about you by heart."

He leaned back in his seat. "Maybe, but I'm really interested to

34

know your spin on them."

"Didn't I say I didn't wanna spoil your good mood?"

"I promise you won't do anything of the sort. Like you said, I've heard it all."

She watched him for a moment, lips quirked and eyes narrowed, but he didn't flinch. She was correct in thinking he knew all those rumors and hyperboles. He'd learned to have his fun with them, devouring the parts he liked and discarding the rest. Nothing surprised him anymore, but he did want to know what image of him she had walked in here with, if he'd exceeded her expectations. He supposed it was a tall order, but his need for her validation was heightened by the simple fact that he didn't want to need it at all.

She sobered, looking down at her glass. "My mother used to say your father created you from venom and shadows, that you grew up to be a great serpent that wasn't to be trusted. Those never scared me much though. My mother is a lover of theatrics."

"Ah, that's where you get it from."

"Mhm." She nodded. "When I got older though, she would say he pulled you from the River Styx, not entirely whole and not entirely human. Others said you were a ghost that haunted your father's district. Or you were something Zeus created in a lab. Then there are the people who swear you don't exist at all." There was a shrug of her shoulders and then, with more dramatic hand gestures, "But my favorite is the one where Zeus summoned you, his own guardian daemon with which he would conquer Khaos Falls."

"Why is that one your favorite?"

She licked her lip. "Seems the most realistic."

He barked a laugh. "You don't think I could have been created in a lab?"

"Not by Zeus." She paused for a moment but recovered quickly.

"Who could possibly put someone like you together, especially if all the other stuff is true?"

"What other stuff?"

"—Did you bring me up here just to stroke your ego because I don't do all that for free."

Chuckling again, he took a long drink from his glass. He could feel her eyes on him, probing, prying. It wasn't often he was on the receiving end of such observation. It was as disconcerting as it was exhilarating. He just wished he could know exactly what she was thinking. He found himself wanting to know everything etched across her mind in relation to him. Unlike his commonplace thirst for knowledge, this was not out of concern or worry. No, it stemmed from something far more selfish and self-indulgent, something he was ill-equipped to name.

When his eyes found hers, she didn't look away, and his breath caught in his throat. Time slowed down, if only for a moment, and he took that moment to truly take her in.

The thick curls were now out, framing her face in the most flattering way. The neon lights that crawled in from below made her brown skin luminescent, and he could see the smattering of freckles that underlined her luminous eyes. With the heart of Khaos Falls beating rapidly beneath them, his own heart sped up too. It was only then that he realized he had nothing to say. Hades not offering to speak was one thing. Hades being left speechless was another thing entirely, a thing that simply did not occur. Until now. Until her.

"Why did you want to meet me anyway?" she suddenly asked.

Truly, Hades hadn't allowed himself to ask that question much less answer it, leaving the blame to Dionysos without a second thought. Now he bided his time with the contents of his glass and a glance toward the flashing lights on the other side of the window.

Once the glass was empty, he set it down and shrugged his broad shoulders.

"I told you," he said at last, deciding upon the simple answer. "You were amazing out there, and Dio insisted I meet you. I trust his judgment."

"As you should. He's sort of a genius. Or a mad scientist."

"The latter is accurate, I'd say." A pause, and then, "And why did you agree to come up and have a drink with me? Even after all those tales you've heard."

"Are you kidding? It's because of all those tales. It's like seeing the minotaur in the flesh."

"So you've debunked the myth then."

"Mm. Are you disappointed?"

"No." It was the easiest answer he'd ever given. "Feels kind of liberating actually. Are you?"

"What, disappointed?" He nodded. She shook her head. "I mean, you don't have sharp teeth or horns or anything like that, which I do feel some type of way about, but I wouldn't call it disappointment."

"That's fair. Are you going to run and tell all of your friends now?"

"Of course not. Who would believe me?" She sold it the best she could before softening again. "Besides, I think it's more fun to have a secret of my own."

"I think we can agree on that. —Though, if you have a - partner you want to impress, I'd completely understand."

She snorted. "I don't have the time for anything like that, but I appreciate the explicit permission. Maybe it'll come in handy someday."

"I hope it does."

He was underestimating her. He could feel it in his gut. Beneath all that conservative intrigue was a raw passion, which he'd stood witness to only an hour ago. He was hungry for it, and while she'd tucked it away beneath a form-fitting gown and an unassuming disposition, the scent lingered in the air. It was not often that Hades felt possessive, but right now, he wanted the privilege of laying claim to that passion. At the very least, he wanted access, and he had yet to figure out how to earn it. Or how far he was willing to go to do so.

At the moment, he would say quite far.

Before he could lean into that though, the door behind them opened, and Thanatos stormed in with a look of grim determination on his face. Hades could tell by the knit of the other man's brow that if he were to pull his phone out right now, he would have multiple missed calls and texts from his friend. Standing, he met him a few feet from the table, and Thana spoke against his ear.

"Tartarus is on lockdown," he hissed. Hades' blood ran cold.

"Since when?" he shot back, turning his head to look at Thana as best he can.

"A couple of hours ago. Full red list."

Hades was quiet for a moment, warring with the information he'd just been given before he remembered where they were. Turning back to Persephone, who stared at them with unabashed curiosity in her eyes, he managed a tight smile as he approached her. She seemed a million miles away now, an oasis he could never reach, but he tried anyway.

Leaning down, he spoke in her ear.

"I'm sorry, I have something - urgent to attend to." He could hardly obscure his disappointment. "Can I - May I get your number from Dionysos?"

She seemed to contemplate it for a moment before nodding.

Then she said, "But don't feel too obligated. We're busy people, and I can't make this a habit."

He certainly hadn't expected that. Not that she wasn't entirely correct. They were busy people, and he was about to be much busier it seemed. To think he could ever make this a habit was a foolishness he could not afford. Nonetheless, the disappointment grew to an overwhelming capacity, and he was forced to choke it down. She didn't look up at him as he straightened.

"Of course. —Thank you for humoring me. Have a good night, Persephone, and - I wish you the best of luck here. If you need anything, we will be happy to provide it."

He turned swiftly on his heel and followed Thana out of the box, wrestling with every urge to look back.

Four

PERSEPHONE

P ersephone stalked into her room, cursing herself under her breath as she tossed her keys on the bedside table, nearly knocking the lamp to the floor. Her words had haunted her since leaving Elysium, crawling across her skin and making her cringe. I cant make this a habit. Who fucking says that? It didn't take a genius to realize how it had come off, and even once she'd realized it herself, she hadn't bothered to try and explain. It had been cold, cruel, and particularly misleading. She'd made Hades, leader of the Underworld and an absolute gentleman, believe that she didn't want to make conversations with him a common occurrence. First of all, it was a bold-faced lie, and second of all, it couldn't be further from the truth.

"Stupid," she groaned, throwing herself on her bed. "What the fuck is wrong with you?"

She could tell by his demeanor that he had been appalled despite taking it in stride. Worse yet, he looked almost... sad. It certainly hadn't been anger though, and she swore she would have preferred anger.

There wasn't much she could do about it now of course, and in reality, while it may have been a lie, it was for the best. This was only her first show. She needed to focus on building on that success. Calliope and the entire cast were counting on her, and she had enough trouble with Zeus as it was. While she didn't think Hades was working against her in Zeus's name, she still couldn't be adding anything else to her plate, certainly not a fucking schoolgirl crush on the leader of the Underworld. No matter how sexy and smart and intriguing he was, no matter how vividly the warmth of his mouth still lingered against her ear now or how clear the sound of his laughter still rang in her mind or... Shit.

It took her hours to fall asleep.

It took her days to wash off her shame.

The good thing was that naturally, a successful show didn't allow for relaxation. In fact, it demanded the exact opposite. Morning workouts and afternoon rehearsals took up most of Persephone's schedule, the rest of it spent scrounging up enough rest to get through it all. On the days when they had a show, Calliope allowed only light rehearsals in the morning hours, but Persephone still persisted with her own routine, all of it demanding and all of it a dream.

The price of success was not at all unreasonable, and every show was as rewarding as the last. While the standing ovations were a beautiful bonus, she was simply happy to be on the stage. There had never been a time in her life when she could not find sanctuary there, dancing amidst the silks before they lifted her into the air, far away from anything and anyone who would bring her harm.

While her more childish fears had been shed, this subtle discomfort in the world managed to make its presence known every now and again. Therefore, tired as she was, she loved every minute of it, but the fatigue always managed to catch up.

It was two weeks before she actually got to sleep in. At least, she was supposed to get to sleep in. Instead, her phone was blaring on the nightstand for the third time in as many minutes, and this time, it managed to rouse her. She reached for the device if only to shut it off before rolling over with a groan.

While Calliope had set her up with an apartment in the Styx District close to the theatre, Persephone still spent most of her nights at Aphrodite's. That wasn't to say she hadn't been just as impressed with the district as she'd been with its leader. She had always imagined the Underworld as some cavernous place, the stuff of nightmares where beasts lurked and smoke billowed from the streets themselves. It was nothing like that.

While the architecture there was much sharper and more unforgiving than the rest of Khaos Falls, it wasn't filled with smog and rats. Its streets were just as impeccable as Hades in his expensive suits and just as striking to look at. Many of the buildings were a stark obsidian or a deep cream, and there wasn't much color to be found apart from the deep purple insignia sporting a full-face helmet and plume that denoted Hades' ownership, but the place still managed to find its charm.

Persephone liked it a lot, but she still couldn't manage to get comfortable. Whether it was her mother or Zeus or something else entirely, she could not pinpoint it. She just knew that she slept better in Aphrodite's house and on her turf. The lavish estate in the Lush District was the closest thing to home Persephone had now.

Her phone rang again, and she knew who it was. She also knew he wouldn't stop calling until she answered. Growling her frustration, she reached over and snatched the phone up, answering the call blindly.

"I'm sleeping," she grumbled.

"Hey, beautiful." Zeus's voice mercilessly assaulted her ear, and she flinched. "How's my girl?"

"How's your wife?"

He sucked his teeth, stewing for a moment. When he spoke again, his voice had risen a few octaves, and it was evident that he was restraining his annoyance. At what exactly was anyone's guess. Persephone liked to keep those options stocked to capacity to the best of her ability.

"What's this I hear about you down in the Underworld so much lately?"

A lazy smile stretched over her face. Ah. "We have a residency down there."

"Spending some time in Elysium too, I hear."

That was what she'd expected. Granted, she'd only been to Elysium twice since the night she met Hades, and it had only been to make up for missing the first celebration. Telling Dionysos "no" was an exercise in resolve, and Persephone didn't have much of that when it came to the younger man. His excitement was contagious, and he threw one hell of a party. Nevertheless, Zeus's curiosity only proved what she already knew. He was still watching her, whether he was in town or not.

"Is that why you're calling?" she asked with a yawn.

He huffed in indignation. "I'm calling because I just got back into town, and I'm already hearing all this—"

"You wouldn't have to hear anything if you minded your own business."

"What are you doin' down in Elysium?"

"Nothing that concerns you, and if that changes, I will let you know myself, Zeus."

"Perseph—"

"I have a show tonight, and I need my rest, so I'm gonna go."

Before he could get another word out, she cut the call and turned down her ringer. Then she rolled over and tried to find some more sleep. It didn't come quickly.

She knew she'd made a mistake trusting him four years ago. Albeit back then, she had been willing to do anything to get away from her mother, and more than that, to go to Terpsichore's school, Zeus's school. Plus, she and Zeus had become friendly in the months prior when he'd started to attend performances in the community theatre. That was where he'd found her. He'd really sold how impressed he was too, but she'd learned by now that Zeus had an unmatched talent for selling bullshit.

When he'd offered her a place for the next semester on a full scholarship, of course it sounded too good to be true. Aphrodite had said it, Adonis had said it, and she had said it to herself a thousand times. Still, it seemed like the only way.

Aphrodite had only just crawled out of the ruin of her father's house and had no means to help her, and Adonis was more interested in living out his own dreams than allowing her to chase hers. Breaking up with him didn't stop him from expressing his disappointment in every choice she made thereafter, especially when she took Zeus's charity. Once Aphrodite came around though, Adonis's disdain and Demeter's inevitable wrath may have done more to persuade her into trusting Zeus than anything else. Not to mention that at the time, she truly believed the city leader wanted to help.

Zeus had admitted that he wanted to see a little rebellion against

Demeter, but he'd made her swear not to tell anyone of his role in her scholarship. He hadn't even put his name on the paperwork, and her naive ass took that to mean that he wasn't going to use it to cause discord in her mother's district. Now, she knew better. Zeus didn't do anything for anyone except Zeus, and what he demanded now was far beyond anything she was willing to do. She wasn't going to be anyone's mistress, not even the king of Khaos Falls.

Persephone managed a few more hours of sleep before she climbed out of bed and into a hot shower. She let the water wash away as much of her fatigue as possible before she found her mind wandering. It wandered to the show tonight, to Calliope, to Dionysos, and... to Hades. Always to Hades.

She hadn't seen him at any of the shows the last two weeks, and if he had come, he hadn't hung around after, nor had he called or texted her. She imagined he must be busy. Or he'd heeded her foolish words and was now keeping his distance. Regardless, understanding did not automatically breed acceptance.

Her disappointment had been all but a physical entity the first show after their little chat. Aphrodite had been forced to scold her for being so moody. Forgive her though. This beautiful man with a beautiful mind had treated her to drinks in his private skybox, giving her his full attention and showing genuine interest in her work, in her. Few had ever done that, and with such sincerity that it lingered long after the words themselves. Then he'd just... disappeared, and again, he had her questioning if he existed at all.

She splashed her face with water before shutting the shower off and reaching out for her towel. She couldn't be twisting herself up over Hades, over anyone for that matter. The show had been going exceptionally well, packing the Pantheon each night, but they could not let up now. They were only a third of the way through their resi-

45

dency, but only increased demand would ensure their stay was continually extended right through to another. She could only hope Zeus didn't come tonight. She simply could not handle the absence of one brother and the presence of the other, especially when the other was Zeus.

"You get some rest finally?" Aphrodite asked, sliding a smoothie across the counter once Persephone entered the kitchen. "You were looking rough, girl."

"You tell me then," Persephone shot back.

Aphrodite gave her a once-over before shrugging her shoulders. "Yeah, you look a little better."

"Thank you." She took a generous drink of the smoothie before speaking again. "You comin' tonight?"

"I might drop by Elysium after, but I've got a meeting with Hephaestus tonight."

Aphrodite looked disgusted, and Persephone had to hide her smirk. She wasn't entirely sure what Aphrodite's issue was with the arms dealer. She wasn't even sure Aphrodite knew herself, but it was always fun to poke at... Well, at least until she remembered that Hephaestus was Hades' nephew, and then her mind was on him and his stupid, charming smile again. Fuck. She shook the thought away.

"A meeting?" Persephone hissed, wiggling her eyebrows. "Oh, I bet."

"Hush up, nasty. You know I can't stand that man. It is a meeting. And really, it's Eros' meeting. He wants to put a couple - investments over at one of the dens. They've been getting some ugly threats over the warehouse we cleared out last week."

"Damn. I guess you couldn't stay a nameless vigilante forever."

"I never thought I could. I'm just worried about the ones we

46

saved. Every time we break up one of these trafficking rings, two more pop up in its place. Zeus won't even take a meeting to discuss city security, which is what we need. He only cares if his shit is protected."

"Not to mention he's a dog himself. For all you know, he makes money off it too."

"Ain't that the truth. But it's cool. I'll keep doin' what I've been doin'. No sense worrying about shit I can't change. I'll focus on what I can."

She didn't know how Aphrodite did it. While Persephone had been forever fleeing from the idea of running her mother's district one day, Aphrodite had made it so that it was as if Oceanus and his district had never existed at all. From changing the name to deconstructing its very foundation, Aphrodite had made the district her own, a safe haven for anyone who could ever need it. Many saw her as simply something to be gawked at and fantasized about. Others knew she was to be worshipped and respected, but Persephone knew the younger woman was so much more than any one idea. She didn't know if she would have made it through her own transition —medical or otherwise— without Aphrodite, even with her mother's blessing. The one blessing Demeter had ever truly given her.

Then again, Demeter had always said that while a son overshadows his mother, a daughter reflects her, so that blessing likely wasn't entirely selfless.

"Maybe you could - talk to Hades about it," Persephone now suggested, looking down at her cup.

"Mhm." She could feel Aphrodite's smug look on her and immediately regretted her words. "Don't come up in here all sad and shit tonight either, actin' like a teenager with all that sighin' and groanin'."

47

Persephone rolled her eyes. "I was trying to help you! And I have not been sighin' and groanin'. I'm just - it's whatever."

"Hey, you told the man to get scarce."

"I did not!" Aphrodite raised her brows, and Persephone withered. "I mean, not exactly like that."

"You should be happy. He listens. Unlike somebody."

"Ugh." Persephone shook her head. "Don't remind me."

"And to be fair, with Zeus out of town and that whole thing going on with Tartarus, Hades no doubt has to hold it all down, on top of worrying Zeus is gonna do something stupid before he gets back."

"Oh, he's back."

Aphrodite perked up, her glare back. "You talked to him?"

"He called me all morning. It wasn't a long conversation though. I hung up."

"Maybe you should talk to Hades about your problem too."

Persephone snorted. "Aphrodite, I don't know the man like that. We had one drink. Really like, half a drink."

"I don't mean talk to him like a friend. I mean talk to him like the man holding Zeus's leash. Maybe he can put him in a damn muzzle so you can get some peace. Think about it. He wouldn't want the woman bringing in all this new money to be unable to concentrate on her work, would he? Besides, it's an excuse to take back what you said about not making it a habit or whatever. That's what you want, isn't it?"

"What I want and what I need are two very different things. Besides, that's the worst possible way to try and start talking to him again. 'Hey, I know I said I don't wanna see you again, but can you do me a favor and fight my battles for me? Thanks."

It was Aphrodite's turn to roll her eyes. "Alright, and what if you do start talking again? Naturally? You gonna tell him, or are you just gonna keep changing your number and hiding out here all the time until he finds out himself and it blows up in your face?"

"I'm not hiding out. I'm comfortable here, and - I can't be changing my number anymore. I'm a professional now. People need to get in touch with me."

"Alright, so my suggestion stands. Whether you start talking again or not, he's your best option, Persephone. In all the ways it matters, Hades is the law in this city. Hephaestus, Achilles, Prometheus, every other security provider in town, they all answer to him."

"And he answers to Zeus. Look, I get your point, 'Dite, and I know you believe he won't turn on me to protect his brother, but of all the stories we've heard, one thing always stays the same. He works for Zeus. Who the fuck am I to disrupt that? Even if we do start talking again, Hades and I? It's nothing. It's always gonna be nothing."

Aphrodite leveled her with a pointed look. "If it's nothing, then why are you so upset you haven't seen him?"

Persephone pinched the bridge of her nose. "—Okay look, it doesn't matter what it is or what it isn't. I don't have the time for this. I have to keep up with these shows and focus on what I can control. I can't control Zeus, and I can't control Hades. All I have is me."

Aphrodite straightened now and rounded the corner, her face serious but soft. "All I'm saying is you don't deserve to be harassed, not even by the king of Khaos Falls, and the only one who can step to him is Hades. It's gonna be really hard focusing on anything if that man don't leave you alone. You know men like that, Seph, men like our fathers. They get everything they want no matter

49

what the cost is, and if they can't get it one way, they'll find another. I don't want to know what that looks like for Zeus. Not with you or anyone else."

Aphrodite kissed her forehead and wished her good luck before heading out of the kitchen, leaving Persephone to sip her smoothie and mull over those words.

Aphrodite was right. Persephone knew that Aphrodite was right, but so was she. Hades and Zeus were each their own brand of trouble, and she should be running the other way on both fronts. Despite that, her mind was far more occupied with the idea of speaking to Hades again than with getting rid of Zeus. Damn. She supposed there was bound to be trouble either way, meaning there was only one thing left to do.

Pick her poison.

Five

HADES

Hades still could not determine which was worse, hearing from Zeus or not hearing from Zeus. He had been made aware of his brother's return the moment it occurred, but any ease that may have graced his mind was all but lost in a matter of minutes. He had expected a call from his brother within a few hours of the notification. It never came, and the problem he had left on Hades' doorstep before he left was beginning to fester.

Tartarus had been on a redlist lockdown for two weeks now. That not only meant that no one from other districts was allowed in without explicit permission from Erebus and Nyx but also that nothing came out which was most devastating. Tartarus specialized in security mainly for the coastal borders of all of Khaos Falls. The entire city was left vulnerable to outside threats without them watching the waterways.

They also guarded the Olympus Port full-time, using it as a base for all naval operations. All they'd wanted was formal control of it to cut the costs being imposed upon them simply for being there.

Zeus had not only denied them that. He had lied first. Their response was not simply swift. It was loud, it was clear, and it was warranted. For the first time since they had been pulled from power, Tartarus was rearing its head. And Hades could not blame them.

Considering they bordered Hades as the only other district on this side of the River Styx, the whole situation made him especially nervous. Erebus and Nyx had always been civil with him, working with him however they could to ensure the city was safe. However, the same could not be said for their two eldest children and future heirs to the district, Coeus and Tethys. Coeus was vindictive and vengeful, and Tethys... Well, she was something else entirely. Unlike Hades, she never let her talents fade into gossip or ghost stories. She always made sure that Khaos Falls knew she was there, alive and well. And formidable.

Of course, none of this had occurred to Zeus when he haphazardly double-crossed them. Or maybe it had. Either way, now that he was back, who knew what they would do.

"Anything?" Hades asked as Charon entered his office, face unreadable as always.

Charon didn't immediately answer. He took a seat across from Hades, extracting an herbal cigarette from his inner jacket pocket and lighting it. His silence was never silent. It surrounded Hades like humidity in the air, sweat-inducing and suffocating. The raven that spread its wings across the front of his throat flexed as he held the cigarette between his teeth.

"No movement in or out," he at last reported. "Even for a red list, Tartarus is pretty quiet right now."

"They're always pretty quiet."

"Then they're very quiet. No deals, no trades, no activity at the port. I managed to get Achilles and some of his men down there to keep any smart guys in check, but he can't patrol the water and the inner districts all at once. He isn't equipped for that. No one is."

"And the family? Tethys's siblings?"

"No one's seen any of them at their usual haunts in some time. They're serious about this lockdown."

Hades ran his hand over his head. "What about Nyx's monthly symposium? They never cancel that."

Charon shook his head, floral-scented smoke billowing from his lips. "Cancelled. Or it just didn't happen. It's a bit unclear. Either way, no one's seen Tethys or Coeus or any of their siblings. You know Iapetos lives in the pleasure dens most days, and yet."

Hades sighed. "And yet."

"My guess?" He ashed his cigarette in the tray before him. "If they do make a move, they'll go to Demeter first. She's the only viable ally they have, and she has access to the only other port apart from the Market District, so we'll keep some eyes around there."

And just like that, Hades was thinking about her again. Persephone. He'd been doing his best not to. He had so much going on, and while he'd failed to keep away completely, sneaking down to several shows in the past two weeks, he'd managed to make it out of the theatre without succumbing to the urge to wait for her. The threat of war had helped in that respect at least.

He'd been forced to focus almost all of his energy on Zeus's return and what Tartarus might do with it. Part of him, the part that sounded a whole lot like Hecate, wanted to blow it off and let Zeus figure it out. However, Tartarus and everyone else knew that the best way to get to Zeus —if not the only way— was to rip the Underworld out from under him. Only then would he flail long enough to have his head separated from his body without a doubt.

Hades knew this, meaning his district was not without enforcement, but he still felt obligated to worry. Hecate told him often about how one day, all of those messes he'd cleaned up for his brother would come back to drown him. He wondered if that day had finally crested the horizon.

"Don't," Charon said, his voice suddenly stern.

"Don't what?" Hades scoffed.

"Whatever you're thinking of doing to try and fix this. You did your part. You hashed out the details with Medusa and gave Zeus your council. All he needed to do was sign a few papers. He ignored that and backstabbed all of us. This isn't your mistake to unmake, and even if it were, you can't because they will never trust Zeus again. He's finally shown his greed to the one district that can call it out, and there is no cleaning this up quietly. It will make us look complicit."

"I'm pretty sure I'm already seen as complicit."

"Not like this, not in a blatant act of betrayal against another district. Against Tartarus."

"We are without security, and our district doesn't have enough bodies to cover the loss. No district does. You just said so yourself."

" Zeus has put the whole city in danger for his own gain. He has to fix this, or else it can't be fixed."

"And if he doesn't?"

"Then when Tartarus comes to you, and they will come to you, you cooperate."

"They'll want him removed from power."

Hades sat back in his chair, gripping the arms and pursing his lips. Charon stamped out his cigarette and mimicked the position. He didn't say what Hades knew he was thinking, but his eyes certainly do, and for once, Hades didn't bother to discount it. With every problem, the common factor was Zeus.

Hades never made problems for himself, never got in anyone's way, and he never went back on his word. More than that, he had always proven himself to be ten steps ahead of everyone else, and Zeus's reign had always depended upon the belief that Hades was an impenetrable shield on his frontline.

While a visit from the elder brother had always been seen as an omen, that visit was always well-earned and never based on fabrication or falsity. He did nothing without proof, and every outcome was given proper justification. But there was no justifying Zeus's actions here, meaning there would be no justifying any actions in defense of him. As of now, Hades' hands were tied.

Cerberus pushed his nose underneath Hades' hand, resting his chin in his lap until the man came out of his head and petted him. Instantly, both were soothed to some semblance of comfort. Hades considered going downstairs for a show tonight. It would do him some good to get out of the office, to keep from dwelling on this. However, he feared that if he went, he would simply dwell on something else —or rather, someone else— for even longer. And far longer than was appropriate at the moment.

While he may have been unable to do anything proactive, he had to be ready to do something reactive if it became necessary.

"Hecate and Thana?" he asked, looking up at Charon.

"Downstairs. He's training a few new guys today, and she's gotta sign off on deliveries."

"Anything I should be aware of going on? In the casino, I mean."

Charon raised a brow. "Not that I can think of."

"You mind if I take the night off?"

He smiled, a sight not near common enough. "Not in the slightest, brother."

Hades looked away. "Flood the streets. Now that Zeus is back, I want to make sure we're tuned into everything. Ask Heph if he can come in and see me tomorrow afternoon. Coeus isn't stupid enough to buy directly from him, but he'll know if Tartarus is stocking up anywhere."

"Will do." Charon stood now, turning towards the door. "Enjoy your evening, brother."

"Will do," Hades echoed.

Though by the time he decided whether or not he wanted to go down to the Pantheon, the evening had escaped him completely. The show had been on for over an hour, and he knew it would end soon.

Rather than try and catch the rest of it, he continued to sit at his desk, staring off into the distance until he could do so no longer. With a frustrated huff, he rose to look down at the casino floor. There was a poker tournament going on in one of the larger rooms, so the traffic in the main area was less dense than it would be later on. There remained enough activity to soothe Hades nonetheless.

He watched patrons at a nearby table squint at their cards, sweat collecting on their brows, glancing around nervously. He could watch a poker game from beginning to end and never get bored, even with the most inexperienced of players. If anything, throwing a few of those in the boat was always entertaining. It gave him an underdog to root for.

Although tonight, not even poker could shield him from all of his woes. Persephone had been clear that she didn't want to spend more time with him, and yet it was all he could think about. It was pathetic. He'd never wanted for anything, content with the way his day-to-day went. In a single night, she threw a wrench in that, and he had no idea how to dig that wrench out. Worse than that, he wasn't sure he wanted to. Maybe he liked denying himself a bit too much.

He decided it best to retire for the night before Charon came back and gave him shit for not leaving, but just as he moved away from the window, he caught a glimpse of someone he'd never seen on the main floor. He nearly lunged for the radio on his desk before rushing back to the window, bringing it to his lips with a shaking hand. He gave the description, then he gave the order.

"Straight up to my office. Now."

Six

PERSEPHONE

Naturally, Zeus attended the show. Although he obviously didn't wish to be seen, at least not by Dio or anyone else with the misfortune of being related to him, Persephone caught him in the crowd with far too much ease. She thought it might be her instinct, drawing her eyes up to the second-floor balcony where he lingered at the edge of the aisle next to the wall. His street clothes and unshaven face did not fool her, but part of her wished they had. The other part of her was glad to have an advantage.

She didn't waste a second once the show ended. She didn't wash up or dress down or any of the normal things she would do on any other night. Instead, she rushed straight back to the dressing room, gathered her things, and scurried out of the theatre throwing sloppy goodbyes over her shoulder. She then ducked inside one of the doors Hades had taken her through after that first show, which led her into the service hallway. Hoping she could find a way up to and out through the casino, she tried to calm herself as she walked along the empty corridors. It was much less comforting here without Hades beside her, but she batted that thought away the moment it registered in her mind. It had become a common occurrence, batting thoughts of Hades away. She wished she could go back to when she truly thought he wasn't real.

These hallways were more maze than anything, but she was dedicated to her escape, listening for the sounds she could associate with the casino. She did hear Elysium, but that was the last place she wanted to go, thinking it was the first place Zeus would go looking for her when she didn't come out of the dressing rooms. She imagined he wouldn't get too close anyway, what with Dio down there, but truly, she didn't know what he was capable of anymore.

Aphrodite's words still echoed in her mind, and a chill ran down her spine.

At last, the sound of slot machines met her ears, and she raced towards it. She was betting on the idea that Zeus would steer clear of the casino altogether if only to avoid Hades, but... Fates, she really had to stop pretending she knew what either of these men would do. They didn't put the city in a headlock with transparency.

As of now though, taking into account both her conversation with the elder brother and the reaction of Zeus himself, Persephone was sold on the conclusion that Hades had no clue about Zeus's obsessive interest in her. Or the subsequent stalking. Seeing as Hades seemed to know everything, it was safe to say that Zeus had not only intentionally withheld that information from him but had thoroughly hidden it, which may just work in her favor. For now.

She clutched her clothes tight to her chest as she hurried across the carpeted casino floor. She kept her eyes straight ahead, only glancing at the marquee above to confirm she was heading for an exit. There weren't enough people up here to keep her from feeling exposed, but there were still enough to make her nervous. She kept moving, dodging bodies left and right until she could make out the glass doors up ahead. Before she reached them, however, two figures stepped in her path, effectively cutting it off and stopping her in her tracks.

"Excuse me?" she said, exasperated. "What's the problem here?"

One of them gestured upward, and Persephone followed it with her eyes. "The owner wants to see you."

Above them, Persephone could see a large, glass box with tinted windows jutting out over the floor, and she imagined this was what the skybox in Elysium looked like from the ground. Of course his office was styled in the same way, offering him an eagle-eye view of all that went on below. She was willing to bet that he had a penthouse in the casino hotel with the same privilege. It certainly explained how he managed to see so much without being seen. This wasn't merely an architectural preference. This was a glimpse at the inner workings of his mind.

Before she truly had time to decipher how she felt about being summoned like this, she was following the two guards up the stairs. She tried to think of what she wanted to say to him, but none of the words form coherent sentences, and she struggled just to find a baseline. It was only once she was stepping inside his office, leaving the guards at the door, that she decided she was pissed.

She ignored the fact that it was geared more toward herself.

To start, he was sitting there behind his desk looking absolutely flawless in a black suit and tie over a red dress shirt. It was obvious he'd been lined up recently too, his hair trimmed and his beard tidy, but those eyes hadn't changed one bit. Again, they were staring at her as though she was something to be marveled at. She wanted to scream.

She also wanted to dive into them headfirst.

"Are you kidding me?" she spat, clutching her belongings tighter. "I don't hear from you for two weeks, and you think you can just summon me up to your office like I got caught smoking in the bathroom?"

He looked genuinely appalled, smile fading and mouth falling open as he floundered for something to say.

"—We - allow smoking in the bathroom."

And how the hell was she supposed to remain mad at that?

Still, she stood her ground, drawing herself up to her full height and giving him a potent glare, one she'd inherited straight from her mother. If he were anyone else, she was certain he would wither to nothing beneath it. But no, he had to be fucking Hades.

"And - you said you didn't want to make this a habit," he went on, his voice tentative as he gestured between them. "I didn't want to overstep."

Any argument she'd armed herself with on the way up here died on her tongue, and defeat began to seep into her skin. She knew what she'd said, and she knew what she'd meant, but only one of those things had been handed over to Hades. She couldn't truly fault him.

But she'd already opened her damn mouth, and now she had to follow through. Didn't she?

"So why are you summoning me now?" she retorted.

Standing, Hades cleared his throat and stepped around the desk.

"I'm sorry," he said softly. "I just - I saw you down there, and - I wanted to go to the show tonight. I'd planned to, but..." He looked down, scratching the back of his head.

She didn't let him off, no matter how cute he looked flustered. "But what? Go on."

He emitted a bitter laugh. "By the time I stopped second-guessing myself, it was over. Then you stumbled into the casino, and —"

"Stumbled?"

"—Well, you know. I mean, you showed up out of nowhere... What are you doing up here anyway?"

"Don't change the subject. You said you would call."

"And you said—"

"I never said not to."

Though it didn't take long for her own shame and embarrassment to start crawling up her throat. She didn't know why she was so worked up over this. She had made peace with the fact that their encounter had been a one-time thing because she'd asked for it to be. She'd just wanted to get home, not go through this, but he was right there, and she couldn't not say anything.

She knew that didn't mean she had to say something so unfair though. She had been trying to convince herself that Hades and Zeus really were two sides of the same rigged coin, but Hades continued to prove her wrong. Even when he wasn't at fault, he took the blame, and he didn't even hesitate. What was she supposed to do with that?

"You're right. You didn't." He met her eyes. "And I should've. I wanted to, but..." He growled in agitation as he dragged a hand down his face, and she had to suppress a shiver at the sound. "I'm a mess. I just - had you dragged up here for anyone to see."

"I don't care about that," she stated firmly.

"I know you don't. That's the thing. I don't either, and I should. There are - things going on right now, and I have to be on top of it.

On top of everything, and I was already so damn distracted by you, I knew if I called, I wouldn't be able to focus at all."

She snorted a laugh. It did nothing to keep the heat from racing up her neck. "Oh, please. Is that really the best you got?"

He mimicked the sound, and despite the tired smile on his face, he looked every bit as intimidating as he did the first time she saw him. When he spoke, his voice was stern and unwavering.

"Are you saying you weren't? That's why you're angry, isn't it? You wanted me to call, even when you knew it would be a distraction. Even when you said yourself you couldn't make this a habit."

She had to pause at the accusation and how quickly the tables had turned, the words lodged in her throat. Why did she have to say anything at all? She'd played her hand, and now he was standing there calling her bluff, and she couldn't even be mad at him.

Suddenly, she felt deflated, staring down at her feet, and she wished she could ascend into the air right now, right through the ceiling. All those warnings she'd given herself came rushing back a minute too late. Getting wrapped up with him would do her no good in the long run. It wasn't even doing her any good right now. And this wasn't about Zeus. It was about the way Hades made her skin hot from five feet away.

"Do you want to change?"

His voice cut through her thoughts, and she looked up at him in confusion. He was pointing to a door to her right, but she still hadn't deciphered what he meant.

"There's a bathroom through there," he went on. "If you would like to change or anything, by all means."

She was about to yell at him again to stop changing the subject, but she suddenly realized she was shivering and not simply from frustration. She'd run from the theatre in very little clothing, and Asphodel was - well cooled. Besides, she could use a breath.

She nodded, tentatively approaching the door as if fearing something was going to jump out. When nothing did, she stepped inside, closing the door behind her. At last, she let herself exhale.

Turning on the light, she found herself in a rather large bathroom. The door and its position in his office had been deceptive in relation to its size. Directly in front of her was a wall, half of it dedicated to a mirror and the other half to a sink counter and cabinets. Stepping over to the sink, she set down her things and turned on the water.

Once her face was cleansed of the stage makeup, she felt substantially better, moving to change out of her final costume and into her street clothes. It was a simple pair of navy blue joggers, a white v-neck, and a light jacket. After all, she hadn't expected to see him tonight, and her evening dress was all too revealing for the climate in here.

Pulling the garments on with a huff, she turned back to the mirror and began running her fingers through her curls, letting them fall loosely around her face. Even once she was satisfied to the best of her ability, she stood there staring at herself, once again chiding her reflection. She didn't want to be angry anymore, certainly not with him, but once that defense came down, what was left to shield her?

She took her time coming out of the bathroom, and once she did, she found Hades on the couch with a large, black dog resting their head on his knee. The dog looked at her, their eyes somehow as scrutinizing as that of their owner's, but they didn't bark or offer much of a reaction beyond that.

"Do you - wash up here often?" she questioned, her eyes still on the canine.

"Not all too often," Hades returned. "I live right upstairs."

"In the casino?"

"In the hotel, yes."

She knew it. From what Aphrodite said about him and his work ethic, she imagined living upstairs was not only very convenient but the only option. It would be necessary to keep him from spending too many nights on that very sofa. Persephone had to wonder why the reigning power of Khaos Falls sat in the Olympus District when Hades did all the work here.

Her eyes traveled back up to his face, snagging on the rest of him along the way. It was the first time she'd ever seen him do anything akin to slouching, sprawled against the corner of the sofa. She could tell he was tired, and while Aphrodite hadn't been able to give her too many details about this business with Tartarus, Persephone swore the severity of it was written all over his face.

"I poured you a drink."

He gestured to the coffee table between them where two glasses sat. She knew her drink just from the look of it, which meant he knew it too. He'd remembered.

As he sat up straighter, the dog moved to accommodate but didn't take his head away from Hades' leg. It was endearing, watching the scene. It was almost as though the animal didn't know they should be afraid of him. Persephone can relate.

"He won't bite, I promise," Hades assured her as he patted the seat beside him, and she didn't hesitate long before moving to sit down. She was tired too.

"What's his name?" she asked, setting her bag down at her feet and picking up her drink.

"Cerberus.".

"He's huge."

Hades smirked. "You should have seen his father. He was my father's dog. In fact, Cerberus's family has been with mine for generations. His brothers still are. He's been with me since he was a pup."

Persephone smiled against the lip of her glass before taking a sip. She reaches out to pet Cerberus but stopped herself, looking up at Hades. He nodded softly, and so she went ahead, running her hand over the top of the hound's head. Cerberus watched her hand descend, but once it did, he moved his head closer before pushing it completely into her hand. She chuckled, and Hades did too.

"He usually doesn't take to people this well," Hades admitted.

"Is he your guard dog?"

"A guardian, yes. And I'm his. It was tradition in my father's family, and it always managed to coincide. A child was born, and a litter was too."

"You said he has brothers. Where are they?"

Hades smiled, and his eyes seemed to go somewhere else, to a memory maybe. She watched, intrigued.

"In the hotel as well. With Hecate, Thanatos, and Charon. I'm sure you've heard of them."

Persephone raised a shoulder, playing off just how much she'd heard about them. What Hades was to Zeus they were to Hades, every bit as imposing and as important to his lore as he was.

"In passing."

"My father always said they were meant to be with me my whole life. Each of them received a pup from the litter as well."

She sat back against the opposite arm to better look at him. "They don't just work for you, do they?"

He shook his head. "As I said, they're my family."

She didn't ask if Zeus got a pup too. She doubted he had, or at the very least, she hoped he hadn't. She also found herself hoping that Thanatos and Charon were better brothers to Hades than she imagined Zeus was as well. At the moment, with his defenses lowered, he looked - exhausted. Maybe even a little stressed. Every time she saw Zeus, he looked like he didn't have a care in the world. Now she knew where all his worries resided, right there on Hades' chest. She almost wanted to reach out and place her hand there, to see if she could lift any of them herself. He interrupted that thought, thoroughly.

"When do you have a night off?"

She looked up with eyes wide, again struggling to catch up to what he was saying. What he was inferring. She had a bad habit of daydreaming and getting lost in her thoughts, a luxury her mother often pointed out. Demeter swore that it would be the first thing that the world would strip her of, right before her femininity. The world hadn't succeeded in taking either of them yet.

And he was patient, eyeing her with a measured curiosity until she caught up again.

"Oh," she chuckled breathlessly. "I don't have nights off."

"Come on, you have to have one."

"And that's about it."

"Would you consider spending it with me?"

She looked at him as though he'd asked her to do a backflip over the balcony railing, mouth agape and eyes as round as plates. He rested his head against his thumb and forefinger, elbow propped on the couch arm. Cerberus laid his head on her lap now and groaned. He was a great wingman.

"You're serious," she concluded, although her own tone was quite skeptical.

"I'm serious," he confirmed.

"We said we didn't want to make this a thing."

"No, you said, but then you got upset with me for it, so I assume that means you didn't mean it or you've changed your mind."

"Why?" She couldn't help but ask. "You said you were busy."

"And that hasn't stopped me from thinking about you. I thought you would distract me if you were here, but the fact is that when you're not here, I wish you were, which is just as distracting if not more so."

She laughed again. "Has that line ever worked for you before?"

"I wouldn't know." He didn't even blink. "I've never used it before, so I suppose we'll find out together."

Her pride was at play now, and it was only incited by the apparent retreat of his own. Of course, she wanted to say yes, but as he'd said, he was as much a distraction to her as she was to him, and what good could come from that? She had already put this entire - desire to bed, and there was still this entire mess with Zeus to think about, but...

"What would we do?" she inquired, petting Cerberus's head once more as she sipped from her glass. It was soothing. "If I decided to spend my night off with you?"

Hades seemed to have already considered that. "Dio's been begging me to try out the new restaurant he's just opened in the eastern vineyard. Maybe you'd like to accompany me."

He was talking about leaving his district. It was said that he rarely, if ever, left his district, and that was one bit of information both Aphrodite and Dionysos had confirmed. Sure, it was only across the river to his nephew's vineyard, but that didn't negate the fact. He didn't truly have to go anywhere at all. She would have settled for dinner here at Asphodel. Of course, she would never tell him that.

"Alright," she at last nodded. "I'm free this Monday. Does that work for you? Do you need to move around your schedule?"

His amusement was the brightest thing in the room somehow. "Monday is perfect. Where should I pick you up from?"

She considered it for a moment. "My place."

He paused. "You mean, in the Harvest District?"

She snickered. She thought he knew everything. "Calliope got me an apartment, here in your district."

"Ah." He laughed as well. "That's who she'd secured it for. I thought it was hers."

"So you know it?"

"I do." Naturally. "So I'll pick you up there, say, seven?"

She suddenly felt nervous. It was real. This was happening. "That works for me."

He raised his glass. "Monday it is then."

She tipped her own glass towards his until the edges touched. "Monday it is."

Aphrodite was never going to let her live this down. She could not find the will to care.

Seven

HADES

Monday couldn't come fast enough, and even once it arrived, the day seemed to drag on forever. And through it all, Hades could not stop thinking about Persephone.

He'd agonized over everything all weekend from his suit to the detailing of his car to the formal reservation at the restaurant, which Dio continually insisted he did not need.

Hades hadn't outright told him what he was going for or who he was taking there, and Dio had assumed he was simply succumbing to the constant pleading. Dio also assumed Hades would bring Hecate along, and Hades hadn't corrected him. It was best this way. He finally had something all his own, a secret he was eager to keep, and he didn't want to ruin it. He also didn't want to bring it into the light only to allow the world to watch it disintegrate into ash. Or worse, allow the world to be the one to set it ablaze.

Though there was still work to be done. A tap on his desk and Hades was drawn back to his office where Hephaestus currently sat across from him. The head of the younger man's cane rested against the mahogany, and he only drew it back once his uncle met his eyes.

"What was that?" Hades questioned, sitting up straighter in his chair.

"I've checked with both Prometheus and the Cyclops," Hephaestus repeats. "Tartarus hasn't made any buys, not here and not on any of the islands. I haven't heard back from Daedalus in Deucalion Heights, but Achilles and I are keeping eyes on the port between the two of us."

"You think you can get someone inside their security compound?"

"We tried. We sent Prometheus to make his monthly delivery to Iapetos a few days ago. No dice."

"So they're outright rejecting ammunition. I wish I could say that soothes me. Instead, it makes me wonder what they've been stockpiling."

Hephaestus shrugged, the right shoulder rising only half as high as the left. "I wouldn't say much unless they're making their own weapons. I keep books on everyone, Uncle, and I don't sell anything high capacity."

"But what about the weapons they use on the borders?"

"Most of them are submerged. I designed many of them to only be used that way, and I built the others myself right where they stand. The bigger guns are mounted into the ground. Even if they fuck around and try to get creative with one of those, I'd be alerted if one of the mounts were damaged or removed, and the gun would immediately become obsolete."

Hades couldn't help but smile. All of his nephews were impressive, but none had been more underestimated than Hephaestus. Zeus and Hera, young as they were, didn't think he'd live to see his second birthday, and considering the story surrounding his birth, Hades dared to believe Zeus had hoped not. Hades had known he would be a fighter though, and he had watched over him in the same way he later would Dionysos and Hermes. Hephaestus had made his weaknesses his strengths, and then he'd strengthened Khaos Falls' weaknesses. Now, he was a renowned blacksmith, overseeing all sales and construction of arms and weaponry in town and doing so with an iron grip so that nothing got out of hand. It wasn't foolproof, but it was safer than the free-for-all that had existed before. In this way, they controlled the flow of weapons and kept those of mass destruction off the streets.

"You shouldn't worry too much about it, Uncle," Heph concluded. "This is all doing what it's supposed to do, make you uncomfortable, and I don't think it's going to go any further than that. They want to send a message, but they won't do anything else if the risk outweighs the benefits. Eventually, they'll need the rest of us. Erebus and Nyx know that. Tartarus isn't interested in putting innocent people in danger for the sake of biting back at Zeus, and leaving the city vulnerable leaves them vulnerable too."

Hades had considered all of this, and judging by the look on his face, Hephaestus knew it. However, Hades wasn't willing to rest, not when Tartarus was the only district to ever pose a legitimate threat to Zeus's reign. After all, the throne of Khaos Falls had sat in their territory for decades before Zeus had taken it... or more accurately, before Hades had taken it for him.

Hades himself had given Tartarus the role in border security as a sign of good faith, but even if Erebus and Nyx kept the peace for the duration of their lives, Hades doubted that Tethys and Coeus would do the same, especially when it was Zeus who held the title of high leader now. Hades had handed it to him like a spoiled child.

For how much of this was he to blame? If he had taken the crown for himself, perhaps...

Well, there was no use going down that road now, was there?

The more Hades turned this over in his mind, however, the more holes he found in his horror. Would one little deal with Zeus truly lead to a war between Tartarus and the two largest districts in Khaos Falls? More than that, Tartarus would be cut off from the Market District and every other neutral district in between. They may find an ally in Demeter, but Demeter's numbers were just as pitiful, if not more so. Tartarus oversaw the borders, but they employed citizens of every other district to do so. The whole thing made no sense, and the only thing Hades had gotten from worrying about it was grey hair. There was nothing more he can do.

Hades surrendered to that at long last.

"Alright," he sighed, standing up. "I wash my hands of it. If you hear anything else, let me know, but beyond that, I put it to rest. It would be rather foolish for any of them to attack Zeus."

Hephaestus gripped his cane and pushed himself to his feet, leaning upon it heavily. Half a smile bloomed across his scarred face. "Or you."

Hades smiled too. "Or me."

After dropping Hephaestus off at the garage level, Hades rode the elevator up to the penthouse of Hotel Asphodel. He had a couple of hours before he was due to pick up Persephone, and he planned to make the most of them. The elevator stopped once more on the casino floor, and Hecate casually strutted in, turning and standing beside him. They said nothing at first, but the moment she tossed him a smug look, he cracked. A quiet laugh left his lips as she bumped her shoulder against his.

"Wear the scarlet tie. I believe it's still hanging on your bedpost from last time," she hummed. "White dress shirt. Oh, and the black vest. It always makes your chest look amazing."

Of course, she knew. Hades couldn't hide a secret from her if he tried. And even when he tried, he always unraveled eventually without a drop of effort on her part. He doubted that would ever change.

"Doesn't my chest always look amazing?" he retorted.

"Don't make me check your ego before your first date. It's not fair to her."

He paused, looking down at his feet. "—So you approve?"

She rolled her eyes. "I have my reservations, but I do think you deserve it."

"What reservations?"

"Oh, you know, only the fact that she's the daughter of Demeter, who puts the food on our tables and wants to eviscerate you the most in all of Khaos Falls. Nothing too profound."

He chuckled, placing a hand just under the back of her neck and brushing his thumb along the column with a sigh. It might be the first time he wasn't more worried than her. He didn't even bring up his concern regarding Demeter and a possible alliance with Tartarus.

"I've considered these things," he informed her, his voice soft.

"I know," she assured him. "I just don't want you to get hurt."

"I know." He turned to look at her. "I promise I'll be the most careful."

She nodded just as the bell dinged and the doors opened onto her floor, right below his own. She leaned up as his hand fell away and pecked his cheek.

"Let me know you get back safe," she demands.

"Will do," Hades agreed, lightly pushing her towards the doors. "Tell Thana to be vigilant."

She grinned as she stepped out, the doors immediately beginning to close. "Will do."

A SHAVE, a shower, and an ironing of a three-piece suit later, Hades stood before the full-length mirror in his bedroom adjusting his cufflinks, altogether satisfied with the outcome of his tedious regimen. It was then that the nerves finally caught up to him, and he took a few deep breaths as he stared at his reflection.

It still baffled him, the fact that Persephone could make him nervous, but he was dealing with it the best he could. He hadn't been on a date in... well, he could not remember the last time he'd been on a date. He just knew that it had been far too long for him to be at all well-versed in the logistics of it. There was a general grasp of baseline expectations, but it ended there. The rest of this was going to be trial and error.

He never thought he would be reduced to such an infantile technique.

With twenty minutes until seven, Hades slipped on his watch and shoes and headed for the door. Cerberus met him there, sensing that it was one of those rare occasions where Hades was going somewhere he could not follow. Hades frowned, kneeling down to get eye level with him and ruffling the fur along his neck.

"Wish me luck, big guy," he sighed. "And as selfish as it is for me to ask, don't wish me home too soon."

Cerberus whined but eventually licked Hades' face, offering his reluctant blessing. Hades kissed his large forehead before pushing himself upright, patting Cerberus once more and leaving the apartment. Cerberus barked once as the door shut.

The elevator ride down to the garage level seemed far longer than it ever had. Hades' fingers fidgeted with the timepiece as he walked. When was the last time he'd been this excited about anything?

Extracting his keys from his pocket, he climbed into his dark SUV and brought the engine to life. He didn't leave the casino often, meaning he rarely ever drove, and even when he did leave, it was usually someone else driving. However, tonight, he'd thought it best that he got behind the wheel himself, making the short trip from Asphodel to the Stoneheart Apartments.

Truth be told, Hades wasn't sure he'd been here since walking the land with Apollo, mapping out his blueprints. Khaos Falls' renowned architect had done most of the structural design in the Styx District since Hades had taken over, restoring it to its former glory and offering it some fresh glory as well, namely in the form of Asphodel. He'd certainly done wonders in this apartment building.

Hades admired the lobby quietly, looking over the more intricate details until his attention was drawn to the arrival of the elevator. He turned just as the doors slid open, and he was instantly stunned into silence.

She was dazzling. There was no other way to put it. If he thought he'd been impressed the first time he saw her on stage, he'd severely underestimated her abilities. Here she stood, making magic in a simple white dress that reached just above her knee, a light sweater layered over it. She seemed to glow through each layer of fabric, as though the sun had reached beneath her skin and taken up residence there. Her long curls fell to one side of her face, the other side braided back tight against her scalp, and Hades struggled to pick his jaw up off of the floor. How was it that she looked both sweet and devastating all at once?

Amidst all this desire to be around her, he'd never paid much attention to his desire for other things. Like touching her, feeling her breath on his skin, tracing the column of her neck with his mouth... That faint feeling of possessive want flickered like a hungry flame begging to be fed. He forced it to the back of his mind when she smiled.

"You're here," she said, lips curling as she stepped out of the elevator.

"I'm here," he managed, his voice hollow.

It took him another moment to move, clearing his throat and gesturing to the door.

"Are you ready?" he asked.

"Are you?" she returned with a raised brow.

He nodded. "Oh, I'm ready. For sure."

Her smile was an image he committed to memory. "Then so am I."

They lingered for several more extensive seconds before he offered his hand. He needed to touch her, to feel her skin against his. To his immense relief, she took it, and with much more confidence than he possessed at the moment, her touch like ointment on a wound.

Trying to keep his wits about him, he led the way back to the car. Opening her door for her, he seized his chance to try and convey his thoughts.

"You look amazing," he breathed as she climbed up into the vehicle and sat down.

She froze, looking back at him with something indecipherable in her eyes.

"I wish I had a better word," he continued, nervous.

"Thank you," she replied, smiling at last before leaning over and kissing his cheek. He had to lock his knees to keep them from buckling. "And you look as handsome as ever."

"-Thank you."

Biting his lip, he forced himself to step back and shut her door before something else fumbled from his mouth. He gave himself a moment to catch his breath as he moved around to the driver's side, his skin tingling where her lips had touched. He really needed to pull it together.

"You know this thing is bad for the environment, right?" she quipped, patting the dash as he slid behind the wheel.

He couldn't help but smirk. "Put your seatbelt on, Persephone."

There were only two ways across the Styx to and from Hades' district. The river separated it from the rest of the city, and a deep canal half as wide as the river separated it from Tartarus. There used to only be one way, but when Hermes and Dionysos carved out their niche in the Market District directly to the west, Hades had another bridge built between the two territories. Tonight however, Hades had made special arrangements to have his private ferry cart them across the water directly into the vineyard just northeast of Asphodel. It was one of the few luxuries he'd allowed himself to acquire when he first took power, and truth be told, a ride down the river every now and again did him good.

He felt Persephone look over at him as he drove directly up to the water, but he said nothing. It was no more than a few minutes before the ferry appeared, coming towards them. Once it docked, its ramp was extended, and he drove onto the vessel. Then it was off again.

The River Styx was at least a soccer field wide, and the current was strong, but the ferry had been designed to overcome that when traveling across. Many superstitions surrounded the river. Hades' father always said that lost souls swam beneath the dark surface, wandering for all time. Other souls had to overcome its treacherous waters in order to make it to the afterlife. Hades didn't know what he believed, but he always loved the stories.

He would always have a soft spot for lore and legends, tales passed down by word of mouth rather than pen and pad. It was why it never bothered him much, becoming a myth. They had already been so integral to who he was to begin with.

They exited the car, and Hades led Persephone up the stairs to the deck.

"So you're this fancy?" she remarked as they approached the railing.

"Have you ever seen the river up close like this?" he asked instead.

She allowed herself to take it in. The sun was just setting, and the glassy surface of the water reflected the deep purples and vibrant blues. Rogue magentas reached their agile digits towards the boat, tickling the underbelly.

"Can't say that I have," she finally admitted.

Her voice had softened, and she looked almost dazed. Her hand grazed his own as they both reached for the railing, and he had to dispel the need to shudder. Whatever this effect was that she had on him, it was as strong as the current far below. He had yet to find a problem with it beyond the obvious, but distractions were far more acceptable when he was willing to stop worrying so much about his brother's next move.

"Do... Are there creatures living down there?" she inquired, her eyes fixed on the water.

"Oh, yeah," he responded, nodding. "Many."

"Like what?"

"Dragons for one."

Her head whipped in his direction with a look of brash bewilderment. He grinned. It felt foreign on his face but not at all uncomfortable. Sucking her teeth, she shoved his shoulder.

"Stop it," she groaned, shaking her head.

His laugh was raucous, a sound so rare that even he was surprised. "You never know."

"I can fashion a guess."

He shrugged, catching his breath. "My father used to say there were. He would scare us half to death."

"My mother used to say it was filled with death."

"Yeah, my parents said so too. My mama caught us wading in once, screamed herself hoarse. We'd done it on a dare of course. Charon was already up to his waist when she caught us. I grabbed him just as the current did. It was the longest game of tug-o-war I ever played."

"And the last, I hope."

He wished he could say yes. "Mm. Come on. We're going to dock soon."

She didn't question him further, slipping her hand into his when he offered and following him across the deck. The simple touch invigorated him in far more ways than one, and the need to touch her more twisted in his gut. All he could do was keep moving. Offering those feelings any attention might keep him from surviving the night.

He must admit though. They intrigued him. No one had ever incited such things in him before. He tucked them away to be inspected at a later time.

The lights of the waterside restaurant's gazebo came into view, glowing like a beacon in the coming dark. The ferry docked just beside it, and the moment they stepped foot on solid ground again, his phone began to ring.

His heart slowed, knowing very well who it was. Digging the device out of his pocket, he saw Zeus's name flash across his screen like a violent cry for attention. Because of course, he would choose right now to finally call. Hades' skin buzzed with agitation, but before he could decide what to do, Persephone spoke.

"You can take it if you need to," she urged, squeezing his hand. "I'll wait right here."

He stared at the screen for a moment. Then he rejected the call and turned off his phone. Looking over at her, he smiled as he shoved it back into his pocket.

"It's not important right now."

She gave him a pointed look. "I know you got a lot going on though. Important matters and all."

He shook his head, leaning closer to her. "At the moment, I'm with the only person who matters."

Eight

PERSEPHONE

Persephone had never been this nervous. Not prior to her first show or even her first audition with Calliope, and honestly, she was beginning to think that "nervous" simply didn't even begin to cover it. How had she gone from keeping Hades at a distance to agreeing to a date with him? A date he planned like a man who was trying to get lucky, and she could admit it. He had done a damn good job thus far.

Aphrodite had alternated between reprimanding her and teasing her for most of the week, but tonight, she'd put it aside and offered to help Persephone get dressed. She'd met Persephone at her apartment with several garment bags. However, Persephone had ultimately settled on her own outfit, pointing out that it was her day off and she wasn't going to suffer through a tight dress and high heels for anyone. If Hades liked her as much as Aphrodite swore he did, he wouldn't care. Still, she was surprised that she'd been correct.

Once she'd laid eyes on him, dressed to the nines in what she would bet was his best suit, she did feel a little bad. That went away the moment he offered her a compliment that somehow eclipsed every other she had ever received despite its simplicity. That was saying something considering it was all Adonis ever did when they were together. She supposed that was why though. She could expect it from others. She didn't know what to expect from Hades.

Everything he had shown her thus far had been contradictory to all the stories she'd ever heard about him. In that, the compliments and the plans and the simple conversations, it all felt so genuine, so rare, so specific to her. She savored each and every one.

And damn, did he look good in that suit.

Their table in Dio's vineyard had already been elegantly set for them beneath the darling gazebo, and her heart flitted around in her throat as they sat down. Hades hadn't reached for his phone since he'd seemingly turned it off, which meant he'd actually turned it off. She removed her own phone from her bag and did the same, pointedly ignoring the several texts and missed calls from Zeus she saw on the screen. She briefly wondered if he might already know something about her plans tonight, but that wonder didn't linger long. Hades stole all of her attention without doing much of anything, and she had not a single complaint about it.

She looked up just as a figure appeared on the short stone path leading up to the main restaurant structure. Once she got closer, Hades seemed to recognize her immediately. He stood, shaking her hand once she reached him.

"Good evening," she said to them both, shaking Persephone's hand as well. "Hades, how are you?"

"Very good," he returned, sitting down again. "Danae, this is Persephone. She's part of Calliope's company. Persephone, this is Danae. She owns the restaurant."

Persephone gasped, standing. "It's so good to meet you. Thank you for having us."

"Oh, thank you for being here," Danae countered with a smile. "I've heard so much about you actually. Dio could not stop talking about you when he was here earlier. He gave me tickets to the show! He didn't say you were the one accompanying his uncle tonight though. This is a wonderful surprise."

"Oh, I didn't tell him," Hades readily admitted, and Persephone knitted her brows. He said nothing further, however, and Danae quickly picked up the conversation.

"As soon as Dio told me you were coming, I prepared my most special menu, so you need not worry at all." She set down a leather-bound menu in front of each of them. "I'll give you a few moments to look."

As Hades opened his menu, Danae smiled at Persephone before reaching for the bottle submerged in a bucket of ice at the edge of the table. She uncorked it with ease before pouring each of them a glass of light-colored wine. Persephone could not pinpoint the smell, but it was certainly a kind of fruit. She took a modest sip as Danae retreated and nearly groaned in contentment. It was absolutely delicious.

"Pomegranate," Hades said softly, and when she looked up, his eyes were on her. "Dio doesn't make much of it, but it's my favorite. I truly think he keeps it in production for me."

When she didn't say anything, instead taking another sip, he continued.

"I didn't tell him I was coming with you tonight because you know how he gets. Excited and - slightly overwhelming at times. The Fates know he would have asked me a dozen questions. Truly though, I didn't want to tell anyone. I didn't want to risk it getting

84

back to your mother or Zeus before we had a chance to see how this—"

"Why Zeus?" She blurted it out before she had a chance to reconsider it.

He sighed, but the guilt she expected to find in his face wasn't there. "My brother has a way of - snatching things out of my hand before I have a chance to enjoy them." He wet his lips, and it was almost as though it pained him to unveil such a thing. "I don't want this -" He gestured between them. "To be the same. I would like to - enjoy it first, if that's alright."

She eyed him warily, and she only just realized how hard her heart was pounding in her chest. She was paranoid. While she continued to hold that there wasn't much to tell about her current situation with Zeus, it still felt like she was hiding something from Hades. And despite the residual suspicion that Hades was attempting to catch her in a lie or get information out of her, she could understand what he meant. If Zeus were to find out that she was seeing someone— anyone at all really but especially his brother— even for one date, she had no clue how he would react. She also couldn't say that she was too keen to find out, no matter how curious her spite made her.

She could not possibly be expected to continue living like this forever though, with him breathing down her neck, calling at all hours of the day and night, and never taking the hint. Four years of increasingly invasive behavior was four too many.

It wasn't as though she'd agreed to anything or promised him something she had failed to make good on. The problem with Zeus was that no one ever told him no, so he didn't know the meaning of the word. More than that, Hades never told him no, and Persephone didn't know what that would mean for her.

Regardless, she accepted that if she continued something with him, she would have to tell him the truth. She could not bear the thought of him finding out from someone else because if he did, it would probably be Zeus, and thus, it would probably not be the whole truth.

"Besides," Hades breathed, effectively bringing her back to the table. "Dionysos, he really likes you, and he put his trust in me when he insisted we meet. If I let you down, I let him down, and I would like to avoid both of those instances, so I would say taking things slow is my best bet."

Persephone softened. "You really have a soft spot for him, don't you?"

He gave a short laugh, shaking his head. "That's one way to put it."

"And he's Zeus's son?"

"So the blood says."

"But you raised him." He nodded. "You did a very good job. He's a good boy."

"He's a handful is what he is." She could tell he didn't like taking credit, which only made her want to offer him more. "And along with the rest of his brothers? Forget it."

"From what I know of Hermes and Dio, they're excitable but very intelligent. Mad scientists to be exact."

He laughed at the callback, and she cherished the sound. "I assume they got it from their mothers."

"Maybe, but it was tended to by an uncle who did his best for them instead of letting them fend for themselves. Now the whole city loves them. Granted, for different reasons, I'm sure, but nonetheless."

He was obviously overwhelmed as he cleaned out his glass in

one gulp before chuckling. "Why are we talking about this, these things? Don't you want to talk about something fun?"

She smirked, refilling his glass with the bottle Danae had returned to the ice bucket. "We're talking about it because it's evident no one has ever given you your due credit, and even if they have, they let you change the subject or dodge it completely. I'm not them, and this is a good lesson for you to learn. Credit where credit is due."

"Do you allow for credit?"

"When it's earned. But I already know you liked the show."

"I liked you." He paused. "I like you."

She appraised him carefully over the lip of her glass. She liked seeing him flustered, yes. It was one of the most endearing things she had ever seen, but she was curious as to just how much it scared him to be so vulnerable. She wanted to protect that, protect him. It was the most natural feeling she had ever experienced, and all because he would never ask it of her.

"Why did you like me?" she asked. "Or - take an interest in me, I guess. The first time you saw me, I was on stage. Why then?"

A moment passed in silence, then another, before he moved again. Pressing the tips of his fingers together, he leaned forward in his chair, gazing off towards the river. She expected some cliche compliment about how beautiful she'd been in her costume or how cool it was to see a woman bend "like that", but she got nothing of the sort. She should know better by now.

"You looked like you belonged up there, in the air." He said it so softly that she was almost convinced he hadn't spoken at all, and yet the air around them was so still that she caught every word. "The rest of us were just - sitting there, feet firm on the ground, like they are every single day even though we - we strive for these great

87

things. We are given these pedestals, and we use them to our advantage. We never settle, and we are never satisfied. We stand on them, hands outstretched, grasping for something higher, something more. We strive for great heights and absurd expectations. We all have our idea of what it means to reach for the stars, but you... No pedestal, no wings, no absurd expectations. You just - do it. You found a way to reach the stars without tearing them down from the sky. When you come down, you leave everything up there more beautiful than you found it. And not just because you wanted to, but - because you were meant to."

He seemed to have gone somewhere else, and she was so keen on finding him there that she didn't recognize the moisture on her cheeks until it reached her lips. She caught it with her palm, but before either of them could speak again, Danae had returned. They smile at her although each of them was quite obviously disoriented. Danae looked at them with apologetic eyes, no doubt under the impression they'd just been fighting, but she took their order and rushed off soon enough.

It was quiet for a while, leaving only the sound of the soft music playing from the overhead speakers, Persephone still turning his words over in her mind. It was as though he'd read them all right off of her bones. It was what she had always wanted, to earn her place in the sky without standing atop her mother's shoulders, without wrecking everything she touched the way her father had accused her of doing. Persephone had wanted to carve her own path among the clouds, and if he was as credible a source as she wanted to believe he was, she had. Right now, she could not imagine it could ever mean more coming from anyone else.

The conversation over dinner between the delicious food and endless wine was far more lighthearted, but Persephone could tell that it had taken a lot out of him to be so honest. There was something else there, something that she was missing, and she didn't quite get it yet. Was it because he himself was a caged bird, one with wings more than capable of taking him anywhere he wanted to go if he would only push open the door he'd closed himself? She wanted to ask, but the moment seemed long past, and after their plates had been cleared, he looked like he'd recovered. At least, she imagined he must have to some extent because he stood then, removing his jacket and hanging it on the back of his chair before holding out his hand.

"I thought you wanted dessert," she questioned.

"I do," he replied simply, but something in his voice made her shudder. In all of this sensitivity, she'd forgotten how utterly sexy he was. "But first, I'd like a dance. If you would be kind enough as to afford me one."

She wasn't sure he was serious at first, glancing between him and his outstretched hand. Though when he didn't rescind it, she cautiously slipped hers into it and stood too.

The music that played was soft, but once he'd pulled her close, it seemed to get louder... No, it definitely got louder, and her eyes darted toward the restaurant suspiciously. A grin spread across his face as he slid his free hand down to the small of her back.

When they moved, it was oddly comfortable. She relaxed into him in a way she hadn't predicted she could. Despite all those sharp edges and hard lines, his body was warm and welcoming. And he looked too damn good in that vest, which was fitted in a way that strategically accentuated his muscular chest and outlined the cut of his pecs. Mixed with his cologne, she found herself eager to be close to him, as close as close could be.

He moved so gracefully too, to the point that she barely realized

89

they'd started to move at all. She was taken aback by just how light on his feet he was. Though he actually wasn't all that much taller than her, his broad shoulders and barreled chest, paired with his overall demeanor, made him look much larger at any distance. Though up close, he looked - celestial? Or divine. His brown skin, several shades darker than her own, reflected the lights that surrounded them like a diamond, and his eyes could warm a village if they so pleased. He was marvelous.

He went slow, and she was thankful for it, far more invested in learning the contours of his body through his suit than anything else. When he spoke, the vibrations against her cheek soothed her, and she struggled to focus on the words.

"Thank you," he said.

She forced herself to look up at him. "For what?"

"For spending your one night off with me."

She smiled. "I haven't regretted it yet."

"I hope to keep it that way."

"And I'm sure you've planned for it."

His laughter reverberated in her chest. "I don't think anyone could possibly plan for you."

She didn't know who stopped first, but they stop moving altogether. In fact, it felt like everything did, the world going silent around them in anticipation. It need not wait long. She was craning up as he was leaning down, a heat pooling in the pit of her stomach. It surprised her, this vibrant desire to sink her teeth into him and watch his walls come crumbling down, to see him vulnerable again. Yet it was hers that crumbled first.

"You should know something," she exhaled, shutting her eyes. "About me. I'm—"

She paused, the word welded into the roof of her mouth. Never had she been ashamed or afraid to come out. From the beginning, she had been open and outspoken about her transition in the Harvest District, hoping it would break down enough barriers to allow Aphrodite safe passage when the time came for her to take over her father's district. And since then, the city as a whole had become far more welcoming. Not to mention the fact that Deucalion Heights was a utopia for queer people, those who did not subscribe to the socially constructed "default". So she rarely thought about it anymore, much less spoke about it.

It was simply an underlying aspect of her identity behind acrobat and dancer and even daughter of Demeter that may have shaped her view of and experience in the world but that no one but her was entitled to. Now she truly knew that freedom. But dating was still new, and she had never found herself having to come out on the cusp of a successful first date. She never felt the need to. But her desire to only proved to her just how much of a thing this was, and how much of a liar she'd been about it just days ago.

Before she could force herself to finish however, he intervened. "I know."

Her eyes fluttered open. "You know?"

"I know everything, remember?"

"—You can't possibly know everything."

His lips curled, and he reached up to cup her cheek, brushing his thumb over the skin there. "I know you're a woman, a good woman, and I like you a lot. I know that you owe me nothing you are not willing to share. And I want you to know that you're safe with me, all of you."

"Then let me say it."

He acquiesced easily. "Okay."

"I'm trans."

It came out on a slow breath, and her body automatically braced for impact. There was no need. He had said as much, but she knew better than to believe someone's word so easily. Still, the relief she felt was immense, and she allowed herself to cradle that for the moment.

He smiled, his eyes glittering with an acute affection, and it warmed her through to the bone.

"Thank you for trusting me," he said softly.

Of course, that shouldn't surprise her as much as it did, but she had learned to expect a more pronounced reaction, whether automatic, aggressively overbearing, or otherwise. It aided in curbing disappointment. Yet as easy as this felt, too easy in fact, she refused to believe she deserved any other reaction than this.

Then he began to speak again, and her heart stuttered several times, alarm bells instantly going off.

"—But... And I do not mean to steal your thunder or anything. I just -" He wet his lips, looking down between them. She raised a brow, already prepared to disengage his touch if need be. Please, no. "I feel that since you were willing to share that with me, I should share with you that - that is something that we have in common."

She blinked, unsure if she was understanding him clearly. Because there was no way he was saying what she thought he was saying. What were the odds of that?

"It's been so long since I've - come out to anyone, and so I tend to forget since I do not share it often, but..." A nervous chuckle left him. "Well, I don't share many things often, and yet, I - I want to share them with you."

"I -"

But she did not know what to say. She had been so focused on his reaction that she never once considered what her own could or should be. Truth be told, she had never had a man come out to her, and she was almost ashamed for how out of her worldview the existence and experience of trans men in general seemed to be. She vowed to work on that.

But for right now, she just wanted the ability to formulate the words she wished to offer him. Words of gratitude, of compassion, of tenderness and overall admiration for him. She felt all this emotion ripening in her chest, a burrowing and blossoming thing she wished to tend for as long as she could. Oh, thank the Fates.

Though Hades did not seem perturbed in the least. Instead, he saved her from having to find the words. Perhaps because he felt the same.

"Can I kiss you now?" he inquired.

All she could do was nod.

Nine

PERSEPHONE

Kissing Hades felt like catching flame.

Yet it paled in comparison to the heat that rose through her once he'd picked her up off of her feet, allowing her to wind her arms around his neck. She had been waiting far too long for this, for him, and she was reeling from the sudden fulfillment. And the sudden need for more.

She threw caution to the wind and ignored her own warnings, melting into him like wax. She gasped into his mouth as his fingers pressed more firmly into her skin, and she had no choice but to take a breath. Looking down into his hooded gaze, she bit her swollen lip, her own eyes flaring with want. She was entranced by him, and every moment away from his kiss felt wasted.

He seemed to feel the same way.

He kissed her again, and this one was far more searing than the first, on everyone's part. Her hand gripped the back of his head, foot dragging along his calf before she reluctantly pulled away again.

"Take me home," she whispered, voice hoarse.

"What about dessert?" he asked although nothing in his voice indicated he was truly disappointed. She wouldn't let him be nonetheless.

"I'll give you dessert. Just get me home."

She need not ask again.

Their hands hardly leave each other as he covered the check and led her back out to the ferry, signaling the captain with the bell on the deck. The man had undoubtedly gone into the restaurant to get a meal, but Persephone hoped he came back soon, otherwise she might have to settle for the deck of his ship.

To their credit, they managed to make it to Hades' vehicle, separating long enough to climb into their respective seats and wait it out. She feared it might kill the mood, this wait, but the tension remained absolutely palpable. She struggled not to bow beneath it.

And she failed.

"Put your hands on the steering wheel." Her voice was stern and non-negotiable.

"What?" he asked, throwing her a look of confusion.

She turned in her seat towards him, removing her sweater and slipping her hand over his thigh. "Hands. On. The steering wheel."

He stared at her still, unguarded and uncertain, though something else flickered in his gaze. She didn't waver. She didn't look away. She simply watched him and waited, meeting his eyes head-on. At last, he cautiously lifted his soft hands and placed them atop the steering wheel. She moved closer to him, leaning across the middle console as she unbuckled his belt with languid movements. He looked down to see, but she immediately reprimanded him.

"Eyes straight ahead," she whispered against his ear before drawing her tongue over the shell. "The moment you look anywhere else, I stop. Do you understand me?"

A bead of sweat collected along his temple. She collected it on her tongue. He swallowed hard, the action visible, and she had to force herself not to trace that with her mouth as well.

"I said, do you understand me?" she repeated.

"I do," he breathed out.

He gripped the wheel tighter.

She let him settle into it before she moved her hands to the band of his trousers, undoing the button beneath. The drag of his zipper sounded so much louder in the thick air of the vehicle, and she could see the strain in his jaw. He screwed his eyes shut as her hand dusted across his length through his boxers, and she clicked her tongue.

"Ah ah, no cheating now," she hissed, leaning in to nip at his neck. "Keep those eyes open for me."

She still held that those eyes were the most dangerous thing about him, but if she could find a way to tame them with weapons of her own, she would. Gladly.

Dipping her hand into his underwear, she cautiously extracted his perfectly sculpted cock, her stomach flipping at the weight of it. A few tender strokes, and he began to harden in the warmth of her palm, her thumb and forefinger kept apart even when she tightened her hold. She narrowly suppressed the moan that knocked against her teeth as she released him, bringing her hand to her mouth so that she could drag her tongue against her palm. All the while, she watched him struggle not to look.

Once she was satisfied with the slick of her hand, she took hold of him once more and began to stroke.

The shudder that racked his body soon rumbled through hers, but she hid it far better than he did. His knuckles had lost all color as they held the steering wheel in a death grip. She pulled back just enough to ensure his eyes were still open, excited to find that they were blown wide with want. She was eager to succumb to them. It would be far too easy. If only she weren't so desperate to see him undone, freed from his flawless facade.

She felt the clench of his jaw in her gut as she picked up speed, the head of his shaft now glistening with fresh arousal. She spread it down the length of him, massaging it into the smooth skin with her thumbs and twisting her fist around him intermittently as she moved down to the base. She brushed her free hand down the back of his neck, heat radiating off of his skin and sweat forming there in its wake.

This image of him clinging so hopelessly to control did things to her that she could never even begin to put into words. She liked this image. She was high off of it. She wanted to see it so much more often. She also wanted to see what he would do once he was able to reclaim control. There was no doubt in her mind that he was already thinking about it.

Or trying to, at least.

"You better not stain this vest," she warned him, her voice soft against his jaw before she nipped at the skin there. "I really love it on you."

"I'm not sure I can help it." He swallowed again. "I think that - is entirely in your hand."

The words rushed out of him on the back of a heavy exhale, and he struggled to catch his breath. She laughed, more so at the delivery than the joke itself, but she adored how he managed to slip it in even on the edge of his own ruin. She liked a man who didn't take himself too seriously. More than that, it was a pleasant surprise to find that Hades specifically did not.

His hips shifted in his seat, which earned another smile from her. She'd never done anything like this before, never felt inclined to, but to watch Hades, godking of the Underworld, crumble around her dainty little hand was a drug worthy of addiction.

Moisture collected between her thighs as her fingers scraped lightly over his scalp. She kissed his neck more fervently, pressing her legs together, trying to find some friction for herself. He must have sensed it too because his fingers twitched, aching to touch her, and it took everything in her to keep from giving him permission, from begging.

The ferry began to move.

His breathing was labored now, and she could almost hear his teeth grinding, struggling to cage the sounds she elicited from him. It only spurred her on. The lewd sound of her fist pumping over him permeated the air as the leather beneath his hands shrieked with distress. She feared he might tear the steering wheel in half. She would also like to see it.

Though she did have a feeling that Hades liked this, not just having his dick handled but denying himself, being denied. And she realized that it wouldn't surprise her in the least. He seemed to thrive in simplicity, but what other luxuries did he actively deny himself in the process?

She bit down hard on his neck, just beneath his jaw, and at last, his lips parted. It was a tumultuous roar held up by pitiful grunts, his voice shattering as he leaned forward. It was impressive, his resolve, and even as she watched it crack at the pace of a rattled windshield, she marveled at it. She wondered if anyone had ever brought him to an edge like this. She wondered if anyone had dared to try.

"Persephone..."

She was so focused on holding her own desire at bay, stroking him fast and firm with her mouth against his throat, that she didn't realize the way he was now throbbing and jerking in her hand. He squirms in his seat, hands twisting against the wheel, his breathing a quivering thing in the air around them. Through her own haze of want, she dragged her tongue over his skin.

"Do you think you deserve it?"

A beat. Only a beat of silence passed before his hips were rising off the seat, his head colliding none too gently with the roof of the car. Still, he kept pumping into her hand until a translucent glaze mushroomed from the swollen head of his cock, slowly dripping down the shaft and over her fingers. He threw himself back against the seat, his moan the most devastating sound she had ever heard. She nearly plummeted over the edge herself when she heard it, watching his face contort with pleasure, his once rigid form doing the same. And all for her, because of her. It was... empowering. He was always beautiful. However, at her mercy, he was divine.

She let him ride it out, and only once he deflated against the seat did she retract her hand, bringing her knuckles to her lips to taste him. It was almost instinctive, not entirely decided upon but inevitable in a way. His eyes, hooded and hazy, followed her hand until she lapped at the drops gracing the skin of her fingers. His body shuddered. Hers did too.

She could not wait to get home.

HADES

I f the ferry ride had been any longer, Hades would have taken her in the back seat, and there was no doubt in his mind about that. He was still recovering when the vessel docked in the Styx District, his hands trembling as they buttoned up his trousers. He was absolutely dumbstruck.

Nothing about tonight would have insinuated that it would end like this, although this felt far more like a beginning. It had never been his goal, and he had been happy just to have dinner and a conversation with her. In reality, he had never felt this comfortable with someone after a single date. Fates, he had never felt this comfortable with anyone after several of them. Even after he'd finished the aesthetic stages of his transition, he was more likely to spend an evening with Hecate than to go out looking for someone to warm his sheets because the emotional connection was already there, and that was crucial to his comfort.

But with Persephone... Well, everything was different with Persephone, but he certainly couldn't say no connection existed. In many ways, far more than he was ready to admit, he was already attached.

He didn't know if it could get any better, but he vowed to find out once they reached her apartment.

He could not remember the last time he'd come so hard. He could still feel the aftershocks running through him at random intervals. He reverted to her prior directions on the drive home, keeping his eyes straight ahead if only to keep from thinking about it too much and running them off of the road. Though as they pulled out onto the street, he slipped his hand over her thigh. And then between them.

She didn't react, but he could already feel the heat there, the moisture, and it somehow managed to ground him. After all, it was almost impossible to tell if what she had done to him had held any effect on her whatsoever until now. But finding proof that it had didn't make him any less hellbent on a comparable brand of revenge.

The side of his finger only just brushed the front of her panties, enough to take note of the dampness there and nothing more. In his peripheral, he caught her sinking her teeth into her lip. Her eyelids fluttered. He pushed down on the gas. His district had never seemed as big as it did right now.

Persephone was prepared with her card key in hand as they approached the main door of her apartment building, buzzing them through so quickly that Hades wasn't sure the door was locked at all. What a tedious thing to take note of when all he wanted to do was rip her clothes off and fuck her senseless in the elevator.

He didn't get a proper look at her apartment. She strode in several steps ahead of him, turning on a few lights and dropping her purse, and his eyes honed in on the valley of her shoulders.

He followed her across the hardwood floor of the open floor plan, oblivious to —yet altogether grateful for— the lack of walls. When she reached her bed in the far corner of the space, he reached down and gripped his belt buckle, which he had failed to reclasp. Slowly, he slid the belt from the loops, the picture of vengeance manifesting in his mind. His voice was low and deep when he spoke. It filled the vast space like smoke.

"Quite something you pulled in the car." Her shoulders tensed. "Did you think you were going to get away with it?"

She didn't answer right away, but as he moved closer, he caught the faint sound of a gasp. He folded the belt into his hand so that he gripped both ends, the loop of leather now menacing as it hung at his side.

"No," she admitted at last after tossing her jacket on a nearby chair.

"Do you think you should be punished?"

She turned to him slowly, and her eyes immediately fell to the belt, widening at the sight of it. He loosened his tie with expert fingers before unbuttoning his vest. He didn't miss the way she swallowed. Or the way her thighs pressed together. His bulge was evident, defined against the tailored fit of his trousers, but he paid it no mind at the moment. She, however, did.

"I asked you a question," he urged, his tone more firm as he dragged the loop of the belt against his palm.

She looked up at him with evident reluctance, and he didn't look away. She may have caught him off guard back in the car, accessing a side of him that he himself forgot existed, but it wouldn't happen again, at least not tonight. He was as patient as they came, and that didn't falter in the bedroom, not unless he allowed it. And now that they were here in her apartment, he was no longer prepared to do anything of the sort.

"Yes," she breathed.

"Yes what?"

"I should be punished."

He appraised her for a long moment, long enough to let her nerves begin to buzz, before he took a seat on the chair, satisfied.

"Do you have a safe word?" She paused at this question he posed before shaking her head. "Would you like some help determining one?" She quickly nodded in the affirmative, and he smiled. It signaled trust, which was a good start. "Remind me, what kind of wine did we have with our appetizers tonight?" he asked.

She took only a second. "Pomegranate."

"Do you think you can remember that?"

"Yes?"

"Are you asking me or telling me?"

She took a deep breath. "Yes, I can remember it."

"Okay. You say that word, and no matter what and no matter when, everything stops. I stop. Okay?"

She nodded, enthusiastic and understanding. "Okay."

Choking up on his grip on the belt, he beckoned her forth. She wobbled on her legs, and he wondered how much wetter she was now. He would have to check on that.

Once she was within reach, he took hold of her hand and guided her to stand beside his legs. Then he reached up, finding a hold on the back of her neck with his long arm and guiding her down to lay over his lap. Catching on, she followed his lead, positioning herself so that her ass was propped upon his thigh. It was amazing how fluidly she stepped into this role, but he was no fool. He only had all this power because she gave it to him.

"I do love this dress on you," he hummed, running his hand down her back.

"It's my favorite," she grunted immediately, and he caught the warning in the words.

He smiled. "Then I suppose we should be careful with it. You did wear it for me after all. I am honored."

He felt her body tense, bracing for the first strike. He took his time, toying with the hem of her dress before he began to drag it up her body. He bunched the fabric around her waist, digits dusting against the bare skin of her back before he allowed himself to admire the expensive black lace of her panties. He curled his fingers around the center of them, knuckles brushing against her slit, and she didn't hold back the whimper it earned.

"You are absolutely soaked, babygirl," he said softly, and her hips writhed against his fingers in response. "You gave me all that pleasure without taking some for yourself."

Though he doubted that was entirely true. He had seen the look on her face just before he'd been ordered to keep his eyes straight ahead. She'd loved every moment of it.

"But let us remember whose territory you traipse through, shall we?"

In one swift movement, he ripped the lace clean off of her body, and she gasped in surprise. She turned her head in time to see him slip the wadded garment into his breast pocket. He shifted the belt to his newly freed hand and guided her head back down with the other.

"Eyes straight ahead."

Her body shivered as he threw her words back at her, but he offered no further instruction. He didn't need to. Even as he landed the first strike right across the center of her ass, a yelp spilling out from her lips onto the floor, she didn't move her head again. She did try to brace her hands against the floor, but she failed to reach, helplessly clawing at the air when he brought down the second strike. His cock twitched against her lower stomach, eager for inclusion, but he tamped down his own desire for the time being. After all, he owed her one, and Hades never failed to repay a debt.

"Clasp your hands behind your back," he directed her.

She struggled to do so, already weak, and he helped her clamp one hand around the other wrist. He then moved his own hand to encircle the front of her neck with a loose grip so as to hold her up. He can feel her pulse pick up beneath his fingers. It delighted him, as if he held her very life between thumb and forefinger.

"Now count."

Persephone did not require elaboration, and that only aroused him further, especially when he recalled just how innocent she'd looked to it all when asked for her safe word. With every strike he delivered to her ass, she called out the number on the edge of a moan, her knuckles sheet white around her wrist the way his knuckles had been around the steering wheel. She got to twelve before the bruises began to bloom, the outline of the belt evident against her skin and the height of her arousal evident against his thigh.

His trousers were soaked through with it, and as he dragged the belt along her slit, the leather came away gleaming with moisture. He didn't want to wear her down too well. He knew she would have to be able to walk tomorrow. And dance and flip and all the other demands of her profession. Not to mention the fact he wasn't even done yet.

"Do you think you've learned your lesson?" he asked, his voice mild.

"—Yes, Sir," she managed, her voice hoarse.

He shuddered at the embellishment. "Rehash it for me."

"This is - your territory. —And you're in charge."

He gripped her throat tighter, pulling her up until he can brush his mouth against her ear. "And tonight, while you remain in my territory, you are mine."

The sound that escaped her was sultry and sweet, spreading over his skin like warm oil, just as flammable too. As much as he would love to drag this out, he'd been waiting for far too long, and his patience was at last wearing thin. If he had his way, there would be plenty of other chances to test her limitations, but tonight, he had already been pushed to his own.

The rest of their clothes were on the floor by the time he pushed her down onto the bed. She stretched out across the sheets, feline, her eyes roving over his form. He could not deny how powerful it made him feel, how invincible. He took great pride in this body he had built and rebuilt, coming so far from the form the Fates had dressed him in. He had been given the greatest of privileges in that regard.

Khaos Falls was home to the best gender surgeons in the Aegean, all of which were leagues ahead in both surgical methods and success rate, and he had also been blessed with the most supportive mother possible and a more than tolerant stepfather which had allowed him to start transition quite young. Needless to say, Hades had taken full advantage, and he had never regretted a single decision he'd made. He had also never yearned for anyone's approval, but right now, he was certainly cherishing Persephone's.

His gaze offered her the same treatment, drinking her in inch by flawless inch. She was every bit as beautiful bare as she was fully clothed, but there was something else now too. It was as though she hadn't only shed her dress but any inhibition that came with it.

"You didn't want to fuck me in that dress?" she purred, drawing her knee up and spreading her legs to give him an unhindered view of her pussy.

"Another time," he conceded. "But right now, I don't have the patience not to ruin it in some shape or form, so we'll have to do without it."

She bit her lip, and the act alone beckoned him forth. He climbed atop the mattress on his knees, taking hold of her ankles and pulling her closer until his heavy erection rested flat against her folds. Her breath caught, but she said nothing, simply watching him maneuver her to his liking. Once he did, he released her legs, lowering himself until their chests were pressed together. He kept his eyes fixed on hers, and with every moment that passed, the pressure in his gut built, right alongside the tension between them.

Do you think you deserve it? Her question echoed in his mind, and he still wasn't sure what the answer was. Yet as much as he liked to deny himself the things he wanted most with the fear that he didn't deserve them, it was impossible to do so now, especially when doing so would deny her too. And with the way she was looking at him, nails digging into his side and pressing him closer, he knew she wanted this as badly as he did.

They lay suspended there, mouths mere centimeters from one another, neither truly breathing until at last, he slipped a hand between them. There was a dense silence in the singular moment before he entered her, and it burst into a chorus of muffled whimpers and restrained groans.

She constricted around him, dragging him deeper as he dusted his lips against hers. He tried to ease into a steady pace, but his eyes snapped wide open as her hand struck his ass, gripping it firmly and driving him into her.

A hoarse laugh left him, a low growl in its wake, and when she snagged his lower lip between her teeth, she took what was left of his patience with her.

Mere minutes was all it took for the sound of his hips clapping against hers to permeate the air, her moans laid out across the bass line unbridled.

"Hades - fuck!"

His control was all but lost to him. Between the hold of her hands and the depth of his desire, he began to relinquish his grip on the reins he'd held so firmly for as long as he could remember. Reaching up, he instead took hold of the headboard, using it as leverage as he drilled into her. She combated her own moans by scraping her teeth along his neck and chest, tugging at his nipple and slapping his ass once more to elicit a groan from him.

"Seph-"

It was severed by a grunt. He drew his knees up, moving his free hand to her shoulder to pin her in place. She caught his thumb between her teeth before it got there, pulling it into her mouth. He gritted his teeth, snarling as her heels dug into the backs of his thighs. Her eyes rolled back, whether intentionally or otherwise. She took him up to the knuckle, moaning around him. Then she receded and bore her throat.

He bit down on his lip as his hand encircled the slender column, her pulse again pounding beneath his digits. Her eyes shone with a hallowed hunger, and he yearned to claim it for his own. She called out, arching off the bed, and his grip tightened both on her neck and on the headboard. Her nails bit into his skin, and she spread her legs wider around him, urging him ever deeper. He didn't need further prompting.

"Ha—" She couldn't finish the word.

He knew she was fighting to hold out, teeth tearing into her lip as her grip loosened on his ass. He didn't slow down, the entire bed shaking beneath them and the frame shrieking in protest, banging against the wall like a battering ram. It failed to dissuade him.

"Cum for me," he hissed on instinct, and the words hung thick in the air.

He stroked her jaw with his thumb even as the other fingers pressed into her throat, his thrusts short and sharp.

"Look - me in the eye, and cum for me, babygirl." Even as he himself struggled to hang on, his tone was firm. It could be taken as nothing other than a command, and when her eyes snapped open to meet his, he knew she understood that. "Now."

"Hades!"

She had been waiting for it. Her walls clenched around him, hands scrambling for perch along his back, her ankles locking against him as she squeezed her legs together. She cried out, wanton and raw, back bowed in a perfect crescent as she unraveled over him. He found his second wind in that newfound warmth, placing both hands on the headboard as he hit the home stretch. She called his name again, clawing at his shoulders, her thighs trembling against his sides.

"Please..." she groaned, hanging on for dear life and taking every rogue and ruthless thrust he supplied her with. "Hades - please!"

"I'm—"

It was as much of a warning as he could manage, so very close to the edge, but she only clung to him harder, rolling her hips wildly up into his. She pleaded with her eyes until they rolled back into her skull again, the most delicious moan spilling over her swollen lips. It was his undoing.

Three rough thrusts, and he went rigid, lightning cracking behind his eyes as he squeezed them shut. His roar shook the open space as he came, her walls still spasming around him. He rode it out with her in tow, their hips rutting against one another until he at last collapsed atop her, panting and slick with sweat. He buried his head in her neck. One of them —or maybe both of them— was shivering.

"Don't - pull out," she breathed, brushing her lips against the side of his head.

"I couldn't - even if I wanted to," he returned, eyes still closed. "Fuck."

"Mm, good?"

He managed to raise his head enough to capture her lips with his own, pouring whatever he had left into it. He caught her hoarse purr on his tongue.

"The best I ever had," he finally relented. And oh, by the Fates, did he mean it.

Eleven

PERSEPHONE

ersephone was *sore*. Deliciously so. She was also still thoroughly fatigued. She woke up at a gradual pace, becoming more and more aware of her surroundings as the minutes passed: the faint light of the sun creeping in through the blinds, the cool touch of the sheets on her bare legs, the smell of Hades' cologne surrounding her, and then... his mouth against her neck.

Suddenly, the events of the night before raced through her mind. The taste of him on her knuckles, the way he'd fallen apart just for her, how fucking sexy he'd looked with his belt in his hand, prepared to take the revenge she had hoped he would, and the thorough way he'd fucked her after.

Everything about it had been far beyond anything she had expected, and by the Fates, she wanted so much more. Despite how sensitive her ass was from his lashes at the moment, she would take it all again. She had never seen anything more delicious than his composed dominance.

Her body reacted before her mind did, greedy hands dragging him closer until he was all but atop her. She bit her lip with a soft groan as that slick tongue of his descended down her body, failing to leave any one area untouched. It swirled around each breast, flicking against her nipples, before drawing a path to her navel. He bit the skin there before continuing, earning a hiss.

"What are you doing?" she asked, her voice raw, even as she guided his head lower.

"Breakfast," he said simply.

A tremor racked her body at the insinuation, thighs parting instinctively as he disappeared beneath the sheet. He found his mark with ease, but he took his time. Of course. Hades was a dynamic lover, and the torture was a large part of that. No one had ever made her feel the way he had in the course of twelve hours. She may not have too much experience, but she was certain she had enough to conclude that, especially considering she'd been afraid that she was immune to most of these sensations. He was very good at what he did, everything he did.

And right now, he was kissing her clit with more passion than she thought anyone capable of, his tongue doing laps around it before he took it between his lips. His fingers parted her folds, and she was already wet, a chorus of moans falling from her lips unchecked.

Her hands did everything they could to find anchor upon his head as he shrugged her legs onto his shoulders. Immediately, her heels were bracing against his broad back when he scooped her ass into his hands. Then his mouth was descending again until his tongue had begun to trace the exterior of her entrance.

"Hades..." His name sounded every bit like the curse everyone around her tended to treat it as, but her tone was far more devout than disturbed. "Please."

He hummed against her, his nose nudging against the ball of nerves he'd just abandoned. He slipped a single hand up along her body to palm her breast, and she was all but aflame. She grabbed blindly for the sheet over them, yanking it away and looking down at him. Their eyes met between the valley of her breasts, and her back arched clear off of the bed. She was usually very self-conscious in this position. Only one person had ever gone down on her before or after bottom surgery, and it hadn't been a particularly enjoyable experience. Then again, sex with Adonis rarely was when he was so focused on himself that she simply felt like a prop for his pleasure. So this was still so brand new. It was impossible not to fear inadequacy.

Yet Hades looked anything but dissatisfied, and she felt anything but uncomfortable. And while she was sure she could attribute some of that to the fact that he intricately understood her situation, she also believed it was just who he was.

He looked absolutely devastating between her thighs, and she had to screw her eyes shut to keep from coming then and there. She knew she could too. It was like he knew her body as well as she did. But she wanted this to last, at least a little longer.

He didn't let her rest though. She had just placed her hand on the back of his head again when he plunged his tongue inside of her, and then her hips were bucking up into his mouth in undignified desperation. Her moans were quick to fill the air, thick with need as she ground against the sturdy ridge of his jaw, yearning for any friction she could get. All the while, his fingers alternated between kneading her breasts and tweaking her nipples, overwhelming her with sensual sensations. His other hand slithered over her thigh until he was able to press his thumb firmly to her clit, and she cried out.

She was shameless in her rutting now, nails scraping across his scalp as she searched for purchase, for relief. She felt it building deep in the pit of her stomach. She knew she would not last long. He must have known it too, smothering his face in her folds and stretching his tongue as best he could.

She hissed his name again, this time in warning, but that was as far as she was going to get. Before she could truly process how close she was to the edge, he was shoving her over, scraping his teeth against her folds as that wretched tongue of his worked across her walls. Then she was screaming out, her entire body up to the shoulders lifting off of the mattress, feet nearly flat against his shoulder blades.

Her orgasm rocked her thoroughly with the severity of an earthquake, shaking her through to her core. Her eyes rolled back into her head as he let her ride it out on his tongue, his hand relaxing against her breast and his thumb still drawing languid circles around her clit. She was babbling a bunch of nonsense as she came down, flopping against the bed with chest heaving and thighs shaking. Pushing himself up into a kneeling position, he stared down at her.

"You like that?" he asked.

"Mm, yes, sir," she breathed, eyelids fluttering.

She could look at him all day, especially right now when the reserved stoicism and polite charm he'd possessed upon their first meeting was now buried beneath raw want and mischievous mirth. Those eyes were impossibly more dangerous than she'd initially believed it seemed, which was saying a whole lot.

He rolled her onto her side. "I got somethin' else you might like."

She already knew she would.

Lifting up her leg, he straddled the one beneath her and slid inside of her with ease. Her toes curled as she clawed at her pillow, his leisurely stroke a blessing and a curse upon her sensitive walls. His grunts were simply another stimulus, accompanying each thrust as they became stronger.

She threw herself onto her back, still twisted at the waist, to find his eyes on her, and that coil in her gut tightened all over again. She bit down on her lip, watching him fuck her with growing vigor, and it was a sight she committed to memory with pitiless greed. His muscles flexing, his dark skin slick with sweat, his chiseled abs contracting with each movement, the faint scars across his chest glistening.

He hooked her leg around his thigh in favor of grabbing her hip, holding her in place so he could drill that thick cock into her with full force. She called out his name, trying to turn over on her stomach completely if only to cling to the sheets or bite down on something, but he kept her pinned as he dug her out. She reached back instead then, digging her nails into his hip, feeling the power he put behind each thrust and getting drunk off it. All she could do was hold on, constantly writhing and moving and searching for purchase. He never slowed down. She never wanted him to.

She coasted to another orgasm in record time, which was unsurprising when he was bottoming out again and again, whipping his hand across her ass with her helpless to do anything but take it. And oh did she take it, willingly, eagerly.

"Hades! You—"

She bit out the words as she came, breasts bouncing in time with his rhythm. She drew up her leg from around his hip, allowing him to get deeper, and he took immediate advantage, knocking cry after precious cry from her mouth.

Reaching up, she braced her hands against the headboard. She knew that he was close. She could tell by the intensity of his movements and the determination on his face. He was galloping towards the finish line, and she welcomed him there with wanton moans and broken pleas. And he delivered, buried to the hilt and relinquishing raw sounds of ecstasy as he shuddered against her. She quivered around him too.

He leaned down over her, finding her lips with his own and smothering them. She gripped the back of his neck, catching his gruff moans on her tongue and keeping him there even as he stretched her out further. It just felt too good. All of it felt too damn good, and she was hooked.

It was well past mid-morning when they finally dragged themselves out of bed, and much later than that when they escaped the steamy confines of the shower. She'd lost count of her orgasms by then, but her legs were still trying to tally them in a series of tremors as she choked down half a pot of coffee. Surely, she'd had more today than she'd had her entire life.

Yet somehow, he looked absolutely flawless in last night's suit, his unbuttoned vest still pristine despite all it endured. His tie hung undone around his shoulders, his top buttons unclasped as well, and still, he was a god among men. If she had less pride, she would demand a picture to drool over for the rest of the day. Instead, she committed it to memory as best she could.

"You have rehearsal this evening?" he asked as he stood from his seat opposite her at the kitchen island.

She nodded, her stomach clenching as she realized he would have to leave. She may have a schedule herself, but he ran one of the most frequented places in all of Khaos Falls, not to mention the district that surrounded it. He was late the moment he left the casino last night.

"How about we have dinner together?" he proceeded nonetheless.

She smirked, cupping her mug in both hands, even as the excitement rose in her belly. "I gave you one night, remember?"

"And I'm asking for another."

"Do you think you deserve it?"

It had the desired effect. He swallowed hard before clearing his throat and looking down at the countertop. When he looked up again though, he nodded.

"I would say so. Wouldn't you?"

She hummed. "If you fuck me again like you did last night, I will not recover by tomorrow's show."

"I promise to go easy on you." There it was, that damned smirk that makes her legs weak all on its own. He didn't know how to go easy on her. "We'll have actual dessert this time."

"Where?"

"At the casino. I'll cook for you."

"Ooh." She wiggled her eyebrows. "I definitely can't miss this."

"Precisely. You can't."

She rolled her eyes. "I might be rehearsing a bit later than usual. We're adding in a new scene tomorrow, and Calliope's really been drilling it."

"I'll have to be there then."

"I'll hold you to that."

He rounded the counter, coming up to wrap his arms around her waist from behind. She leaned back on the stool, resting her head against his shoulder. It was amazing. After what she'd seen last night, the merciless and domineering man with a belt poised in his hand, she cherished these moments of warmth. She liked both sides of him, very much, and they each took damn good care of her.

He kissed her cheek then her temple. "How does 8:30 sound?"

She nodded. She would agree to just about anything he said right now when he was touching her with all this tenderness, but she truly did want to see him again. It was almost sad really. She already missed him, and he hadn't even left yet.

"That sounds perfect," she sighed.

"Good. Don't be late."

Her lips quirked. "Well... I am known to lose track of time."

She watched as he brought his hands up in front of them after a brief pause and removed his watch from his wrist, setting it on the counter before her. "Now you have no excuses. So either you're on time, or you're in trouble."

She turned her head and nipped at his jaw. "Yes, sir."

THE OPEN FLOOR plan of Persephone's loft was very much intentional. It offered her the chance to refine her craft in the comfort of her own home when she was away from formal rehearsal. Once Hades left, she used it to her advantage, stretching out her muscles extensively as she tried to work out what was left of their eventful evening.

Her mother called several times during, but Persephone ignored her, unwilling to speak with the woman right now. Her legs were still wobbly, and it only served to push her mind back to the night before over and over again. It had been magical, plain and simple. Any expectations she had held for the evening had been met and then stomped through the ground, and she could not wait to see Hades again. It was worth it. All that risk was worth it.

And she'd be damned if she tainted her current excitement with her mother's venom.

Nevertheless, she made up for the guilt of distraction in the best way she could. She ran through the routine at least twice, utilizing the silks that now hung from her high ceiling to emulate the aerials she performed in Ferocity. It helped her clear her mind and recalibrate her focus, but above all, it soothed her. Not that Hades hadn't because he certainly had, but this was where she lived and thrived, within the role and above the ground. It was the only solace she knew that housed no guilt. And it was the one she had found all on her own when she'd needed it most.

She felt marginally more prepared for rehearsal by the time she was done with her final stretches. She was readying her gym bag to head to the theatre when there was a knock at the door, and her heart jumped in her chest.

Logically, she knew it wasn't Hades, but logic wasn't much fun right now. He had effectively drawn out the dreamer in her, mainly the parts she'd dampened to make room for reality, parts she had tried all too hard to cage outside of work despite the success it had led her to. These efforts were mainly due to the ever-present sound of Demeter's voice in her head, but the ghost of Hades' mouth did well to muffle that. He'd said she was made to fly, and she knew this to be true. She just - never fully believed it before meeting him, viewing her own unyielding doubt as a necessary abundance of caution. It seemed so silly now.

She pulled her bag over her shoulder, slipping Hades' watch inside, just as the knocks grew more persistent, and any hope of it being him died right there on the hardwood floor. Soon enough, she knew exactly who it was, and she seriously considered hiding. However, her pride wouldn't allow her to do anything of the sort, so she took a deep breath, straightened herself, and marched towards the door just as the knocking turns to banging. When she opened the door, Zeus immediately pushed into the apartment, his face red with rage.

She rolled her eyes.

"Where the hell have you been?" he roared the moment the door closed behind him.

She kept a distance between them, crossing her arms over her chest and leveling him with a hard stare. She wasn't about to give him any footing, especially considering he'd only use it to find another step on the back of her neck.

"I imagine right here where you found me," she offered, her tone bland. "Oh, but I also might be, I don't know, working."

"Oh, yeah? Working?" He sneered. "What's this about you having drinks with my brother?"

She didn't react, at least not outright, but her heart surely did a swan dive into the pit of her stomach. She realized however that he was asking about drinks rather than dinner, which meant he didn't know about last night. That was good. That made this easier.

"Which?" she asked.

"What do you mean which!"

He took a step forward. He had several inches on her, and he had at least a couple on Hades, but he was not nearly as imposing. He looked every bit like a large child throwing a temper tantrum. She treated him accordingly.

"I mean which," she went on, nearly yawning. "You have more than one, don't you?"

"How many have you had drinks with!"

She rolled her eyes again and looked away. "If you mean Hades, then yes. He owns Asphodel. I perform there. He invited me for a drink. I accepted it."

"And?"

"And that's far more than I owe you, Zeus. I gotta go. Is that all?" He took another large step forward, and with the door at her back, she had nowhere to go. She still didn't move, refusing to give him the satisfaction of backing her up against it. Her heel came off the ground however, prepared to give him a hard knee to wherever she could land it if need be. She was fed up. This had to stop.

"I made you."

Her brows knitted together. "Excuse me?"

"You would be nothing without me."

"Has anyone ever told you that you think too highly of yourself?"

"Am I wrong?"

"Very."

She choked down the bile crawling up her throat, her fingers tightening on the strap of her bag. She honestly thought he might strike her, and he appeared to think he might too.

"You think you don't owe me your life, but you do," he growled. "The moment you took that money—"

She stepped forward now, so suddenly that he recoiled. "I didn't take shit from you. You made an offer and lied about the catch. Don't come in here with that mess. I tried to pay you back—"

"With someone else's money!"

"What does it matter? If you wanna wait on my paycheck, fine, but that's what you'll get, Zeus. Take it or leave it, but I am done with this. I don't want you. I will never want you, and you damn sure do not own me."

He was flustered now, floundering, and all he could do was repeat his words. "I made you, Persephone! Everything you are, I made you!"

"You made me regret ever meeting you. Nothing more. And from what I hear, Hades made you." She looked him dead in the eye, and while she may have been pushing it, her anger didn't care. "Which means he can unmake you. I'm sure he would hate to hear you're harassing his associates, in his district at that. And before you say 'it's my district, I run everything' or whatever childish thing you're about to say, it isn't. And you don't. You're just a little boy playing Fate while your brother wipes your chin and keeps your hair out of your face. You are nothing without him. You have nothing without him. I am everything without you. That's what it means to make someone."

The look in Zeus's eyes was deadly, but no more than what she had seen in her mother's. Or her father's the first and last time he struck her. She wasn't afraid of Zeus. She wasn't afraid of much of anything anymore.

Stepping aside, she reached back and pulled the door open for him. He stared at her, seething, but she didn't look away. She certainly hit a nerve. In fact, she was almost certain she hit all of them. Still, he finally scrounged up just enough poison to make her blood run cold.

"This house you think you built is made of nothing but sticks and stones," he growled, pointing his finger at her. "Whether you made it or not, I can bring it crashing down on your head at a moment's notice. I can unmake you. That's what matters now, and if you even think of telling my brother, I'll show you exactly what I mean." Another step forward. "Because remember, Princess, Hades does for me. He has always done for me. You honestly think you can change that?" His smile was sharp as glass. "You're just another business venture, and my brother has plenty of those to choose from. I'll make sure he tosses you out the moment you become more trouble than you're worth. You're tiptoeing that line pretty close now, so if I were you, I'd be really careful about how you speak to me."

"Get out," she growled.

His smile only widened. "I want you at Lonzo's restaurant at 8 sharp tonight. Do not make me come back here, Persephone. You won't like what that looks like."

She maintained her glare, but the lump in her throat rose exponentially. She couldn't speak. It felt like ages before he stalked out, and he tried to grab the doorknob to slam it closed, but she held firm. He was jolted by the force, and when he glanced over his shoulder at her, she slammed the door in his face.

"8 o'clock, Persephone!" he shouted through the barrier before his footsteps began to recede.

She leaned against the door, shuddering out a breath. It was quiet now, but she knew it wasn't over. It would never be over if her pride was her only weapon, and she had to swallow said pride and accept that.

Being afraid of Zeus and being afraid of what the leader of Khaos Falls was capable of were two different things, and they had to be treated as such. She had no power where the latter was concerned. Gambling everything she had worked so hard for just to avoid admitting defeat was as arrogant as it was foolish, and it was exactly what Zeus was doing. She could not make that same mistake. She could not be like him. She wouldn't.

She had to come clean to Hades, and she had to do it tonight.

Twelve

HADES

H ades leaving his office before the sun set was not simply uncommon. It was unprecedented. And he had now done it twice in as many days. Not that everyone in the casino noticed. He had always been the very definition of a higher power here, working unseen but always incredibly felt. No, the divergence weighed far more heavily on Hades himself than anyone else, and he felt almost uncomfortable, stripping off his tie and rolling up his sleeves as he entered his kitchen. He doubted he needed so much time to prepare a late dinner, but if he was honest, he was nervous, which would be funny if it weren't so invasive. The first date had gone so well. How was he supposed to follow that up?

He had rarely —if ever— made it past the first date, and not entirely for lack of trying either. From the beginning, something would be missing, and by the end of it, he would be sure that there would be no salvaging it. That was the pattern he'd become accustomed to. For a plethora of reasons, he had consistently struggled to connect with anyone beyond a surface level. The only exceptions had been Hecate, Thanatos, and Charon, and not a single complaint about that had ever passed from his lips. Nor would it.

But then... Persephone happened.

She had changed everything, quickly and irrevocably. And all in all, for the better. All of a sudden, with a relentless determination, he wanted for more. And not only that, he wasn't willing to settle for anything less.

He heard the elevator ding just as he pulled the lamb out of the oven, setting it atop the stove. He glanced at his watch — Or rather, he glanced at his wrist where his watch should be only to find the faint outline in his skin. Looking towards the balcony doors instead, he found that it was not yet fully dark out, so he knew it couldn't be her. He looked up as the elevator opened, knowing it could only be one of three people with card access to his suite. To his surprise, it was two of them, Thanatos and Hecate entering in full formal attire. Hades halted his movements and turned to them fully, brows raised.

"Going out?" he asked.

"My sister's annual auction, remember?" Hecate explained.

He had indeed forgotten. Granted, Hades tended to forget Hecate had a sister. She and Circe had only found out about each other a few years ago, well after they were both already grown, and the former didn't make a habit of coming around. Hades only ever saw her when he had business with Medusa's Sarpedon District. In that, it was difficult to see her as anyone other than Medusa's right hand.

"We came to see if you wanted to come," Thana went on, flopping down on the couch only to be immediately reprimanded by Hecate for rumpling his suit. He shrugged. "Bring Persephone. I assume that's why you left your office before midnight for the first time in ages. Apart from, you know, going out last night and going to her shows, but that only serves my point, doesn't it?"

Hades picked up a head of lettuce and launched it at him, which Thanatos caught with a grunt. Hecate's glare passed over both of them.

"I just made dinner," Hades pointed out, gesturing to the counter before him. "And she has a show tomorrow. She'll want to rest."

Thana snorted. "As if you're going to let her rest."

Hades smiled. "I promised."

"Probably because he wore her out last night," Hecate hummed, softening now.

"Hush, the both of you," Hades huffed, catching the lettuce when Thana threw it back.

Though, the air seemed to thicken as he set it back down, the three of them eyeing one another. Hecate tilted her head, inspecting Hades.

"She's something, isn't she?" she asked, her voice saturated with something Hades couldn't quite place. Then, "Something serious."

Immediately, he felt the sweat trickling down his neck. He told himself it was from the heat of the oven at his back, but he knew better. He may have already heard Hecate's thoughts on the matter, but that didn't ease his apprehension.

"I don't know," he answered honestly, bracing his hands on the counter. "Can she be?"

"What do you mean?"

He shrugged. "I don't know what it means, to feel this way about someone. It feels-"

"Selfish?"

Hades looked up at Thanatos, whose face was screwed up in

126

questioning confusion following his suggestion. Though the two of them said it all in the eyes. Thana knew. He understood. How, Hades did not know, but he was given no time to investigate that.

"Because it isn't," Thana went on, his expression clearing. "You only think that because you've never had something for yourself. You, Hecate, me, Charon. We put everything we have into this place, this district, and that's no complaint. It is our home, the home your father wanted for us, but he never would have asked you to do it on your own."

Hades smiled. "I have never done it on my own."

"You know what I mean, brother." Thana stood up, smoothing out his suit solely for Hecate's benefit, conveyed by the look he spared her before he looked back at Hades. "He would have wanted you to be happy. Your mother too. And if she were here to see what we're seeing, from that night you met this woman to now, she would say the same thing. There is room for her, Hades, for Persephone. And if there isn't, you better make some, because you deserve to be happy, not just content."

Hades looked down at the counter again, shaking his head. He was lucky to have them. He had always been very lucky, and he told himself that it was enough. Through the years, he'd believed that this little bit of luck was more than he deserved, and asking for anything more was not only selfish but ungrateful. Yet here they were, the people he trusted most, telling him otherwise. How could he deny it then?

Whatever existed between him and Persephone, he wanted to see it to fruition, and he wanted to make it work. Everything about her inspired this. He thought them opposites at first, but the truth was that she was so many of the things he wished to be. Brave, bold, free. She never let anyone clip her wings, and because of that, for the first time in his life, he was questioning why he ever did.

When he looked up, Thana was grinning. He realized he was too.

"Is that a 'yes, Thana, you're a genius, and you're right, and I'm gonna listen to you'?"

Hades and Hecate both rolled their eyes though their smiles betrayed them.

"It's not even close to all of that nonsense," Hades replied, "But it's a - 'I'm going to try and take the one bit of good advice you've ever given'. How's that?"

Thana smirked and patted Hades' chest. "That's a start. We'll work on it. Now, we should get going, love, or else we'll be late, and if there's anything I hate more than your sister's last-minute invitations, it's that fucking glare Medusa gives people when they show up late. Or - show up at all. Medusa really doesn't like people. Not that I blame her."

Hades laughed. "Okay, but first. Can you taste the lamb? I need to make sure it's perfect."

Thana is already moving towards the pan. "Absolutely. They feed you nothing at these things. We pay so much to lick an empty plate, I swear it. The portions are a nightmare."

Hecate scoffed. "Get all of that complaining out now because I do not want to hear it once we get there, do you understand?"

Thana took a large chunk of meat and stuffed it in his mouth before speaking around it with a large grin. "Yes, ma'am."

Thirteen

PERSEPHONE

Persephone's phone continued to ring nonstop as she approached the imposing towers of Asphodel, Demeter's name flashing across the screen on a loop. It was almost 8, so Persephone assumed that soon enough, Zeus's name would be interspersed, but she tried not to think about that for the time being. Or at all. Once she was safe inside the walls of the casino, she could not care less about what he did.

She'd gone home, quickly, after rehearsal for a quick shower, but she was edging very close to late. Unlike with Zeus, the thought of being late to dinner with Hades both thrilled her and scared her, uncertain of what her punishment would be if she lingered in the elevator a little too long. However, once she arrived, she realized she didn't have that option.

She left her phone in the car and sauntered into the casino, this time able to take it all in —or at least, a good amount of it— without the need for an immediate escape. She even had the chance to actually admire the black and violet carpet pattern that her feet had carried her across the last time. Still soft beneath her flats, you would never know that thousands of people trampled over it with drinks sloshing out of their glasses daily. Hades' people kept the place pristine. She wasn't surprised.

The casino was large, much larger than it appeared from the outside, and each room felt like a whole new world. The various card tables buzzed with traffic and anticipation, most of them intense and inaudible amidst the siren song of the slot machines. The slots had various themes from pop culture to a uniform default, and the sounds seemed to fill the air in a heroic harmony if one only listened close enough.

When she entered the main room, her attention was automatically drawn upward toward the nest where Hades dwelled, but of course she saw nothing. Her gaze continued to climb up the walls to the high ceilings and silk banners that hung from them, Hades' crest billowing in the air conditioning. Like the man himself, everything in this place was absolutely majestic. And now that she knew him, she could see that it was a direct reflection of its owner. Her heart clenched. She could not wait to see him.

Once again, she was intercepted, but the guards were much kinder and far less imposing this time, leading her up the stairs. She thought they were going to Hades' office again, but instead, they led her into a side hall across from it where an elevator resided. Judging by the seclusion and the fact that a key card was needed, she imagined that it went straight up into his penthouse. The guards did not immediately board it however.

Persephone stood there idly as the woman on her left spoke into her radio, and only a few minutes later, the elevator descended and the doors opened up in front of her.

There stood Hades, looking as dapper as ever in a navy blue

waistcoat and matching tie secured over his white dress shirt. She had no clue how he did it with such simplicity, and again, she felt underdressed in her strapless baby blue dress.

He smiled and offered his hand, pulling her into the elevator and thanking his guard with a wave. The two guards waved back before turning and heading back down the hall. Hades let the doors close before pulling her even closer and capturing her lips with his own. She melted on impact, gripping his elbows for anchor with a groan. When he pulled away, that devilish smirk was still perfectly in place.

She wanted to sit on it.

"You look amazing," he said, brushing his fingers down the side of her face. "And you're on time. How was rehearsal?"

"What would have happened if I wasn't? On time?" She completely sidestepped his question in favor of her own.

His eyes glittered with mischief, the corner of his mouth curling upward. "Be glad you don't have to find out. You know what they say about curiosity, what it does."

"Yeah, but considering you already did that yourself last night..."

The look on his face shot heat straight down between her thighs. As did the tone of his voice. "You want that punishment, don't you, babygirl?"

"Mm, does it involve that belt again?"

"Yeah. This time I tie you up with it and make you beg for my attention."

She moaned without truly meaning to right there in the elevator, leaning into him. Goodness, he wasn't just turning her on, he was turning her into something else. It was impossible to keep her mind from wandering, conjuring up image after image of what last night's sequel might look like. The things she could do with him, the things she would let him do to her...

Her eyes darted down to his belt as if compelled to before they return to his face. Somehow, she'd forgotten all about Zeus and her mother and any other problem that awaited her outside. Here, in his tower, she was safe. The only immediate danger was what this man before her might do to her panties before they reached the top floor, and she was more than willing to fuck around and find out.

From the moment the doors parted again, she knew the place was huge. It opened into a short entryway, flanked at the end by the kitchen on the right and the living room on the left. Past that was more living room in addition to the dining room and the balcony. Three hallways branched off these main spaces, and she could only imagine his bedroom. For now at least.

"This is gorgeous, Hades," she breathed as she moved deeper into his space, staring around the living room. Her eyes soon honed in on the dining area. There were candles lit upon the table, and it was set with the utmost attention to detail. The food looked absolutely delicious, and she would say that he gave Danae a run for her money, but Persephone could be biased. Either way, she was ecstatic.

Hades took two wine glasses off of the counter and offered her one before guiding her towards the dinner table. She saw another unopened bottle of pomegranate wine on a tray beside a plate of actual pomegranates that had yet to be cut. She was exceptionally impressed with the spread he had put together, taking her time in admiring it before sitting down in the seat he'd pulled out for her. She could no longer remember the void idea she'd had of him before all this, but it paled in comparison to the man in the flesh. Lucky her.

Dinner passed in a haze of wine and laughter, and they eventually wound up sitting out on the balcony on two very comfortable chairs. Another bottle of wine and the freshly cut pomegranates sat upon a table between them although neither had touched them yet.

Persephone found herself enjoying the view of the River Styx District more thoroughly than ever before. Despite the monochrome design across most of the buildings and the fog that engulfed it from the river, it was soothing. Like the elevator and his penthouse, it felt safe, an impenetrable fortress where they could rule and reign.

"Did you like it, growing up here?" she inquired.

He smiled. "Very much so. It's much the same too. Few people know of them, but there are a lot of hidden gems here in the district. The hot springs, the wildlife preserve, a few museums. There was always something to do here, and always a lesson to learn." He laughed heartily. "Though I cannot tell you how much trouble Thanatos and I would get up to. Charon often got dragged into it, and Hecate either planned the whole thing or managed to get us out of it. Either way, my mother had her work cut out for her."

She looked over at him curiously. It remained bizarrely difficult to integrate the reality of him with the legend. In the latter, he was never a child. Shit, he was never really human. He simply was. Or wasn't.

Truly, she felt like the man beside her and the leader of the Underworld were two very different people. She'd heard of the things he'd done, mainly for Zeus, and none of them matched up with the being before her, the man who touched her like his favorite flower until she was stripped bare and then made all her wildest fantasies come true. She smiled to herself. It was almost like she had unlocked a side of him all her own, one she would certainly like to keep.

133

"Did you like growing up in the Harvest District?" he asked, and she realized he was looking at her now too.

She nodded. "It had its wonders. Growing up by the coast was fun every summer. I spent most of my time in my Aunt Hestia's library though, especially when my dad was around, before I transitioned. It was - it's where I felt safe, you know?"

The look of pure adoration in his eyes didn't escape her, and she ducked her head as heat flooded her cheeks. Though when he spoke again, her eyes darted up.

"You're very—"

"Don't tell me I'm brave," she interjected, immediately soothed by his soft smile. "The only reason I'm brave is because the world is cruel, and that isn't something to glamorize. Being my mother's daughter shields me from a lot of it, but sometimes, that just makes it feel worse. I don't want to be brave. I want to be seen."

He grew quiet, and at first, she wasn't sure what he was thinking. She imagined he could understand, but she also knew his experience and hers may have differed in far more ways than they reflected one another. He looked contemplative, as if turning her words over before responding. She didn't fear whatever came next, waiting patiently and sipping her wine. After all, the hardest part was long over.

"I can admit I never really considered it that way," he finally admitted with a soft laugh. "You know, I - it just... I have hidden myself my entire life, not because of my gender. That was the easy part for me. But simply because I did not know how to exist in the world with other people. I did not know how to be who my family needed me to be without becoming something bigger than what I was. Even once I - had the body I wanted, it still wasn't big enough. I needed to become something else, something - formless, some-

134

thing. Which meant I could not be a person. Nor could I be someone to other people." He turned to her fully. "So I don't think you're brave just for being. I think you're brave for - wanting to be seen."

Persephone held his words in her hands like precious pearls, sorting through them to make sure that no stones or pebbles had slipped their way in. But no, he was as genuine as ever, and she wasn't sure why that was so difficult to believe, but she did. At least, she wanted to.

"But regardless, you will have that here, with me," he continued. "I - can't promise I'll never make a mistake because I will not pretend as if our experiences are identical, but I can promise that I'll be willing to learn from it, to listen and make sure that you always feel heard. And I want you to know that - I didn't go looking for that information, and that is not something I would ever use against you. It was merely part of what I learned of your mother's district, of her family. It had no bearing on my attraction to you, good or bad."

A soft laugh escaped her. "I figured as much, and - I believe you. I mean, I don't really think about it often either, but dating is - well, it's still new to me really."

His lips curled. "It's new to me too, but we can figure it out together, right?"

"I think so, yeah. We've done alright so far."

Hades accepting her didn't make him a hero, not in the slightest. Just as accepting him did not make her one. She would not reward him or anyone else for being a decent human being, but that didn't minimize her relief.

Yet, knowing he knew all along without her ever having to agonize over explaining it to him made her feel foolish for hiding the truth about her ties with Zeus. That felt so minuscule in comparison, although she imagined both men might believe otherwise. Who she was should never be as controversial as what Zeus was doing, how he constantly harassed her to the point of distress. Years of her life had been threaded with that stress, and all because she had believed him to be someone other than what everyone else had warned her he was. Granted, she had done the same for Hades, but he had yet to make her regret it. That only made it clearer to her. It wasn't her judgment of character that was at fault. It was Zeus. If Hades was the man she believed him to be, he would see that too.

And if not, none of this would work anyway. It couldn't.

"I have to tell you something - else."

She blurted it out without fully committing to it, but once she did, she knew it was time. Turning in her chair to face him, she set down her glass on the tray. He seemed to sense the seriousness of it, setting his glass down as well and mirroring her position in his own chair.

"It's about... Well, I- I don't really know how to explain it." She pushed a trembling hand through her hair.

"Take your time," he encouraged although she could see the confusion in his eyes.

Still, she accepted his encouragement. She gave herself a minute to gather her thoughts, but even when she started again, she didn't know if she was saying what she meant to. "Remember how I told you that I went to Terpsichore's School before I started with Calliope? I mean, I - I didn't actually start there. I started in a community theatre, but I wanted to go there. I just - I couldn't... oh, for Fates' sake."

"Hey." She looked up at him as he leaned towards her, reaching over and taking her hand in his. "It's alright. Whatever it is, just tell me."

She nodded, clearing her throat and taking a deep breath. "It's Zeus."

It wasn't entirely what she meant to say, but she felt that if she didn't get that out of the way first, she would implode before she could explain anything else. Hades sat up straighter, ears perked as he stared at her. He didn't release her hand, and she can't read his expression, but she imagined a million things were going through his mind, and she simply could not find the words to explain fast enough.

"What about him?" he finally urged.

"Well, when I - when I wanted to go to school, my mother cut me off. She was set on it, not letting me go. Even with my savings, I couldn't afford to pay the tuition on my own, and I didn't have anyone I could go to for help then." She squeezed his hand instinctively. He squeezed right back. "He came to me, Zeus. We'd met at the community theatre, and I thought he was my friend. He owned the school, and he said he could put me on a full scholarship. I - I should have known there was a catch, that he-"

"No." Hades' voice was so firm that it stopped her in her tracks. "Don't do that. Don't blame yourself. Tell me what he did."

She only realized then how close she was to breaking, whether from anger or shame or both. All these years of Zeus's unwanted attention were finally catching up to her, and she hated it. She looked down at her knees, her chest tightening.

"Now he won't leave me alone. The whole time I was away with Calliope, ever since I got back, he just - he's everywhere. And - if he isn't there, he has someone watching me. That's what he did these last two weeks, and..."

She took a moment to breathe before continuing. He waited.

"He showed up at my - apartment after you left today. I don't even know how he found me there, but - he heard about us having drinks, and -" She swallowed hard. "I was supposed to meet him at a restaurant in Olympus at 8. Obviously, I came here, but - he said he would make sure I never forget that he can bring it all crashing down on me if he wanted. And - I'm not worried about that, what he can do to my career or anything, but - I don't want him to ruin this, and - I don't want to lie to you. I don't want you finding out from him or anyone else, and I don't want to start trouble between you and your brother. If you want me to go, I will, but I can't - I..."

She looked up at him now, unsure of what else to say, uncertain of what he might do. He didn't speak, not immediately, and she realized then that she wasn't sure she wanted him to. She also realized that she meant what she'd just said. Although she knew she needed help, she didn't want him to get involved if it brought trouble for him. She didn't need saving at the expense of his safety. She just wanted to be honest with him, and she wanted to be honest with herself about the fact that she didn't want to lose him.

And right now, everything about his body language told her that he was fighting not to flip the table between them right over the balcony railing.

HADES

H ades was livid.

He let nothing show on his face, but his palms pressed into the arms of his chair with unnecessary pressure. He felt it buzzing beneath his skin, an unmatched anger that he refused to act on. He did not act out of anger, certainly not for Zeus, but his brother was crossing a line that Hades never thought he would.

Except...that wasn't true at all, was it? Because Hades knew his brother. He knew what his brother was, and he had enabled him for as long as they had known one another. Every tryst and encounter and extramarital affair, Hades had found out about. He had never spoken a word about them to anyone, and even when the fruits of such engagements had literally shown up on Zeus's doorstep, Hades had been more willing to take those children into his own home than to force Zeus to own up to his mistakes and take responsibility for his actions.

Of course, Hades had also known that those children deserved better than anything Zeus would have ever been capable of offering, and Hades, who already had a habit of choosing to do things himself to ensure they were done well, had truly wanted to be a father, fearing it was not something that would have happened otherwise. And... as ashamed as he was to admit it, he liked the idea of being better than Zeus in that regard. Of being more. Because regardless of how devoted he was to denying it, the fact was that Zeus had never been an ally to him. He was Hades' first adversary.

Though Hades began transitioning young, Zeus never missed an opportunity to make him fight in the dirt for his masculinity. Literally and figuratively. And for a long time, he was able to convince Hades that it was inevitable, that he had to fight for it, because men like Zeus owned it inherently and men like Hades had to earn it. Now, he knew better, but that old rivalry remained.

Maybe that contributed to the guilt he carried around, the reason he worked so hard to keep this promise to his mother even though he knew better than to believe she would approve of this method.

For all that, Hades also accepted that no matter how long it had been since he had stopped demanding his masculinity from Zeus or anyone else, Zeus would always have power over him. This was his world, his city, and Hades would never do enough to earn his respect much less his own freedom. Not as long as he believed it was Zeus's to give.

But all this hardly mattered right now. Whatever ills existed between him and his brother were irrelevant to this current situation because nothing could justify what Zeus was doing to Persephone, and nothing would justify Hades sitting there and doing nothing about it. He may have never known Zeus to outright harass anyone, but the younger brother's devolution had been evident from the start. Was it not simply a matter of time before it came to this?

It was a shame really. He'd just told Persephone not to blame herself, and here he was. Although he could say for certain that he had far more to do with this chain of events than she ever could. He was his brother's keeper, after all.

"I'll talk to him," he said at last, but she was immediately shaking her head.

"I don't need you to talk to him." Her voice was stern, so much so that his gaze was drawn to her. "I don't need you to get involved, Hades. I can handle this myself."

"You shouldn't have to."

"You're right, I shouldn't, but I am, and I can handle it."

"It's not about whether or not you can handle it." His voice was calm as the Aegean despite every nerve ending in his body sparking with electricity. "Zeus is a monster of my making, and-"

"Hades, you can't do that!" He was shocked as she stood up, her fists bawled at her sides, brows knitted in frustration. "He isn't your anything! You are not responsible for him. You did not make him do anything. You may have given him everything he has, or at least protected it, but what he does with it is not up to you. The man he is now is the man he chose to be. Just like you're the man you choose to be, and are you really gonna choose to be his whipping boy?"

He opened his mouth but closed it again. It was not like these weren't things he didn't know, or at least they weren't things he hadn't already been told. Though not even Hecate had ever put it so bluntly. The desire to protect Persephone didn't go away, but there was now some hesitation. He chose his words more carefully.

"You can say all that to me, and you're correct, but that doesn't negate the fact that you shouldn't have to handle it, by yourself or otherwise." His voice was steady, some of the anger having subsided. "And if I'm being honest, I don't think you can handle it, which has nothing to do with you. Whether he's my doing or not, his actions are not to be tolerated. The fact of the matter is that he won't listen. You told him no, and he refused. Now it's a matter of persecution."

"And that's your job?" she grunted, but she did sit back down.

He nodded. "I made it my job the day I started protecting him from said persecution."

"What's talking to him going to do, Hades?" She shook her head again. "It's only going to look like I ran crying to you like I can't handle myself. Everyone will know, and I'll look like the girl who used the leader of the Underworld as a shield. I won't."

"Who in Gaia is going to know, Persephone? You think if Zeus wanted anyone to know, I wouldn't by now? Hell, I usually know things even if he doesn't want me to, but this..." This, he hadn't even suspected, and he was ashamed. Still, he kept his focus. "No one has to know anything, and even so, you're not going to look like the girl who used me as a shield. You and I have a-"

He realized then that he didn't know what they had. Two dates and great sex hardly constituted a relationship, but what else could it be? What else would he want it to be? He supposed it would be up to her. Nonetheless, he exhaled and continued.

"You came to me because you wanted to be honest with me. What I do with that information is my choice, as you said."

"And then Zeus goes and throws a tantrum, no doubt painting me as some harlot. All he has to do is tell the truth, Hades. I took that money."

"The trustee of your school offered you a scholarship, Persephone. It's not like he handed you cash in a bag in a back alley, and even if he did, you don't owe him anything!"

It was the first time he'd ever raised his voice in her presence, and he could see it on her face that she realized it too. She looked taken aback, not quite afraid but not entirely comfortable. He sighed, letting his face fall into his hands for a moment as he composed himself. He wasn't this. He wouldn't be this.

"I'm sorry," he said.

"You should be," she returned curtly. "But in all of this, raising your voice is the only thing you should be sorry for, Hades."

So much passed between them in that singular moment of silence. They were arguing over barren ground, each attempting to take possession when both of them should simply let it be. However, he of all people knew how difficult that could be. Ignoring Zeus was literally like ignoring the big, white elephant in the room. At the moment, it felt like listening to the ticking of a time bomb and doing nothing about it.

"No." The word sounded like law when it fell from his lips, and she straightened. "I said I wouldn't let him take this from me, and I meant it. Not now, not tomorrow, not ever. I don't care where or how he tries to take it, he won't."

"So then what? We just - continue seeing each other at secret locations? Or holing up in here? Dodging him until he gets bored? I don't even think I can go back to my apartment after tonight."

"I want to be with you. I want us to be together."

She stared at him, her eyes expectant as she opened her hands in confusion.

"Do you want to be with me?" he asked instead. "I mean truly. Do you want a relationship with me?"

"I wouldn't be here if I didn't."

143

"Then be with me. Without hiding."

She snorted. "So you want me to publicly use you as a shield."

"You're not using me."

"See, Hades, you say that, but the fact of the matter is you don't know when you're being used. Zeus has been using you for years."

"You assume I don't know that, but the fact is that I do. I just didn't care to stop it before."

"And now?"

"If I have to choose, I choose you. And I choose me. Because I know he wouldn't choose me and my happiness, but - in this way, I can be sure."

"So it's a test?"

He chuckled, picking up his glass and draining it. He hadn't prepared for all of this tonight, and he hated to be unprepared. It garnered unnecessary stress.

Setting down his glass again, he fixed his gaze on hers. "Look, you either trust me or you don't. You're going to find fault anywhere you look because this is not an orthodox plan. Yes, it could make us both look bad. It could backfire. A lot of things can go wrong, not least of all where your mother's concerned, but I'm willing to take that risk. And truly, I want this. I want to go to your shows without worrying about people wondering why. I want you to be able to walk through the front doors of the casino as you please even when you don't have a show. I want to be with you, and that has nothing to do with my brother, but if it gets him to take the hint, that's a welcome bonus. If it doesn't, I'll handle him some other way."

"And what way would that be, Hades?" Her voice softened. "I do realize that he has as much power over you as he does over me.

If not more so. And - being us, who we are? Do you honestly think he would never use that against you or me?"

He wet his lips. "No, I do not put it past him at all, but again. What is the alternative? Living in fear? Denying ourselves this - this beautiful possibility when we both know it will not matter either way? If he decides to take it that far, nothing we do or don't do will matter. Because as you said, we do not control him."

He could tell she hated having her words recycled, but she begrudgingly nodded, knowing he was right. They both were.

Hades was surprised with himself though for sure. He had been fighting this internal war for most of his life, and in a single night, his entire vantage point had shifted. For a woman he had met less than a month ago.

Though perhaps this was simply the final straw, and all that weight was at long last just too heavy for him to carry any longer.

You deserve better. We all do.

Hecate had been right too, so many times, but she and everyone else had been patient with him. He had cost them all so much time. How much better would his boys' childhoods have been if they hadn't still been subjected to Zeus's influence and the constant reminder that he had rejected them? How much better off would Athena and Ares be? And Hera... Fates, he could not even imagine. So many people hanging at the end of Zeus's whims, and Hades had convinced himself that it was simply how the world worked.

No, not anymore.

"So... you don't want to hide away in your fortress anymore?"

He blinked and realized then that she was smirking. He matched it.

"At least not full-time, and even if I do, I want this to be as much your fortress as it is mine." He gestured towards the pent-

145

house through the balcony doors. "And - if you wanted to stay here instead of that apartment, I would feel much better about your safety. Because whether we should have to deal with it or not, we are."

The smirk fell slightly, but he didn't take his eyes off of her. He knew that what he now offered was a huge step in this very new relationship, but if Zeus had resorted to entering his territory unannounced and harassing her at home, Hades was not willing to put anything else past him.

Of course, there were also more personal benefits to the arrangement if she agreed to it, and he did want to live his own life, free of his brother's ill will. It would be a learning experience above all, but if he could take it on with her at his side, he had nothing to fear. He gathered all of that and somehow managed to convey it in the reprise of a few small words.

"I choose you."

Fifteen

PERSEPHONE

I *choose you.* His words held so much conviction that Persephone lost her breath. He was so - sure. She'd never heard anyone say something with such certainty, and certainly not in regard to her, not even her mother. And her mother was always so sure about everything.

In a world full of trap doors and false bottoms, stability was a lighthouse in the dark she always feared running towards because it often took the shape of a tower to be locked away in. The idea of planting her feet firmly on the ground scared her more than the act of falling in the first place, but right now, looking at him with all that certainty in those sharp eyes? She found no fear to afford it.

Nonetheless, she still wasn't certain about the proposed arrangement as it stood.

It wasn't that she wanted to hide their relationship. Even the prospect of moving into his home didn't sound as farfetched as it might to someone else. She lived in his district, and he lived in the casino, right upstairs from her workplace. Not to mention, this place was huge, and she doubted he would object to allowing her a space all her own. It was convenient for a vast number of reasons, not least of all being closer to him. They had so little time together as it was. Stealing a few extra hours each evening was nothing to turn her nose up at, and while her own desire to be near him as often as possible made her uneasy to an extent, that was only because she'd never felt this way about someone before.

She'd had very few relationships, but all of them had felt ephemeral and aimless in the end except one. Her relationship with Adonis had turned out to be no more than an extension of her relationship with her mother, a gilded cage that both had been so sure she would submit to. Both had been disappointed, and both had tainted her idea of love in irrevocable ways. Yet, it didn't feel that way with Hades, no matter how hard she looked for the warning signs. For a man willingly chained to the whims of others, he was very protective of her freedom.

The problem was that she felt as though she was simply being thrown around from one keeper to the next, at the mercy of every rogue wave her mother and Zeus threw at her in the treacherous sea that was Khaos Falls.

Persephone knew Hades did not seek to own her or cage her, to chain her to a wall, but his intentions could never suit his image. He was known to be ruthless, every bit inanimate in the tales they told of him. Zeus's shield, his personal daimon, the wraith of Khaos Falls. Even if they both knew of the sincerity of their bond, no one else would. It could be more harmful to her career than Zeus's attempts to bring it all crashing down, and while she wanted to be with Hades, she wouldn't pay the steep price of everything she had worked for.

Zeus could say what he wanted, but his money did not make

her. With or without Terpsichore's school, she would have wound up here. It may have taken her longer, but she would have found a way to claw out from beneath her mother's thumb and into the air. She just wished she would have waited now and found that alternative rather than hand the reins to Zeus. Now, in order to claim them back, it felt like she had to hand over the reins to Hades, and she was simply trying to decide whether this perception was correct or if she was making excuses.

"I'm choosing you," he said again, his voice soft. "And I'm not saying that we can't still be together if you decide against this. If you don't want to make it public, I have no qualms about that."

"I just don't want to feel like I'm leaving his chains for yours." The guilt threaded through her the moment she said the words, and she looked down at her hands. "The same way I felt like I left my mother's chains for his."

"That's the last thing I want to do, Persephone. I don't want to tie you down to anything."

"But I want to be tied down to you."

The words came so naturally that she almost questioned if she'd said them at all. But it was the truth. She wanted to do this with him, to have a real relationship. Casual sex was fine, but it had never really been her thing, and she was curious to know what stability felt like. Specifically stability with him.

Wanting Hades and being with Hades may have been two different things, but only one of them offered the stability she sought. The thing was that it was because of him that she wanted that stability at all. Looking at him right now, there was no doubt in her mind that if she was with him, she wouldn't have to worry about what came next. He would be there no matter what. She realized then that she was as sure of him as he was of her.

"I mean, you know, not in a physically restraining way," she at last cleared up with a sheepish smile.

"Oh, really? Because you sounded really enthusiastic about the idea of using my tie to-"

"Shut up."

He chuckled, and the tension seemed to disintegrate between them. She laughed too, but her cheeks were no doubt flushed red beneath her skin.

He held out his hand. "Come here."

She eyed him for a long moment before standing, taking his hand and allowing him to guide her into his lap. Her legs hung limp between his, her toes grazing the ground as he wound an arm around her waist. Her body's reaction to his touch was instantaneous, muscles unraveling and pupils dilating. There would never be a time when she could be this close to him and remain unscathed. She knew this, and the reality was that - she didn't want to.

One of the most beautifully bizarre things about being with Hades was that although it felt dangerous being so close to him, it also felt like the safest place she could ever be. The danger was thrilling, the security was soothing, and everything in between was an infatuation waiting to happen.

His dark skin glowed in the moonlight, not unlike hers, and she basked in the sheer artistry of it. She didn't know why he would call her closer now when they were attempting to have a serious conversation. It was damn near impossible to think with him so close, infiltrating every single one of her senses and seeping into her bloodstream. Of all the things her mother and aunt had warned her of in this world, they had never warned her of this.

They had warned her of Hades, yes, but they had not warned her about the sheer power of passion. Even Aphrodite had flitted over such intense emotion and fervent feeling. They never warned her to be wary of just how ready she would be to burn for someone. Then again, she doubted anyone but Hades could possibly have an effect such as this. Perhaps that was the real reason he was to be admired from a distance.

Her eyes were unwavering as they met his, and the two of them seemed to stay that way, in soft silence, for ages. Even the wind stopped blowing, as though it too held its breath, awaiting some grand defining moment. At last, he looked away, his eyes falling upon the tray on the table, the pomegranates piled on the plate beside their wine glasses. Glancing between him and the fruit, she caught the slick movement of his tongue over his lips. He slowly reached over into one of the pomegranate halves, scooping out some of the seeds. They glittered like rubies in the light, rich juices dripping down his fingers but never falling from his skin. The droplets clung to him as though they knew nothing else, and never wished to.

She could relate.

"Do you want this?"

She inhaled, and her body tightened once more, an invisible cord winding around her chest. He wasn't speaking about the seeds when he asked this question, and she knew it as well as he did. She shivered against him, her voice now low and thick with anticipation.

"Yes."

Her answer was simple, but it encased entire worlds, heavy as it landed in her lap. Every fiber of her being screamed the affirmative again and again, leaving no room for denial, for doubt.

151

He looked up at her. His eyes had darkened considerably. She imagined her own had as well.

With his fingers suspended in the air between them, he asked once more, a subtle urgency underscoring the words.

"Do you want this?"

"Yes." She didn't hesitate this time. "Yes, I want this." She was little more than scorched earth in the wake of her own desire. "I want you."

His hand moved in slow motion. He twisted his fingers as they approached her lips, which parted for him as though it was the most natural reaction they could have. He slid the seeds into her mouth and across her tongue. Her eyes fluttered shut.

Her lips enveloped him, teeth scraping the offering from his skin with an astute eagerness. A single drop of nectar finally broke free of his draw in a way she never could, in a way she never wanted to. It trickled down her chest through the valley of her breasts. It had yet to cool by the time it reached her navel. Everything he touched was not only destined to burn but to burn forever.

Though she was far too captivated by the taste on her tongue to worry about that. Dionysos's wine was divine, but its flavor could not even begin to hold a candle to the fresh fruit on Hades' fingers. Light and sweet, yet it fell heavily into the pit of her stomach. Like a promise.

It tasted like all of the things her mother warned her about with hints of all the lines she should never cross. It tasted like damnation and divinity and an unfailing devotion to both.

And she wanted more.

She sucked his fingers clean, and she kept sucking, the hand at her waist clamping down upon her. His nails bit at the skin barricaded behind her dress, her hips shifting against his thigh. She braced a hand against his stomach as he slowly pulled out of her mouth. Then he brought those same fingers to his own lips, taking them in and leaving her panting.

Her own digits curled into his vest, the rigid fabric of the garment keeping her from him, but when she tried to move, the hand around her waist tightened. It took everything in her to combat the whine climbing up her throat. Unfortunately, she resorted to burying her face in his neck, and so she missed the moment when he extracted his fingers from his mouth and slipped them beneath her dress.

She gasped as those devious digits landed on her inner thigh, tracing a path toward her heat. It took her a breadth of a second to realize just how wet she was for him already, teeth sinking into the juncture of his neck as she fisted the collar of his waistcoat.

She had no clue which was more unnerving, the agility of his fingers or his impenetrable composure, but the stark mixture of both was enough to have her whimpering against his skin. His knuckles bumped against her clit through her panties, which were substantially damp already. Her body writhed, helpless, against his immovable form, and she had to force her hips to remain in place, to keep from bucking against the exploration of his touch.

Neither of them said a word, and not a word was needed, but if she could beg, she would. At the moment, her tongue had forgotten its purpose beyond collecting the salt upon his skin.

He showed mercy at last —if one could call it that at all— gripping the center of her panties and brushing over her bare folds in a most tantalizing way. She gave in to the need to roll her hips, but the moment she did, his grip on her thigh became bruising, holding her firmly in place. She beat a fist against his broad chest and felt the rumble of his laughter. She bit down harder on his neck. He never stopped stroking her folds.

"Hades..." she forced out, tugging hard on his tie before she wrapped it around her fist.

"Yes?" he asked as though they were out to fucking breakfast. "Did you need something?"

"For you to stop - fucking teasing me."

"Ah, I see. And where are your manners? If you don't mind me asking."

"Hades!"

"Babygirl, I'm not sure what it is you're asking of me. I-"

She tore her face from his neck, pulling back enough to press her forehead to his. Her eyes bore into those dark pools with the embers burning at the bottom, but she did not waver.

"I want you to fuck me - with those fingers you have in my panties."

"Ah."

There was no warning before he plunged two of those fingers into her, pressing the pads of them into her walls so hard that she bucked her hips with a loud cry. Long and thick, he worked them inside of her at a slow pace as she struggled to catch her breath. She clawed at his chest, the hand that had been tucked between them now seeking perch in the back of his vest. He did not break eye contact, and it felt like a challenge.

However, it was a challenge she was going to lose, by way of forfeit, because he was as good with that hand as he was with that tongue. And that belt, and that cock, and every other damn weapon he'd brandished against her. She would move into this Fates-forsaken penthouse tonight if it meant he kept doing things like this to her.

154

She wanted to scream, to reprimand him for all of his continuous teasing, but her voice failed her. He dragged her dress further up her thighs until he was able to see what he was doing. Then his thumb found her clit, and all hope was lost.

She cried out into the cool night air, squeezing her thighs around his hand. None of this perturbed him in the slightest, his concentration unscathed, and he merely pushed deeper into her as he stroked her throbbing clit. She gritted her teeth, but soon enough, she was actively riding his fingers, seizing her pleasure and taking what she needed.

She came with a withering wail before she claimed his mouth, conquering it with teeth and tongue alike. He reciprocated with a tangible hunger as he pulled out of her pussy, eliciting a groan. In the space she created for the sake of breath, he brought those fingers between them. Again, it was his mouth that took them, sucking them clean as his eyes locked on hers.

She had never been so needy in her life.

Even as her thighs continued to shake amidst the aftershocks, she adjusted her position so as to straddle him fully, and he didn't interfere this time. She fumbled for his belt, unbuckling it while he was preoccupied with cleaning his palm. By the time he got his hands back on her hips, she had freed him from the confines of his boxers, and he was pulsing in her hand. She licked her lips, torn between gratitude and greed, as she admired his slow rise to attention, the moonlight catching the light scars at the base. Her patience dissolved into nothing, and as much as she wanted to taste him, she knew damn well where she needed him. He had no one to blame but himself.

He seemed to read her inner turmoil, his lips curling and his eyes flashing, but he only squirmed beneath her in his seat, making no move to start or stop her. She surged forward and kissed him again. Then she wound her hips down onto his cock, catching his groan between her teeth like a prize.

There was no easing into it now. She rode him with reckless abandon, throwing her head back as her hands gripped his neck and head. His hand left her hip and left her cold, but she gasped when it yanked down the front of her dress. He shoved up the fabric of her bra until his mouth found her breast, teeth tugging her nipple before ravishing it with his tongue. It was carnal and crazed, and she reveled in every moment of it. She loved to see him lose control.

She called out, her nails unforgiving against his scalp as she bounced higher, harder, faster upon him. Soon, he had both hands on her hips again, guiding her up and down his shaft. She spread her legs wider, as wide as she could within the boundaries of the chair, taking him deeper. Her eyes rolled back, her sensitive clit glancing off of him and eliciting a guttural groan. She would risk it all for this. There was no doubt left about it.

His mouth moved to her other breast, and she was careening towards the edge. His fingers spread her ass and strained her folds, and she knew his trousers must be a mess by now. She growled his name through gritted teeth, but he only returned it around her nipple, slapping her ass once and nearly shoving her into oblivion. She only just held on although she didn't know why. Perhaps it was because she hated how fucking easy it was for him to make her cum when it was usually such a struggle to get there even on her own. Or perhaps it was because he would be behind two orgasms. Maybe it was a mixture of both.

Tearing herself away from his mouth with a whimper, she grasped his head and tilted it upward so he could look at her.

"Cum with me," she demanded, but her voice broke as he hit

her spot again. Still, she clenched her jaw and braced herself enough to make the demand again. "Cum with me - Hades. Now."

He nodded. All he could do is nod, his eyes fathomless and unfocused, his nails clawing at her skin. He all but lifted her now, almost all the way off of his dick before slamming her back down over and over in quick succession, A raucous moan ripped from her throat before she managed to sink her teeth into his shoulder. She failed to hang on though when he grabbed her hair and yanked her head back.

"You want to cum with me-" he breathed. "You're going to do it - out loud, Persephone, so that you - and anyone else who listens knows who this pussy belongs to..."

Bastard! Another blinding light preceded this orgasm as well. It turned her moan into a shriek and her body into a tremor. Hades turned his head into her neck, roaring against her skin and sending wave after wave of shivers through her lithe frame. She felt him pulse and jerk inside her, his quick pumps probing her sensitive walls until the softest warmth painted them. They rode it out in misjudged movements and rogue ruts, but nothing had ever felt so good. She didn't think he could top last night. Now she wasn't sure he would ever stop seeking to ruin her.

She went limp against him though her frame continued to quiver, and he slouched back against the chair, wrapping his arms around her. His hoarse laugh tickled her neck. "I think the whole casino heard you."

"Me?" She scoffed, peering out of one eye although she didn't have the strength to raise her head enough to see him. "You were loud as fuck too."

"Definitely not as loud as you."

157

"You wouldn't let me cover it!" She shut her eyes again, exhaustion overtaking her. "You're cut off."

"Oh, really?" He ran his hand down her back. "Well, I did say I'd take it easy on you."

"You call that taking it easy on me?"

"As opposed to last night?"

"Hades, you don't know how to take it easy. Definitely not with me."

"I can only do my best. How I get when I'm around you is strictly instinct."

"A very primitive one."

"Are you complaining?"

"Mm."

The sound was noncommittal, but her hand curled against the other side of his neck nonetheless, her lips pressing into his skin. He hummed before standing up. She was far too tired to look where they were going, but she trusted him, whatever he planned to do.

His first stop was the bathroom where he undressed them both fully before climbing into the massive bathtub in one corner. She was already dozing off by the time he finished washing her, the smell of his soap soothing and seductive.

She reveled in the attention he afforded her, from drying her down to dressing her in one of his shirts and placing a bonnet on her head. This wasn't usually something she would let herself indulge in, being so dependent on anyone no matter how small the acts seemed to be, but he looked genuinely eager to take care of her. And she had to admit it was nice. She deserved this. She deserved good things and a good man who put her first.

He carried her out of the bathroom, her head resting against his shoulder, exhaustion pulling her down further by the moment.

Moments later, he laid her on the softest bed she had ever been in, and she hummed her content.

"Is this your bed?" she inquired lazily, eyes still closed.

He snorted. "No, you're sleeping in the guest bedroom."

Her eyes snapped open at that, only to find him untying his robe at the foot of the bed, his gaze fixed on her. She glared at him, which was difficult considering how fucking sexy he looked in that moment. He grinned as he removed the garment, hanging it on a hook by the door.

"Where else would I put you, Persephone?" he returned, coming to stand beside her.

"Shut up and come to bed, Hades."

Though she did not wait for him to obey now, reaching up to hook her hand around his neck and pull him down on top of her, relishing in the sound of his laughter and the weight of his body atop hers.

"Keep that up, and you won't be getting any sleep tonight," he warned.

"Shh."

She felt him reaching out, and then the lamplight shut off, leaving them in complete darkness. They settled into the sheets, wrapped around each other as he pulled the comforter over them. Persephone burrowed into his warmth with a content sigh, and she suspected that this might be her favorite part of the night. The sex was amazing of course, but seeing him soft —and for her— brought her a kind of joy no one and nothing else ever had.

She was glad she didn't have to choose between one or the other.

Pressing one last kiss to his chest, she sunk into him and fell into the best sleep she'd had in a very long time.

Sixteen

PERSEPHONE

Persephone woke up to the heavenly smell of something cooking, and it took her a long while to accept the fact that she wasn't dreaming. Once she did, she climbed out of bed and sauntered into the kitchen to find Hades hard at work at the counter, cutting fruit in a pair of sweats that rode far too low on his hips, or not low enough.

She didn't even think he owned sweats, and she wondered how many people would be surprised at this particular development. How many people had truly seen the leader of the Underworld outside of his pristine, tailored suit? She doubted very many. Maybe she should keep a journal. Or write a book.

In place of a shirt, a towel was tossed over his shoulder, and she stood in the archway for the longest time simply admiring him. Even with something as simple as breakfast, he was focused and composed. His hands moved over his work the way a pianist's would over his keys, and she doubted he had ever done anything half-assed in his life. She would bet every dollar in this casino that he hadn't. Regardless, she could definitely get used to this.

He seemed to sense her presence because without turning around, he took a mug from the cabinet and filled it with coffee, adding just the right amount of cream and a dash of sugar. He did it as though he had been doing it for years despite the fact that they'd only had coffee together once the morning after their first date, and she'd made her own cup. Like her drink order in Elysium, he'd remembered.

He'd been taking in these tiny details about her as easy as a breath. She had no clue if it was that or the sacred soreness between her thighs or his physique in those sweats or a mixture of all of it, but she had to force herself to grip the counter before she jumped him right there over the stove. He turned around just then, smiling as he set the mug on the counter.

"How did you sleep?" he asked.

"Like the dead," she grunted, picking up the cup. "And you?"

"Similarly, and in no way unpleasant."

She hummed in content at her first sip. "I am - deliciously sore, Hades."

"Then I fulfilled my duties."

She raised a brow. "Mhm... You know not everything is work, right?"

He seemed confused by the statement. "Of course not. I didn't mean to imply that you were work. I only meant that-"

"Hey." Setting down her cup, she reached over the counter for his hand with a soft smile. "I know what you meant, but what I'm saying is that - it's more than that, right? You're too hard on yourself to begin with. You think your entire purpose is to please people, and it isn't." Her smile widened. "Even if you're really good at it."

There was something akin to relief in his eyes as he squeezed her hand, bringing it to his lips and pressing them to her knuckles. Again, there was that warmth he had put on display for her in their most private hours. It made her feel like the keeper entrusted with a crucial secret, and she wanted to protect it with everything she had.

"What do you have, before the show?" he questioned now, loading a plate for each of them.

"A few run-throughs this afternoon," she replied, snatching a piece of fruit off the plate as he set it down in front of her. "Nothing too heavy, but if my legs give out on me tonight, I'm blaming you fully."

He smirked. "I'll be happy to take the credit."

She glanced up at him. "And you'll be there?"

"I will."

The feeling that rushed through her was all-consuming, and she relaxed into it with a wide grin. She took another bite of melon and nodded.

"Eight o'clock sharp, Sir," she went on. "Don't be late."

"Hm, I am known to lose track of time."

"Oh?" Holding up a finger, she stood up and raced back into the bedroom. When she returned, she had his watch cradled in her hand. He laughed heartily as she rounded the counter, taking hold of his wrist and securing the accessory in place. She then ran her fingers over the band of his sweats and pressed a kiss to his chest.

"This is a look," she purred. "But now you have no excuses, do you?"

"None at all." Running his hands over her arms, he licked his lips. "How do you feel about - a few drinks in Elysium after? Maybe even a dance."

Her eyes glittered with amused excitement as she laughed. "Are you telling me that Hades, the man, the myth, the legend, dances in clubs? The slow dancing I believed just fine, but that?"

He scoffed. "Hey now, I was born with the rhythm, same as you. I have a move or two. I just have little use for them."

"Now that's a lie."

"And surely to a professional, they aren't all that impressive."

"I'll be the judge of that." Though, she paused, toning down her expression. "So... you were serious then, last night. You wanna be seen with me. In public."

He nodded. "That's right."

"Everyone will see us."

"Yes."

"Everyone will know."

"Mhm."

His patience was a thing to behold. It persisted through the length of her silence.

She knew what she'd said the night before, and she'd meant it, but that didn't negate the apprehension that accompanied such a commitment. He let his hands fall from her shoulders as if not wanting to pollute her thought process, and she appreciated it, but the moment his touch was gone, the panic became more tangible.

She was only just making a name for herself in this city, namely with the people who frequented Elysium. How quickly would she become no one other than Hades' woman? She had spent so long being no one other than Demeter's daughter that the thought terrified her. She trusted Hades. She could not imagine he would ever ask her to live in his shadow, but perhaps that was because he had become so comfortable living in that of others. Either way, it wasn't him that she was worried about. It was everyone else.

But as she looked up at him, she realized that it was not

everyone else that mattered. She knew that regardless of when they decided to make it public, the gossip would still be waiting for them. And if she was being honest with herself, she would never be more ready than she was right now.

Cupping his cheek, she nodded and pecked his jaw. "Okay. You can take me dancing."

His grin lit up his entire face. She had never seen anything like it. All of this was worth it if she got to see more of that grin.

He kissed her with that vibrant fervor she was quickly falling in love with, and she melted into his arms. No matter how high up above the stage she flew, she had never felt higher than when she was with him. Part of her thought he was simply too perfect. The rest of her was just glad that he was hers.

"Mm, now I have to go get ready," she hummed, pulling away from him reluctantly. "And you're going to behave and not join me in the shower this time. I do not have enough stamina to go another round with you before showtime."

"I suppose I'll save it for after then," he smirked, holding her hand loosely until she slipped out of reach.

"Oh, you better."

She knew it in her heart. Tonight is going to be special.

BY THAT NIGHT, all of Persephone's worries had faded into the background. To start, it had to be her best performance to date. She felt lighter than she ever had, gliding above the stage, suspended from her silks and swinging from ring to ring. The excitement in the air was electric, spiriting towards a magnificent crescendo. She could feel Hades in his usual seat far below, staring up at her in awe. She could also feel Zeus in the back of the theatre, eyes boring deep into her form, but when she was up here, it wasn't about them or anyone else. It was about her. It was about freedom. To fly or to fall.

By the time her feet touched the ground again, her heart was pounding and her skin was slick with sweat, but you couldn't wipe the grin off of her face with a sandpaper towel. The resounding applause only increased in volume as the cast regrouped at center stage, taking their bows and waving their thanks. Once the curtains closed, she retreated to the dressing rooms, but she still felt like she was floating, the rest of the night spanning out before her beneath the bright stars bursting behind her eyes. There, fatigue was kept at bay by a giddy excitement that she was meeting for the first time.

She was just about to undress and don her robe when Calliope appeared, taking her in a hug.

"You absolutely killed it! Again!" she shrieked, jumping up and down so that Persephone had no choice but to do the same amidst her own laughter. "You did that! It was amazing!"

The taller woman's dark curls tickled Persephone's neck as they pulled away, both of them grinning from ear to ear. She had never seen Calliope this wound up after a show, and she eagerly fed off of that energy.

"Big news," Calliope hissed. "Terpsichore is out there with two very big talent scouts, Thalia and Clio. No one that's planning to take you away from me of course, but they recruit dancers for temporary projects like music videos and things like that."

Persephone's eyes widened. "Are you serious?"

"Yes, girl, and they want to talk to you! T told them all about you, so they had to come out, and they absolutely ate up the show. I

165

promised I'd bring you out as soon as you were ready. Sound good?"

Persephone tried to gather her bearings before eventually flinging herself at the woman, squeezing her. Calliope hooted with laughter, jumping up and down again.

"I'm assuming that's a yes!" she shouted before they disengaged.

"Absolutely, are you kidding me?" Persephone breathed, wiping tears from her eyes. "Uh, can I meet you out there in a minute?"

"Yeah, for sure. We'll be right out in front of the stage, okay? They're going to love you, I just know it!"

Persephone smiled as the other woman flitted away, offering praise to the rest of her performers as she went. Once she was gone, Persephone went out in search of Hades in the side hall where they'd first met, near the door leading into the service corridor. She found him there waiting again, and she ran into his arms.

"What's wrong?" he immediately questioned, his voice one of concern. "Why are you crying? Did something happen?"

She chuckled, patting his chest as she pulled back.

"Something amazing," she assured him, meeting his eyes. "Terpsichore brought talent scouts tonight. They want to meet me."

He cracked that damn grin again, and her knees grew weak, as did the rest of her. She was greedy for it. It was nothing more than impulse when she grabbed his tie and tugged him down so that she could smother his lips with her own. He picked her up off the ground just enough to make it comfortable, only releasing her when she pulled back. His gaze was hooded, and he looked absolutely delicious. She had to force herself to focus on not shoving him into the service hall and fucking him senseless. It was easier said than done.

"What I was going to say before I was so rudely interrupted was that this doesn't surprise me in the slightest," he sighed, brushing a hand over her cheek. "You were absolutely - otherworldly out there. I told you. It's like you have no business on the ground at all."

A soft laugh escaped her. "You, sir, have a way with hyperboles."

"I mess with nothing of the sort." He pressed his lips to her forehead. "You were amazing, and you deserve everything that is coming your way."

She gave him a grateful smile, but soon, her face fell. "Zeus is here."

"I saw him. And he saw me, so I'd like to think he's smart enough to take his leave, but if not, I'll deal with it. You don't have to worry about him as long as you're here, Persephone."

She nodded. "I know." She chewed her lip for a moment. "Will you tell him?"

"About us?" She nodded again. "Do you want me to?"

"I think that's up to you. I have no problem telling him."

"Yes, but I imagine we both know how nasty he can be, and I would rather spare you any further stress."

"I don't need saving."

"I know, but do you want me to save you?"

She rolled her eyes. "Do you want me to save you?"

He smiled. "I can't be saved."

She let her forehead fall against his chest, and he wrapped his arms around her for as long as she kept it there.

"Are you ready to go?" he questioned after a few moments.

She looked up. "Oh, no, they're waiting to meet me right now, the scouts. Calliope is out front with them."

"Ah, do you want me to wait here?"

"I can meet you upstairs. Calliope will probably walk up with me." She sighed. "Although I really wanted to run home for a quick shower."

He was quiet for a moment before he reached into his jacket pocket, extracting his key card. He slid it into her hand.

"Once you're done here, you can go upstairs and shower," he suggested. "I'll have Daeira, a member of security, stay down here with you. She can escort you up through the service corridors."

"I only have the dress I came in," she groans. "No makeup, no -" She leaned closer, wiggling her eyebrows. "No panties."

His lips quirked. "Well, I've taken care of the latter. The dresser in my bedroom, second drawer from the left. I got you a few things, for if you decided to - stay over more often."

She was nearly stunned into silence, struggling to suppress a smile. "I cannot believe you."

"I like to be prepared."

"You're lucky you're cute."

"Am I?"

"Does that mean you acquired makeup as well?"

"Unfortunately not. Picking panties for me to take off of you is one thing. I wouldn't insult you by trying to pick your makeup. But if you need me to, I will ask Hecate to bring some up to the suite."

Her heart fluttered as she stared up at him, shaking her head with a smile. There was some tinge of magic to everything at the moment, the fear of bringing their relationship out into the open morphing into a fervent anticipation. She was ready to run through that wall and be done with it so that she could continue to enjoy this, enjoy him.

"Okay..." she acquiesced. "Maybe just a little bit of eyeliner. And some gloss. Thank you."

He chuckled. "It shall be done. Now go make things happen. I'll make sure my brother is gone, and then I'll be waiting in Elysium for my dance."

She winked up at him. "I wouldn't miss it for the world."

"You better not... But just in case." Removing his watch from his wrist once more, he placed it upon hers. "Don't keep me waiting too long."

"I wouldn't dare."

Seventeen

HADES

Hades found Zeus lingering just outside the main theatre doors in the hall leading back to the casino. Zeus looked relatively annoyed and impatient, and Hades felt the same emotions ticking beneath his skin. He refused to let them flicker across his face in any capacity.

"Ah, brother," he greeted, and Zeus visibly cringed, his back to Hades. "Long time, no see. What brings you down here to my casino unannounced?"

Zeus turned around, his pale skin reddening. His soiled expression was a stark contrast to Hades' cool composure, and while he had never said it aloud, Hades was glad for the severe lack of resemblance to his stepbrother.

"I didn't think you ever left the nest while you were here," Zeus said through gritted teeth, not quite looking at Hades. "What are you doing here?"

"I don't think you're around enough to know what I do within the walls of my casino, Zeus, so I'll ask again. What brings you here? Did you finally think it important to fill me in on your - rogue escapades?"

From one breath to the next, Zeus's cold expression returned. "I simply wanted to see the show, brother. I've heard so much about it."

"Yes, I figured that was the reason the first time you showed up here even if you didn't have the decency to let me know, so I'm wondering what could possibly compel you to come again? Not to imply it's not an amazing show because it certainly is. I can understand the need for an encore."

Zeus seemed to realize that Hades knew more than he was letting on, and Hades should hope so. He was laying it on rather thick in his humble opinion. There was a single second of panic that flashed through his eyes before that characteristic smug smile uncurled across his face in the laziest way possible.

"Well, I have to say, I'm really intrigued by the star of the show Calliope's dragged out of whatever hole she found her in," Zeus stated matter-of-factly.

"Oh, no hole," Hades countered, his voice still as warm as ever. "Persephone attended Terpsichore's school actually. Or, I suppose in a sense, your school since you refused to let Terpsichore build it in Olympus without marking it as yours too. I remember the deal rather vividly in fact."

"Is that right?" Zeus hardly gave anything away, and as well as Hades knew him, he had no clue where this conversation was going to end up. "That's impressive. Have you been talking with her too, brother? You seem to know a lot about her."

"She's given the casino another avenue of vast wealth. It would be disgraceful for me not to talk with her…"

"Of course. Always so personable, Hades, it's a wonder people don't speak more highly of you."

"They would have to get to know me before they could speak of me at all. That doesn't stop them of course, but people fill in the blanks however they see fit, right? You should know. Your children do that all of the time."

It was only when Zeus's vein became prominent upon his temple that Hades realized how hard he was clenching his fist behind his back. He didn't often throw things like that in Zeus's face. In fact, he never did. And if Zeus were more like Hades, he could use this simple loss of filter against the elder, but he wasn't. Hades had to be grateful for that.

Still, he exhaled slowly and reclaimed the reins of his control, unwilling to give Zeus the benefit.

"Well, it's getting late, brother, I don't want to keep you," Hades went on. "Come on. I'll walk you out."

"Oh, no need," Zeus quickly countered. "I'm not ready to go just yet."

"Oh? Coming up to gamble? We know how well that usually goes for you though, don't we?"

Zeus gave a hollow laugh. "Actually, I wanted to meet the star, so I'll just-"

"I don't think that's going to be possible."

It was more stern than intended, but Zeus latched onto it immediately, like a dog being thrown a bone. Suddenly, it didn't matter who revealed their intentions first, and Hades felt ashamed either way. While Persephone hadn't outright told him not to tell Zeus, he would rather forego it if possible. She didn't owe Zeus anything, and Hades didn't either. More so, he hated to speak of her when she wasn't present, especially under the circumstances.

"Why is that?" Zeus inquired, and while his voice was calm, the look in his eyes was anything but. It was ravenous. "I don't mind waiting."

"She's busy with Calliope, and then I believe she'll probably want to retire for the evening."

"Again, you seem to know a whole lot about her."

"And like I said, I spoke with her. We-"

"Oh." That spark in his eyes seemed to catch flame, and Hades tried to suppress his unease. Why did he still let Zeus make him feel so fucking inferior? "Please don't tell me you've got a thing for her, brother. That's - no, that can't be it."

"I'm only-"

"She's not your type. I can tell you that right now."

Hades raised a brow. And took the bait. "What does that mean exactly?"

"She's a circus performer for one. That's nowhere near the uniform, calculated order you endorse, is it?"

"I own a casino, Zeus. Chaos sort of comes with the territory."

"So you're saying you do?" He boomed a laugh, and Hades had to remind himself that it was all a smokescreen for Zeus's own growing indignation. "You have got to be kidding me."

"I'm beginning to sense that you have a bit of an issue with the woman, Zeus."

Zeus's features slowly fell into a sneer, and seemingly fed up with the back and forth, he moved to shove past Hades. "Run along back upstairs, brother. This might be your little playground, but don't forget who runs the school, as you said earlier. Just like you, what business I have with Persephone is—"

The words died in the air.

Zeus' eyes widened as his back hit the wall, his airway

constricted by the concrete press of Hades' forearm against his throat. Although it wasn't written all over the elder brother's face, Hades was just as surprised as he was. He was not one to strike, much less strike first. Never strike first.

He had certainly never put hands on his brother, not without a targeted incitement and physical initiation from Zeus when they were younger and Hades was still trying to figure out what type of man he wanted to be. Oddly enough, it was through these short-lived brawls that he realized he did not want to be the same type as Zeus.

It was also when Hades had begun studying his brother's weaknesses, learning his pressure points and vulnerabilities with the understanding that Zeus would always be bigger and stronger in one way or another. He had told himself that he needed a way to defend Zeus from himself. Now he knew he also needed a way to protect everyone else.

He was using that knowledge now, and not just because he wished to defend Persephone. At long last, Hades had had enough.

He was tired of exposing himself to this level of manipulation and stress, of bowing to the whims of this child before him and losing himself again and again in the process. And he was tired of having to be perfect, constantly clean and kempt and calculated, composed and consistent at all times. He was tired of being denied grace or room for error while men like Zeus traipsed around this world unchecked and unaffected by anything anyone else had to deal with. He was tired of breaking himself over the waves Zeus created for his own fucking amusement. And he was tired of feeling obligated to sacrifice his own happiness for his brother's.

Zeus did not deserve that. Zeus did not deserve anything from him.

They stared at one another for what felt like centuries before Hades spoke, his voice like smoke.

"You have no business with her, Zeus, not anymore. As long as Persephone is under my roof... No. From here on out, no matter where she is, you will not harass her. You will not call her. You will not text her. You will not show up to her apartment." Zeus's eyes widened. "You will not bully her, you will not tail her, and you will certainly not insult her. You will not do any of the pathetic things that men like you resort to doing when someone tells you no. It's time you learn the meaning of that word."

Zeus opened his mouth to talk, and Hades pressed harder against his neck as he reached for his radio with his free hand, clicking a button on the side. He shook away the lingering guilt of having put hands on Zeus, letting his anger settle over his skin like armor. He would not berate himself for taking action. Whatever change had overtaken him was for the better. He had never been able to stand up to Zeus, to put his foot down, to say no. However, he could not live with himself if he failed to do so now.

"She doesn't want to see you, Zeus," he pushed. "You already know that. And she didn't ask me to get involved. In fact, she had hoped I wouldn't have to, but I have let you make these foolish decisions for far too long. It will not happen here, and it will not happen with her. Regardless of my relationship with her, she does not deserve to put up with the likes of you." Two security guards rounded the corner as Hades eased his grip. "Now, whatever debt you think you have to settle will be settled with me or not at all. As for now, you are going to leave my casino, and the next time you want to visit, you will call."

Hades shoved him away, and the guards immediately seized him with no questions asked. Agamemnon and Leonidas were the two

175

that came swiftly when Hades' emergency button was pushed. Large and imposing, they dragged Zeus away even as he tried to break from their hold.

"Don't forget who I am, brother!" Zeus roared. "I could destroy you! I could—"

"Before you make a threat, Zeus, I would implore you to remember who usually has to carry them out for you," Hades said slowly. "Good night, brother."

Zeus continued to shout at him, spiteful and arrogant, but Hades paid him no mind as he straightened his jacket. After all, he had a date to get to, and he would hate to keep Persephone waiting.

Eighteen

PERSEPHONE

T he meeting with Terpsichore and the scouts passed in a blur, and Persephone hardly believed she was awake the entire time. Once they left, she struggled not to race through the service corridor as Daeira led her to the penthouse elevator. She took a quick shower once she arrived upstairs, washing off the evening before donning the little red number she'd come to the casino in. She'd just finished pulling the straps on when she heard the elevator arrive and the doors open. Then a woman's voice called her name — Hecate.

Persephone knew of Hecate. Her name was as commonplace as that of Hades. The difference was that Persephone had seen the woman a time or two around the city before coming to work at the casino, namely at Aphrodite's various events. She was a face one could not forget with her luminous, dark brown skin and alluring brown eyes.

Despite this, they hadn't talked much, if at all, beyond a few words amidst group conversation and certainly not under these circumstances. If she was honest with herself, Persephone was nervous. Hecate was imposing in her own right, but she was also Hades' family, meaning this was an important first impression.

Persephone opened the bedroom door to find the shorter woman standing there with a broad smile and a bag in her hand.

"Hades sent me up with some goodies," she said, moving into the room and towards the bathroom.

Persephone followed, curiosity piqued. She looked over the woman's shoulder as Hecate began pulling out various lipsticks and eyeliners. Persephone wondered if Hades had forgotten to specify she only needed a few things or if Hecate simply liked to be as prepared as he did. Either way, Persephone appreciated it. Although Hecate seemed to read the question off of her energy because she looked over her shoulder with a wry smile.

"I don't have much in the way of foundation that wouldn't be absolutely insulting to both of us, but I wanted to be sure you had options," she explained before tilting her head. "Your skin is a gift though, girl, and your freckles are gorgeous, so I'm not too worried."

Persephone flushed, looking down at her feet with a smile. Makeup had always felt like a necessity. Even after coming out and acceptance in Khaos Falls became the prevailing opinion, passing in public remained a lifeline she had been all too eager to cling to, and she hated when people looked too close. It felt like they were always looking for the flaw, the clue, the proof that she was exactly who she said she was.

The worst thing was that if they were actually doing this, she knew they would never be satisfied either way. She never felt like she passed as well as Aphrodite, and while her mother's critiques had only ever been to aid her, they sometimes tended to do more harm than good.

She had been completely spoiled in Deucalion Heights as well where "passing" had all but been alleviated from the local lexicon, and people were free to present however they wished without being expected to pay in social constructs and stereotypes. No one asked invasive questions or policed expression. They just lived.

Her home city seemed to be making its way there since she'd returned, but it was difficult to rectify the place she'd grown up in, the place where her dad had existed, with the place she occupied now. It was going to take some time for her to trust it.

Luckily for her, Hades' opinion had gained a bit more weight than anyone else's as of late, and she knew he didn't expect much, but she hated to admit that she still craved that validation.

"Thank you," Persephone replied, sifting through the eyeliner selection. "I hope you live in the casino too, and he didn't send you out somewhere."

"Oh, yeah," Hecate chuckled, moving out of the way to give Persephone full access to the mirror. "I'm right downstairs in the suite below. I share a suite with Thanatos, and we share the floor with Charon. We like the arrangement. It's been the same since we were children really. I would always sneak out of my room to pile in with the boys. I felt safer that way."

"So you all grew up together then? I mean, I figured as much, the way Hades talks about you all, but still."

"We've pretty much been together all of our lives, yeah. Even when Hades and Rhea moved to Olympus, she made sure we could stay together. None of us really had the best home life if any at all, and she never shied away from taking us in and making sure we were cared for."

"I'm really glad he had you all while he was there then, in Olympus."

Although Persephone didn't point out the obvious, their eyes met in the mirror, and she was slowly becoming convinced that Hecate could read minds.

"We still had to share him more than we liked," she said softly. "Being Zeus's big brother was - is a full-time job, you know."

Persephone swallowed. "So he's been doing that his whole life too."

"Just about. Since we were all about eight or nine. Zeus was only a year younger than Hades, but he acted no more than half that. It wasn't just annoying either. It was - cruel. And he always knew Hades would clean up after him, which only made him do more damage."

"That hasn't changed, it seems."

She nodded sadly. "We try to tell him, and I think deep down he knows, but..."

"But he thinks it's his purpose," Persephone finished with a sigh, setting the eyeliner down without putting much on. "Like it's all he's meant to do."

"Exactly." Hecate ran a hand over her head, her braids arranged in a tight pile atop it. "He-"

She was cut off by the sound of her radio crackling, and she ripped it from her hip as a voice said "-think we got a counter." Rolling her eyes, Hecate huffed.

"Thana, can you get that, love?" she replied, holding down the side button of the radio. "I'll be right down to help."

She returned the radio to her hip and smiled at Persephone in the mirror, both of them wanting to return to the conversation but knowing it was better they didn't. Truly, she didn't like speaking of

180

Hades like this when he wasn't present, and she could tell Hecate felt the same.

"I should both get going," Hecate concluded. "Do you want me to walk you down?"

Persephone shook her head with a smile. "No, you go ahead. I know my way, and I don't wanna hold you up from a potentially eventful evening downstairs. But thank you again for the makeup and everything. I really appreciate it."

"Anytime. You need anything at all while you're in this casino, you give me a call or a text. You're never alone while you're here." She reached into her purse on the counter, pulling out a business card and setting it on the sink. "That's my number. Don't be shy."

Persephone grinned. "I won't. Thank you."

"And-" She paused briefly, her smile still present although she seemed to be warring with something. "Thank you."

"For what?" Persephone raised a brow.

"Everything you've done for him already. It's good to see him genuinely happy. You're - good for him, and I'm glad he has you."

Hecate's words lingered on Persephone's mind long after the other woman left, and she stood in front of the mirror for an absurdly long time, alternating between staring at her reflection and checking the watch once again secured around her wrist. She knew Hades was waiting for her, but it took her some time to gather her wits and enough courage to leave the suite and head back downstairs.

She didn't know if he talked to Zeus, but she knew that if he had, there was no turning back now. Regardless, she wanted to be with him, to be in his company and surrounded by his energy. The night had been a good one, all things considered, and she wanted to end it with him. She focused on that rather than the excess because all things considered, that alone was worth it to her.

She made her way into the service corridor, her clutch cradled in her arm. Once the music from Elysium began to beat through the walls around her like a strong heartbeat, she started to tense, but she kept moving forward.

Yet something felt eerie in the empty halls, a tense silence just beneath the bass. She tried to ignore it, her own heart pounding in her ears, but as she turned the final corner leading to the Elysium elevator Hades had first led her onto, that eerie feeling intensified. She only had time to inhale before she felt someone behind her. She was about to turn around when a familiar voice stopped her cold, a large hand snatching her clutch from her grasp.

"Just walk out on your own, Persephone. You're coming with me one way or another. We both know that. I really don't want to make it worse for you or - anyone in this casino, so please."

HADES

Hades intermittently glanced down at his wrist only to become more frustrated each time he found nothing there. The lights in Elysium were beginning to give him a headache, or make one worse, and he could hardly sit still.

"Ephialtes, what time is it?" he called over to one of the servers near the skybox bar.

The man, hunched over and hardly meeting Hades' gaze, hurried over.

"Just four minutes past midnight, Sir."

"Thank you."

Ephialtes scurried away again as Hades stood up, moving to the railing that overlooked the dance floor. He caught a glimpse of Dionysos and Calliope dancing near the corner of the room, Terpsichore not far away. Even Apollo was sitting at his reserved table near the back of the room tonight, another man beside him whispering in his ear. His sister Artemis, who rarely made an appearance in Elysium, sat on the other side of him watching the crowd with keen eyes. Though everywhere Hades looked, there was no sign of Persephone.

He walked around the bar and into the back room where they stored some of the liquor, closing the door behind him so that the music was marginally softened. Pulling out his phone, he dialed Persephone's number for the fourth or fifth time, worry and confusion filling his lungs at a steady pace.

No answer.

He huffed and ended the call, dialing Hecate's number next. She answered on the second ring.

"Hey, is Persephone with you?" he asked hopefully.

"No, love, why?" Hecate returned, and he could tell she had already retired to her suite.

"She hasn't shown up yet."

"What?" Her tone of voice made Hades' stomach turn. "No, I left her in your suite at around... Thana, what time did we deal with that card counter?"

"Dunno, probably about half past ten or so?" Thana's sleepy voice came from somewhere close enough to the phone that Hades heard him perfectly.

"She said she was on her way down," Hecate continued. "Couldn't have been later than 11 for sure."

"Was - everything okay?" Hades questioned. "Did she look alright? Did she look - I don't know, nervous or anything?"

"No, no, nothing like that. She was - she looked happy."

Panic clouded his mind, and it immediately went to Zeus. How could it not? Zeus had been angry, humiliated, and absolutely throwing a tantrum. And he would be desperate to reclaim the control Hades had seemingly seized from him tonight. He would not let this go unpunished. But Hades had never thought...

He had to stop putting things past his brother.

Hecate was saying something in his ear, but he wasn't listening.

"I'll call you back."

He didn't wait for an answer, hanging up and leaving the back room. He made his way out of Elysium and upstairs to security headquarters where he found Agamemnon manning the cameras.

"Agamemnon, are you and Leo sure that Zeus left when you walked him out?" Hades inquired without preamble. "That he didn't come back?"

Agamemnon didn't miss a beat.

"Oh, yeah, we're sure, boss." He nodded firmly. "We watched him drive away, and I let everyone on perimeter duty know that he wasn't allowed back in without permission straight from your mouth."

Hades trusted his word. Hades trusted his security. No one, least of all Zeus, would be able to get past them. However, that didn't make Hades feel any better about where Persephone was, especially when he received a text from Hecate stating she'd checked his suite again and Persephone was nowhere to be found. When Hecate asked if he wanted her to come down, he replied in the negative before looking back up at the screens.

"Review the tapes for me, please," he sighed, sitting down beside Agamemnon.

They went through the recordings from the external cameras, confirming that Zeus had both left and had not come back within the last several hours. There were only two entrances onto the property, both of which were heavily covered by cameras. Of course, that wasn't to say someone working on his behalf had not made their way inside, but that would of course be much harder to pinpoint.

Hades gripped the edge of the desk but suppressed any emotion, directing Agamemnon to next review the tapes from within the casino, namely the service corridors. However, before he could begin, Hades stopped them. There was no need. In the corner screen, he saw a familiar head of thick curls and a notable red dress. He pointed at it.

"Bring that one up on the main screen and rewind a bit please," he commanded.

Agamemnon did so with expert efficiency, and Hades watched Persephone exit one of the side doors from the service corridor nearest Elysium. She had been on her way then, but something had changed.

She seemed in good shape, but she was walking quickly, as if in panic. They moved to the next camera, the one in the parking garage, and Hades' heart plummeted into his gut as she climbed into her car and pulled out of the lot. Just like that. No one with her, no one following. She just - left. There was indeed a decent amount of relief to know she was safe, but after that, the dread set in. And rather quickly.

She'd changed her mind.

"Thank you," he said curtly to Agamemnon, clapping the man's shoulder as he stood.

Hades made his way out of the security room and back up to his office, the idea of returning to his apartment unsettling. He knew remnants of her would be strewn through every part of the place, and he was not ready to face that just yet. He could hardly fathom the idea that this was it.

He sat down on the couch in the dark, pouring himself a drink and listening to the bustling sounds of the casino floor below him. It did not soothe him as easily as it usually did, but he refused to acknowledge that.

At some point, the door opened, and he realized he must have dozed off, his glass still clutched in his hand. Hecate didn't say anything. She simply sat beside him and poured herself a drink as well. Cerberus came in close behind her, coming to rest his head in Hades' lap. Hades ran his hand through the hound's fur, shutting his eyes and letting it center him some. Hecate clinked her glass against his and brought it to her lips.

"I'm sure there is a perfectly good explanation," she hummed after a time.

"Yes," he agreed. He would of course respect it regardless. But… "That doesn't mean it will be one that I like."

Twenty

PERSEPHONE

I t was well past midnight when Persephone reached the stark white house on the hill, its pearlescent pillars glittering in the moonlight. Beautiful as it was, she knew that nothing of the sort awaited her inside. Another car pulled up shortly after her, but she didn't turn around. No doubt the one sent to fetch her had taken another route entirely out of the casino, and out of the Underworld. Persephone had warned that Hades would have cameras everywhere, and while the little exchange in the hallway would be one thing, the image of her being escorted out against her will would be something else entirely.

A disturbance like that would have certainly brought the district down upon them like a pack of hellhounds. Now that she was here, part of Persephone wished she would have just let it happen. However, she knew that she had to face this, otherwise it would only be worse later, and she had enough on her plate.

She entered the house and already knew where she was meant to go, allowing her feet to carry her through the dark halls and down to the dining room. The light at the end of the hall called to her, soft footsteps echoing in her wake, and she had to fight the urge to turn around and tell her escort that his job here was done. Instead, she kept walking until she entered the correct room, met by the precise sight she had expected to be greeted by.

"Ah, there you are. It is about time you graced me with your presence. I suppose I should be grateful to the Fates that my daughter has made time in her busy schedule for poor old me, yes?"

Demeter's voice was sickly sweet, but Persephone could see the sharp glint in her eye like a viper ready to strike at a moment's notice.

The leader of the Harvest District sat at the table, imposing as ever, her slender neck dripping in jewels as though she had just returned from somewhere important. Her thick, dark hair was pulled up and arranged into something intricate, but Persephone focuses her attention on the red-painted lips that twitched with indignation and the fathomless glare that cut through her like butter.

Demeter wasn't angry. No, she was most likely angry weeks ago. Right now, she was spiteful, apathetically so, and that was the most dangerous thing she could be.

"Hello, mama," Persephone greeted softly, moving to stand at the other end of the table. "Auntie."

She now greeted Hestia, who stood off to the side, her expression unsettled. She managed to flash her niece an apologetic smile as Adonis passed Persephone to stand on the other side of Demeter. Persephone didn't look at him, but she did grab her clutch from his hand as he passed. He looked back at her, surprised, but she kept her eyes on her mother.

It was hard to look at him, and not because they'd broken up on less than respectable terms, but because he'd taken his hurt feelings and given them to Demeter to use as a weapon. She had done just that ever since.

"I hear you've been spending quite a lot of your time south of the river, Darling," Demeter went on, clasping her hands together. "In Casino Asphodel no less."

"I work there," Persephone surrendered. "Which I've just finished, and I'm exhausted, so if you wouldn't mind rescheduling - whatever this is-"

"Oh, no, no. You ignore my calls, my texts, my very existence, and you expect me to believe you would have come on your own?"

"When I had time, yes."

"No, see, you make time for your mother, or she makes it for you, Persephone."

"I have a job, Mama, a life, and I-"

"Yes, so I've heard. A job isn't all that keeps you in the casino, is it? Having drinks with the rabid dog who runs it now as well, are we? Privately at that. Has he given you a room there too? Is that where you were coming from when Adonis found you, or was it his own room?"

Persephone didn't answer right away, forcing her hands to remain unraveled at her sides. She had been so worried about Zeus's tactics for knowing her every move, she had forgotten to shield against Demeter's just as well.

Though Adonis's role in all of this quickly clicked into place. He was the only one Demeter would dare send into the Underworld, into Casino Asphodel, and he was the one person Persephone would not look for because she wouldn't expect her mother to be so blatant, sending someone Persephone knew, but he had seen more than enough it appeared.

"It is no one's business but mine," Persephone said now, her voice rough.

Demeter chuckled. "Don't be naive, Persephone. You may get to play pretend on that stage, but the moment you step off of it, this is real life. He is the most dangerous man in Khaos Falls, on the leash of the dumbest man in Khaos Falls, and you-"

"Not to me."

Demeter shot up onto her feet, fists slamming against the table. "But to me! Do you forget where you came from, who gave you life, who gave you the means to be who you are in a world that would rather see you and women like you rot in the shadows? Is there no gratitude for me now, daughter, no-"

"You tried to imprison me here!" Persephone suddenly shrieked, catching them all off guard. She'd never raised her voice at her mother, even at her most angriest. "You kept me from going to school, from doing what I loved, and I had to figure it out myself!"

The ice in her mother's eyes was impenetrable. "And is this how you figured it out? Falling into bed with the enemy? Are you-"

"I did no such thing, and if you truly think so little of me, I don't owe you an explanation—"

"I am your mother!"

"Then act like it!"

The silence fell like a hammer, and then there was nothing but their heavy breathing and a tangible tension. Demeter stared at her, wide-eyed as though Persephone had slapped her across the face. Or as if she would have preferred Persephone had slapped her across the face. Either way, it took Persephone only a moment to take it for what it was, an opportunity.

"I had a dream for myself, one not tethered to you and your legacy, and you hated it. You hated the idea that I wouldn't follow in your footsteps. Because that's what it was all about, right? Why you paid for the hormones and the surgeries and the clothes? That's what having a daughter meant to you, that you would have a carbon copy of yourself to take your place when you left this world instead of a son to overshadow you."

She only waited a second for an answer, and when it did not come, she continued.

"But you didn't, Mama. You won't. Now, you taught me a lot. You made me this strong, this brave, this bold. I am your daughter, but I am not you, nor will I ever be you. I am doing what I love, and Hades - that's what he wants for me. He never demanded anything of me. I met him the night of my first show, and he supported me from the very moment I stepped on that stage. I'm not going to ask you to understand. I am not going to ask for your blessing. You can do what you want because either way, that is exactly what I am going to do. For me. You have your power here, and I have mine on that stage. Up in the air. And I will not cut myself down for you or anybody else."

She never broke eye contact, and while Demeter didn't either, something shifted behind her catlike gaze. Persephone couldn't decipher it for the life of her. She didn't know if it worked for her or against her. All she knew was that her mother's silence was as deafening as it had always been, and she had no clue what to do with it but claim it for her own.

"Now, it's late, and I'm tired, so all I ask of you is - if you're not coming to Asphodel to watch me perform, to support me in any way, I would appreciate it if you stayed away altogether."

At last, her eyes slowly turned on Adonis only for a moment before she turned on her heel and left the dining hall. In her peripheral, she caught the faintest smile on her aunt's face.

She had just reached the entrance hall when she heard footsteps racing behind her, but she didn't stop.

"So you're with him now?" Adonis asked, his voice hollow.

"I am," Persephone returned without hesitation, her eyes set on the front door.

"Why, Seph? I get why 'Dite left, but you... We had it all."

"No, you had it all." She turned sharply on her heel if only to look him in the eye when she told him what he didn't want to hear. "There's a reason you're here alone with my mother, Adonis. You want a doll to play with, and I'm not the one or the two. I don't fit in your box nor do I want to. That's not gonna change."

"I would've given you anything."

She snorted. "I can get it all myself, as you can see. You knew that though, and you couldn't stand the idea that I wasn't some trophy wife you could show off like a new fucking sports car."

"I loved you, both of you. I still—"

"And that wasn't enough. You thought because of who we were, you could play house with us and we'd think ourselves lucky just to be loved by you because no one else would. You bet on that bullshit, and you lost. Let it go. We have, and I'll tell you. I don't miss a damn thing."

His jaw clenched. "He'll hurt you."

She flashed a tired smile, neglecting to point out Adonis had done far more of that than Hades ever could. "After what you've done to me tonight, and the past few weeks, him hurting me is the last thing you should be worried about. I'd stay out of Asphodel, Adonis. I'm not telling you again."

Before he could conjure up another word, she pushed through the doors of her mother's house, and this time, it felt far more like freedom.

Twenty-One

HADES

Hades managed to keep his nerves at bay until he was standing in front of Persephone's door, holding two coffees that suddenly seemed pointless now. Despite a sleepless night, anxiety spiked like a shot of adrenaline through his system, keeping him upright and alert. He told himself he was here because he didn't like to leave things up in the air. He liked understanding. He liked finishing what he started. He liked close-ended questions and clear, concise answers. He liked closure.

Therefore, driving to Persephone's apartment first thing in the morning seemed to be the only option.

Not that he didn't question the decision because of course he did. He didn't want to push limits and cross boundaries the way Zeus had. After all, Hades knew she left Asphodel of her own accord, and she hadn't called or texted him since. It was pretty clear she didn't wish to talk to him.

Though maybe he'd come because - he didn't really expect her to answer. Maybe he didn't expect her to be there at all. It would make more sense that she would find sanctuary with Aphrodite in order to avoid both brothers, but... If she wasn't here, if she didn't answer, it became easier to confirm his suspicions and justify running back to being a myth, one created solely for the benefit of his brother.

Hades could not deny it. Last night had scared him as much as it had scared Zeus. Never had he treated his brother that way. He could probably count on one hand how many times Zeus had heard the word 'no', but not a single instance had involved Hades saying it. He was a coward. He had no qualms about coming to terms with that, but that didn't change the fact. He didn't know who he was without Zeus, and so maybe he did need his brother as much as his brother needed him.

It would be easier this way. That was what he told himself now. If he couldn't keep his promise to Persephone, at least he could still keep his promise to his mother. But...

How could he possibly return to serving Zeus after everything that had happened? Persephone was likely not the only victim. She certainly wouldn't be the last, and she still deserved protection regardless of her relationship with Hades. All of them did.

Hades would not be able to look himself in the mirror if he went back to enabling Zeus to that degree. Between his harassment of Persephone and his inflammation of the situation with Tartarus, Zeus had gone too far in every way he possibly could. So Hades had to stand his ground. Even if it drew the eye of his younger brother's ire. Even if it got Hades killed.

Yet that was neither here nor there right now. Right now, he only cared about Persephone. They were adults, and he was not about to give up on the best thing that had ever happened to him over a possible misunderstanding. He had to be certain.

He took a deep breath and shifted both cups to one hand before he knocked on the blue-paneled wood. He waited patiently, counting out the seconds in his mind and focusing more on the numbers themselves than the time that passed. He knocked only once more, but once he hit triple digits again, he steeled himself and prepared to retreat, setting the coffee down by the door.

Before the cup touched the ground, however, the door cracked open, wild curls and a sleepy gaze appearing above him. Persephone offered a bashful smile as he straightened awkwardly, and he tried to match it. He doubted he succeeded. She opened the door completely and stepped aside to allow him entry, both of them looking at the floor instead of each other. He walked in, setting the coffees on the counter before he turns to her.

"I'm sorry," she croaked before he could. "For not calling or texting or - trying to explain."

Hope constricted around his heart, but he didn't acknowledge it. He remained true to his nature, which ensured that he could suppress and solve and afford nothing to the emotions incited.

"You don't need to worry, Persephone," he assured her. "You had every right to change your mind about us. I only came here to clear the air so that you don't have to stress about coming into the casino. I don't want you to feel uncomfortable. You'll still be protected there, very much welcome, and I-"

"Hades, hold on," she said, holding up a hand as she rubbed her eyes with the other. "Wait. That's - that isn't what happened. My mother - She sent Adonis to get me, and I didn't want him, or her, causing a scene. So I went. I would've called you on my way there, but he had my purse and my phone, and - I should've made time. Or gone back to the casino after, but I was just exhausted by then, and I didn't want to talk about it or have you worrying too... which I'm sure you did anyway, so I apologize for that. I just figured I'd come to you when I woke up. I'm sorry."

He halted, blinking several times before he refocused on her. Well, that...

It seemed too easy, didn't it? Things were never that easy, not for him, and her not changing her mind made much less sense. Whether because of Zeus or because of him, he'd been willing to bet on it. He'd — well, he'd doubted her. And he'd doubted them.

But as he'd reminded himself earlier, they were adults. And things could be that easy.

"But - I saw you leave the casino alone," he managed.

He was almost ashamed to admit that he looked for her on the cameras, but rather than be upset, she smiled.

"That's why I told him to let me drive myself. I knew if you saw them pushing me out, you would have come running, and I didn't want that trouble for you. I figured I could just talk to my mom and be done with it."

He squinted at the ceiling, raising his hands. "—She couldn't just call?"

Her smile turned sly. "She has been. I haven't been answering or - wanting to talk to her because I knew what she would say. She figured this was the easiest way to get me to go to her, and I guess she was right. In a way."

"Oh." He was still processing.

"I told her about you, about us."

That was going to take him a moment. He leaned back against

the counter, bracing both hands on its edge, tongue poking out of one side of his mouth. He didn't miss the way she tilted her head, those gorgeous curls following the movement as her lips curved further upward. She picked up the coffee with her name on it and drank as she watched him. Finally, he inhaled deeply.

"You told her about us?" was all he could come up with.

"Mhmm," she hummed against the lid of her cup. "And my auntie. And - my ex too, but I don't think that matters too much in the long run."

"Adonis." Another tidbit he'd managed to pull from the Harvest District gossip mines like a scarf from a hat. It didn't matter much then either. "I gotta say I'm surprised she'd send him."

"That's why she did it. She knew I wouldn't expect it either, but he's apparently been watching me for some time. Zeus wasn't the only one keeping tabs on who I was having drinks with. But I did tell him he'd stay far away from Asphodel if he knew what was good for him."

"Oh?"

Her eyes flashed, and her voice lowered. "My boyfriend is kind of a legend around these parts. I wouldn't come looking for trouble with him if I were - well, anyone."

The title triggered a feeling Hades couldn't quite put a name to. It fluttered in his stomach and made him puff out his chest a bit, to his shocked horror. He cleared his throat and rubbed the back of his neck.

"And - what did she say? Your mother."

"Actually, she didn't say anything, and I know my mother. That's probably the best possible response she could have had."

"And if she does something?"

"What is she gonna do? She's protective, not stupid. This whole thing is bigger than her daughter dating when she's dating the leader of the Underworld."

"But I doubt she would care too much if you were dating anyone else."

"You're probably right, but facts are facts. When it comes to revenge, my mama goes big or goes home, and she knows she can't go big here. Coming for you would be an act of war. She isn't gonna put her district at risk. You have the largest district in the city, and she has your brothers on either side of her. There's no gambling with that, not if you wanna win."

"I would never—"

"I know that. Doesn't mean she does, and I'd rather use that to our advantage, at least for now. Once she calms down, that might change, but I doubt it. She really does not like you."

He snorted. "Tell me about it. I mean, I'd never even laid eyes on you when you lived in her house, and I doubt that was merely coincidental."

She placed a hand on his chest, and he breathed out on impact. It did soothe him, the idea of an unspoken truce in place of Demeter's blessing. Demeter was a far bigger threat than Zeus could ever be on his own. Because of that, one question still lingered.

"And - you're sure she wouldn't move against us? Even if Tartarus gave her a legitimate reason?"

Persephone chuckled. "Oh, baby, the only people my mother might hate more than you are Nyx and Erebus. Fates, I'm almost sure she talked down on them twice as much as she talked down on you."

He was perplexed. "Are you kidding?"

She raised a brow. "Nyx letting her husband, an outsider, co-rule her district? Then agreeing with that same man to accept the terms of their district's removal from power? Yeah, she ain't letting that one go. Especially not for a war. She would rather stand back and let y'all kill each other. Which, if I remember correctly, is what she did last time."

Hades had severely underestimated his capacity for relief. It surprised him just how big the wave was that washed over him at that moment. He had all but completely disregarded the possibility of Demeter joining Tartarus if things went awry despite it being one of the first things he'd considered before meeting Persephone. Yet now, he could put that fear to rest more or less. For the time being at least. If he was lucky, things would die down before it got to a point where he would have to take it up again.

"And what about Zeus?" she asked.

Hades inhaled sharply. "I told him... Well, not outright, but I doubt he'd believe anything else after what I said to him. Or did to him."

She raised a brow before her lips curled into a grin. "Ooh, put your foot down, did you?"

"I did." A soft chuckle left his lips. It felt - good. All at once, his guilt left him. "I'm not saying he won't blow up your phone-"

"Oh, he has."

Hades glared at the floor. "By the Fates."

"Hey. What did I tell you? He isn't your responsibility."

"But he is, Seph. Men like him—"

She took a firm hold of his face. "Men like him built a world centering themselves on the backs of people like you and me, people who he sees as beneath him. But he also needs us to make that world work, and I'm not doing it anymore, Hades. Neither should you."

"But I did do it. For years. I did nothing to control him, and I - I handed this city to him like a toy to play with. I gave him everything."

"And what was the alternative? That you go up against him? That you tell him no, and he kills you, and no one bats an eye because he's Zeus and you're a myth?"

"I -" He wet his lips, shaking his head. "My whole life, I have had to take the blame. I have had to carry the - the weight of his world, despite the fact that - from the moment I told that world I was a man, I was expected to inherit all of his sins. And all the sins of every cis man who has ever come before me. The 'normal' ones. The standard, the default. And people told me that - that this was what it meant to be a man."

"No, it is not." She shook her head, bringing their foreheads together as he screwed his eyes shut. "You are a good man, Hades, with a good heart, and you do not have to be anything else. Not for Zeus. Not for anyone. You do not have to accept that blame nor do you have to accept their idea of what kind of man you should be. Why should you have to carry their sins when they never have to?"

He could not answer that. He did not know. All he knew was that he wanted to be good. To be good. For Persephone, for Dionysos, for Hermes, for Hecate and Charon and Thanatos. He had just wanted to be good. Now, he wanted to be better.

But fear and then guilt and then duty had reigned over his life, creating this illusion that he was in control, that he had any power at all when the truth was that he had always been strung up by strings that Zeus pulled.

And maybe his mother knew that too. Maybe she knew he

would never have the kind of power his brothers did. Maybe she knew this world would never allow it, and so she made Hades vow to her not that he would be loyal to Zeus for Zeus's own good, but that he would be obedient to Zeus for his own good.

That was not going to work anymore. That was not a promise Hades would be able to keep because it was not the promise he had made to begin with.

"Let it go," she whispered, her breath against his lips. "I get why you feel the way you do, and I'm all for you calling him on his shit, but I need you to remember he's a grown-ass man. If you can't change him, it's not up to you to hold his hand until he gets it together. It will kill you, Hades, and I'm not cosigning that. I've learned to love my mama from a distance because I know I have to have boundaries. If I don't, she will drain me of everything I am. Don't let Zeus do that to you. He's already taken enough." After a brief pause, he felt her shrug. "Besides, all you gotta do is stay out of it. The city will handle him. Tartarus can't be the only one waiting for a shot at him, and I know that's your brother and all, but... something's gotta give, baby."

He chuckled in spite of himself. "How are you so - calm right now when he's blowing up your phone and shit?"

"Oh, I blocked his number right before you got here. And you're here, so... I'm good."

He rolled his eyes before reaching up to cup her cheek, her hands moving down to cradle his neck. His sheets had been so cold the night before. To feel her warmth again, to breathe her in, it felt like a revival, a resuscitation. He didn't know how he ever thought he'd be able to just walk away from her. If she stopped touching him right now, he might disintegrate.

"And if he shows up here?" His voice was as tender as his touch.

"I'm barely here anyway."

"But you come here to rest. That will be very difficult to do if he's banging down the door at all hours." He paused a moment before his face softened. "Will you still consider it? Staying with me? If not, I understand, but I'll insist on either getting you a room at the casino or making it easier for you to get to and from Aphrodite's every night. My driver would probably be grateful to spend more time actually driving."

"You don't think we're moving too fast, moving in together?"

He shrugged. "I think we're two levelheaded adults who can figure it out together. There's more than enough room for both of us to have our own space if we need it, and if it doesn't work, we can make other arrangements. But you'll be closer to work, and I'll make sure you're getting quality sleep. As will I."

She glanced up at him. "And how do you intend to do that?"

He grinned at last. "I'll wear you out every night."

"Mm, I think I'm gonna need a demonstration before I commit to anything."

"How much time you got right now?"

She glanced down at her wrist where his watch was still secured. "A couple hours."

"I think I can work with that."

"Yeah, but will my legs be working by the end of it?"

"For the most part."

She pushed her lower lip out though excitement lingered just beneath the surface. "So... you ain't mad at me for ghosting you?"

He was about to assure her he wasn't when a much better idea graced him.

"Oh, I never said I wasn't mad at you."

He slipped into the role with ease, taking what opportunity she offered him as she gave him a questioning look. He dropped his hands from her entirely, a mask of stoicism sliding into place across his features. He wanted her, and he wanted her bad, but he had just enough patience to drag it out a bit longer.

"Put your hands on the counter, Persephone."

Twenty-Two

HADES

S he didn't obey right away, frozen where she stood, those bright eyes wide with awe. He could see it in those eyes that she had not expected this which made him all the more proud for enacting it in the first place. He liked to catch her off guard, to surprise her and keep her on her toes. Considering how well she did those things to him, it was nice not to be entirely without means of retaliation. And he was not going to waste this particular success.

She watched him remove his jacket and roll up his sleeves before at last turning around and pressing her palms into the countertop. He simply took her in for a time, allowing the anticipation to build for them both. Then he stepped up behind her, chest pressed to her back so that he could feel the shuddering breath she released.

"Do you accept your punishment?"

Her voice was hoarse. "Yes, sir."

His knuckles traced a path down her spine as he unbuttoned his shirt at the slowest possible pace. He shed it from his shoulders before dusting his fingers down her arms with the lightest touch, her hips shaking against his as his hands left her wrists to tease the hem of her pajama shorts.

"Don't worry," he whispered against her ear. "Your honesty will be taken into account."

Yanking her shorts and panties down, he elicited a deep moan from her, and that patience he was depending on immediately began to dwindle at a much faster pace. He slapped her ass once if only for the sake of calling it punishment before he unbuckled his belt. She seemed to have adopted an instinctive response to the sound though, her body trembling visibly as a whimper escaped her. He folded the belt in half and snapped it, and she instantaneously threw her hips back.

"Fuck, Hades," she groaned, dropping her head.

"I haven't even touched you yet, baby."

"Do you even have to?"

"Are you saying I shouldn't?"

"Don't put words in my mouth."

"That's the last thing I'm tryna put in your mouth right now."

He smirked at the sound of her purr, reaching between her thighs and stroking her lips. Her knees bent, threatening to buckle, and she dropped to her forearms on the counter. He kept his touch light, but she was already wet, coating his fingers in light arousal. He took his time exploring her folds, and in time, she started grinding down into his hand. Only then did he pull away, earning another groan.

"You gonna take what I give you?" he questioned.

"Yes. Yes, I will."

"Everything I give you?"

"Yes, Sir."

She knew damn well what she did to him too, and she didn't skimp on it. Bringing his arms around her, he held the belt in front of her face.

"Open your mouth."

She did so hesitantly, and he peered around her to watch. Then he carefully slipped the leather between her teeth. She took the hint and bit down.

"If this belt hits the counter, I stop. That means the only reason it should be hitting the counter is if you need to say your safe word. Do you remember what that is?"

She nodded.

"Good girl."

Freeing his cock from his trousers, he slid it between her thighs, both of them sighing in a mix of contentment and exasperation. The moment there was adequate stimulation, he began to harden. He reached around, guiding his tip through to the other side and tapping her clit generously on each trip. His stroke started slow, and she mumbled around the leather, her hand darting down to grip his. He halted.

"Uh uh. Put that hand back where it belongs."

She was quick to oblige, slapping it back down on the counter, but her hips pushed back against him, insistent. He held out nonetheless, figuring that if he ate up enough time with foreplay, he might be able to curve the urge to fuck her into a stupor that might hinder her work tonight.

He... wouldn't make any promises, aloud or otherwise.

The patience was thin, and her body was begging, and he just wanted to be inside of her. After another minute of agonizing friction, he was at his limit. Pressing a hand between her shoulders, he bent her forward further. She spread her legs at once, giving him enough room to guide his swollen head to her entrance and push inside.

"Fuck, Seph..."

Dragging her back up by the hair, her muffled moans met his ears as he started to thrust. His hands wrapped around the fronts of her thighs, holding them in place so that he could speed up. Soon, it was sloppy and desperate and absent any control whatsoever, but the way her walls contracted around his dick was the only thing he could focus on. Her body sagged against his as she struggled to both keep her hands on the counter and the belt between her teeth. His fingers found her clit again, and she tossed her head back, a cadence of cries caught in her throat. He wanted to collect every single one of them.

"You cum for me - before that belt hits the counter - and we can call it even."

She wasted no time, working back against his cock and down against his fingers, gripping the edge of the counter and using it to her advantage. He slowed his own movements, letting her lead, and she didn't take it for granted.

She unraveled with a scream like shrapnel that bled around his belt, piercing the air in every direction. He held her to him to keep her from collapsing, and she used that aid to keep riding him, bouncing mercilessly on the balls of her feet until her body at last went rigid, then limp, in his arms.

Once she'd settled into his embrace, the last of her moans fading out, he gingerly took the belt from her mouth and planted a kiss on her cheek.

"We even?" she breathed.

"Yeah, we're even." He took each of her arms and pulled them behind her back. "But we aren't done."

Securing her wrists with the belt, he stepped out of his pants before turning and marching her into the living room area. He pushed her down on her knees atop the chaise near the balcony doors, her face down against the cushion. Straddling the furniture, he remained standing, the head of his erection knocking against her folds. Winding the free end of the belt around his fist, he slid unceremoniously inside of her once more.

She called out freely now, turning her head and attempting to look at him over her shoulder.

"You slick bastard," she moaned, biting her lip.

"Who are you calling slick?"

He pushed his cock as deep as he could, and her mouth fell open as her eyes rolled into the back of her head. He leaned forward, his own lips parting as spit spills from them over her ass. He uses the lubrication to massage her hole, continuing to stroke in her pussy, tremor after tremor racking her body. He loved to see it. He loved to know he had this effect on her.

Tentatively, he sunk his thumb into her, and her chest momentarily came off of the chaise.

"Fuck, Hades!"

"You want me to stop?"

"—Don't you - dare!"

"What do you want?"

"Fuck—"

"What do you want, Persephone?"

"I want you to - fuck me - harder."

His dick twitched inside of her. "Say it again."

"Fuck me harder!"

He slid into a whole other gear before she could inhale, slamming into her with reckless abandon. Everything he'd felt the night before, the anxiety, the apprehension, the uncertainty of the future: it all got thrown down and worked out in a furious sequence. It may be the first time he hadn't held back in any discernible way, putting his full strength behind the swing of his hips. It echoed in the sound of them colliding with hers. She strained against her bonds, burying her face in the cushions before her, his name a broken hymn against them. He sunk his thumb deeper into her ass as he leaned back, the coil in his belly tightening to capacity.

"Hades, I'm - I'm gonna cum. I'm gonna —"

He only pounded her harder, laying claim to what was his and what would always be his if he had any say in it.

She rose up, her chest parallel to the chaise as she cried out, her orgasm rushing through her until the fruits of it painted her thighs. Her body was still convulsing when he pulled his thumb free and released the belt, grabbing her hips and drilling into her with short and quick thrusts. He only had a few more in him before his back locked up, straight as a rod as he roared out in overwhelming pleasure.

She moaned his name again, both of them collapsing in a heap onto the chair. A gentle quiet consumed them, absorbing their labored breaths. His skin was slick with layer upon layer of sweat, his shaft still pulsing, but he had never felt better in his life.

She'd chosen him too.

He freed her arms, and she groaned as she stretched them out, gripping the top of the chaise and pushing herself up. He pressed soft kisses to what skin he could reach along her side, trailing down over her hip. He had no clue how much time had passed, but he imagined they'd cut deep into that couple of hours. Then suddenly, she cried out.

"Hades!"

"Are you gonna be late?"

She didn't answer. He looked up at her when the silence began to worry him, but she wasn't looking at him. She was staring out the balcony doors.

"Seph? What is it?"

He clambered up onto his knees beside her, following her gaze. The city spanned out before them, Casino Asphodel rising above it on the horizon. There, amidst the hotel tower and the casino's dome, billowed a thick, black cloud of smoke.

Twenty-Three

PERSEPHONE

P ersephone kept her distance. It was difficult to watch Hades walk through the ruin, his face ashen and expression stoic. People were talking to him, but she could tell he hardly heard them. He directed them as he always had, but his eyes were glassy, absent of the life she had fallen so fast for. It pained her to see him this way.

It had taken hours for them to put the fire out. While no one had died, several people had been injured and taken to the Healer's District. Most of the damage was isolated to the Pantheon, but a large part of the dome had been badly damaged as had a wall in Elysium. The casino as a whole had to be closed for the time being, and while the fire department had deemed the hotel safe as it was on the opposite side of the property, Hades had offered all of his guests a refund and a free stay later down the line as a safety precaution. More accurately, he had instructed Thanatos to do so because beyond what was absolutely necessary, he was hardly speaking at all.

It was late by now, and of course, all of Persephone's shows were canceled for the foreseeable future. At the moment, she could hear Charon speaking with Apollo, a built man with a head of tight curls and flawless dark brown skin. She knew him of course. Everyone in Khaos Falls did, and she also knew he'd designed Casino Asphodel from top to bottom.

He was appraising the damage alongside his contractor, attempting to offer Charon a realistic estimate on repairs. Something told Persephone that it was good he was here, and when he offered Charon a timeframe she just missed, the latter looked relieved. Persephone moved closer to Hades as Charon approached him.

"He says the structural damage is minimal," Charon explained. "We can block off the affected wing and use the rest of the casino once we air out the smoke, but he says they can get the dome and Elysium good to go in about 6 weeks. The Pantheon will take a bit longer, but they'll work as quickly as they can. It has to be repaired with great care due to the use of acrobatics in the theatre."

Both Charon and Hades glanced at her, and Hades reached for her hand. She slipped it easily into his just as Hecate appeared before them. Persephone couldn't read her face, but she imagined that Hecate was as confused and upset as Hades. They built this place together. She could only imagine how Dionysos was going to feel when he heard about Elysium, and Persephone... Well, she was trying not to think about what it meant for her.

Without the Pantheon, their residency was more or less over, which limited her options as to what to do next. Even if she returned with Calliope to Deucalion Heights, there was no telling where or when their next show would be. She could wind up across the Aegean at any rate, and that scared her. She was just getting comfortable in her hometown again, and she and Hades were moving forward with one another. She wasn't ready to leave. She wasn't ready to put a hold on her dreams though either.

She decided not to focus on that right now.

Thanatos appeared, and it was evident that he'd been in the damaged part of the building at some point. His black suit was now grey with ash, and soot stained his white dress shirt as well as his cheeks. He looked tired but in good spirits, and he clapped a hand on Hades' shoulder.

"Got the last of the guests out," he reported. "Rebooked a good amount of them for later next month, and there weren't too many complaints. You alright?"

Hades sidestepped that question. Persephone squeezed his hand. "The word on Tartarus?" he asked.

"Still on lockdown," Charon stated. "I reached out to one of my informants but have yet to receive a response. Should we move forward with a lockdown of our own?"

"No." His voice was firm, leaving no room for debate. "We will not be made to look weak. And if they're still in lockdown, it would do no good. I won't punish the rest of the city for their stupidity. I want the tapes gathered and gone through. Everyone should be talked to. I want to know what area was targeted and by how many people. I want reports on the injured, including staff, and I want to ensure any expenses, medical or otherwise, are taken care of without them having to worry."

"It will all be handled, Hades," Hecate interrupted gently, placing a hand on his chest.

Persephone felt the immediate effect Hecate's touch had on Hades, his muscles relaxing and his shoulders dropping several inches from his ears. Somehow it soothed her too, and she brushed her thumb over his knuckles. She met Hecate's eyes then, and they both seemed to be thinking the same thing—they needed to get him out of there. He needed to rest.

"Let's go upstairs, Hades," Persephone offered up, placing her other hand on his arm.

"She's right," Hecate added, curling her fingers against him. "You need time to rest, to clear your head. We all do, and there's nothing else we can do until the cleaning is done. Tomorrow, we can tackle things head-on."

He seemed to consider it for a moment, and Persephone could tell he was chewing on the inside of his cheek. She'd never seen him do that before. Then again, she'd never seen him in a state like this before. She doubted anyone had because no one had ever attacked the River Styx District. This was what he looked like after a disaster struck that he couldn't have anticipated much less avoided, sullen and shaking, and she would do anything in her power to keep from ever having to see it again.

At last, he nodded in agreement, and Persephone felt herself expelling the breath she'd been holding. He turned to Thanatos with final thoughts poised upon his tongue, but Thanatos cut in before he had to say a word.

"I'll check up on the cleaning crews, make sure we've got everything cleaned up and blocked off."

Hades nodded once more, his eyes wandering over their heads toward the rubble. Water still rained from the roof, and piles of ash and debris waited to be cleared. He clutched Persephone's hand harder. She didn't let go.

At last, he allowed the two women to lead him toward the service elevator, dropping his gaze to the floor in front of him. The smell of smoke lingered in the air, sticking to their clothes and following them through the space. Once they were in the elevator, he exhaled the heaviest sigh, and he seemed to shrink substantially.

He put an arm around each of them, resting his head against the cool panel of the wall, and both women moved closer to him. They caught each other's gaze for a moment, mutual gratitude smoothed out in the space between them. Persephone didn't know if she would have any clue how to help him without Hecate. They were still learning about each other, and she was still processing the whole event herself. While she could handle his stress when it came to her, this was so much bigger than Zeus's temper tantrums, especially if the Tartarus District was responsible.

They promised not to think about that tonight however. Tonight was for rest. Tomorrow would be something else entirely.

When they reached the suite, Persephone found that all of her bags had been placed neatly in Hades' bedroom, which soothed her immensely. She had told Hades it could wait, but he'd called Aphrodite himself to ask her if she could gather Persephone's things from the apartment, and Aphrodite had been more than eager to do so if only to get Persephone out of there. Aphrodite hadn't stayed long, but it had been good to see her, and she'd left with the promise of stopping by the next day so that she could hear all about Persephone's visit with her mother and see if there was anything she could do to help.

"You should go take a shower," she whispered to Hades, her heart aching over just how lost he looked at the moment, standing in the hallway.

"Mm," he hummed, finally turning his gaze on her. "Will you join me?"

She nodded, her lips curling. "In a minute."

He offered a dramatic roll of his eyes but obeyed nonetheless, stalking off through the bedroom and towards the master bathroom. Hecate watched him go before looking at Persephone. The two of them shared a worried look before they each smiled, the expression strained at best.

"Has this happened before?" Persephone questioned despite knowing the answer, sitting down on the bed.

"Oh, you mean someone trying to burn down Asphodel?" Hecate quipped, sitting beside her as they both laughed. "No, nothing even remotely close."

"I mean him. Like that."

Hecate sobered some. "No, I can't say it has, not like that. Honestly, the last time I saw him this - lost is when his mother passed. And before that, his father. He doesn't get lost. He's the one that leads the lost."

"That's soothing."

She giggled. "We'll get through it though."

Persephone wet her lips. "Who do you think did it?"

"Thanatos swears it was Coeus." Her sigh told Persephone that she wasn't so sure. "It's the most logical explanation. Who else would be so stupid?"

"What about Zeus?"

Their gazes drifted together all at once, Persephone herself surprised at how easy it was to ask that question, but the doubt was palpable between them. Zeus simply wasn't stupid enough, and he certainly wasn't smart enough either.

"That man has never gotten anything past Hades," Hecate concluded. "Even if he roped someone else into doing it, there is no way Hades wouldn't trace it back to Zeus if he did it. The idiot wouldn't risk it."

That much, Persephone could agree on. Zeus may be on the

cusp of an epic temper tantrum, but he wouldn't risk his place at the top of the food chain. Hades was his meal ticket, the very throne Zeus sat on carved from his bones, and it would be self-destruction to try such a thing. Going after Persephone was one thing, but to target Asphodel? You would have to have a death wish.

"But you don't think it's Coeus," Persephone confirmed.

Hecate smirked. "No, I think it's his sister. Tethys is far more calculated and three times as smart as he is."

Persephone hadn't had too many encounters with Tethys, and she preferred it that way. Tethys was a wolf in wolf's clothing, but if she did do this, she seemed to forget her district only remained standing because Hades was far more forgiving than his brother and stepfather.

"Either way, Zeus made a big mistake fucking with them," Hecate continued with a sigh. "Just because he didn't plant the damn bomb doesn't mean this isn't his fault. Whatever trouble comes to the River Styx can certainly be traced back to that jackass."

Persephone laughed lightly, but she knew it to be true. Hades was so wrapped up in freeing her from his brother that he had hardly focused on freeing himself. She couldn't allow Hades to continue slaving over the man's every whim when he wouldn't allow her to. That wasn't how this worked. She knew it wouldn't be easy though. Zeus had been her problem for only a couple of years. He'd been a burden on Hades' back for decades. That didn't simply go away. Even once the weight was removed, he would still have to learn to walk without it.

"You should go to him," Hecate whispered, the sound of the water now evident in the air.

Persephone nodded, standing up and turning towards the bathroom door. Though she halted after only a step, turning back to Hecate.

"You should too," she said.

While it sounded as natural as can be, Persephone's heart had ticked up several speeds, thudding against her ribcage in a raucous beat. She had no clue why she said it, but she didn't at all regret it, her gaze unwavering upon the other woman's. At the moment, she was worried about Hades, and Hecate seemed to have a calming presence for them both. It was much easier not to think about the show and the casino and everything else with twice the distraction, and truly, Persephone wanted Hecate around right now, in any way possible.

"Join us."

Hecate seemed genuinely surprised at the invitation, and she didn't immediately respond. Her thin lips were parted slightly, brown eyes swimming with awe. Persephone found herself surprised at just how eager she was for the woman to agree, but she suppressed whatever that may look like all over her. Hecate then simply rose to her feet, gaze fixed on Persephone.

"Safe word?" she inquired.

Persephone wet her lips, relief washing over her. "Pomegranate. And - you?"

A smirk. "Dagger."

Then Hecate pushed her towards the bathroom, following close behind.

Persephone could make out Hades' hulking form through the steam, and a chill ran down her spine at the prospect of what was to come. It only just dawned on her how painful it would be if he were to reject her, if he were to reject them both, but she choked down that fear. It was too late to turn back now.

The shower was large with multiple heads lining the walls, various water pressures descending upon his body all at once. She and Hecate locked eyes yet again, and it almost felt like a sanctuary of their own, found when everything around them was moving too fast.

They undressed like that, finding comfort in one another before Persephone opened the shower door. Hecate entered first, sliding her hands up along Hades' back as though she'd done it a thousand times. Persephone was willing to bet it was far more than that, but she took a moment to simply admire them and the unadulterated adoration that poured from Hecate's gaze. How did he fail to realize just how loved he was?

Though from there, her appreciative gaze fell to other details of Hecate's frame. The soft dark brown skin, the gentle curves, the sheer length of the dark locs that fell down her back, excluded from the bun that sat atop her head. Persephone hummed her content before moving around the two of them, her palms pressing into Hades' chest once she stood before him.

His eyes were already filled with a shallow curiosity, no doubt recognizing Hecate's touch. Once he saw Persephone however, those eyes widened as he realized what was occurring. Persephone could laugh at the slow dawning that overtook his face, but she only smiled, pressing her lips to the skin between her splayed fingers.

"I brought some extra hands if that's okay," she purred.

She could tell that he had several questions poised upon his tongue. He wanted to ask her if she was okay, if she was sure, if she remembered her safe word. She answered all of them by sliding a hand up around the back of his neck and dragging him down to capture his lips with her own. He relaxed into her as Hecate's hands appeared between them, smoothing over his abdomen. One slipped lower along his hip until her dainty fingers were able to take hold of his shaft at the base.

She began to stroke him slowly, and Persephone caught his groan on her tongue. She reached for his hand, guiding it to her breast. He needed no additional prompting, groping and squeezing, kneading the flesh between his fingers. She moaned against his mouth, and Hecate's hand sped up slightly.

He came to life in her hold, hardening as he pumped into her palm. His other hand came up to cup Persephone's neck, but as he tried to back her into the wall, she pushed him back instead. He gawked at her through heavy eyelids, and she only winked before she began to kiss down his jaw, his neck, his chest.

Hecate was still working her fist over him when Persephone's lips reached his waist, the water cascading down her back. By then, his hands were braced on the wall in front of him, and his breathing was shallow. His eyes had followed her descent, his mouth falling open once she looked up at him through her lashes. Hecate peered at her around him, smirking when she caught the other woman's gaze. Her hand stopped halfway up his cock before moving back down to the base now. Persephone took advantage of the space left for her, dragging her tongue along the underside of his head, catching drops of arousal as she went. A shuddered breath fell over her from above, and pride swelled in her chest. She smoothed her palms up his legs from knee to hip, gaze still locked on his. Until his eyes began to flutter.

Persephone's tongue swirled around his tip in a most tantalizing way until his hips were trembling. She knew he was fighting to stay still, and she savored it, her nails raking over his skin. She was growing to crave the power she managed to take from him, pulling it from his hands with unbridled ease to claim it as her own. With it, she could move mountains and drain rivers. With it, she could bring a myth of a man to his knees. The only thing that prevented the latter was Hecate holding him upright with a power all her own.

Persephone at last took him into her mouth, sucking generously, allowing him to adjust to the dual sensation of this and Hecate's hand. She felt the other woman's gaze on her again. Moments later, their paces were synced, and Hades' fingers were curling against the shower wall as his groans became more persistent. Persephone took more of him, teeth scraping over his shaft as her lips came up just short of Hecate's fingers. Despite the palpable tension, the silence was comfortable, only the sound of Hades' breathing becoming more labored in the air.

Hecate's fingers receded further as she leaned into him, pushing his length deeper into Persephone's mouth. Persephone gagged as he hit the back of her throat. It took her only a moment to adjust, but she felt his hips jerk harder into her at the sound as he clamped down on a groan. She smiled around him.

"I know you want to fuck that pretty little mouth."

Hecate's voice dripped over them like warm honey in a tone Persephone had never heard, and this time, Hades was not the only one who shuddered. Persephone's nails dug harder into the backs of his thighs. She still managed to relax her throat as Hecate moved her hand back further, guiding his hips into a decent pace. Persephone's hands climbed up to grip his ass, urging him on until she felt him in the back of her throat once more. He rewarded her with a choked "Seph-" before he again sped up, pumping into her mouth fully.

"That's a good boy," Hecate breathed. "Let it go."

She released his cock completely, allowing him to stroke until Persephone's nose hit his groin, earning a loud grunt from behind his gritted teeth. His hand came off the wall, hovering above Seph's head, and she nodded in encouragement through watering eyes. Soon, his fingers were tangled in her hair, and he relaxed further, knees bending slightly as he set his own rhythm. The heat of his gaze poured into her like molten gold, and her nails bit deeper into his ass, whimpering around him. He took the hint, his thrust more forceful, his balls grazing her chin each time. She stretched her tongue out, gagging again, her eyes falling shut as tears gathered at the edges.

"She takes it so well, doesn't she?" Hecate hissed, her hands roaming his body again.

Persephone could sense the arousal in the other woman's voice, and she found herself wondering what kind of effect this had on Hecate. How wet she was.

She reached out instinctively, resting her hand against Hecate's thigh just as Hades bottomed out in her throat, her eyes rolling back in her head. Once she recovered, she moved her hand between Hecate's legs, the other woman stepping sideways eagerly to allow the access. Persephone was elated to find Hecate's thighs slick with want, the other woman shivering beneath her touch. Pressing her palm against the skin just below Hecate's stomach, she let her thumb find her clit, massaging it and drawing the first unhinged sound from the other woman.

Hades' reaction was immediate, nearly on his tiptoes as he shoved his cock as far down Persephone's throat as possible. Her hand slowed, but Hecate soon took it in her own, guiding the motions and pleasuring herself with Persephone's touch.

It was intoxicating, from the atmosphere itself to the growing symphony of sounds. The pace quickened, and the pressure built at a rate to match. Tears flowed freely down Persephone's cheeks as she hollowed them, sucking him down now as he fucked her mouth. More out of desperation than anything, she turned her hand, slipping two fingers between Hecate's folds and curling them inside of her. Hecate's hips bucked, her yelp ricocheting off of the tiles. She was riding Persephone's fingers within moments, nails clawing at Hades' chest. Hades now had both hands buried in Persephone's curls, tightening his hold as he rested his head against the wall. His balls slapped her harder, and she hummed around him, using the vibrations to enhance his pleasure. She had to admit, she was surprised by her own ability, but she didn't question it now, taking all that he had to offer her in stride.

He came first, and he came hard. With a sharp thrust and a firm hand keeping her forehead pressed into his abdomen. She swallowed and kept swallowing, though there was little to collect, focusing on the feeling rather than the absence of air. She pressed her digits firmly into Hecate's walls, thumb more fervent against her clit. The other woman rutted against Hades as she took Persephone's fingers, her wanton moans now spilling forth unchecked. It was yet another dose of power, the high making Persephone feel monolithic, even on her knees. Two of the most powerful people in Khaos Falls, and they were coming apart around her, for her.

"Damn, Seph," Hades grunted.

He pulled out of her, and she took a moment to rest her head against his thigh, gulping down air. He combed his fingers through her hair, his knees still shaking against her. Once she gathered the strength, she pushed herself to her feet, moving around him to walk Hecate back into the wall until their chests were pressed together.

Persephone could now focus on her ministrations, but she reached back and took Hades' hand first, dragging him up behind her. She plunged her fingers deeper into Hecate's pussy, and the other woman's eyes burned into hers before she pulled Persephone into a bruising kiss.

Hades' mouth found Persephone's neck, his large hands bracketing her hips. He pressed his length against her ass, still —or again — thoroughly stimulated and semi-hard. She rolled her own hips with a moan, body pressed between both of them, her skin buzzing with electricity. His hand slipped over her ass and down between her thighs, his thick fingers teasing her folds from behind as Hecate's teeth tugged on her lip.

Before Persephone could demand that he stop playing with her and give her what she wanted, Hecate's hands are on her ass, pulling her closer as she bucked and ground her hips right through a shattering orgasm. She cried out, head falling back against the wall as she came, her juices pouring into the taller woman's hand.

Persephone's mouth attacked her neck, nipping and sucking until Hecate's finished riding it out. Once she did, Persephone withdrew her fingers, turning to push them into Hades' mouth. His eyes were obsidian pools as he took the offering with eager haste. Persephone's thighs rubbed together. She hoped they weren't tired yet. She had so many ideas she wanted to get through tonight.

Twenty-Four

HADES

The journey from the shower to the bed was a blur. Hell, the journey from the casino floor to the suite was a blur, but neither more so than the journey from silence to...this.

He could admit he was surprised, not simply by what was now occurring but by the fact that Persephone seemed to be running the show. She directed them with nothing more than the movement of her body and the touch of her hands. Hades was keen to melt for both, but he never thought Hecate would be so weak for it too. That may be the biggest surprise of them all. Regardless, they'd certainly accomplished what they set out to do. He had all but forgotten about the chaos downstairs. For now.

Their collective movements were as fluid as water, falling into a writhing pile of tangled limbs and sultry sounds upon his sheets. From one breath to the next, he was on his back, and Persephone was lowering herself down onto his face, taking a seat on his jaw. She looked down at him with mischief in her eyes, as though she knew just how badly he wanted to be inside her. Nonetheless, he wouldn't dare complain, as eager to please her in this position as any other.

He stretched his tongue out before her obediently, curling the tip against her clit and eliciting a guttural moan from her just as he felt Hecate's hand around his cock, lining him up with her slit. He took Persephone's clit into his mouth, and Hecate took the whole of him into her pussy, their collective cries falling over him like heavy rain. Hecate snatched his hands from where they clung to the sheets, pressing her tits into his palms as she began to move. Again, she and Persephone fell in sync, and if he weren't so overwhelmed with the dual sensations, he would wonder just how much of this they had planned beforehand.

Persephone soon gripped the headboard, grinding down against his mouth. He relinquished her clit in favor of sweeping his tongue over her folds, scraping his teeth across them along the way before he pushed his tongue inside of her. She didn't miss a beat, riding it the way Hecate rode his dick, claiming every ounce of friction she could find.

His hands ventured down Hecate's abdomen when she leaned back, and as she braced her hands on his thighs, he sought out her sensitive clit and began to massage it. Her hips were immediately more insistent, rolling between both points of impact in need of the friction. After watching how quickly Persephone had made her cum, Hades was hungry to unravel her himself this time. They had robbed him of all control, and he basked in it. While Hades had never shied away from being useful, he was still used to holding the reins. He could admit that Persephone and Hecate were the only people he had ever been any kind of submissive for, the only people he had ever wanted to be submissive for, in any capacity. It made this all the more fitting.

And all the more alluring too.

He didn't know who came first this round. All he knew was that Persephone was swirling her hips at the same time Hecate was bouncing hard on his cock, and his senses were overloaded in a very short amount of time. Then he was coming undone inside Hecate, calling out against Persephone's walls as she covered his face in her own orgasm.

Even with his eyes in the back of his head and his body trembling, arching off of the bed, he lapped up every drop that he could. He felt the fruits of Hecate's climax streaming down his shaft and across his thighs. She slapped Persephone's ass with a hoarse groan as the brunette moved down Hades' body far enough to crush her mouth against his own, kissing him deeply until his head spun. He was still dazed when she pulled away, his beard slick with her.

"You still got somethin' for me, Baby?" she asked.

It took a moment to catch his breath. "You know damn well I do."

They moved like cogs in a well-kept machine. Hades slipped out from beneath them, playfully shoving Hecate down on her back against the pillows he'd just been pressed into. Persephone needed no guidance, lowering herself down between the other woman's thighs and leaving her ass up for Hades' access. He licked his lips, eyes trailing along the arch of her back. She slipped her hands beneath Hecate's ass, pulling her closer. Hecate's eyes were fixed on Persephone as she fisted the sheets, her chest rising and falling quickly in anticipation.

Hades only watched at first, hands lax at his sides. Persephone gave Hecate's slick folds a long, languid lick. Hecate bit her lip, and it was evident how hard she was fighting not to buck her hips. She looked up at Hades for a brief moment, and he smirked. Then, right before his eyes, her face was contorted into shock and awe, then unbridled pleasure.

He took hold of his shaft as Persephone went to work on Hecate's clit, and he was hard again before she even slipped her fingers down to toy with Hecate's sensitive lips. He moved closer, slipping his cock between Persephone's cheeks, proud to hear her whimper amidst her ministrations. He spread her open with his thumbs as he gripped her, grunting in time with each roll of his hips. He dragged it out for the sake of them both, having found the utmost joy in their foreplay thus far. They may have each drawn an orgasm out of the other, but that didn't negate the need. He wanted to see her legs shaking all over again before he thrust inside of her.

She didn't disappoint.

When he finally dragged his tip down through her folds, she was slick with fresh arousal that coated the length of his erection. She shifted her hips back towards him, but he matched the movement, keeping just out of reach. She looked back at him with a pout, but he reached forward with a quickness, gripping her neck and guiding her face right back down into Hecate's pussy.

"Don't hold out on her now," he commanded, although it took him a moment to realize he'd spoken. "Fuck her with your tongue, your fingers. Make her cum again."

"Hades—" she whined, throwing her hips back, but he pushed her down further.

He knew when she touched down by the gasp from Hecate, her hips jerking upward into Persephone's mouth.

"Be a good girl, and give her that tongue now, Baby," he coaxed. "Then I'll give you this dick. That's what you want, right?"

That was all it took. Her head snapped forward, and Hecate's cry let him know Persephone was in her now. He didn't relinquish his hold on her just yet, relishing in the sensation of her head moving along with her strokes. Only when he was certain she was focused on her task did he guide his cock to her entrance, ramming into her without warning. She shrieked against Hecate, whose heel was now digging into Persephone's shoulder, but Hades kept her head pinned down. He was already moving, his thrusts coursing with the command he'd reclaimed as their cries warred around him.

Persephone's hands fumbled and eventually found Hecate's, threading their fingers together. They held onto one another for dear life, Hecate's mouth frozen open in a silent scream. Hades released Persephone's curls at last, taking hold of her hips as he fucked her harder. And fuck, she felt good. He thrust into her as though he'd been deprived for days rather than hours, and he may as well have been. With her, always with her, he was insatiable, and the amount of time he could go without being inside her felt as though it were shrinking. Dramatically.

"Ah! Fuck - yes, Seph!" Hecate howled, which spurred both Hades and Persephone on. He anchored them in place with his bruising grip. Otherwise, Hecate would have been driven through the headboard with the way he was drilling Persephone, the sound of their skin colliding now echoing through the room.

Hades knew the moment Hecate came this time, her moans violently severed as she convulsed against the sheets, back arching off of the bed and the whites of her eyes visible. Persephone mewled as she lapped up Hecate's offering before she reared her head and called out into the air.

"Hades - right - there! Please! Don't stop - don't —"

He didn't. Of course he didn't. He pounded into her pussy with merciless thrusts, sweat pouring down his face in the midst of his exertion. As her upper body came off of the bed, Hecate slipped down under her, her mouth quickly latching onto Persephone's breast as her hands slid down her sides and around her ass. She spread her apart for him, Persephone's arms giving out so that she collapsed hopelessly against Hecate, clawing at her shoulders as their mouths crashed together. Though it wasn't long before Persephone was breaking away to beg and plead for release.

"Come on, baby," Hades snarled, whipping a hand across her ass and eliciting another raw moan. "You're gonna cum for me, right? Aren't you?"

"You better," Hecate demanded, her body still shaking beneath them. "I want to see both of you cum. I need to."

Her voice, in tandem with Persephone's sounds, had him teetering on the edge. Gathering Persephone's hair in his hands, he hoisted her up enough to allow Hecate to ravish her breasts once more. He then put every ounce of energy he had left behind each thrust until Persephone's shrill cries spilled out into the space, her walls constricting around him in a vice grip.

Hades barked his pleasure, leaning over her as she milked him too, his body erupting into a fit of unchecked tremors. Together, they fall apart, wave after wave of ecstasy rolling through them until they collapsed beside Hecate in a mess of slick skin and heavy breaths.

And content. There was also content.

They eventually managed to crawl up further on the mattress, Hades slipping between the two women with a satisfied smile. The day had caught up with him, but the thoughts were pleasant as he drifted off to sleep, the burden left laying on the bedroom floor.

Twenty-Five

HADES

I t was nearing noon when Hades slipped out of bed, quietly dressing and leaving Persephone and Hecate sound asleep. They had worn him out well enough for a few hours of rest, but dreams —or, more accurately, nightmares— of the fire had roused him all too soon.

He'd tried to drift off again to no avail, and so rather than lay there ruminating, he decided it best to go downstairs and see if he could be some kind of productive. He could only be distracted from the situation at hand for so long, no matter how well Hecate and Persephone had done that for him. Now, there were answers he needed to find. And quickly.

Since arriving yesterday, he'd hidden his emotions well enough, as well as he always had, his rage and pain a rogue current beneath a placid surface. He'd asked questions, given directions, and inspected the damage without so much as a frown. He couldn't show weakness now. It was the one thing whoever did this would want to see, and he had no plans of giving them such a privilege, no matter who it was.

That still didn't mean there wouldn't be scars.

Casino Asphodel wasn't simply the heart of Khaos Falls. It was the heart of Hades himself too. The worst part was that he knew whoever had done this must have known that too. No one had ever attacked his district before, meaning it would have taken very little to make a statement. There were easier targets in the Styx District, far more accessible targets that would have put him on edge and inspired fear among his people, no matter how brief. However, to attack Asphodel? And in such a way that visible damage would linger for an extended period of time? It was bold, it was brutal, and it was an act of war.

It was also a personal wound he felt deeper than any blade could ever reach.

He'd just stepped off of the elevator on his office floor when his radio crackled on his hip.

"You available, Boss?" Atalanta's voice questioned.

"Yeah, I'm here," Hades returned once he freed the device from his belt and brought it to his mouth. "What's going on?"

"Zeus is here. He insists on seeing you."

Of course he was. Hades removed his finger from the button on the side of the radio as he entered his office, breathing out through his nose.

No matter the reason, Zeus shouldn't be here. Hades had enough on his plate right now to worry about, and his brother's temper tantrums weren't going to help. However, it was impossible for Hades not to be suspicious. Zeus may not be stupid enough to pull off something like this himself, but it didn't mean he wouldn't get as much joy as he could from it either.

Hades didn't want to hear the younger's shallow attempts at faux concern. He just wanted to be left alone.

But he was still a novice when it came to telling Zeus "no", and as much as he hated to admit it, to feel it, there was a substantial amount of guilt over the other night. And an overwhelming need to believe that his brother actually cared about him.

At last, he responded. "Bring him up to my office."

Hades sat down at his desk, running a hand over his head. In an effort to calm his own nerves, he tried to focus on the delicious soreness that ached in every inch of him. It worked for a time, and a large part of him wanted to walk right back upstairs and fall into bed between Hecate and Persephone. He buried that desire under an abundance of caution as Zeus appeared on the landing.

The leader of Olympus looked well rested, but there was a crease between his brow that Hades didn't understand. Zeus wasn't smiling. He didn't look at all excited to be here. Hades didn't chalk it up to genuine anything just yet. He clasped his hands atop his desk and waited.

Zeus entered the office, but he didn't say anything just yet, collapsing into the chair opposite his brother. Atalanta, sleek as a cheetah and just as powerful in a brawl, walked in behind him, a red folder in her hands. She placed it in front of Hades.

"Stills from yesterday's video," she explained. "Leo sent the footage to your computer before he got off, so you can review it when you're ready."

Hades nodded, opening up the folder. "Thanatos?"

"He was just checking on the contractors, but he's probably on the floor now."

Hades looked up. "The contractors have already started?"

"Yeah, they were here about 7 or 8, mapping things out. Apollo himself too."

That shouldn't be so surprising. Apollo had always been about his business, and if he said he could get it done, he wouldn't waste a moment doing so. Still, it was definitely a relief, and Hades allowed himself a moment to breathe without letting the emotion boil over onto the surface.

"That's all, Atalanta, thank you."

She nodded once, throwing one last suspicious glance at Zeus before leaving the two brothers alone in the silence. Hades didn't look at Zeus immediately, instead spreading out the pictures in the folder across his desk. Zeus lasted all of a minute.

"Why didn't you call me, Hades?" he demanded, although his voice was wary.

Hades wanted to ask if he meant the way Zeus had called him when he'd betrayed Tartarus, but he held his tongue on that particular matter. It wasn't worth the breath.

"I didn't call anyone," Hades returned, the nonchalance impeccable.

"The place nearly burned down, and I had to hear about it on the fucking internet?"

"In case you've forgotten, Zeus, I threw you out of here the other night."

"Yeah, but you let me in today, so I assume we've made up."

"Is that so?"

Everything he didn't say is written in his eyes when he finally looked up to meet his brother's, and Zeus visibly shrank in his seat. Odd, how conscious Zeus was of the power he had been handing Hades in increments over the years. How much was it now? And why did Hades still feel so hopeless despite it?

235

Zeus seemed to contemplate something for a moment, gripping the arms of the chair, before he huffed out a heavy breath.

"Alright, look, I'm sorry for the other night," he sighed.

"The other night isn't the only problem, Zeus," Hades chided, looking back down at the pictures.

"Well - I'm sorry about before too."

"And I'm not the one you should be saying sorry to."

"Then I'll tell Persephone I'm sorry—"

"You won't. You're going to leave her alone is what you're going to do, and not just because she blocked your number."

"She—" He caught himself and took a moment to think, for once. "So - you're really with her or something then?"

"Is that what you came here for, Zeus? Because I really don't have time—"

"No, Hades, that's not what I came here for. My brother was targeted. We're a united front, no matter how many times we bicker. And - no one comes between us. That's what we said when Mom died. That's what you said."

Hades' jaw clenched. It was the only sign of his indignation. Zeus always knew exactly what to say to bring his big brother back into the fold, but the most dangerous weapon he had in his arsenal had always been their mother, especially when Zeus called her as much. Mom. That was who she was when it was the two of them, Zeus and Hades. To others, she was simply Rhea or his stepmom when Zeus spoke of her. It sounded all too much like shame.

It wasn't like anyone needed the distinction, and not simply because the death of Cronus's first wife had always been a hot topic. With Rhea's beautiful Black skin and natural hair, there was no way one could mistake Zeus for her son by blood. Still, she had loved Zeus as much as she had loved Hades and Poseidon, and she

236

had been the best mother she possibly could be for them all until the very end. That included Hades' vow. Whether it had been blown out of proportion or completely misconstrued remained up for debate, but the foundation remained. They were to take care of each other.

Or at least, Hades was to take care of Zeus, no matter what.

"I appreciate the concern, brother," Hades at last conceded, "but I don't have anything more to share with you at the moment."

"So you don't know who did this yet?" Zeus countered, face screwed up in confusion.

"No, I —"

Hades stopped, focusing his attention on a single photo with a single figure in it. He could tell right away it had come from the camera in the hallway behind the theatre, one of the most likely places the fire had started. There were three other stills of the same hallway featuring the same person, tall and thin, dressed down in black with a hood over their head. No one came into the casino looking like that. While the dress code wasn't written in stone, it was widely understood and religiously respected. Besides, no one wanted to come in here looking desperate. That was the quickest way to lose whatever change you came in here with.

"Come on, Hades, we know who did this," Zeus groaned, running a hand through his light brown hair. "And yeah, before you say it, I know it's my fault. The deal with Medusa and all, but to be fair, Coeus lied to me first. He didn't even—"

Zeus seemed to realize then that his brother was paying him no mind at all. He stood up, curiosity adorning his features as he rounded the desk to stand at Hades' shoulder. He looked down at the pictures of the man in the hallway, brows knitting. Hades couldn't make out a face, but judging by the progression of the photos, it was possible that there was a frame missing with a better chance of identification.

Hades turned his attention to his computer, booting it up as Zeus pulls one of the photos closer to him.

"Do you recognize him?" Zeus asked. "I mean, do you think you've seen him before?"

"Can't tell," Hades responded, preoccupied with the input of his password on the screen and the scan of his fingerprint on the keyboard. "See if you can find any other photos of him in there, from any other part of the casino."

"Where did it start? The fire?"

"That hallway."

He could feel Zeus looking at him, no doubt in bewilderment, before he began looking through the photos, comparing each person he found to the suspect in question. Hades pulled up the footage that Leo had sent to his drive, glancing down at the picture for the time-stamp before seeking out that particular clip.

"Found him again," Zeus said, sliding another photo over to Hades.

Hades looked down at it, recognizing one of the service hall-ways between the Pantheon and Elysium, the hallways Persephone frequented. His blood ran cold. The figure was still covered from head to toe, hands tucked in the pockets of his jacket and chin tucked in against his chest.

Hades couldn't even estimate a proper height from this angle. He was surely shorter than Hades and thinner than Zeus, but that hardly narrowed it down at all. Hades would give the guy this: he was care-ful. He seemed to have at least a vague knowledge of the camera positions, adjusting his body as needed to ensure no part of him was exposed. There was also no footage of him actually planting an explosive or setting anything aflame, meaning he'd found somewhere between cameras to do his work. It was impressive.

It was also frustrating.

Zeus kept combing through the photos, and Hades played the clip, looking for anything that might help to identify the person. He found no luck there, but he checked the timestamp for the pictures in the service corridor and searched for that clip next. When he found it, his heart thudded in his chest.

The lighting was far better here, and he knew that all he needed was one tiny slip-up, one movement of the person's hood or tug of a sleeve. Just one.

Zeus was watching now too, both of them riveted as the person appeared in the hall and began walking toward the camera. Hades gripped the computer mouse hard, his other hand curling into a fist against the desk. He swore he was holding his breath. He thought Zeus might be as well.

The man moved closer on screen, but every inch of him remained obscured, no slipping, no adjusting. He was about to walk out of frame, and Hades felt his blood begin to curdle. Then the door at the other end of the hall opened in the shot. The person turned his head on instinct.

He turned it just enough to give Hades and Zeus a clear look of the other side of his face. He seemed to realize it too because he quickly jerked his eyes back in front of him, hurrying out of sight. But not before they get a glimpse of the ink along his neck. The distinct tattoo, climbing out of the collar of his shirt and up the side of his face into his hairline, was emblazoned in Hades' mind. It sketched the vaguest of memories behind his eyes, but he failed to fill in the blanks and color it in. But he knew that tattoo. He knew this man. Why did he know him?

Zeus suddenly started rifling through the pictures.

"See if you can follow him," Zeus snapped, evidently feeling the confused look Hades gave him. "The parking lot or something. Tell me if he's driving a town car, maroon."

Hades obeyed, more so out of a need to do something than any real understanding. However, when he found himself watching that very man climb into a very maroon town car, he paused the clip and sat back, exasperated. Zeus looked up then, a picture in his hand. Hades didn't doubt it was of this very clip.

"Midas," they both said at the same time.

Midas, who turned everything he touched into golden flame. Midas, who notoriously worked under Coeus.

Hades shook his head. "Why would Coeus send his own guy, someone that we could recognize?"

"Because Midas is his best guy." The younger's eyes remained on the screen. "And we almost didn't. If anyone could pull this off without being caught, it's him, and if it were anyone else but us, he would have, right?"

"Nyx and Erebus never would have given the green light on this, Zeus."

Zeus looked at him now as though he'd said something blasphemous. "Are you trying to say Coeus has never done anything without his parents' approval? Or Tethys for that matter? We - I fucked them over. If all their parents were gonna do was go into a lockdown and put the city in timeout, why wouldn't they go out behind their backs?"

"And you've considered this a whole lot, have you?"

Zeus threw up his hands with a heavy sigh. "Yeah, well as I

copped to before, I fucked up. Granted, I thought they'd go after the port. Or - try and make a deal with Demeter for the northern docks. I don't know."

Hades bit back a lecture. They hadn't discussed it, his little deal with Medusa. Denying Coeus was one thing, but cutting him out of a deal Zeus and Hades had already agreed to was treachery in its worst form. Not only did it inspire retaliation and further betrayal, it degraded Zeus's integrity beyond the low it already sat at, which was saying something. It didn't do Hades' integrity any good either for that matter.

It was far too late to pick it apart though. What was done was done. Now they had to deal with this. However, Hades wasn't completely convinced of Zeus's take on the matter. It seemed far too easy, and Hades had never taken well to easy.

Standing, Hades gathered up the photos, carefully extracting the one from Zeus's fingers, and packing them back into the folder. He could see Zeus's confusion in the corner of his eye, but he didn't address it until he'd set the folder aside.

"We can talk about this more later," he said plainly, straightening his tie.

"What do you mean 'later'?" Zeus scoffed.

"Exactly what I just said, Zeus. I don't know how else to say it."

"So you're just - not gonna do anything!"

"I never said that, but I'm certainly going to need more evidence than a picture of a masked man in a maroon car."

"So you don't trust me?"

"I didn't say that either."

"You don't have to!"

"Because if you're right, trusting you is the reason why we're here in the first place!"

241

It was only when the silence fell between them that Hades' voice echoed back to him, showing just how loud he'd become. Another first really. He'd scolded Zeus before, sure, but he wasn't the type who lost his temper so easily. He hadn't slept much though, and Zeus's constant pushing wasn't helping him resolve his own reservations. It was confirmed though. Their relationship had certainly changed, and looking at Zeus right now, Hades had no interest in reverting back to what it was. Looking at him made Hades sick.

"I'm not going to make a decision on a whim," Hades resumed coldly. "That is where you and I differ, brother. That is why we are still here at all. If one of the heirs of Tartarus did this, I will find out. Otherwise, I will keep looking, but we are not going to go to war at noon on a weekday because you identified a fucking car. Do you understand me?"

Zeus said nothing for a long time, and Hades kept his eyes trained on his brother's face. He could not back down. He could not let this get swept aside. Zeus had to understand. He was not allowed to make any foolish decisions right now. It could cost them all far too much.

It could cost them everything.

At last, Zeus turned away, but before he could head for the door, Hades gripped his arm.

"I said, do you understand, Zeus?"

Zeus gritted his teeth. Then he nodded, and once Hades released him, he stalked out of the office and down the stairs, pouting all the way.

It was just another thing to worry about. That was what Hades told himself because somehow, that had always made it okay.

Though it felt like this time might be different.

Twenty-Six

PERSEPHONE

Persephone stretched as her eyes fluttered open, adjusting to the darkness of Hades' room. She knew it must be well into the day by now, but his blackout curtains made it nothing short of a guessing game. She glanced over at the clock on the end table. Half past noon. She groaned before rolling over the other way, right into Hecate's still form.

Persephone froze, fearing she might wake her up, but Hecate giggled and turned to look at her, eyes dancing with amusement.

"You're awake," Persephone hissed, relaxing back into the pillows.

"Barely," Hecate hummed, stretching out herself now. "You two nearly killed me."

Persephone smirked. "That good, huh?"

"Mhm. Plus, it's been a while."

She clucked her tongue. "There is no way you and Thanatos weren't rolling around with each other here and there, right?"

Hecate snorted. "I meant like that. We never have the time to go that many rounds, and it's been a while since we've had - company."

"Ah." Persephone's eyebrows raised, lips quirking. "Well, I'm sure we can work on that, make this more of a habit."

They grinned at one another. "I'd appreciate it. I'll even bring the toys next time."

"You better."

A pleasant silence fell over them as each of them seek out their phones, checking for messages or missed calls. Without Zeus or her mother hounding her, the only notable notification was a text message from Aphrodite stating she would be by in the afternoon and that the news of Asphodel had spread like wildfire across the city. Persephone wondered about the details, but she wasn't ready to look at the news coverage or social media posts just yet, especially from show critics. Setting her phone down, she stared up at the ceiling.

"You think he's okay?" she asked.

"I think he wants to be," Hecate returned as if she'd been wondering the same thing. "And I think he'll tell us that he is. That's what he does, but - this place is his home and his heart. It's the one thing that was his. Not his father's or his mother's or Zeus's. He built this, and to have someone try and take it from him, no matter the reason... It's - personal."

Persephone turned on her side to face the other woman. "I could feel it, when we were driving over here. He wouldn't say anything or - show anything, but I could feel how - afraid he was. It scared me too."

"It used to scare me too." Hecate turned to her as well. "I guess it still does. I used to believe that it should. And not because he doesn't handle the emotion well but because - he doesn't handle the emotion at all. To him, every problem is tangible. He's used to being in control, to being the anchor when everyone else is being thrown around by the waves, and to him, anything less than that is a failure. And this is... It's big. It's the biggest thing to ever happen to him. Not to Zeus or to his parents or even to the district, but to Hades personally. This is a man they say is immortal. Imagine what could happen if a whole city starts questioning that."

"What can I do?"

Hecate smiled. "That's the beauty of you, Seph, and - how he feels about you. I think you can do anything you think you need to. You sense things like that, you can put your foot down. You can make him face it, but-" She grabbed Persephone's hand. "You don't need to try and fix him. Even if he needs it, and I don't think he does, but... That's not your job. That's not anyone's job. You just need to let him know that he can be himself with you. Apart from that, business is always gonna be business."

"I'm still trying to wrap my head around the fact that he feels somethin' for me at all."

"Oh, it's more than something." She chuckled. "I don't know all the details, but whatever happened the other night with him and Zeus, it was because of you." Persephone frowned, but Hecate squeezed her hand. "Hey now, that is not a bad thing. The first time he's ever stood up to Zeus? We've been trying to get him there his whole life, and you did that. You don't have to make him stronger, Persephone. You make him want to be stronger on his own, and that is more than enough. You just gotta let him be."

It was Seph's turn to laugh. "You're really good at this, you know? The talking."

"It comes with the job." She smirked. "I do the talking, Charon does the listening, Thana does the doing, and Hades brings it all together. We had a lot of practice with each other. How else do you think we run this place? You think your man is downstairs greeting people? Please."

Persephone laughed harder. "I definitely would never picture him doing a thing like that."

"We all have our roles. We've settled into them alright."

The brunette sobered now, looking up at the ceiling. "Looks like I'm gonna have to find a new one for now."

Hecate frowned now. "Oh, right. The show."

"Yeah. Calliope will probably wanna go back to Deucalion Heights without a venue." She remembered how distraught the other woman had been in their short conversation the day before. "Either to work on something new for the time being or to tend to the other productions she has going right now."

Hecate's brows knitted. "Why not one of Aphrodite's places?"

"I wish we could, but even if she has the space, we can't just set up acrobatics anywhere. The stage has to be made for that."

"And there's no other place in Khaos Falls like that?"

"Not that I know of. That's why it was so important we get the extension here."

Hecate was quiet for a moment, but Persephone could hear the cogs turning in her head. It soothed her to no surprise. That was Hecate's entire charm. She knew how to make people feel safe. More than that, she knew how to make people feel like they deserved to be.

"I'll look into it," Hecate said finally. "Don't give up hope yet. I'm not gonna let you leave town without doing everything that I can. Dio and I have a few tricks up our sleeve we might be able to pull for something like this."

Persephone grinned, her heart fluttering. "Don't play with me now."

"I would never." Hecate squeezed her hand once more before releasing it and sitting up in the bed to look at her. "Until then, if you get bored, you can always work with me down in the casino offices. In a paid position of course. The amount of people you deal with daily is entirely up to you, and the job is pretty straightforward. You're smart, and you have a business degree already, don't you? I could teach you in no time."

"You mean that?"

"Oh, that's nothing, Seph, of course. It's just something to do, to keep your mind busy."

Persephone couldn't explain how much that meant to her. It wasn't that she was giving up on her dream. If Calliope insisted on her returning to Deucalion Heights for the offseason, she would. However, a chance to stay close to Hades —not to mention Hecate and Aphrodite as well— was something to keep in mind. It was a choice, and she needed choices. She appreciated it more than she could ever say, and she had come to love Asphodel as an extension of Hades. It was the first time she'd ever been genuinely happy in her hometown, and she would do anything to savor it.

"On one condition though," Hecate went on, now turning back to the bed with the most mischievous look Persephone had ever seen on anyone's face. "And it's important."

She raised a brow. "And what is that?"

"You help Dio and I plan Hades' birthday party."

She realized then that she didn't even know when his birthday was. "And - when is that?"

"Three weeks from now, the third of next month, but we want to

247

have the party just before so he's not expecting it. Especially with this going on, I think he needs it."

Persephone grinned wider now, nodding eagerly. "I'm in."

BY THE TIME Persephone and Hecate made it downstairs, Aphrodite had arrived, and she embraced Persephone the moment she saw her on the landing outside of Hades' office. Hecate said goodbye to them and entered the office with haste. Persephone only caught a glimpse of the casino owner where he sat at his desk, Charon and Thanatos at each shoulder as they all looked over something in front of Hades. She tore her eyes away and focused on her best friend.

"You sure it wasn't your mama?" Aphrodite huffed, cupping Persephone's face. "You still haven't told me what went on with her."

She was absolutely right, and Persephone conceded.

"Come on, girl," she sighed, taking Aphrodite's hand. "I'll tell you everything over coffee. Upstairs out of earshot."

"Oh, we goin' to the penthouse?" She smiled at last. "Okay, let's do that."

Persephone cut one more glance through the window of Hades' office just as he looked up. She waved at him, and he smiled bash-fully, offering a wave back. She gestured towards the elevator, and he nodded before turning back to a talking Thanatos. She liked to know that even in his darkest hour, she could still make him smile. It made her feel better about her own strife.

Once she and Aphrodite were settled in the living room with fresh coffee, Persephone unwound fully, dragging a hand through her hair.

"You look beat, girl, what's up?" Aphrodite asked, raising a perfectly shaped brow.

"I don't have a job," Persephone chuckled although there was nothing funny about it. "Just a couple of nights ago, I'm standing in my mother's house telling her I made it, and then this happens."

"And again, are you sure she had nothing to do with it?"

Persephone didn't answer right away, pinching the bridge of her nose. Was it possible that this was Demeter's real response to everything Persephone had thrown at her the other night? Yes, but she'd already assured Hades that Demeter wouldn't do anything to jeopardize her status or the peace in the Harvest District, especially when Persephone left on her own. If things were different —maybe even if she knew about the whole mess with Zeus— that might be another story, but as it stood, Seph doubted it.

Her mind did wander briefly to Adonis, but as childish as he might be, he wasn't that stupid, and he looked like he'd taken her threat to heart that night. Besides, Demeter would kill him before Hades ever got the chance, and if Demeter didn't, Persephone might do it herself.

"Naw," she returned at last. "My mama is proud as all hell, but she's not that."

Aphrodite rolled her eyes. "So she just dragged you outta here by your pigtails or what?"

Persephone snorted. "No, no. She sent Adonis to 'fetch' me."

"Oh, no." They both laughed. "Are you serious? I know he threw a tantrum."

"I drove there myself, but he had the decency to hold it in until I was on my way out." She wet her lips now, looking over at her friend. "I told them about Hades."

The other woman gasped, nearly choking on her coffee. "And?"

249

Persephone shrugged. "Adonis did his thing, but my mama didn't say a word. I think my auntie's alright."

"She's always alright with you though. That woman loves you, like for real."

"Don't I know it."

Hestia was the quiet saint of the Harvest District. Many knew about Persephone's transition, but few knew of Hestia's. She'd guided them all, Demeter included, through the whole thing. Persephone had been in awe when her aunt had first come out to her, but it had helped her put her own pieces together. Hestia had spared her so much pain and confusion. Sure, her father returned more than enough of it, but that didn't negate Hestia's contributions. She went unnoticed by almost everyone in general, but that was her strength. That was how she made things happen.

"So Hades thinks Tartarus did this?" Aphrodite pressed on.

Persephone exhaled slowly. "Honestly, I don't know what he thinks. We didn't really talk about it... Actually, we didn't talk about it at all. Hecate thinks so though. She's betting on Tethys."

"Mm, now that I can see."

Both of them nodded with a mutual look of disgust.

"Hades was gonna review the tapes from yesterday," she recalled although her voice was still distant. "He very well could've cracked the case by now."

"Let's hope," Aphrodite set her mug down on the table between them. "And Zeus? He back off yet?"

"I blocked his number. Hades got on him the other night though too, and I'm willing to bet he'll do it again if Zeus comes around here."

"So you're staying here for good then?"

Persephone glanced over at her to find the other woman grinning, and she rolled her eyes. "It was supposed to be more convenient for work."

"And—"

"And hush your mouth." Aphrodite giggled as Seph shoved her shoulder lightly. "You're here for him. Be real about it at least."

Persephone shrugged. "It's still... I mean obviously, I'm serious about it. I never would've told my mama if I wasn't, but there's still that fear that - especially now without a job, I'll just become Hades' woman."

"You don't ever have to be just anything, Seph. I know this is an unfortunate example under the circumstances, but Nyx has never been just Erebus's wife."

"It's her district."

"And Erebus is - Erebus. His family is practically royalty in Old Crete, and they run the place now. He came here for her, and he's never tried to overshadow her. Hades damn sure won't do it to you."

"You're forgetting we're talking about Hades though. I don't wanna have to screen interviews for 20 questions about him for the rest of my life."

"Most people don't even think he's real, so you should be more worried about people calling you a liar."

"'Dite..."

"Okay, look. I can't promise that won't happen, but I can promise you can say no." She reached over and patted Persephone's leg. "Here's what you gotta accept, Seph. You're always gonna be Demeter's daughter to somebody, and you might always be Hades' woman to somebody else, and Fates, you might even just be Aphrodite's best friend to others." Seph rolled her eyes again, but Aphrodite was unperturbed. "But what matters is who you see when you look in the mirror. —And if you don't see it, I will be happy to point out that you're a fucking superstar."

"Ugh." Persephone let her head fall back against the chair. "I hate when you say shit like that. I don't even have an argument."

Aphrodite snickered. "That's the point. And I'm just glad I don't gotta worry about you in that apartment anymore."

"I can promise that you won't have to worry ever again. If I ever leave here, I'm coming straight home to you."

"Damn straight."

And at the moment, despite all of this uncertainty, Persephone felt like she just might have it all. Not only that, but she felt like she might just deserve it too.

Twenty-Seven

HADES

The sun was beginning to set when Hades headed back to the penthouse, feeling worn out and exhausted. The last few hours had been little more than a circular argument that led them to the same conclusion they'd all apparently walked in there with. And truly, Hades felt worse than he had at the start of it.

The doors opened to the elevator and out stepped Aphrodite, to who he offered a smile.

"You look a mess," she stated matter-of-factly. It made him laugh.

"I feel it," he returned, running a hand over his face. They were quiet for a moment, and the elevator doors closed again, leaving them on the landing. She stared up at him, observant, and he stared too, expectant.

"Thank you," she said finally.

"For what?" he questioned, brows knitted.

"She and I have been through a whole lot. She's family, and she's - happy. That means a whole lot to me."

"I think it's me who's supposed to be grateful."

"Oh, you absolutely should be." They both chuckled. "Seriously though. If there's anything you need, you can call."

He raised a brow. "Is this an alliance?"

She rolled her eyes. "My alliance is with her, and it's rooted in a lifelong bond, so fuck this up, and we'll be enemies before you can blink. Eternally."

He nodded, a tight smile on his face. "That's fair."

"And know it only applies to you and your district."

He knew what she meant without having to ask. She already had her formal union with Dio

and Hermes, and she and Poseidon were respectful neighbors. Neither of them needed to specify who it didn't extend to, surely not right now.

"Just - watch out for each other," she sighed, patting his arm.

"You have my word." Before she could leave him there though, he put a hand out to stop her. "Can I ask you something though?"

"What is it?"

"Do you - honestly think Demeter would do something like this?"

She laughed softly, meeting his eyes. "I asked Persephone the same thing, but truly? Naw, I don't. Demeter is many things, but reckless is not one of them. She knows what it would look like if she were to attack you for something like dating her daughter. I mean, she loves Seph, don't get me wrong, but her district has always come first. If that weren't the case, she wouldn't be this angry to begin with, you know?"

He nodded, trying to find some relief in that assurance, but there was little to be found. It only enforced the story that had already begun to fall into place.

They bid each other good evening, and Hades continued upstairs, finding Persephone laying down on the couch. The TV was on, but she seemed in and out of sleep. He smiled, moving to sit on the recliner before she reached out an arm, beckoning him over. She pulled him down atop her the moment he was close enough, and his head fell against her chest. Immediately, he relaxed into her, feeling her lips against his head as he closed his eyes.

"Tired?" she asked, running a hand over his back.

"Very," he huffed. "I'm not complaining though."

"Do you ever?"

"I see no sense in it really."

"It's a very human thing to complain every now and again."

"Hmm."

He felt her lips turn upward against him before she moved her hand over his head. For the moment, all the stress and anxiety washed away as though she simply wiped it off with her palm. He hummed his content, wrapping his arms around her middle as he turned slightly on his side to relieve her of most of his weight.

He didn't want to think about the state of the casino or of Tartarus or of Zeus. He only wished to remain here with her and pretend nothing outside of the penthouse existed. This was the first time he'd ever felt that way. While he'd always desired to be left alone, it did not mean he was not lonely. The sounds of the casino were his company beyond Hecate and the boys, and that was his comfort in a world that felt far too small to accommodate him sometimes. Now, Persephone had become a sanctuary for him without him ever meaning for her to. He'd known from first looking at her that she was special, but he never could have fore-seen this.

"How did it go?" she questioned after what seemed like forever, her voice a soft lull that washed over him with renewed warmth. He must have started to drift off. "Did you find anything?"

"Yeah." His thumbs stroked her back thoughtlessly. "Video of a man who works under Coeus."

She froze, fingers idle against his scalp. "Seriously? Just - like that?"

He sighed heavily. "No, not just like that. —Zeus identified him. By a tattoo and a maroon car. I mean, I recognized him after the fact, but..." She seemed to sense that there was more he wanted to say—or rather, needed to say as he wasn't sure what he wanted to do anymore. He should say it too. Maybe he couldn't say it to Charon or Thana or Hecate because to say it meant he'd been consistently debasing their trust in him for years, but if he said it to Persephone, maybe he could begin to break that cycle. Or at least prevent it from continuing with her as well.

"Do you think he did it?" he asked at last, his voice fragile.

"Zeus?" She took hold of his chin, guiding it upward. "Do you think he did it?"

He still couldn't meet her eyes. "I - don't know. A week ago, I would have said no, but - something has changed between us."

"Because of me."

He shook his head. "That's not - it isn't that simple, and it isn't your fault. Even if it were, it wasn't for the worst." He forced his eyes up to hers. "I denied him. I've never denied him even when I should have, but I did this time, and he took it as a personal strike. In his mind, I may have very well declared war myself."

"But you didn't, Hades. Forget Zeus for a moment because you won't be able to go down that path until you hear this, and I mean really hear it. You are not the problem. He is. I am being as blatant as I possibly can about that, and it is the only thing I am willing to do for you. Because I will not be to you what you have been to him. I will not be your enabler. If he did this, you have a choice to make. If you let it stand, this will continue until you either give in or lose everything. He doesn't care about you. He only cares about what you can do for him. You threaten that, and you are as much an enemy as anyone else because that is what he was taught. He is the king. Everyone else exists to serve him, and when they cease to do that? They have to be disposed of."

She allowed him to lay his head back down, to marinate in the cold, hard truth to his heart's content, to let it seep into the core of him and calcify there. She resumed stroking his head, her heartbeat soft against his ear, and he clung to it. He let it soothe him, even when he knew he didn't deserve it.

Zeus was very much a monster of his making, and he was now tasked with setting it right. If Zeus was responsible for the fire at the casino, it was an act of war. And it has to be treated as such. Whatever that might look like under such circumstances, it was crucial that Hades have a plan in place, multiple plans. First, he would need proof. He'd meant what he said to Zeus. He never made any decisions, especially those as critical as this, based only on a few pieces of disputable evidence.

"He's forgotten one important thing though," Persephone whispered.

"Hm?"

"He may be the king, but you built the throne. You sized the crown. You gave them to him, and you can take them away."

Hades breathed out slowly. He'd forgotten that too.

257

Twenty-Eight

PERSEPHONE

P reparations for Hades' birthday party had been much easier than Hecate and Persephone had both anticipated. For one, Aphrodite and Dio had been more than willing to help. It was easier to be sly too when Hecate had informed Hades that Persephone would be working with her for the time being. While he'd felt bad about the fact Seph couldn't do what she loved, he'd been supportive of the decision. After that, the two women could plot and scheme the details of the party to their hearts' content without him wondering what they were doing. Needless to say, they spent much of their time in Hecate's office with Dio and Aphrodite on video call.

With the contractors and engineers making absolutely astounding time with repairs, Hades was currently in good spirits, but Persephone knew he needed something to celebrate. He also needed to be celebrated. In a way, it was all of them telling him that they were behind him.

While Persephone had refused to disclose what Hades had

confided in her, Hecate had been able to garner the basic gist once Persephone assured her she thought things would be different now. It was the only thing they had to look forward to when they were all under attack.

Tartarus still hadn't lifted the lockdown nor had they spoken out about the attack despite the rumors floating around. Persephone didn't know if that was a good thing or a bad thing, but she knew that eventually, the other shoe was going to drop. They just had to be ready for it.

Dio was setting up the wine fountain when she walked into Elysium, decorating the bottom with fresh Pomegranate seeds. Persephone took a moment there, remembering the night on Hades' balcony. Carefully, she dipped her fingers into the bed of seeds, scooping some up and taking them into her mouth. She closed her eyes and savored the taste. Sweet and light, they fell heavy into her stomach, like a memory.

"Hey, do not disturb, Seph," Dio warned playfully, smoothing out the space she'd touched as he bumped his broad shoulder against hers. "But you're just the person I wanted to see."

"Please don't tell me there's a problem," she groaned.

He shook his head, grinning wide. "No, I talked to Thalia last night. She wants to see you next week about a music video. She said I could tell you she was gonna call."

Persephone inhaled sharply, her eyes wide. "Dio, don't play with me."

He scoffed. "I do not play — Well, not about that! Besides, you can't be that surprised. Everyone knows you're free right now, and you're a hot topic. We'll have a drink later though, yeah? We're on a time crunch."

She chuckled even though her face was aflame with anxious

259

excitement. "Thank you for telling me, and you are doing a wonderful job. Your uncle is going to love it."

"I hope so." All at once, Dio softened, his eyes growing shiny. "He deserves it, you know, to have something for him. People sort of forget about him. I mean, I know he prefers it that way, but - I think it's alright every once in a while, for him to remember people care."

She smiled up at him. "He's lucky to have you."

"You flatter me."

He gave a dramatic bat of his lashes, and she giggled. Persephone wondered what it would have been like watching Hades try and raise this boy who most often appeared to be his polar opposite. Either way, she was glad they'd had each other.

"He's lucky to have you too though," Dio stated, disrupting her thoughts "You seem to be a very good influence, and don't bother playing modest. I've heard it from everyone."

She scoffed. "Who is everyone?"

He only grinned again before looking at his watch. "We've only got a couple hours."

"How are y'all getting him down here?"

"Apollo's going up to get him. He's gonna tell him he wants him to come down and check out some ideas he has for the new floor plan. Uncle doesn't even know it's done. Hecate made sure Apollo wouldn't tell him until tonight."

"And you don't think he suspects anything?"

He snorted. "Absolutely not. He trusts us. That's a good thing of course. This is the only evil we've ever used it for."

Persephone sobered. "Did - someone tell Zeus?"

Dio rolled his eyes again, and Persephone only just remembered who his father was. "Even if someone did, I doubt he would come. The party isn't for him, so - not really his scene."

"Good point."

"Oh, and Eros says he'll bring the cake down just before we're ready to cut it. It's huge, and he doesn't want it getting bumped or anything beforehand."

"Did you see it? Did it match the design?"

"Down to the felt."

"Perfect."

As she finished up with her own decorations over an hour later, her phone buzzed in her pocket. Persephone extracted it to find Hades' face and name flashing across her screen. It was wild. They'd been together and in the closest of quarters for weeks now yet she still got butterflies in her stomach when he called or texted. She grinned unabashedly at her phone before slipping into the service hall, answering his call and putting it to her ear.

"Yes?" she answered, her voice low and slow.

"Are you working?" he asked, just as low, and his voice sent shivers down her spine.

"I am. And you?"

"Very much so." He paused only a moment. "But I miss you."

She bit her lip. He'd become more and more affectionate lately, and she couldn't say she was complaining. "Oh yeah? How much?"

"Enough that I'm thinking of skipping out on the rest of the day."

"Ooh, sorry, baby, Hecate's showing me the big books today. I'm about to learn all about the algorithms these college kids use to try and steal all your money."

"Ah, now that's a good lesson. Has she started calling them dickhead juniors yet?"

"Since the first slide."

While it may have been for a good reason, she hated lying to him, but she vowed to make up every moment to him once this was all said and done. As in, the moment this party was over and she could get him upstairs. Or maybe just into the elevator...

"You like working down there then?" His tone had grown more serious.

"I do. Don't get me wrong. I miss the stage, but it'll hold me over until I go back." She thought of the news Dio had given her but decided to hold off on telling him. Today was his day. "I like spending time with Hecate and meeting vendors and - coming home to you."

She could hear his smile through the phone, damn him. "I do like that part."

"Mhm, I like taking that suit off of you, roping you into baths just so I can-"

"Okay, don't tease me now."

She laughed softly. "Oh, I'll show you exactly what I'm talking about as soon as we get home. I promise you that. I don't bluff, boss."

"I know damn well you don't. Bless the fates."

"I gotta go before Hecate comes and drags me back into her office."

"Mm, you two better behave down there."

"Yes, sir."

She hung up just as she heard him greet Apollo. She glanced at her screen. Right on time. Stepping back into the club, she allowed herself a moment to take in the scene.

For all the quick repairs, Elysium looked better than ever. Both Dio and Hecate were no doubt thrilled to be close to reopening, and

Persephone was willing to bet that the rest of Khaos Falls was thrilled as well. Traffic was still decent on the casino floor, but she and Hecate spent a good chunk of their day fielding calls from various businesses, civilians, and even the Khaos Falls Daily newspaper to see when the Pantheon and Elysium would be revived. Today was a good day for many reasons. After Hades' party, they could fully commit to opening up again.

Persephone was ushered by Hecate towards the center of the room as the lights came down. The crowd had grown to a few dozen now, all of whom had some kind of notable relationship with Hades or who might come to appreciate one. Hecate and Persephone had been very particular about the guest list, wanting no one who might sour Hades' mood anywhere near it. It was why Zeus hadn't received an invitation.

Moments later, the lights came up just as Hades and Apollo appeared at the edge of the railing that fronted the balcony adjacent to his skybox.

"Happy birthday!"

The words boomed through the space, and Persephone drank in the sincere shock and surprise that was etched on Hades' usually composed face. Confetti spilled from the rafters, fluttering around in the air conditioning as music began to play. Persephone waited until Hades' gaze fell upon her, and she grinned. A moment passed. Then he grinned too.

What felt like an eternity later, she blinked, and he was gone from the balcony. Then she was being swept up in his arms. She giggled against his assault of kisses across her face and neck as everyone around them offered a collective "aww". Persephone had to remind herself that they had never seen him like this. In fact, they had never seen the two of them together. Pride swelled in her chest as she seized his face and planted her lips on his.

"You think you're so slick, don't you?" he hummed against her lips.

"Oh, more than that," she returned, gesturing around them. "I just proved it."

He rolled his eyes but kissed her again.

"Get a room!" Dio yelled from somewhere, but Hecate immediately cut him off.

"No! They aren't allowed to leave for at least 4 hours! I want the doors guarded!"

Laughter bubbled up around them as Persephone stared into Hades' eyes. If she would have known then, the first time she laid eyes on him, that he would be this important to her, she may have run in the other direction from the jump. She was glad she hadn't known. The surprise was well worth it.

She kissed him once more before they found themselves parted by the crowd, Persephone finding Aphrodite as she entered and Hades greeting the rest of his guests.

"I'd never seen that man smile in my life before he met you," Aphrodite hissed as they watched him. "What have you done, girl? Actually don't answer that. I don't need to know."

Persephone snickered and lightly smacked her arm. "Anyway, thank you for the help."

"You know I like to make things happen. This was pretty easy if you ask me. Plus, telling you no is hard enough. Telling Dio no? Impossible."

"I know that's right. And I doubt anyone else could've gotten him a functional wine fountain that size on such short notice."

"You know he has one of those in his living room, right?"

Persephone pushed on. "And the tapestries? Hecate and I looked everywhere for that color. Not even Apollo could help us."

"Okay, that was a complete accident. Eros ordered the wrong ones for Psyche's birthday. That boy wouldn't know plum if it slapped him in the face." She paused. "And it did."

"Shit, I'm glad you mentioned him. I almost forgot the chocolates. They're Hades' favorite. I'll be right back."

She handed Aphrodite her drink before rushing towards the stairs. Eros made exquisite holiday chocolates, and on her first night staying with Hades, she'd found a stockpile of them in his pantry. She had immediately called Eros and asked him for his best party arrangement, which he had been most honored to deliver. To find out that the mysterious —and, to an extent, terrifying— leader of the Underworld had a sweet tooth for his chocolates had seemed to be quite the milestone, and Persephone had shamelessly milked it for both the chocolates and the cake he'd eventually agreed to make.

Once she reached the top of the stairs between the two skybox areas, she signaled one of the servers with a smile. The man followed her behind the bar to the back room where she'd stored two carts earlier. One cart was piled high with various types and shapes of chocolate. The second sported an entire model of Casino Asphodel, complete with the hotel tower, made out of decadent white, milk, and dark chocolates. It looked stunning, and Persephone had stared at it for nearly fifteen minutes when Eros had first brought it by.

She was filled with excitement as they pushed the carts into the elevator, moving them down to the first floor. She found Dio in the crowd, and once they locked eyes, she gestured between the chocolate cart and the DJ booth before pointing to Hades. Dio nodded immediately and moved towards the booth while Persephone and the server were joined by a few more servers, who put the carts atop one of the elevated platforms.

"Uncle," Dio's voice boomed once the music lowered. "Will you please direct your attention to the southern corner and your beautiful girlfriend, please?"

Everyone followed the instruction, and Persephone's eyes gleamed when Hades found her. He began moving closer as Dio also demanded that Eros join him, and they reached the platform at the same time. Hades was immediately smitten with the model, calling out with elation and hugging the younger man to everyone's surprise as people clapped and cheered. It was impossible not to emulate Hades' energy, and Persephone was beginning to wonder if maybe, he and Dio weren't all that different at all when they were comfortable. She wanted to see more of him when he was comfortable if that was the case. The light in his eyes could contend with the brightest stars.

"You found my stash, didn't you!" Hades hollered to Persephone with a whooping laugh and a giddy expression that nearly floored her. She nodded, grinning. "This is stunning. I—"

But suddenly, everything... stopped. The crowd quieted, and Persephone searched face after face, following their gazes to the main door. It was ajar, and there seemed to be a growing hiss of voices there as a guard spoke to someone in the hall. The tension erupted like a plume in the center of the room, spreading outward at a rapid pace. Of course it did. This was the site of an explosion hardly a month ago. For Persephone —and most likely Hades and his three closest friends as well— that fact was only intensified by the appearance of Zeus in the doorway.

He was drunk. Persephone didn't need to see him up close in

order to ascertain that. He stumbled in, his pale skin red as a cherry tomato, and he was pushing past the guards with a growing aggression. Hades' face fell, and Persephone's heart plummeted into her stomach. It was the worst thing she'd ever seen. She watched it in slow motion, the bright grin turned to ash, replaced by this ruin of an expression. She should have known better. Of course, Zeus would find a way into the party if only to bring it all crashing down.

Her eyes scanned the room again until they found Hecate's. The message between them was clear. They needed to get rid of him.

Twenty-Nine

HADES

H ades knew before he even turned around what was happening. He felt it in his chest like a spike through his back, puncturing his lungs and leaving him breathless. When Zeus stumbled into his line of sight, there was a physical pain that accompanied it, and for the longest possible second, he was rooted to the floor.

"Brother!" Zeus called, his gaze wild and unfocused. "Where is my beautiful brother!"

The comfort of the past hour was burned to ash, but from it rose a familiar facade, resilient as ever and goal-oriented. Right now, the goal was to control what damage Zeus might do there.

Hades quickly threw his eyes on Dionysos, who still stood with the microphone, and nodded. Dionysos didn't hesitate, and moments later, the music erupted around them again. Hades then moved towards his brother with quick strides, the crowd parting between them without daring to meet his gaze. This was the Hades that was expected, the one people thought they knew, and while that fear dragged across his skin like barbed wire as he passed them, he wouldn't acknowledge it. He swore he would deal with Zeus from now on, and he wouldn't go back on it now. He couldn't.

He felt Persephone behind him, but he didn't ask her to stay back. Part of him wanted to, but that part simply wasn't large enough to halt his progress. He needed the support too. He needed to be reminded both of what he would lose if he didn't stand up to Zeus and who would remain when his brother was gone.

Hecate and Thanatos were feet away by the time he reached Zeus, catching him around the middle and all but carrying him toward the door. Zeus didn't allow it however. He swung his arms, and it caught Hades off guard. He released his brother, and Zeus forced himself upright as best as he could.

"No invite, brother?" Zeus slurred, blinking repeatedly.

"You're drunk," Hades said simply, his voice quiet yet firm enough to be heard.

"That doesn't answer my question." Zeus almost sang it before belching. Then he turned on Persephone. "Ah, the beautiful Persephone. Long time, no see, Princess. Too comfortable hiding under my brother's skirts now, huh?"

"Zeus." The way Hades said his name caused Zeus's head to snap towards him as if on instinct, a party trick the elder had been practicing for decades. "I am only going to tell you once. You need to leave."

"You gonna have me carried out like some scum off the street again, Hades?" And there it was, a challenge wrapped in a sneer of privilege. Zeus swayed on his feet and gawked around at the club. "Hey! I see you've put the place back together too."

"Surprised, brother?"

"Impressed actually," Zeus hiccuped, patting Hades' chest

before his eyes fell down on Persephone once more. "You're really doing well for yourself. Don't need me, do you?"

"Have I ever?"

That got his attention. He looked up at the elder with wide, red eyes and surprise on his face, but this time, Hades felt nothing but relief. It was the truth. He knew that now. Everything he had, he'd built for himself atop the foundation his father had left for him. Cronus had left him nothing, his mother as much as she could, but in the end, Hades had created this. He had built the Styx District anew with only his friends to aid him. He owed them so much more than he owed Zeus. Hell, he owed Persephone more than he owed Zeus, and he wanted to do right by that. He would. He vowed it.

And the bolder Hades grew, the weaker Zeus appeared.

Yet there remained a strong urge to ask him the question that had plagued Hades for weeks. He hadn't seen Zeus since they reviewed the tapes, Hades and the others gathering what evidence they could. Midas still hadn't been found, but Hades felt that taking their time would work in their favor in the end. The longer Hades put off an attack on anyone, the more anxious Zeus would get. And the more prone he would be to making a mistake that could unveil some truths.

"You—" Zeus started.

"As I said, brother, I'm not going to tell you again," Hades sighed, a white-knuckle grip on his composure in place. "It's my party, and I would like to enjoy it with my family, so—"

"What about me!"

Zeus was practically foaming at the mouth. His voice was a scratched and torn thing, high-pitched and childish as it clashed with the music. Hades was well aware of the onlookers, but his eyes remained firm on his brother's bloodshot gaze. He knew now that there was no coming back from this. Not only was this his brother, this was the leader of Khaos Falls. Everyone here was witnessing the man who controlled their city throw this temper tantrum. They were also watching Hades' response to it.

The news would spread. Any credibility Zeus had left would be lost, and all power of his bond with Hades would deteriorate. And how could Hades clean up that mess when to do so would be to betray himself and everyone who trusted him?

He placed a hand on Zeus's shoulder and steered him back out into the hall. Thanatos, Hecate, and Persephone followed, shutting the doors behind them.

"We are family!" Zeus went on, striking his own chest with his finger so hard that Hades thought he might break it. "You're supposed to look out for me! That's your job."

"No, Zeus, it isn't," Hades returned.

Hades wanted to hit him. He wanted to hug him. He wanted to scream and shout and plead with Zeus to love him as he had loved Zeus.

However, it had clicked at long last. That was not possible. Zeus was not capable. He took and took and took. He had nothing to give. He was a glutton for sacrifice and accountable to no one. They — no, he, Hades had allowed Zeus to play Fate for so long that Zeus knew nothing else. Nor would he ever know anything else, certainly not at Hades' hand. Hades could only hope that he hadn't let his mother down, that he wouldn't start now.

"You are not my job," Hades asserted, his voice somehow level. "You are my brother, and we were supposed to take care of each other, but - it's only ever been about you. I have done everything I can for you, but you will never be satisfied, and I can no longer feed you. I will not. Certainly not from my own plate."

271

"Hades—"

"I'm sorry, brother, but you have to figure it out on your own now."

"You're just gonna leave me! Is this what you're gonna do, huh! After what you said when Mom—"

"Don't, Zeus. I've made my peace with what I told my mother."

"She told you—"

"She didn't tell him to kill himself for you!" Persephone shrieked, and only then did Hades feel the way she shook beside him. "You're a childish little brat, Zeus, and you don't deserve a damn thing he's given you!"

Zeus looked at her as though she'd slapped him. Judging by the way she curled her fist, Hades summed up that she'd considered it.

"You think you can speak to me about childish!" Zeus roared, louder than he'd been thus far, and Hades tensed. "You! Mommy let you play dress up for—"

Hades wasn't entirely sure how the next few moments played out as they all seemed to blur behind a red tint. One minute he was moving forward, and the next, Zeus was rolling around on the ground, dazed and unable to sit up. It took Hades a moment to register Persephone's raised fist, her body several steps in front of his, Hecate and Thana staring at her in awe. Zeus's hand rested loosely against his jaw, but Hades was sure he'd just about lost consciousness between her strike and his own intoxication. Hades reached out carefully, taking her hand out of the air and into his own before brushing his thumb over her knuckles and bringing them to his lips. Then he turned to the guard beside the door.

"Can you get him out of here please?" he requested softly. "And just so we're clear. He is not allowed back on this property without my express permission. If I am unavailable to give a verbal 'okay', he is to be turned away by any means."

The guard nodded fervently before calling for backup on his radio. It didn't take long for several other guards to arrive. They carted Zeus away, leaving Hades' mind reeling. Persephone placed her hand on his chest, and as expected, he exhaled. And he felt lighter than he had in a long time yet not entirely light. He knew this wasn't the end, but he hoped it was a beginning. If he could do it once, he could do it again, and he could keep doing it until Zeus realized he was serious. For now, they would continue to gather the evidence. But for tonight, he went back to enjoy his party.

To his relief, his guests welcomed him back into the festivities with open arms and warm smiles, mainly by following the example of Dionysos and Aphrodite. He ate chocolate and drank wine and laughed and joked with all of his nephews. He danced with Persephone and Hecate and Aphrodite and Athena, and they sang him a birthday song in front of the biggest cake he'd ever seen.

He'd thought it was a real poker table when Eros had wheeled it in, and it was absolutely as delicious as Eros' chocolates were. In all these years of skipping or completely forgetting his birthday, dinner with his family being the only exception, he never thought he was missing out on anything. Now, he thought he could make this an annual thing. More than that, he wanted to.

By the time he and Persephone stumbled into their suite, he had all but forgotten about Zeus's visit, and she took care to dampen the rest of the memory. They reached the hallway floor before he landed on his back, her mounting him. She ran her hands up his chest with a devilish grin.

"Careful with those hands now, baby," he warned with a smile. "They're dangerous."

"Mm, not to you," she started but seems to reconsider. "Well, maybe to you, but in a very different way. Just remember to stay in line, yeah?"

"Of course."

Soon, they were surrounded by discarded clothing, her hips rolling down against his, teasing his hardened shaft. The alcohol they'd indulged in all evening had the suite spinning, but he was only focused on her.

"This is the birthday present I was waiting for," he groaned, licking his lips.

"Is that right?"

She hummed, leaning down to kiss his chest and take hold of a nipple between her teeth. He hissed, spanking her ass twice before his hips bucked wildly. It was no lie. He'd wanted her all night. In fact, there were very few moments when he didn't. On any level, he had never wanted anyone with such vigor, such - urgency.

Pleasures of the flesh did not often draw him. They had always been something he could live without, and he knew that this need stemmed solely from his fathomless feelings for Persephone. He gave himself over to them with a willing recklessness, and they became an entity all their own, battering his ribcage from within.

He reached for her hips, but she caught his wrists, pinning them to the floor with a sly smirk. He could hardly suppress a shudder.

"Wait," was her simple instruction, and although he tested her hold briefly, he did obey.

She ground harder against his cock, her slick folds leaving a trail of arousal along the underside. He let his head fall back against the floor, eyes hooded, a guttural sound growing in his throat. Soon, panting breaths echoed through the hall, and he dug his heels into the carpet. She moves up higher and higher until his tip snags against the edge of her entrance, eliciting a pronounced moan from her that has him gritting his teeth. Still, she continues with her teasing, her hands moving from his wrists to tangle her fingers in his. This constant struggle for dominance each time they undressed was a thrill he'd never imagined enjoying so much. He wasn't used to being challenged. Now he yearned for it.

Soon enough, her hands were braced firm against his as she worked herself against him, sound after hallowed sound pouring from her parted lips. He cursed under his breath but didn't fight, the desire to be inside of her at war with the thrill of being so very close. When she finally did sheathe him, he was completely caught off guard. His roar shook the space around them, but she didn't give him time to adjust, riding him hard and fast.

When she released his hands to brace her palms against his thighs, he was too far gone to do anything but grip her hips and hold on. She looked devastating, head thrown back and breasts bouncing, a sinful song staining the air above. She moved with a poised grace he had learned to associate with her, but seeing it in this light was an entirely new experience.

He watched in delight as the first tremor racked her body. She came, calling his name like a hymn before she collapsed against his chest. He inhaled a large breath. Then he reached for her hair, tugging her head back to capture her lips in a searing kiss.

She groaned into his mouth, and he was already pushing himself up off of the floor. She clung to him as he stalked into the bedroom, ravishing his neck with tongue and teeth until he pulled her away and shoved her face down on the bed. Her attempts to turn over were thwarted by his large hand on the back of her neck.

"Uh uh," he grunted. "You got yours. Now it's time to get mine."

"Mm, this is how you want it, birthday boy?" she purred, propping her ass up.

He slapped it with his free hand, once with his palm and again with the back of it, and she whimpered. He kept her on her knees at the edge of the bed as he secured her hair in his fist. His knuckles pressed into her neck, keeping her cheek pinned to the mattress. Stroking his cock, he ran the head through her folds from front to back several times before sliding his shaft through her cheeks. She shivered with a gasp, and he teased her as she had teased him. Her fingers curled into the comforter, toes curling against his thighs before she spread her legs further apart. He stepped closer. Then he dragged his head down again until he could slide into her pussy, their collective groan rising like smoke. With a rough tug of her hair, he rammed his hips into hers, taking no time to ease into it.

"Fuck, Hades!" she damn near sobbed, banging a fist against the mattress, the comforter still clenched in it. "Please!"

"What?" he grunted. "Should I stop?"

"Don't - you dare - fucking - stop!"

As if he intended to.

He yanked her up further, further until he could get a hand on her breast, squeezing it. She threw her hips back into his to the best of her ability, meeting each stroke with eager fervor. Leaning against him, she gripped the back of his head, scraping her teeth none too gently against the side of his jaw as he sped up his stroke and tweaked her nipple. It felt too good. He wanted it to last forever. But he also needed a place to put all this power he felt inside of him tonight, power she'd inspired.

He pushed her back down, a sharp yelp signaling her surprise. Crawling atop her, he pinned her down by the shoulders and hammered into her with ruthless thrusts that had her moans saturating the space unadulterated. He growled, low in his throat, the sound of skin slapping against skin almost as loud as she was. He didn't slow down. He raced for the edge, addicted to the way her sensitive walls spasmed around him. She screamed his name again, her second orgasm sending shockwave after shockwave through them both as she bucked and writhed beneath him. He went harder still, desperate and demanding, until his own orgasm ripped through him with a careless cruelty.

"Fuck, Seph!"

It was a sharp cry that cracked his voice wide open as he rode it out, fingers gripping her shoulders hard enough to bruise as she buried her own deeper into the sheets. When he finally collapsed beside her, she glared at him before relaxing her body.

"Bastard," she grumbled.

"Are you complainin'?" he chuckled breathlessly, gathering her in his arms. She only sucked her teeth. "Besides, it's my party, right? I get to do what I want."

She turned in his arms to face him, though he found that her features had softened.

"Did you enjoy it then?" she asked.

He quickly nodded. "I did. Very much. —All I ask is that the chocolates be brought upstairs first thing tomorrow."

She rolled her eyes. "Don't worry. I made sure they were secured." She paused a moment, biting her lip. "You wanna take tomorrow off? Roll around in bed with me some more?"

He licked his own lips, the thought alone sending shivers down his spine despite just having cum. He knew what she was doing and why she was doing it, and for once, he could not find a single reason worth arguing, much less turning down a day at home. Although more accurately, he could never find a single reason worth turning down the chance to spend more time with her. He nodded again.

"As long as there's chocolate," he declared.

She chuckled, lightly smacking his chest before she pulled him into a kiss. He held her closer and melted into it, soaking up every ounce of passion she offered him and offering the same in return. He may have figured it out then. Or maybe it had been when he'd first found her in the sea of party guests as he stood on the balcony in Elysium. Either way, he knew now. He loved her, and there was nothing he wouldn't do to protect that.

Thirty

HADES

H ades slept in the next day. It had been a long time since he'd done anything of the sort, but he was grateful for the rest. When he woke up, he immediately rolled over and sought out Persephone's warmth. She curled into him like a flower to the sun the moment he touched her, and their first fuck of the day was quick and rough and filled with passion. She opened up fresh scratches on his back, and he felt himself losing more and more control each time he got lost in her. Just like she demanded him to. He eagerly paid the toll.

He was about to follow her to the shower when his phone began to ring. He knew by the tone that it was Charon, which immediately put him on high alert. Charon wasn't in the habit of calling him before seeing him in the morning. If there was an urgency, it was deferred to Hecate or Thana. Hades lunged across the bed for his phone, answering the call.

"Yeah?" he grunted, turning on his back.

Charon's tone was all business. "We found Midas."

Hades froze. "Where?"

"In the Harvest District, preparing for a trip it seems. He's downstairs in the security office now."

"I'll be down in fifteen."

The moment he stepped into the shower, Persephone sensed the shift in his demeanor, and he didn't attempt to hide it from her. He explained the development, and she urged him to hurry down, but before he climbed out of the shower, he had a thought.

"Come with me," he stated although it was not entirely a command.

"What?" she questioned, looking up at him.

"I want you there," he stated. "I mean, I - I know you don't want a leadership position, so you can say no, but if you do want to go, I'd like you to be there."

Her lips twitched as she continued to lather her body, but she didn't answer immediately. He waited patiently.

It wasn't that he wished to involve her in the mess per se. It was that he wanted her and everyone else to know that they were equals, that he trusted her to aid in making decisions, especially those that affected them all. He didn't want her to feel out of place in a district he hoped she might call her home.

After a moment, she nodded. "Okay, but - for moral support this time."

"That's acceptable," he sighed with a smile. "But I want you to know that if you want to do this together, I would like that. I trust your judgment and value your opinion."

"And my fists?"

His smile widened. "Very much so."

"As you should." She humbled, leaning up to kiss his cheek.

"And you're right. I don't want a leadership position, but we support each other, and I want to do my part."

"I'll take what I can get."

She smirked. "You better."

For once, it was a quick shower, and in ten minutes, they were exiting the bathroom. In twenty-two minutes, they were walking into the security office where Thana, Hecate, and Charon stood around the small table in the corner. Sitting with his back to the door was the tall, slim man with the discernible tattoo clawing up his neck. He squirmed in his chair as Hades entered, and when the leader of the Underworld rounded the table, the man's eyes immediately fell to his lap. Persephone moved to stand at his shoulder, just as imposing.

Hades felt stronger than ever.

Taking a seat opposite Midas, he rested one ankle on his knee and leaned back, threading his fingers together and resting his elbows on the arms.

"You know what I want to know," he began with a slow breath. "Let's just make this a very simple transaction."

"I'm not saying anything," Midas immediately shot back.

"You are." Hades didn't falter. "How you decide to say something is up to you. I know you work for Coeus, but you know I know that too. You knew it when you walked in here that day, and it's hard for me to believe you would be so careless as to let yourself be identified, especially considering you were so careful not to let the cameras see you start the fire. Therefore, I would be inclined to say that you wanted to be identified as one of Coeus's men as a countermeasure. What I want to know is who paid you to be their countermeasure, Midas."

Judging by the man's demeanor and the substantial lack of

surprise, Hades would say he was very much correct in his assumption. Midas remained quiet although his hands gripped the arms of his chair hard. Hades breathed out heavily, tapping the tips of his fingers together.

"Do you want money, Midas?" The man's shoulders fell, but he didn't look up. "You were getting ready to leave town I imagine, which leads me to believe that your - employer called you last night. They may have been spooked or upset, and they told you to run... far. Maybe they had been housing you, protecting you, but they realized they couldn't protect you from me. And they were right, so make this easy on yourself. Because I don't want you. I want a name."

"I want to leave," Midas growled.

"You don't talk, you don't leave," Thanatos said, leaning down beside Midas until his mouth hovered next to the man's ear. "It's that simple, my man."

Hades stood suddenly, and Midas jumped. At last, he looked up at the man looming over him. He swallowed hard.

This was one of the few instances where it paid off, what Zeus had done to Hades. Hades made himself a myth, but within it, Zeus made him a monster, passing off his most heinous and repugnant traits onto his older brother so that he could play hero any chance he got. That would be rectified in time, but first, Hades had to make good use of his reputation. Even if it meant uncovering a truth that hurt him more than it could ever hurt his brother.

"You think I'm stupid, Midas?" Hades asked, and his tone was a cold wind in the room that had his culprit shuddering. "There are two people it could have been. I call them both, tell them you gave them up the moment I got a hand on you, and we can see which gets to you first. Or you tell me, and I send you on your way. No one ever has to see or hear from you again. You choose, or I choose for you."

Hades could see the man warring with himself, frantic and fidgeting as he weighed his options. He'd evaded them this long. There was no doubt in Hades' mind that he was considering his odds of making it out of this office with his dignity intact. He wouldn't, but Hades didn't point that out just yet. He let him sweat a bit before speaking again.

"Tethys must have paid you quite handsomely, hm?" he asked, pressing the pad of his thumb against his lip. "I can't imagine it would come cheap, usurping your loyalty from her brother and using it to get you here. To attack my casino, my district. She knew it was a suicide mission one way or another, and I just wonder who would pay more for your spine — her or Coeus. Once she finds out—"

"It wasn't Tethys!"

Hades could see how Zeus and Midas might have gotten along. For one, their egos seemed to mirror one another in the confines of their outbursts. Midas looked ready to stand too before Thana's strong hand on his shoulder pinned him in his seat.

All of this was almost too easy, but there was little doubt left to cling to. All Hades needed was for Midas to say it. It ended much the same way. The only difference was that Tartarus had the chance to be an ally rather than a liability.

"Then who was it, Midas?" he questioned, skirting around the desk to perch at the edge beside the man. "Who ordered you to bomb my casino?"

"I can't - tell you!" he nearly whined, the veins in his neck threatening to burst.

"Because he'll kill you?" Midas's eyes widened. "Here is what you keep failing to account for. If you do not tell me, you won't live long enough for him to kill you. You endangered countless people, people I care about, people I would kill to protect twice over."

There must have been a change in Hades' voice that Midas sensed because he threw himself back in the chair and put his hands up.

"It was your brother, man!" he shrieked, shaking his head. "It was Zeus!"

Hades drew in a breath through his nose but didn't waver. "Go on."

"He paid me - big money. Huge. More than all my years with Coeus combined. He said all I had to do was take out the theatre, make sure it couldn't be used. Elysium was a bonus. He - he wanted me to plant it right before some show there, but - I couldn't do that, so I just did it when I saw you leave."

"You couldn't do it, huh? Why, Midas? Did you think I might spare you if you didn't kill anyone?"

Midas deflated, and Hades could tell he was on the verge of tears. Coward. Not because he was crying but because he was only crying for himself. "I - I know I'm not making it out of here alive, okay? I've heard the stories! I know!"

Hades surveyed him for a moment.

Yes, that was the rumor. People who came into the casino in possession of a problem for Zeus didn't usually leave, with or without it. Although more accurately, they didn't leave and go home. Many of them were many miles away from Khaos Falls. Others failed to heed Hades' warnings and had been swallowed up by Zeus's personal guard. The rumor was important though, he supposed. Or it was to Zeus's reign. Hades thought he could afford to keep it alive a bit longer.

He smiled. Midas's face fell into one of terror.

"Get him out of here."

Before Midas could manage another word, he was out cold, and Thana was on the radio calling Agamemnon and Leonidas. Within ten minutes, they had carted Midas to the service corridor and down the elevator to the garage, never to be seen again. At least in Khaos Falls. For now.

Charon removed the tape recorder from his pocket, hitting the "stop" button and setting it on Hades' desk. Evidence was important when you were planning what Hades was planning. Evidence was the crux of legitimacy.

Persephone had remained quiet throughout the entire meeting, but she moved to stand in front of Hades now. He could read the question in her eyes.

"He'll be on a ferry headed out of the city by tonight," he assured her.

She raised a brow. "So you just - send them off to be someone else's problem?"

"Not entirely. What do you know about Heraklion?"

She stared at him, understanding slowly donning on her face. "My mama said the only way to get there is on the back of a death wish, and it's a one-way trip."

He nodded. "His fate remains in his hands, he doesn't fall at mine, and the city is safe from him. It's the best-case scenario, I would say."

She smiled, nodding. "You are very good at this."

"I've had a lot of practice."

She moved to sit down, and Hades crossed his arms in a moment of thought. He had to be very careful where he treaded next. Now that he had his proof however, he could —no, he must move forward with the plan that had been coming together in his mind for the past few weeks. It was bold, and it was ambitious, and it would change everything in a most irrevocable way. There was no room for error.

"Hecate, call Nyx," Hades at last said, eyes distant, still on the future. "Let her know that we're coming to dinner if she will have us. Make it discreet. No one outside of this room is to know of it." Hecate nodded. "Charon, I want eyes on Zeus from sun up until sundown and every hour that falls in between. I want all of his movements tracked and noted. No exceptions."

Charon nodded too.

"What's the move?" Thana questioned.

Hades' words held worlds within them. "The only move we have left to make."

Thirty-One

PERSEPHONE

Despite Hades' insistence, Persephone hadn't attended dinner at Tartarus. While she liked the idea of being directly involved in the politics of the district she resided in, it wasn't something she wanted to make a habit of. She'd attempted to find the meaning in it when she'd accompanied Hades downstairs to interrogate the arsonist, but it reminded her too much of the destiny her mother had tried to prescribe to her. She would gladly give her input when necessary, but she would rather leave the leadership to Hades and his council. They were more than capable. They'd made it this far without her.

Her only concern at the moment was ensuring that Hades stood his ground against Zeus. This dinner seemed to prove that he was. Once he handed over his blueprint to Nyx and Erebus, there really was no going back. Nonetheless, she did her part that night when Aunt Hestia invited her and Aphrodite out to dinner.

It had been a welcome surprise. Persephone missed her aunt and hated that this line in the sand drawn for her mother had to extend to Hestia as well. Hestia hadn't lectured nor warned nor mined for information. She had simply enjoyed the company of her girls, and they had done the same. It had been a breath of fresh air, something Persephone had needed after everything going on the past few weeks.

Before dinner concluded though, Persephone did take the time to brief them on Hades' next steps. She'd asked his permission to do so, and he had been eager to give it. She figured if she told them, not only could she make sure they were prepared, but they could also do the same for her. She would of course need to have this conversation with Demeter as well, and so she sought their advice on how best to tackle the subject with her mother. In the end, they had all agreed that it was best to handle it head-on, but they each knew it could only really go one way. Persephone would simply have to push through it.

Throughout the night, her mind had continued to wander to Hades and Hecate and their dinner in Tartarus. She'd been eager to get home and check in on him, but she'd still expected to get back to the casino well before he did. Instead, she found him in his office, tugging at his tie and staring down at several documents.

She walked in, moving around to lean against the desk at his side, undoing his tie for him with expert fingers. He looked up at her with a tired smile.

"How did it go?" she asked.

He leaned back in his chair, expelling a heavy breath as if the knot of his tie had been holding it hostage. She took note of the lines in his face, the thickness of his beard, the slight droop of his eyes. He had never looked older than he did right now, and she knew he had the weight of the world on his shoulders. If she could alleviate him of it, she would, but she knew he needed to choose to put it down himself. All she could do was show him what the finish line looked like if he did.

"I think it went well," he concluded, licking his lips. "They're supportive of our agenda. Granted, we had to make a few promises, but none that were unexpected."

"You knew what they would ask for before you walked in there." It wasn't a question.

"I never would have walked in there if I didn't."

"But - they've been locked down for weeks. How did you know they would even see you?"

"I made some educated guesses and calculated risks, I assure you, but after I knew it was Zeus, everything else made much more sense."

"To who?" Definitely not to her.

He chuckled, taking her hand in his. "The lockdown was a tactic, nothing more. They knew they would put us on edge. They just wanted what they were promised, and they figured I would inevitably work it out and fulfill that promise with a few extra bells and whistles for the trouble."

"Fair enough."

"My thoughts exactly. But when the bombing happened, I think they knew they had a choice to either break lockdown and declare their innocence or let me find the culprit on my own. If they chose the latter, they could milk the chaos that the bombing caused for their own gain. Again, they were betting on me coming to them."

"They trusted you to. To do the right thing, the right way."

He nodded once after a brief pause as if he hadn't considered it that way. She wasn't surprised. It was why she'd pointed it out.

"Whether it was to accuse them or make peace, Nyx knew she would have gotten her audience."

"So she knew you wouldn't have just attacked without talking to her."

He nodded again, exhaling heavily. "I'm sure many people in Tartarus feared that, but Nyx and Erebus know better. While there remains some - bitterness about the way Zeus has handled his charge, they know who I am. They know how I do things. I came to Nyx and her father when we took power. I was upfront and honest with them, and I showed them what would happen if they fought it. Then I negotiated the terms of the transfer, and I gave them as much as I could without failing my cause. They know I always state my purpose before I do anything, and unlike Zeus, they still believed it would apply to them even now. They gambled on that, and they won."

She looked at him, awe in her eyes before she burst into laughter. "You are something else. Are you sure you're real? Because you got me questioning it again."

He looked up at her, and beneath all that fatigue was a glint in his eyes, one born purely from excitement. It made her heart flutter, as well as her stomach. That was the glint he got as he kissed down her body, hands following his trail, tongue hot against her skin. She loved that damn glint. He answered only with a kiss to the inside of her wrist, and she shivered. Yep, definitely real.

"I talked to my aunt a bit after dinner," Persephone offered almost breathlessly before she forgot to, moving to perch herself on his lap. She nearly purred when he wrapped his arm around her waist. "She thinks my mother will go for it, after she goes off for a bit of course, but I'll talk to her first thing tomorrow."

"What opposition would she have?"

"Well, it's you for one." They both smiled. "But I think with the terms you're offering, she'll see the benefit of good business."

"That's all it is at the end of the day. I'm not trying to buy your mother's approval."

She brushed her hand over his cheek. "You don't need it. You have mine."

He leaned into her touch, offering a tight smile. She knew that turmoil lay behind those beautiful brown eyes, rife with questions he still poses for the world and for himself. What he plans to do is big, bigger than he's ever dared plan, and he'll be the face of it. No more hiding in the shadows, no more disguising himself in darkness, no more being used as a vehicle for the conquest of others. His solitude will be compromised, his sanctuary under constant scrutiny. The world he shaped for his brother will be destroyed and built anew. It isn't what he wants, and that is exactly why it is the only viable option. It's the only way for Khaos Falls to know peace. And for him to as well.

"Tomorrow, after I speak with my mama, we're going to celebrate," she said, her fingers tracing along his eyebrow.

"Oh yeah? What are we celebrating?"

She offered a wry smile. "You."

"Didn't we just do that?"

"Mm, you're right." She hummed in faux contemplation, eyes climbing to the ceiling before she looked back at him. "Then us. And the future."

His lips twitched. "I think I can get on board with that."

"Oh, sorry, did I forget to mention it's not a choice?"

She wrapped her arms around his neck as his body shook with laughter. Fates, she loved this man.

"I promise that even when others think I'm in charge, I will never forget who truly is," he mumbled into her neck as he buried his head there.

"I appreciate it. But don't worry. I have no problem setting the record straight."

"I have no doubt about that."

She didn't tell him anywhere near enough how he inspired her, to be stronger, to be better, to be kinder. She doubted he would believe her if she did. Hecate and Aphrodite both had said much of the same thing countless times — they were good for each other.

Persephone never thought anyone would be good for her. Seeing her mother thrive after her father's departure and Aphrodite rule all on her own absent her father's influence had led her to this conclusion that she would only be hindered by personal attachment. Especially to a man, which her mother swore would never do any woman any good.

She knew that was what she was supposed to believe. Adonis had only enhanced that, always expecting her to fit into this box he himself had constructed, the doting wife who picked him up and carried him through to his own power and place in the world. When it wasn't her, he had turned to Aphrodite to both be that for him and convince Persephone to be that too.

He had been greedy and naive, and both Seph and Aphrodite had departed from Demeter's house with the intention of it being just the two of them, staking their claims and chasing their dreams without the convoluted connections of people who would demand they come to heel. People like Adonis, like their fathers, like Demeter, like Zeus, each of whom had created this falsity in Persephone's mind about what it would be like to love any man.

But Demeter, who laid that foundation, had never known a man like Hades, who reminded Persephone that there were in fact men who understood what it was like to be on the outside looking in. Men who had been forced to fight for everything they had including their identity, to carry the weight of the world with the hopes that society would grant them nothing more than the simple right to exist if they held it aloft long enough. Men who wanted to be good, not just for themselves but for others.

Hades was not perfect, it was true. With Zeus at the helm, she knew he must have done many questionable things to earn both his masculinity and his reputation, but he had never allowed those things to change him, to turn him cold, to turn him ugly. He was good, not just to her but to anyone given the opportunity to truly see him. More than that, he wanted to be, and he was proving that right now. He was trying to recreate the world in his image, and while he may have thought it no better than one made in Zeus's, she could not think of any world she would rather live in.

How was she ever to know she would find the very antithesis of every person who had ever harmed her hiding in the depths of the notorious Underworld, wrapped in a riddle and shielded by legend? What a pleasant surprise. She was determined to protect it at all costs.

"We're partners in this," he uttered against her lips. "Equals. Regardless of how involved you decide to be, I make no decisions without coming to you first."

"I trust you to make those decisions," she stated, eyes fluttering open. "You have to trust yourself too, Hades. I'm not saying I won't help you, but this is your move, your path, and you can do this. People believe in you. That is why Tartarus agreed, why Aphrodite did, and why your nephews will too."

"And your mother?"

She chuckled. "She may not see everything I see, but by the time I'm done, she'll see what matters right now, which is that you're a good leader."

His expression shifted into something akin to confusion. "And what do you see?"

"That you're a good man."

"And do you think a good man can do this?"

"I think you can do this, Hades." She pressed her lips to his forehead. "Only you."

Persephone took her newfound determination with her to her mother's house the next morning. As breakfast was served, Demeter talked about mundane happenings and generic gossip as if Persephone had never left home in the first place, but Persephone knew she was stalling. Maybe she thought she could eat up whatever time Persephone had without having to commit to anything, but Demeter failed to understand what was occurring here. Persephone had no issue clarifying for her. She had all the time in the world right now.

"Mama," she urged before Demeter could go off on another tangent about Apollo's planned renovations for the local sports arena. "You've been at it for an hour. Let's talk business now."

Demeter leveled her with a stare that once would have sent Persephone scurrying from the room. Her eyes narrowed atop her high cheekbones, the dark skin that bracketed them crinkling visibly. Persephone did not flinch. She did not squirm. She stared straight back at her mother.

Demeter's silence had always been a more devastating weapon than anything that could come out of her mouth. That had not changed. What had changed was Persephone. Demeter had power, but she did too, and she no longer came to see her mother without it.

"Hades gave you fair terms, I would say," she went on when Demeter didn't speak.

"Yes, it would seem so," Demeter said slowly, her long fingers tapping against her glass.

"But..."

Demeter rolled her eyes. "Persephone, you ask me this knowing my history with Hades."

"No, I don't. In fact, I don't think you have a history with Hades. I think you have a history with those who preceded Hades, and you're holding it against him because he's the only one left to hold it against."

"History repeats itself, Darling."

"If that were the case, you wouldn't be perpetually upset with me." The elder scoffed. "Now that is not fair."

"Neither is your treatment of him, but this isn't about fair, Mama. We've given you this deal for two reasons and two reasons alone. I love you, and Hades respects you. We are trying to make it so that history stops repeating itself. We will do that with or without you."

"Oh, is that what this is?" She snorted, and Persephone's blood boiled. "Because what it looks like is two brothers fighting over a toy, and this city is not a toy, Persephone."

"And you would rather have Zeus playing Fate—"

"I would rather have neither of them!" Demeter slapped her hands against the table. "If he trusts you so much, why not elevate our district, let a grown woman handle things, and when I die, you can do the same?"

"Because you have a grudge against everyone in this city, unfounded or otherwise."

"And yet they remain fed. They remain supplied. I can separate business from personal life just fine, and—"

"Mama." The tone of Persephone's voice stopped her mother

cold. "You cannot defend yourself to me. You are a great mother and a great leader, but you have biases, ones that cannot be rectified right now."

"I may have less biases if I didn't have to worry about idiots undermining me all of the time."

"And that's a fair point, which is why we are offering you—"

"You are not offering me anything I could not take for myself!"

"Yet you haven't—"

"You are children, all of you! I have been around longer than each and every one of you! All three of those brothers, you, Aphrodite. You two learned from ME. I have watched the crown change many hands, and I have watched it corrupt each and every one of them! Hades is no different!"

"So why would you be?"

Whatever Demeter saw in her daughter's face now must wipe the answer she'd readied on her tongue clean off, and Persephone was overwhelmed with gratitude. Even if she refused to let it show.

She would not deny the fact that Demeter made good points, but she also knew her mother. She had never done anything without ulterior motive. She needed control. Too much of it could spoil her, and Persephone had seen it, not only with herself but with her aunt.

She looked over at Hestia, who sat beside her sister with her head bowed and lips pursed. They had discussed it the night before, predicting every possible objection Demeter would have. They both knew the truth. She could lead her district. She could not lead a city, lest it be brought to its knees before her to do her bidding first and foremost.

This limitation on her power had been the only thing to keep Demeter in check. If she had the numbers and the resources to go to war with the sons of Rhea, she would have done so years ago. She may not be Zeus. She would certainly make a better leader than him, but every other leader in Khaos Falls would too. The fact of the matter was that trusting Demeter was as difficult as trusting their current leader. It just looked different. It looked like safety, and that was far more dangerous.

"If it weren't for Hades," Demeter hissed, eyes flashing, "we would not be in this situation to begin with."

"This isn't up for debate, Mother," Persephone continued, calm even as her mother seethed with rage. She'd brought a page from Hades' book with her, keeping her composure, clinging to it. "As I said, we are going forth with or without you. This is a courtesy. It is an assurance that I have your best interest in mind."

"That does not mean Hades does," Demeter growled, but Persephone could see she was beginning to wane.

"But he has my best interest in mind, and so it coincides."

She tilted her head. "Do you honestly believe that man cares for you, Persephone? Do you think that—"

"I do because he does. He and I will do this together, as equals, and—"

Demeter cut her off with a barking laugh. "Persephone, darling, please, you cannot—"

"That isn't up for debate either."

The dining hall felt smaller than it ever had, the tension suffocating. Persephone held strong though. She would not let her mother run away with this conversation. She may never be able to crawl back out. That was what Demeter does. That was what Demeter was capable of. Persephone now had to show her —and herself— what Persephone was capable of.

"You expect me to sit here and submit to this - this promise that when I die, Hades will inherit my district!"

297

"No, I will."

"He will lord over the entire city!"

"He will see that it has peace. My birthright is mine. That is also not up for debate."

"You don't want it!"

"No, I don't, but I am your daughter. I'll fulfill my duties in whatever way I have to. I'm just not leaving the stage to do it."

"Then how can you be sure! How can I!"

"What other option do you think you have?" They stared at each other for ages before Persephone sighed. "I am not asking you to trust him, Mama. I am asking you to trust me."

She knew Demeter may not think it fair, but it was all there was left to do. The elder continued to stare her down, but still, Persephone did not yield. She waited, her patience impeccable and her resolve impenetrable. She was not backing down, not today, not ever again.

Demeter reclined in her seat.

"Expansion all the way to Chimera Street," she stated, repeating the first line of Hades' offered terms of her alliance.

"Yes," Persephone confirmed. "That includes Terpsichore's school."

"But you want to give Terpsichore full control of the board and finances."

"Yes. Zeus has been shortchanging her ever since it opened. It's her school. She'll pay your property tax at your rate, but nothing more."

"And - who gets Olympus once this little - feud is over?"

Persephone fought the urge to roll her eyes. "Let us worry about that, Mama. You will get all the details the moment they happen, I'm sure." She smiled. Her mother did not. "Can you agree to that?"

"On one condition."

Of course. "What is that?"

"If, at any time, I do decide I have a concern, I want to be able to speak to you directly about it."

"That's not a problem, but again, I want you to remember that when it is business, I am not your daughter. You aren't going to strong-arm me into agreeing to anything, and I won't promise you anything without Hades' agreement."

"Is that what it comes down to? You're going to let a man—"

"Nope, we're not doing that." At last, Persephone stood up, pressing her fingers into the tablecloth as she met her mother's gaze head-on. "You and I have had our share of horrible men, cis men specifically. And I know why you're worried. I heed your warnings, but I am going to say this once and only once. Hades is not my father, and I am not that scared little girl I used to be. Some decisions we make together. Some decisions we make on our own. Where the city is concerned, he has the final say, and I stand by that because I trust him to make those decisions now. He knows he's made mistakes, and he's trying to fix them, but he doesn't need me or anyone else spoon-feeding him the right thing to do. But we do communicate, and we do compromise, and how things work between us doesn't have to make sense to you, but you will respect it. You will respect me. And I will not speak to you if all you are going to do is tear him down. Or tear me down for that matter. Is that understood?"

It had to end now. They both knew it. Demeter had run out of excuses, and Persephone wouldn't take another anyway. Moving down the table, she kissed both her aunt and her mother on their cheeks. Then she bid them good day and exited the kitchen, aware of their glances. It was only once she reached the front hall that she heard footsteps behind her. She knew it wasn't Adonis this time, so she fully expected her mother to come charging into a whole new argument right there inside the door. She came to a halt and turned around, only to be swept into her aunt's arms.

"I'm proud of you," Hestia whispered into her hair. "I've always been proud of you, and I always will be, but - damn."

They both laughed as they pulled apart, Hestia's eyes welling with tears.

"I wouldn't be here without you," Persephone assured her, her own eyes pricking. "You're as brave as they come, Auntie."

"Oh, I don't know about that, but - you make me wanna be. Just - don't be a stranger, alright? And don't ever think you can't come home. I don't mean if things go wrong. I just mean - to know it's still here."

Persephone nodded. "And - you're welcome across the Styx anytime, you know."

Hestia laughed now, looking down at the floor. She seemed to be considering something. When she looked up again, the tears had begun to fall, and Persephone wiped them away with her hand before Hestia swatted it away playfully.

"I was at the first show," Hestia whispered under her breath.

"What?" Persephone's eyes widened. "Why didn't you tell me? I could've gotten you tickets. You could've sat with 'Dite."

"First of all, I'm capable of buyin' my own damn tickets." They chuckled again, and Hestia shook her head. "And second, I just wanted to witness it all, to make sure it was everything you wanted it to be. Everyone loved you. And by the end of it, I knew you were safe. You were where you belonged, and - that's all I wanted for you, all I ever wanted for you and for Aphrodite. I wanted you to be able to walk through this world and never question that you had a place in it."

"I don't - anymore. I don't question it, and I don't think I ever will again."

"Well if you do, you call your auntie right away. Got it?"

Persephone grinned. "I got it."

As she left the house of Demeter, Persephone found herself giddy with excitement. She hadn't just proved her worth to her mother. She'd proven it to herself. Without the stage, without the silks, she still had her wings. And as her aunt had said, she still belonged. That didn't mean that she couldn't fly. It just meant she had a place to land.

She never knew how much she wanted a place like that until now.

HADES

The office was quiet. It wasn't Hades' main office hovering above the casino floor but rather the one beneath the casino where Hades' most exclusive meetings were held, those not for show of force or public diplomacy. Instead, it offered the utmost privacy.

Hades' family sat quietly around the large conference table, Poseidon and Amphitrite at one end and Hades at the other. Between them on either side sat Dionysos, Hermes, Hephaestus, Athena, and Ares. Hades was relieved that the latter two had shown up at all. He looked between each of them, pride and nerves tangling together behind his eyes. He doubted he had ever been forced to have a more difficult conversation with them, but it had to be done.

"I gathered you all here because I love you all," Hades said after a long time of contemplating. "I also respect you. While I would rather you keep what we discuss here today quiet for the time being,

I will not force you to. I will be clear that this is going to take place no matter what."

He let that sink in for a moment, but no one spoke, each of them watching their uncle in patient anticipation.

"I am removing Zeus from power," he proceeded. No one reacted outright, but Athena squirmed in her seat, and Poseidon's eyes widened. "That has already been decided, and I do believe it is the best course of action at this time. Of course, this means many things are going to change. I will take control of Khaos Falls as a whole, but decisions will not be made without taking every leader's opinion into consideration, and each district will be given full sovereignty over its own affairs.

"First though, I would have to appoint a new leader of Olympus. I know Zeus has made many promises to several of you, and I want to honor your expectations as much as ensure the safety of your district. So I ask first and foremost, Hephaestus." He made eye contact with the man. "You being the eldest, do you want control of Olympus?"

Hephaestus stared at his uncle for a long time. Ares' eyes were firm on the desk with his brows knitted, and Athena stared straight ahead at the wall over his shoulder. Hades allowed Hephaestus to consider it for as long as he needed, and at last, Hephaestus shook his head.

"That's never been for me," he concluded. "I've made peace with living outside of a district leadership position, and I've grown to like it a whole lot, so no, Uncle. You appoint the leader you see fit, and I'll help them as I help you."

"Well then, I have something else I'd like to speak to you about when we have more time. You can think of it as a promotion from your current dealings, for the good of the city."

Hephaestus nodded. "Of course, Uncle, I'd like to hear it."

Hades returned the gesture before he looked between Ares and Athena. "That brings me to my next question then. Do you two think you can do this together? Run Olympus?"

Athena was the first to respond when Ares seemed to have no intention to, but her voice was thin. "I - I believe we are capable of anything, Uncle, but I doubt Hera would be at all thrilled."

"Let me handle Hera. She is of no concern to me right now. I am planning for the future. Your futures. You are who I'll leave the city to when I'm gone, and I need to know each and every one of you can hold your own."

Ares looked up at Athena at last. Hades knew they can. When Ares wasn't around his mother, and he and Athena weren't around his father, they got along just fine. They may not be blood, but they were family. However, he knew they each had their reservations about this coup in general, and Athena was also the first to voice them.

"With all due respect, why now, Uncle? I - I trust you have your reasons, and I also trust your judgment, but - is this about the deal with Tartarus? Shouldn't we be focusing on them right now? I mean they attacked the casino. That's a call for war, and we need a united front. Removing him now might show weakness."

Hades looked between them all, his eyes landing on Dionysos, who hadn't looked up from his hands in his lap. While he was very much a people person, he was no politician, and he'd always hated this part of the leadership. It was why he and Hermes worked so well together, and why he needed Hermes in the first place. But Hades worried how he would react when he found out what Zeus had done to Elysium, even if it hadn't been about him at all. While Dio did a great job of pretending he no longer cared about Zeus's rejection, any reiteration of it always made him uncomfortable. Hades wished more than anything in that moment that he had taken the boy aside prior to this meeting, but it was too late now. He had to continue.

He huffed. "It isn't just about the deal with Tartarus. I've made peace with Tartarus, and they will be lifting the lockdown shortly."

"What?" Athena scoffed. "But they-"

"They didn't." She gave him a quizzical look. Dio did too, looking up with those big eyes fixed on Hades. "Zeus is the one that attacked the casino." The air in the room seemed to disappear, and now everyone's eyes were on him. "He paid one of Coeus's men a lot of money to frame Tartarus, but he made the call."

"Just because you stood up to him?" Dionysos croaked, his face falling, and Hades' chest hurt.

"I think it was a lot more than that to him, son."

They were quiet for a long time, and Hades let them all ruminate until at last, Athena spoke up once more.

"I know what you're doing is the right thing to do, Uncle," she assured him, meeting his eyes. "But it is difficult. I - we have been loyal to Zeus our whole lives. And - he took me in when I had no one. You've done a lot for me too, and I trust you, but still."

"I understand that," he returned with a sympathetic look. "I have been loyal to him most of my life as well, and this is not a decision that was made lightly, and it certainly was not made easily, but I am asking you to trust me now. I have done everything else I possibly can to make Zeus see the error of his ways, but lives are at stake now. He's grown vengeful, and that can't pass." He leaned forward in his seat, resting his forearms upon the table and clasping his hands. "This particular decision regarding the leadership doesn't have to be set in stone. We can renegotiate the terms as we go, draw lines if we must. The territory is going to get smaller. Tartarus will take the port that Zeus originally promised to them as a sign of good faith. Demeter is going to expand some in order to minimize any losses that might be caused by whatever financial disasters we find in Zeus's wake, but there will be room for you as long as I live. I promise you. Both of you."

The two of them were quiet again, but eventually, they nodded. Not to their uncle but to each other. He smiled.

"Good," he said. "That's good. That's what I wanted. Now." He looked to Dio and Hermes. "You two, I have something for you as well."

"You know you don't have to bribe us, right, Uncle?" Hermes asked, raising a brow. "Our loyalty has always been to you."

"Oh, I know, and this is not a bribe. It's a benefit for us all. I'll give you access to any plot of land this side of the river for another vineyard and another port. It should help increase trade and production, and it will keep us out of Tartarus's way until things truly settle."

Dio recovered quickly, grinning as wide as his face allowed, and Hermes clapped his hands. Hades couldn't say he wasn't relieved. He'd do anything for that reaction.

"Thank you, Uncle," they both said before fumbling a high five.

"We'll do right by you always," Dio added, sobering as quickly as he could.

"Speaking of which," Hades continued, trying to hide his smile. "It does come with a condition. I need you two to get with Apollo and make plans for another theatre. Having only one doesn't cut it. It cost us a lot. Not only can we alleviate that hurt in the future, we can create more spaces for entertainment. It may also give people more reason to visit, right?"

Dionysos hooted with giddy laughter. "Absolutely!"

It went about as well as Hades expected it to. Making them happy had been of the utmost importance to him, and he was glad he'd been able to do it. Turning to his baby brother, who had been quiet this entire time, he furrowed a brow.

"What do you think, Si? Amphi?" he inquired. "Any objections?"

The two looked at each other before turning to him and shaking their heads. The relief on Poseidon's face was evident and outright. Hades knew he hated confrontation and stayed away from Zeus as much as he possibly could for that very reason, but Hades also knew that his baby brother had his own concerns, concerns he felt he was never able to voice. Hades had fought hard to give Poseidon his territory in the opposite corner of Khaos Falls if only to ensure he had a place that he could go to get as far away from the other two. He often wondered if Poseidon had believed it was because Hades himself had wanted the distance, but that couldn't be further from the truth. He simply believed Poseidon would be happier that way.

The fact remained. Hades had allowed his caretaking of Zeus to rob him of all of his time with Poseidon. He had effectively neglected his blood brother in pursuit of Zeus's happiness, and that was certainly not what Rhea had made him promise. Hades hated that it took so long for him to realize it. He'd missed out on so much. He just hoped there was still something to salvage.

"Thank you, Hades," Poseidon said at last, his baby face a picture of serenity. "I think you're doing the right thing, and - we're behind you. No matter what, we trust you."

"I know, little brother," Hades returned with a soft smile. "I'm just sorry it's taken me this long."

"Better late than never, right?"

"Right. —Are you ready for your condition?"

Poseidon managed a lopsided smile. "What's that?"

"The two of us have dinner once a week, and then, we all have family dinner at least monthly. Is that reasonable for you all?"

They each signaled their agreement in turn, Poseidon more enthusiastic than Hades had seen him in a long time. He'd fully embraced his choice, but for the first time, he was proud of it. He knew for sure now that he was doing the right thing. That he could be a good man and still do good for his family. He did not have to be a tyrant. He did not have to be Zeus.

"Alright, that's all then," he sighed. "By the end of the month, it all changes. I'll be by to see you all soon enough."

Athena stopped him. "And - if it doesn't go... If he doesn't go quietly?"

Hades could not deny that he had failed to consider that possibility, but even now that he attempted to, he could not come up with an answer that would appease anyone. Because it did not matter. He had to follow through with this. There was no going back or changing plans. One way or another, Zeus would be removed from power, and Hades had made peace with the risks that came with that. Or at least he wanted to believe he had.

"He will," he stated with a firm nod. " I think my terms for him are quite reasonable. He will still live comfortably in the city, and if he can learn from his actions, I might give him more freedom here in my own district. Regardless, none of you will have to worry."

He knew Athena probably had more love for Zeus than anyone in this room save Hades himself. She may not have been his kid, but he had always been more attentive in raising her than he had been with any of his sons. This was hard for her without a doubt, but she was the most rational and intelligent person Hades knew. And he knew she understood that this had to happen.

"Just know this," Hades continued. "As long as I breathe, you will be taken care of, and you will want for nothing."

As the others filed out of the room, Dionysos hung back, and Hades approached him with curiosity in his gaze. As soon as he was close, the younger man turned to him and wrapped his arms around his middle. Hades was only surprised for a moment before he embraced him. No matter how large Dio got —and he was large, taller than both Zeus and Hades with twice the bulk of a bear cub— his uncle still struggled to see past the boyish features he'd possessed since youth. In fact, he still held fast to that youth to this day.

It was Dionysos who had taught Hades how to love in a warm way. He only wished he would have had more time with him, with all of his nephews, that he would have stood up to Zeus the first time he'd given up on Hephaestus or made Dionysos cry. That should have been more than enough. The worst part was that Hades knew Dio would never fault him. Still, Hades wanted to do right by him, by all of them, the way they had always done right by him.

"Thank you, Uncle," Dio breathed again, resting his head against Hades' chest. "I'm proud of you, you know. You - I wouldn't want anyone else but you as my dad."

"And I could not ask for a better son," Hades assured him, his voice thick with emotion.

"I promise I'll make you all the pomegranate wine you want."

Hades chuckled. "In the end, that's what this is all about, you know."

When Dio pulled back, his eyes were red, and his cheeks were damp. The boy with the biggest heart and the biggest need to please, he was every bit a better man than any who had raised him — or refused to. Hades patted his cheeks and brushed the tears away.

"I am proud of you," the elder said. "I am so proud, Dio. You make me proud every single day. Don't you ever forget that."

Dio grinned through his tears. "Not just for the wine?"

"No, son, not just for the wine. That's an added bonus, but I'd be proud of you no matter what you did. And remember, you're my boy, always."

They hugged again for a long time before Dio pulled away at last, and they headed back up the stairs toward the casino.

"What are you gonna do now?" Dio inquired, slipping his hands into his pockets.

"Mm, Persephone wants to go out to dinner," Hades replied.

That impossible grin made a comeback as he patted his uncle's shoulder. "You know, I'm really glad I introduced the two of you. She's a good influence."

"And I am grateful to you every day for it." His laughter lingered in the air. "Come on, walk me out. I have to meet her in the garage, and I believe I'm already late."

They made their way through the casino, and Hades felt a peace he had never felt. Things were looking up and falling into place. He put an arm around Dio's shoulders and kissed his forehead, exhaling as they exited the building.

The sun was setting now, and Hades checked his watch, which continued to change hands between him and Persephone to this day. As they came to a stop beside his car, a much smaller vehicle than the SUV he'd driven on their first date, he looked back toward the doors. No sooner did he do so than was Persephone exiting out of them, coming towards the two in a sleek black dress and a wild smile. They were both successful today. He could see it in her face. He smiled too. Dio elbowed his side with a grin.

"She is amazing," Hades breathed as though the nudge knocked it out of him.

"Don't mess that up, Uncle," Dio warned.

"I wouldn't think of it."

Persephone waved at them both before gesturing towards Hades' car.

"New ride, huh?" she called out across the garage.

"I was told this one would be better for the environment," he returned with a grin.

Dio howled in some generalized celebration before running towards Persephone with his arms spread wide. He was no more than a foot away from her when there was a loud boom that echoed through the parking garage. It sounded like a bomb.

Or a gunshot.

Thirty-Three

PERSEPHONE

T ime slowed down.

Dio was running towards her. Then he wasn't. Why wasn't he running towards her?

The shot rang out. His face contorted in confusion. His body fell forward, and from one breath to the next, Persephone was catching him in her arms.

What was most chilling about the moment was the silence. That was all there was outside of the shot itself. No screams, no cries, no shouts, no yells, no breaths. Or at least, none that she could hear. It had all been muted.

She dropped to her knees, cradling him to her chest as she turned him over to look at his face. He looked up at her with dull eyes and a slack jaw, and he tried to smile. It was stained. Someone had stained that beautiful smile. All she could see was the blood. Everything was red.

Then the silence was shattered in the most violent of ways, disrupted and destroyed by a wail. Hades' wail. The ground shook.

She felt like it might give way beneath the sound. It pierced her straight through, hitting her heart and leaving her cold. Her blood turned to slush in its wake.

She didn't know how much time passed. At some point, Hades had Dio in his arms, and Dio was clinging to him, and Persephone was calling for an ambulance. Security was swarming the parking garage, but no one saw. No one realized the danger, the dread, the destruction. No one knew what had happened. They only knew that something was terribly wrong. They misunderstood. Dionysos had been hurt. Everything was wrong!

Persephone did not remember how she got to the hospital. When her conscious mind started working again, she was in a stark white hallway pacing while Aphrodite, Hephaestus, Amphitrite, and Hermes alternated between sitting and standing around her. Hecate was on the phone at the end of the hall near the door, and Thanatos was leaning against the wall watching her and talking to Poseidon beside him.

How did they all get here?

Charon looked like an omen in front of the doors that Asklepios and his staff had wheeled Dio through. Hades had refused to let him go alone, but Persephone didn't know how far they had allowed him to follow. She didn't know what to do with her hands. She didn't know what to do without Hades.

She could not even begin to think about what they would do without Dionysos.

The only sound that rivaled the one Hades had made in the parking garage was the wrathful shriek of Athena as she blew into the building. Her rage shook its very foundation, and Persephone flinched.

She'd never seen the younger woman in anything other than

perfect composure. At the moment, Athena looked like the smallest thing could turn her to ruin... Or cause her to turn everything around her to ruin. Or both.

"Where is he!" Athena demanded from a nurse, and Persephone could tell by the hollow scratch of her voice that it wasn't the first time. "Where is he! Tell me now!"

The nurse tried to reason with her, but there was no reasoning. Nothing about this could be reasoned with. There was no rationality to a world without Dio's laughter, to a day that imbibed his pain. Athena screamed again and again, and Persephone felt the tears slip down her cheeks in hot streams. She wondered if love alone could heal a gunshot wound. She would not mind trying.

Athena started towards the swinging doors, but she was halted by them swinging out towards her. Hades appeared, disheveled and distraught, and again, he looked so much older than he was. Everyone halted. The air in the hall thinned. He held up his hands.

"Asklepios says he's going to be fine," Hades croaked after a long moment, and a collective exhale echoed through the space. Persephone's lungs burned with the strain.

"Where is he?" Athena demanded again, but her voice had softened —or rather, weakened— thin as an eggshell. It could crack at any moment. "Can I see him?"

Hades gripped her shoulders. "A little longer. You can go in first, as soon as Asklepios gives the okay."

Athena seemed to war with it for a moment before she nodded. Then she hugged Hades around his middle, and he wrapped his arms around her shoulders.

Persephone's mind kept racing. She was afraid of what happened when it stopped. She wasn't sure she knew how to deal with that.

She looked down the hall again and met Hecate's gaze. She was still on the phone, no doubt trying to get confirmation from security, but they already knew. Each and every one of them knew who was responsible. The bullet had not been meant for Dionysos. He had intercepted it without meaning to. No, that bullet had been aimed at her, at Persephone. Dionysos had saved her life.

She would switch places with him right now if she could.

Persephone only sat down when Hades did, taking the chair beside him and taking his hand in hers. It was shaking, and she squeezed it, running her thumb over his knuckles. She could almost pretend that her hands weren't shaking too.

She didn't know what to say. She knew what had to happen next, and she knew that he knew it too, but what could she possibly say to make that any easier? How much more prepared could they be in a few weeks than they were now?

She was angry. Of course she was angry. While she had resigned herself to putting nothing past Zeus, she never could have imagined this. The recklessness of it all was so on brand yet so out of bounds that she simply could not comprehend what it meant. He was so much more than a privileged brat who wouldn't take no for an answer, but his ability to hide behind that made him all the more dangerous.

All these years, he'd stood at the head of Khaos Falls, loved by a few too many and avoided by most. No one trusted him, but everyone thought that because he was rich and handsome, everything else could be tolerated. He was the fun guy, charming and graceful, while all other atrocious traits defaulted to Hades. Chaos could reign as long as it didn't clash with his, and Persephone was disgusted by it. There was always a cost to pay, but no one ever cared who paid it as long as it wasn't them. They were all guilty of it, and now they were all paying the price. It was the only way to get them where they needed to go.

Hades scratched his beard with his free hand before smoothing over his mouth. "My boy." She barely caught the words he muttered. She could almost hear his heart hammering in his chest, and she knew what he was thinking. Still, she waited patiently for him to say the words.

"He saw us there, all of us," he breathed. "I'm sure of it. He saw us there, and he waited. He waited for you. He knew he couldn't stop me, us. He—"

"He's a coward, Hades," she intervened as gently as possible. "He is a coward, and you are doing what's right."

"But I haven't, not yet. The longer I let him stay in this city, the more harm that comes. It has to be dealt with tonight. This has to end."

"Hecate doesn't have the proof yet—"

"I have enough proof to last me a lifetime. He has been shoving the proof in my face and down my throat for years now, and I just wouldn't look at it. No more."

"That isn't how you work."

He looked at her. "The way I work put us in this position in the first place."

"You aren't him, Hades. You never will be, and I will never let you believe that is a bad thing."

"—Then I will go get the proof myself."

She knew he'd made up his mind. She also knew that Zeus was a loose cannon with not a single thing left to lose. What he'd done tonight proved that, but hitting Dionysos? He must have known by now what Hades would do. He must have known that he was no longer safe. It was common fucking sense. Dionysos may be a god in Khaos Falls, but no one loved that boy more than Hades. In this instance, hitting her may have been a better outcome for Zeus. But if Zeus knew that too, who knew what he might do the moment he saw Hades?

She moved to squat down in front of him, cupping his face. He seemed to brace himself, as though fearing she would lecture him or try to stop him, hand him an ultimatum that might break him in two. She brushed her thumbs along his cheeks.

"Just come home to me," she pleaded.

He looked at her for a long time, trying to calculate what that meant, attempting to see if he could draw the permission he needed from it. Then, once he had, he nodded, soft at first then more vigorously before he leaned in and kissed her hard. She fell into him, her hands on his neck, and offered his tongue all the words she could not say. They parted far too soon for her liking.

"Watch over him," he requested. "And Athena."

"I will," she assured him.

He stood then, gesturing to his three closest companions.

Hephaestus stood too, and Poseidon moved to his brother's side. They needed no further instruction. The group of them followed Hades out, and Persephone's chest began to tighten. The next time she saw any of them, everything would be different in an irreversible way. Until then, there was no peace. There couldn't be.

Her eyes darted over to Athena, who stood beside the swinging doors, her arms crossed over her chest and her brows knitted together. Her face was obscured by her loose black curls falling down around her head, but her shoulders shook visibly. Persephone doubted herself as she stood, making her way toward the younger

317

woman. She wondered if Athena blamed her, if she was angry with her for being the one out here while Dionysos was the one in there. Persephone would understand if she was.

She approached her anyway, grabbing a few tissues off of the nurse's desk and offering them to her. Athena immediately started to swipe at her eyes, but when it did no good, she took the tissues, muttering her gratitude.

"I'm not about to stand here and try to feed you some bullshit that may or may not make you feel better," Persephone assured her. "And as much as I care about him, I won't pretend I have any idea what you're going through. —And if you blame me, I—"

Athena snorted a sharp laugh before she looked up, her brown eyes bloodshot and buried under a grief that startled Persephone. The tears continued to fall without Athena's permission despite the rigid control she had over every part of her body, her shoulders set back and her feet squared and her wild curls falling obediently to either side of her slender face. There was an angry red tinge to her rich brown skin, and her jaw clenched every now and again, but she finally spoke.

"He thinks the world of you," was the first thing that came out of her mouth, and it seemed to surprise them both. "— I - I thought he had a crush on you in the beginning." Her brow quirked. "But he just really loved working with you and Calliope and the rest of the cast. He talked about the show nonstop, and it - it broke him when the Pantheon burned down and Elysium got closed, and it was like - like—"

Persephone remembered Hades. "Like someone cut off one of his limbs?"

Athena perked up. "Yeah, exactly like that, and I didn't get it. I couldn't. I tried, and I wanted to, but I just couldn't 'get' it. I don't really get most of the things he's passionate about, the vineyards or the clubs or the parties, not the way that he does or the way he wants me to, but I love his passion. I do, and so I keep trying. I always will. I want to make him happy and be in it with him because he's - he's my best friend."

Her voice cracked at last, and Persephone sensed there was something more there, but she didn't push. She doubted she could give any more of a push than a gunshot if there was something Athena needed to say, and it was probably not Persephone she needed to say it to anyway.

Athena shrugged. "I don't know. I guess that even though we're complete opposites in many ways, he's taught me a lot about what it means to love yourself. Ugh, it sounds so stupid."

Persephone smiled. "It doesn't. I think he's taught me a good amount of that too."

Athena softened. "He said you taught him. —I just - I don't know who I would be without him. And I feel like this is my fault. I trusted Zeus too. I..."

She appeared to war with something, looking down at the floor, and eventually, she shook her head. Persephone placed a hand on her shoulder, speaking softly.

"There's only one person at fault for any of this, and I know that you know Dio would say the same thing. The point is that he's gonna be okay, and when all of this is over, you'll still have each other. We all will, and we have to let that be good enough."

Athena only nodded, leaning back against the wall, and Persephone let it rest there. She returned to her seat, and Aphrodite came to sit beside her. Their hands found each other as fatigue began to catch up with Persephone.

"It all changes tonight, huh?" Aphrodite asked, her gaze as distant as her best friend's.

"Yeah," Persephone conceded. "For the better. It has to be for the better."

She would tear this city in two if it changed for the worst.

Thirty-Four

HADES

The SUV was silent as it covered the short distance between the neutral Healer District and the neighboring Olympus District to the north. Hades stared out the passenger window, privy to the intermittent glances he received from Thana in the backseat and Charon behind the wheel. Hecate's presence directly behind him was an immovable pillar. While it was usually his job, she was the one that tethered them to the ground tonight. He focused on that now. He needed it.

The pistol resting on his thigh was heavier than it had ever been although he'd like to think he didn't need it. After today, he knew better than to assume, but it signified exactly what all of this had come to. His constant coddling, his disregard for the concerns of countless others, his willful ignorance... It all came down to this. Now, he was the only one that could make this right.

As they reached the main street of Olympus, which led all the way up to Zeus's estate, the other vehicles in his caravan branched off. The place would be surrounded within minutes, but Hades was going right through the front door. It was crucial that he looked Zeus in the eyes when he tore the crown from his head. It could not end any other way. It had always been him or Zeus, and both of them had always picked the latter.

Maybe for Hades, it was easier than risking defeat. Maybe it was easier than facing his mother in the afterlife. Maybe he feared failing. He'd come to see however that it wasn't about picking himself or Zeus. Today, it was about picking Dionysos. Tomorrow, it was about picking this city.

They reached the dramatic golden gates at the foot of the hill, Zeus's massive mansion visible sitting atop it. Charon rolled down the window, and Hades recognized the man in the security booth as Demokrates. He wasn't just any security guard but the head of Zeus's entire security team. Hades had foreseen this. Zeus knew he was coming. It worked out exactly as the elder needed it to.

Hades didn't hesitate to climb out of the car and round it to the driver's side. Demokrates extended his hand, and Hades took it, a good sign.

"I'm going to be straight with you," Hades said, his tone firm. "I'm going up there, and I'm going to take him down. I won't kill him if I don't have to, but he will leave this city tonight, one way or another. I'll offer you a job here and now. First, you'll escort my men inside, and then, you and your men can continue to work here for Athena and Ares at a higher rate. Let's say a - 30% increase to start, to be revisited in six months then once a year thereafter." Demokrates raised a brow, and Hades knew that Zeus had never done anything of the sort. "Your choice, but I'm only offering it once. This all plays out the same way, and I know you know that."

Demokrates eyed him warily, but it only took him a moment to nod his acceptance, and Hades knew it was no secret what Zeus had done today, not to his security team. Even if he hadn't shot the most beloved club owner and winemaker in Khaos Falls, working under Zeus was more a necessity than a privilege for most. Hades hadn't worried how they would get through Zeus's frontlines. He just wondered how much it would cost him. Compared to what he had prepared for, this was not steep at all. Demokrates shook his hand again before picking up his radio, his eyes still on Hades.

"Open the gates," he commanded. "All of them."

Then he followed his own order.

Hades clapped his shoulder before returning to the car, and they proceeded up the lane to the circular driveway that fronted Zeus's home. They climbed out once Charon parked, and Hades caught glimpses of the other SUVs flanking the place, coming through each of the other two gates. He tucked his pistol in the shoulder holster beneath his jacket as the security guards at the front door opened it for him. Ganymede, who had worked for Zeus under a number of titles for years but was also a close friend of Dionysos, met them at the center of the entrance hall, yanking the earpiece from his ear.

"He's upstairs in his study," he whispered to Hades, his eyes red. "He's - he's drunk, and he's just - going off on everyone, waving his gun around." He paused a moment, and his lip trembled. "Is - is he - Dio... Is he okay?"

"He will be," Hades assured him. "Here is what I need from you right now, Gany. Pack my brother a bag with his five favorite outfits, and leave it here at the door. Then get out of here. For now at least. I'll be in touch."

The young man nodded and quickly moved past him. By then, Poseidon had entered the house, and he met Hades at the foot of the

323

stairs. They traded only a glance before proceeding, leading the others toward Zeus's study.

The moment they reached the third-floor landing, Hades could hear his brother's shrill shouting. When they rounded the corner into the hall housing his study, he saw Hera leaning against the wall, her head pressed back against it. She looked up as if sensing their presence and immediately rushed toward him.

"What did he do?" she demanded in a low hiss, concern and confusion threaded through her face. "What happened?"

"He shot Dionysos," Hades said although he didn't expect Hera to care much. She'd hated that boy since he'd shown up in Khaos Falls. "He was trying to shoot Persephone."

"Wh - why? Why would he do that?"

Hades could see it in her eyes: she knew why, but they didn't have the time to discuss it at the moment. At this point, the specifics didn't matter to Hades. His nephew was lying in the hospital, and the man who put him there must be dealt with now.

"Hera, I would be delighted to speak with you tomorrow so that I may lay out how things are going to be from now on, and I'll answer any questions you truly want the answers to, but right now, I need you to either stand aside or leave."

"What are you going to do?"

"My brother has seen his last day in Khaos Falls. Would you like to join him?"

She stared at him for a long time as if attempting to discern whether he was serious or not. Her eyes then drifted over his shoulders, no doubt to lock with Charon's for a moment before they turned back on Hades.

They had both enabled Zeus in ways rooted in fear, and he could understand her hesitance. She may not be in love with Zeus, but she had loved him once. That short amount of time had been far too much. He'd used every single moment to convince her of her worth, or lack thereof, and she'd been feeding those fears ever since. As was the case with Hades, many in the city had an idea of her that was far from the truth due to his brother's presentations. And like Hades, she didn't know who she was without Zeus. She had been forced to build her entire life around him too. Once he was gone, she would have no choice but to start over from scratch.

It would not be easy, but if she could accept Hades' terms regarding the district, they could try and figure it out together.

She shook her head. "No, I do not wish to join him."

"And I assume you don't care to see him off either," he continued, and she shook her head again. "Good. I'll call you in the morning, alright, sister?"

She nodded, and he kissed her cheek before she moved off toward her room. There had never been much pronounced feeling between them since she'd married Zeus, but there was a tremendous respect. They had survived this nightmare together in so many ways, and while she may not be happy with every part of his plan moving forward —namely the roles in Olympus— he had hope that she would learn to love her freedom again.

Hades now turned to the others. "Wait here for Demokrates."

"I'll go with you," Poseidon immediately piped up, but Hades put a hand on his shoulder.

"No, brother, this is on me."

They stared at each other for a moment, but when something else shattered in Zeus's study, Poseidon nodded and stepped back. Hades continued down to the large oak doors on his own, Zeus destroying what he assumed was furniture on the other side. He waited for a moment of peace, or as close to peace as it could get, and entered the room.

It was in complete shambles, as was its master, who immediately raised his pistol as he swung around to face the door. One look at him, and Hades knew he could never pull his own gun. Not just because Zeus would shoot first but because Hades never would have been able to pull the trigger.

"Put it down, Zeus," Hades said, and although it was a simple command, it was a command nonetheless.

"You took everything from me!" Zeus screamed after he realized who stood before him, eyes wild.

"I didn't. Not yet."

"You - you think you can just - come in here, and... You can't do anything, Hades! I'm in charge! Me!"

"Not anymore, brother."

It was hard to look at him. Hair mussed, face flushed, eyes unfocused; he looked every bit as out of it as he sounded with his slurred words and stark stuttering. Hades almost felt sorry for him. Almost.

But then he thought of Dionysos, innocent as the day he was born, and he remembered that Zeus had been prosecuting the boy for that alone ever since Zeus learned of his existence. He thought of Persephone and how close Zeus had been to taking her too. And then he thought of all the times he himself had tried to please his brother only for it to never be enough.

"You can't do this!" Zeus cried, tears welling up in his eyes, his hand shaking. "You can't! This is my city!"

"You nearly killed him, Zeus."

"I was aiming for her!"

"You think that's a viable excuse?"

"She—"

"You would have answered for that just the same."

"Look at what you've - you've let her do to us! You let her come between us!"

"You let you come between us. You and your ego, your pride, your greed. You chose all of that over me again and again, brother, and still, I put you first every time. I will not do it anymore, not at their expense. What - what you could've taken from me today is -" He felt it; the pain, the agony, the fear crawling up his throat, everything he'd choked down as they carted Dionysos away. He forced it down once more. "It's irreplaceable. I will not gamble with their lives, not for you and not for anyone else, not ever again. Put the gun down, Zeus."

Zeus did not obey, but as Hades moved closer, his resolve strengthened. If Zeus was capable of shooting him, he would have done it today rather than go after another. He would have ended it then. He had to know Hades would come for him, and he'd risked it anyway. If Persephone had died, Zeus believed he would be all Hades had again, but all he'd done was disprove that theory. The truth had never been more clear than it was in this moment.

The barrel of the gun touched Hades' chest before Zeus realized his brother wasn't bluffing. He pulled the hammer back, but Hades disarmed him in one swift movement, gripping his wrist and using the same arm to deliver a strong elbow to Zeus's jaw. Zeus stumbled back, tripping over his chair and hitting the floor with a groan.

"You'll be on a ship tonight to Naxos," Hades explained, setting the gun down on the desk. "You'll have enough money to get you on your feet and some clothes I've had packed for you."

"Demokrates!" Zeus called. But Demokrates would not come. At least not yet.

"My guards will escort you into the city to a place I've arranged for you."

"No," Zeus grunted as Hades stood him up, but it was hollow and broken.

"I will have eyes on you. I will know every single time you eat, sleep, breathe—"

"Demo—"

Hades gripped his jaw, forcing Zeus to look him in the eye. "—and if you ever even think of coming back to Khaos Falls, I will come to you again as I do now, but unlike now, I will bring no mercy with me."

His eyes bore into Zeus's until he found the fear, lurking there beneath the crystal blue surface, and he called it up with expert efficiency. It was crucial. This was the moment, the transfer of power, and power was the only thing Zeus had ever understood. He must understand this.

And he did because for a moment, his face cleared, and he looked back at Hades with the ghost of a grin on his splotched face.

"I guess - you're finally a man now, huh, brother?"

Hades suppressed the urge to sneer. He'd let Zeus have it. This would be the last time he or anyone else would question his masculinity.

"Demokrates!"

It was Hades who called upon him now, and this time, Demokrates appeared in the doorway with three of Hades' own men. Zeus's eyes widened as he glanced over his brother's shoulder. When he looked back at Hades, his face was chalk white.

"You - promised—" he began, but Hades stopped him.

"I promised to look after you. My promise is fulfilled, Zeus.

Otherwise, you wouldn't be breathing right now. You are your own responsibility going forward."

Patting his cheek, Hades turned and shoved Zeus into the arms of his men. Demo stepped back, allowing them to cuff his former employer.

"And I'd be careful in Naxos, brother," Hades stated. "I hear they don't take kindly to bullies, and they're swift with their justice. In fact, from what Erebus told me when we had dinner last night, it's brutal. His brother is the one who makes sure of it, and he's looking forward to welcoming you to the city."

Zeus shouted again as they hauled him out of the room, but Hades tuned it out. He turned to look out the window at the green slopes that led down to the sea. The city could not be seen from here, not the way it could be seen from Hades' penthouse in Asphodel. He had always been in charge of seeing the big picture, he supposed.

He wondered if perspective could have helped his brother in the beginning. He knew it was too late to speculate on such things though. Now, he had to turn toward the future. He held it in his hands, and he had to do so with great care. Many were counting on him. It was what he had always feared, being the one that good people looked to. It still terrified him, but today had taught him that there were worse things worth his fear.

WHEN HE ARRIVED BACK at the hospital alone, he found only Hermes and the two guards he'd stationed there in the waiting room. The younger man stood when he saw his uncle approaching, slipping his phone into his back pocket. Hades embraced him the moment he was close enough, and Hermes instantly released a shuddering breath. It was not often he showed his more vulnerable emotions. He had been through things that Hades could not even imagine before he reached Khaos Falls and his uncle's care, but when it came to his brother, everything was different. Hades understood that intimately.

When they parted, some of the tension hanging off of both of them seemed to have disintegrated.

"He's been awake about an hour," Hermes explained softly, his brown eyes moving over to the swinging doors beside the nurses' station. "He needed a lot of blood. Asklepios wanted to put him back to sleep to manage the strain on his heart, but he wanted to see you first."

Hades nodded, squeezing his shoulder. "Go home and get some rest. I'll see you tomorrow, and - any help you need with the district, you just call. We will handle it together."

"I know, Uncle." He chewed his lip a moment before offering a half smile. "So you're the leader now, huh?"

"Not just yet, but by tomorrow afternoon, I will be."

"And - Zeus?"

"I assure you that he will never step foot in Khaos Falls again."

Hermes nodded his head, and Hades left him with a small smile before heading through the doors into the patient hallway. A nurse met him on the other side, and she led him through the corridors until they got to Dio's room. Hades heard him before he saw him, his laugh weak and his voice thin. But he was still laughing. Hades focused on that.

Athena was sitting beside him to no surprise, and they both looked up when Hades appeared. Dio grinned wide, reaching for his uncle and pulling him into a light hug.

"Careful now, son, let's not overexert ourselves," Hades warned, hugging him all the same. "Don't worry, I saved up for that one."

"Of course you did."

"Is it done?"

Athena's voice was steel. Hades found her features stern and unwavering even as Dio reached for her hand and began to play with her fingers. He knew she was struggling with this for more than a few reasons, but he also knew that the answers were the only way to appease her when she was like this. Athena liked results, and she liked logical paths to acquire them. Her pragmatism was unfailing, but he acknowledged that it came from a good place.

"It is," Hades assured her. "He is gone from the city for good, and tomorrow, I'll make the announcements."

Athena tilted her chin down in a curt nod before she stood. "I should go. My new job starts tonight, and I have to make sure we don't let the dust linger too long. I told Ares I would meet him at the house."

She leaned over to kiss Dio's forehead before walking around to hug Hades. There was so much he wanted to say to her, but she was there and gone before he could blink, and then it was just him and Dio. Dio offered him an apologetic smile as Hades sat down beside him on the bed.

"She's not taking it very well," he admitted, playing with his own fingers now. "I think she feels guilty. She doesn't say it, but that's her guilty face. She'll be okay once she sees me good as new, I think."

"I think so too."

"So - you ready for tomorrow, Uncle?" His eyes still held all that boyish excitement even now. "It's a big day for all of us. Asklepios said I probably can't be there though."

"It's a simple announcement, Dio. There won't be a parade or anything, and - I need you here resting. I need you to get better."

"I will."

They were quiet for a time, Hades staring down at his shoes as he tried to rifle through the many emotions he'd endured today amidst all of the others he'd forced himself to ignore. There was guilt there. There was also anger, sadness, fury, grief, fear, and so much in between. He felt like he'd been failing Dio forever, and it was worse because Dio was the only one who never complained, who never asked for better, who never asked Hades to do something.

It was as if he read Hades' mind.

"You know this isn't your fault either, right, Uncle?"

Hades raised his head. "I still can't help feeling like it was though, Dio."

"I'm sure both of us could make a great case, but the bottom line is that you didn't pull the trigger, and I don't blame you. I think I have a say in it."

"Yeah, I think you do, son." He scratched his chin. "But if I had done right by you long ago, he never would have had the chance to pull that trigger."

Dio sunk deeper into the pillows at his back as if trying to make himself small. It didn't do much good, but Hades gathered the intent regardless. And when Dio spoke again, his voice was light and small.

"When I would get sad that Zeus wanted nothing to do with me, you always told me that it wasn't about me, it was about him, and I should never think of myself as unworthy. Now, I'm telling you.

That's why I wanted you to come back. Why I waited up to see you. I didn't want you to go to bed thinking it was your fault."

Hades dug the heels of his hands into his eyes as they began to water.

"I - I know I never say anything about it, but Uncle, you're way too hard on yourself, and you shouldn't be. I wouldn't - I wouldn't be here without you in the first place. I never would've made it this long. Hermes either, and probably not Heph. Ares and Athena might've killed each other without you too, so - whenever you think you failed, I just want you to remember that that's impossible. Because you've never failed me. I don't think you can."

Hades looked up at him, reaching over to cup the side of his neck with a watery smile. "It's because of you I learned to love at all. You will always be a part of me, Dionysos, and I will always protect you. Always."

"I know, Uncle." He gripped Hades' forearm. "You're gonna be an amazing leader, and I know that because you already are. And you're worth ten of Zeus, which is why you don't have to do this alone. We've got your back."

Their foreheads came together as Hades soaked it in, allowing himself to accept the fact that this was real and Dionysos was still here breathing. That was more than worth everything that came next. Because Dio was right. He didn't have to do this alone. As much as he mourned losing a brother, he knew he had gained so much more. It was worth leaving the shadows for.

Tomorrow, he would announce himself as the leader of Khaos Falls.

Tonight, maybe he could finally get some sleep.

Thirty-Five

PERSEPHONE

U pon arriving home, Persephone attempted to calm her nerves with a hot shower though it hadn't done much good. All she'd done under the spray was think about what could be happening in Olympus and the many various outcomes it could produce. She'd known there was nothing else to do but wait for Hades to return, but that hadn't put her any less on edge.

The day had felt a lifetime long, hours stretching out into eternities that had aged her with a threatening haste. How it was still the same day was beyond her, but with each second that ticked by, she was convinced that time had slowed and all of the world had turned its eyes on Khaos Falls.

While she knew Dionysos was okay now, she did not know what to expect of tomorrow. She had faith in Hades of course, but she would never underestimate Zeus again. The worry in her gut would not allow it. What she needed right now was to know Hades was safe. Everything else felt so minuscule and irrelevant without that confirmation. Without him, tomorrow mattered very little to her.

She was sitting on the bed in her robe when she heard the elevator doors open. She was on her feet in a second, rushing through the living room, and before she took another breath, she was in his arms.

They stood there holding one another for a lifetime, saying nothing at all. The sound of their hearts falling into sync was the only thing Persephone could hear apart from his breathing. She savored both sounds, allowing them to soothe her worries for as long as she could before she broke the silence out of necessity.

"How did it go?" She presented the question tentatively, her face buried in his chest.

He didn't answer immediately, but she felt his heart kick up beneath a heavy exhale. She ran her hands down his back, allowing him to settle.

"As well as I could hope for," he replied in time, resting his cheek against the top of her head. "But it's done, so…"

"I'm proud of you."

She knew this was difficult for him for a host of different reasons. She also knew he carried a lot of guilt over the timing and all that led up to it, but she didn't blame him. She could admit that she was still processing the fact that it could have been her, that it should have been her, lying up in that hospital, but she was here now. She wouldn't let him burden himself with something that didn't happen no matter how close it was to doing so. Dionysos wouldn't blame his uncle either. That, she knew.

She pulled back, slipping her hands over his neck and looking into his eyes. She found his fatigue there, right alongside his worry for what came next. Tomorrow would be nearly as difficult as today. He could handle it though. He was the only one who could.

"I'm—" he began, but she shook her head.

"Don't," she whispered. "Don't you dare."

"Seph—"

"I won't have it, Hades. I refuse. What happened happened. It's done now, and we have to move on, move forward. You did the right thing, and now you have to continue to do so, every day for the rest of our lives."

He stared at her for a moment, his fingers curled into her sides before he nodded in acquiescence. Then he smiled.

"You're going to make a good leader," he relented.

She smirked. "I definitely won't debate that."

Shaking his head, he swept her up off of her feet, winding his arms around her. "I mean it. I want - I need you beside me. And - I don't mean I want you to give up your dream. I want to make sure you can still perform, but I don't want to do this without you."

"Nor will you have to." She leaned up, pressing her forehead to his. "I am by your side always. No matter what."

"But I want to know you're choosing this and not—"

"I'm not choosing this, Hades. I'm choosing you. This is just a benefit. I was only ever against taking over for my mother because she had ulterior motives and strings attached to her legacy. She made me choose between me and her. I know I don't have to do that here. I know you'll look out for me just as I'll look out for you and every person who does the same."

"I will. I just - I don't want to hold you back."

She chuckled. "Now you're giving yourself too much credit. You can't hold me back. Only I can hold me back, and that is the last thing I am doing here. I am completely in love with you, Hades, and I will choose you for me every single day, but I will never choose you over me. Not you, and not anyone else."

His lips curled upward further. "You love me?"

She rolled her eyes before gripping his tie. "Don't try to be slick right now."

His laughter was a salve for her soul. "I love you too."

"Mm, yeah?"

He nodded. "Mhm."

"Prove it."

He perched her on the counter with a sly smile. "And how would you prefer I do that?"

She only smirked, placing a hand atop his head and guiding him to his knees. He didn't resist, sinking down as her legs parted before him. She undid the tie of her silk robe, leaving herself exposed to him, and he did not take it for granted. His lips touched down upon her inner thigh, coasting upward toward her core. She blinked, and he was pressing his tongue against her clit, massaging it with a thoroughness that made her buzz in place.

"Hades - oh—"

She leaned back on her hands, struggling to remain present in the moment as he pushed her toward ecstasy. Her head rolled back, eyes fluttering shut as his hands slipped beneath her thighs.

He handled her like he hadn't eaten in days, sucking her clit into his mouth until she was a mess of continuous moans and rogue rutting against his lips. She pleaded with him, although she had no clue for what, only yearning to be closer. Reaching a hand out, she placed it on the back of his head just as he plunged his tongue inside of her.

Her body reacted accordingly, shaking and jolting around him as a cry split the air. He burrowed as deep as he could, face moving from side to side and igniting every inch of her. His chin, his cheeks, his nose; each of them stimulated her, and she had no hope of holding out.

She came in a rush of strangled cries and helpless rolls of her hips, but he didn't stop. He lapped up every drop that she offered him, his nails digging into her skin.

At last, she found the strength —or the desperation— to drag him up, claiming his mouth with the same hunger he'd shown her as she tore open his shirt and yanked the knot of his tie free. Once the fabric fell from his shoulders, he wrapped his arms around her, grinding his erection into her sensitive folds and tearing sound after wanton sound from her lips. Fates, the things he did to her. She could drown in him if allowed. And he could damn sure drown in her.

She reached down between them, unbuckling his belt and shoving down his pants as his lips scaled her neck. Once she freed it, she took a firm hold of his shaft and delivered a series of eager strokes. His mouth instantly found hers again.

She reveled in the song she caught on her tongue until he batted her hand away with a growl. It was the only warning she got before he entered her, every single inch buried inside her drenched pussy. She let out a muffled shriek before sinking her teeth into his lip, but that only spurred him on. Suddenly, he was plunging into her with ruthless thrusts, and all she could do was claw at his back and shoulders in search of an anchor. She released his lip if only to call out into the open air. It wasn't long before she drew blood.

He didn't seem to notice.

Just tall enough to bend her to his will atop the counter, he held her by the waist and all but folded her in half atop the counter even as she remained upright. His arms were hooked beneath her knees, leaving her immobile and unable to do anything but take it. And oh, did she take it. Gladly.

The sensations were both overwhelming and all-consuming, and she was a glutton for each and every one of them, her nails digging into him wherever they could reach. Eventually, she resigned to holding tight to his biceps for dear life, her eyes rolling back and her moans stalled by breathlessness. That was when he picked her up, catching her completely off guard and slamming her down on his cock again and again, her clit glancing off of him every single fucking time. He hit her with four or five quick strokes before sound managed to escape her, a tattered scream that hung in the air around them. If this was him fucking all of his frustration out, she would gladly invite him to do so more often. She wrapped her arms around his neck as best she could, completely at his mercy, the clap of their bodies colliding loud and lewd.

"Hades! Fuck!"

He growled in response, a vibration that hit her neck and shot straight down into the pit of her belly. She wasn't at all prepared, and white light eclipsed her vision as another orgasm crashed through her. She cried out, and he seemed to chase it, his thrust skipping a beat and going rogue before she felt him throb and jerk, cumming with a strained whimper.

Then his mouth was on hers once more, and she melted into him, holding him close as he was overtaken by euphoria. She could feel his orgasm ravaging his frame, and it affected her in the most damning ways imaginable. She could not get enough.

He set her back on the counter, their foreheads resting together and their heavy breaths entangled between them. She looked up into his eyes once her body allowed it and submerged himself inside that gaze, in absolute awe of his divinity. He was beautiful. He was hers.

He picked her up off of the counter, and she immediately wound her legs around his waist despite their trembling. Then he carried her towards the bedroom, their bedroom.

"How the fuck are you walking right now?" she groaned.

"Adrenaline." He shrugged, still out of breath. "Now my turn."

"Your turn to what?"

"Ask you a question." She rolled her eyes as he deposited her onto the bed and collapsed beside her. "Would you mind if I - took the day off from the casino tomorrow?"

"Mm, you gonna do me like this all day?"

"That's the plan."

"Then I don't mind at all." She smiled, licking her lips. "But only after you make your announcement, leader of Khaos Falls."

He smiled too. "Deal."

She looked at him with nothing less than admiration in her eyes. She loved him. There was no denying it any longer. There was no need to. Every breath she took was laced with it, and it reverberated in her chest at all hours of the day and every minute encased in them. This man who was once only a chapter in Khaos Falls' folklore had broken her wide open, taking her heart in his gentle hands and laying his lips wherever he thought might have hurt before him. She loved him, and there was nothing left to debate, no regret left to cling to. All they had now was the future, and not a soul alive could take that away from them. She knew he'd make sure of it, and she would too.

"Thank you," she said softly, her eyes fluttering.

"For what?"

"Giving me a soft place to land when I need it."

"Trust me. The pleasure was all mine. As long as you drag me up to where you are every once in a while."

She kissed his temple. "Deal."

Epilogue

HADES

The vineyard's restaurant had been decorated in a decadent elegance, the lights low and the air warm. Three tables had been lined up at the center of the empty dining area, each of them adorned by a majestic centerpiece, the other tables pushed back towards the walls to leave ample space for both the dining and the dance floor.

"It looks good," Hades whispered as he gingerly placed his hands on Dionysos's shoulders. "Though I am certain you had nothing to do with this because I clearly remember telling you not to be doing anything for another few weeks at least."

Dionysos held up his hands, immediately grimacing and letting the arm still in a sling fall slowly back to his body.

"I swear I only made a call, Uncle," he stated, looking back at Hades. "Honestly, does this look like something I'd do myself? There's hardly any color and not a single wine fountain."

Hades smirked and rolled his eyes, kissing his nephew's temple before steering him towards the table.

Athena was already at the table, punctual as always, and she stood to pull out the chair beside her for Dionysos. He sat with haste, leaving Hades to make his way to the head of the table on his own. He hardly minded, greeting the other members of his family as they entered and joined them.

It was their first official family dinner, which they had been planning for a couple of weeks now, and he had decided the occasion should be marked with some luxury. He had called Danae straight away to arrange it, and she had been more than happy to host. Hades also knew Dionysos would appreciate being able to visit the vineyard amidst his strict ban from work until he was fully healed.

He had continually tried to negotiate with Hades, pointing out that his work consisted of very little manual labor. Additionally, even Asklepios had cleared him for regular activities, having given Hades a full rundown of the advanced technology used to repair the damage Dio had suffered.

But Hades had been adamant, informing his nephew that he was planning to force everyone to take some much-needed time off before the real work began. Including Athena. Dionysos agreed quite quickly after that.

The first two weeks of his reign had been pleasant enough. Or at least as pleasant as he could have hoped. There had been many questions to answer, many fears to soothe, and many relationships to mend. However, Hades had been given the best help throughout the entire shift, and he was quite content with where things currently stood.

It wasn't perfect of course. Demeter would remain a wild card for the time being, but he and Hestia had hit it off well enough. It seemed they had a lot in common, and they shared many ideas and understandings of the city they resided in. She was going to be an excellent addition to his inner circle.

As for the River Styx, it was still running well, Hecate, Charon, and Thanatos taking up any slack they had to while Hades focused on the city. It wasn't as big a task as it had once been now that he had ensured the districts would be overseen by their leaders and citizen boards without any interference from him. They would come to him if they needed basic necessities or resources, but beyond that, he would not chain them the way Zeus had. And he would not mine them for his own gain as Zeus had either. Everyone seemed to like where this was going so far.

Aphrodite came in with Eros and Psyche in tow, taking their seats beside Persephone's, which was at the head of the table beside Hades. They left one seat between for Hestia.

Poseidon sat on the other side, Amphitrite adjusting his tie when Hades reached them, greeting them both with warm pleasantries. Ares, Hermes, and Hephaestus then arrived, and Persephone and Hestia followed soon after.

Hades tried to gauge Persephone's face, knowing she had tried to invite Demeter who had obviously turned them down, but she simply gave him a wide smile as she approached. They would discuss it later he was sure. For now, they would enjoy the family they did have to share the evening with.

He took her in his arms once she was close enough, kissing her cheek as she wound her own arms around his neck. He inhaled the scent of her perfume which was deeply present although it was different from what he was used to. And yet familiar too...

"Is that-"

"Pomegranate?" she filled in with a smile against his cheek. "It is."

"I really like it."

"Yeah? I was hoping so because I do too."

"Mhmm, I like it a lot."

When she pulled back, their eyes met, and the world around them seemed to quiet. It was good at that when she was in his arms. Or maybe she was good at calling the quiet.

Leaning up, she pressed a soft kiss to his lips, which earned a whistle that Hades strongly suspected originated from Dionysos. When they pulled apart, they found the entire table looking up at them. Hades cleared his throat and reluctantly released her before turning to them.

"I see we're all here now," he began, his fingers curling into the lapel of his jacket. Persephone rested a hand on his shoulder. "Thank you all for coming. I—"

"Uncle," Hermes interrupted with a grimace, raising a hand with one finger extended. "Sorry, but - you know this is a family dinner, not a formal meeting, right? You can speak to us like... Well, not like that."

Others snickered under their breath, and Hades blushed. "I - I have to admit, I'm not very good at it. I - this is the first time I've had my entire family together in a room, I think."

He looked down at the table, contemplating his next words for a moment before he picked up his glass of bubbling champagne.

"Well," he sighed. "Listen, I know things aren't gonna be easy movin' forward. A lot is changing. A lot is evolving, growing, moving, etc. I know that, and you do too, but I have complete faith in every single one of you. And I wanna thank you for making this transition as easy as possible for me personally. I - love you all. Dearly, with everything in me, and my primary concern will always be doing right by each of you, so... A toast." He raised his glass, and the others at the table followed suit. "To this city, for what it is and what it will be when we are done here. May our future generations see all of its potential come to fruition."

Aphrodite cut in now, raising her glass higher. "And may your reign be long and prosperous."

"Here, here!" Dionysos immediately added, downing his glass before anyone else. He then raised the empty glass and barked, "To Hades!"

Everyone else echoed him. Even Persephone grabbed her glass with haste to raise it. "To Hades!"

It would take some getting used to, this attention. As would the faith that these people instilled in him. He would do his best to honor it, but worry would follow in his wake regardless. How could it not?

He would use it to his advantage however. It would drive him to do his best and remind him who he was doing it all for.

Dinner commenced thereafter, scores of food and drink making their way out of the kitchen and to the table endlessly. The chatter of his family was a most welcome sound to Hades, and every time he glanced over to see Dionysos talking and laughing, he was filled with a fresh feeling of gratitude.

He and Poseidon also indulged in the longest conversation they had had in years, speaking of their districts and their current interests, their hobbies, and things they missed from their childhood. They spoke of their mother without Hades being burdened by guilt, and they spoke of the future as if it was an inevitable thing. He enjoyed it thoroughly. It made him feel invincible.

At some point, the two brothers found themselves alone at the edge of the table while everyone else moved to the dance floor or the dessert table to mingle further. Hades took the opportunity to really look at Poseidon, to commit this image of him to memory. He looked so much like their mother when he smiled that wide grin. He possessed her nose and her deep laughter.He had his father's colored eyes and smooth, light brown skin that looked healthy and luminous. Hades was glad to know he was relatively comfortable in the Atlantis District and little stress from the rest of the city had reached him.

"I miss her," Poseidon said suddenly, tossing a side glance at Hades. He need not explain himself or elaborate on who he meant.

"I miss her too," Hades admitted, folding his hands in front of him. "I still keep lilies in the house, to remind me of her."

Poseidon smiled. "Me too. I used to just - bring 'em home without thinking about it. I didn't even realize how often I did that until Amphi pointed it out. But - every time I look at them, I feel better. Lighter. Like - I don't know... Like—"

"Like she's there," Hades finished. "Like she's there, and she's letting us know things are good."

"Exactly."

After a beat, Poseidon placed a hand on Hades' shoulder.

"She would be proud of you, you know," he said softly. Hades inhaled a sharp breath. "And she would be happy that we're here right now, together, and that - you're trying to fix things. Make this place better for all of us."

Hades tried not to let his eyes water. "Thank you for saying that, Brother."

"I mean it, Hades." Poseidon looked at him hard. "And I want you to know that - I love you. I wouldn't trade you for anything in the world, and I - I'm sorry. For running away and for—"

"Hey, don't do that. You didn't run away. I wanted you to be happy, and I never wanted you to put up with the shit I had to. I carved out your district where I did for a reason. I wanted you to be comfortable. That was my only concern when it came to you, and that isn't to say it was right. I should have been more present, more responsive, but... I am happy that you put yourself first, Poseidon. It is what I wanted and what she would have wanted too."

Poseidon nodded, but Hades knew it would take some time before both of them began to relinquish all this guilt they had been carrying around their whole lives. Maybe they could help each other.

"Well, thanks for looking out for me," Poseidon said at last.

Hades smiled. "Thanks for being so easy to look out for."

"Mm, well, I'm pretty low maintenance, you know. Plus, you had a lot of help once Amphi came along."

"That I did. I'll have to thank her personally for picking up most of the slack."

"Speaking of which..." Poseidon looked towards the dance floor. "If you don't mind, Brother, I'm gonna go and ask my girl for a dance. Maybe you should do the same."

Hades smiled, his eyes already seeking Persephone out. "Yeah, I think I will."

When Hades found Persephone, she was standing at the end of the dessert table, picking at some chocolate-covered fruit. She looked up at his approach, her eyes immediately twinkling with the smile that soon spread across her face. He returned it, holding out his hand.

"May I?"

She wiggled her eyebrows and slid her hand into his. "You may."

They moved to the edge of the dance floor before he took her fully in his arms, stepping into the music with ease.

"Have I mentioned how proud of you I am?" she hummed as she rested her head against his shoulder.

"Every time you see me," he teased, turning his head to press a kiss to hers. "Not that I'm complaining."

"Mhm, you better not be."

They moved in comfortable silence for a time, the sound of their family chattering around them a welcome addition to the song they moved to. Though it also reminded Hades of the stark absence they would likely have to endure for a long while at these dinners.

"I'm sorry," he blurted before he could think about it. "About your mother not coming."

After a few moments, Persephone slowly lifted her head to look at him. There was a sad smile on her face, one he knew he had no aid for.

"Don't be sorry," she said. "Nothin' has changed. Mama and I have been like this for years now."

"But you miss her."

"Oh, I'll always miss her, and I know she misses me. She - my mama is good. I know she is. There are just - things she hasn't healed from and refuses to even inspect much less talk about. Maybe one day, that changes, but - it has to change before we can do anything about our relationship. For now, it's above me."

He nodded. "I am proud of you too, you know. For - being able to see that, for helping me to see that too. With Zeus."

"Well, listen, your situation was a bit different, wasn't it? I mean, at least Zeus gave you the illusion of purpose, of - doing what was right. My mama never gave me that. She just always spoke about my future as if it was hers, and it was already written with no room for input from me. There was no illusion, no deceit. She was upfront about her motives from the start."

349

"I get that. And - I do believe she's a good mother, but I think that maybe she fears that isn't good enough, you know? She grew up in a different time with different expectations, and she only wants to be remembered and to be celebrated for what she's done. She doesn't want anyone else to get that credit, and she's right about that. —And maybe there is something I can do there."

She raised a brow. "Like what?"

He shrugged. "I don't know yet, but… Your mother wants her flowers, and she deserves them. But she thinks she needs to live forever through you to get them, and that's not true. So -"

"So you're gonna kiss ass?" She smirked.

He offered a lopsided grin in return. "I mean I'm not sayin' all that, but - if there is a way to make your mama see that I do support her and appreciate her, maybe it goes a long way. And maybe it don't, but - I wanna try. Not just for you but - for me. For our family, current and future."

Her smile widened. "I really am so damn lucky."

"I think it's me who's lucky."

"It's not a competition."

She leaned up, kissing him with a slow-burning passion that set him ablaze. The room seemed to fall away around them, and then there was only her. His whole world, his present and future, all wrapped in a red dress and secure in his arms, and he was happy. A year ago — Fates, a few months ago, he never could have foreseen this, but for once in his life, he did not feel like simply existing. He was alive. Persephone had quite literally dragged him up out of the Underworld and into the land of the living, and he vowed to pay homage to that every single day.

Acknowledgments

As I write this, my mind is still trying to catch up with the reality that I am actually at this stage in my very long writing career. Despite the longevity of the dream, writing nearly every day for the past two decades, this is the first manuscript I've actually completed. I was always so immersed in the worldbuilding and character creation that I never made it past that, but being that I've been in my house 24/7 for the past year, it makes sense that I was finally able to hunker down and Get. It. Done.

I'm thankful for the friends I've made through this journey, and I hope to nurture those relationships in the future. As an introvert who struggles to initiate conversations as it is much less sustain them, it's been difficult being isolated for as long as we have been, but I've found good community across all social media platforms. Thank you to everyone who has welcomed me into the writing community and showed genuine interest in this little project of mine. It kept me going on days when I just wanted to quit and be done with it, and now I'm here actually publishing something? This is a gift I will cherish no matter what happens next.

After months with this story, I grew tired of it quickly, but by the end, I'd fallen in love with it all over again, which signals growth in my opinion. This isn't a story I would call tame, but it's probably the tamest thing I'll ever write, and that's a guarantee. I've always loved mythology, but Hades and Greek mythology have forever been special. To be able to reimagine the Greek pantheon (partly in my own image) and share a fresh take on these stories is a dream come true, and I hope you enjoy the ride as much as I have thus far! I can assure you that this is just the beginning!

About the Author

R.M. Virtues is a mythology junkie, lover of love, and creator of worlds. He writes fantasy and paranormal romance about underrepresented characters who get to live and love in a history unabridged. When he isn't busy conjuring romances, he can be found watching horror movies, playing fantasy video games, or eating Korean BBQ. He currently lives in Las Vegas, Nevada with his Funko Pop horror collection. You can find him online at rmvirtues.com or @rmvirtues on Twitter, Instagram, TikTok, and Patreon.

 twitter.com/rmvirtues

instagram.com/rmvirtues

patreon.com/rmvirtues

 tiktok.com/rmvirtues

Also by R.M. Virtues